SCARLETT FINN

Also by Scarlett Finn

TO DIE FOR...
TO DIE FOR TRUTH
TO DIE FOR HONOR
TO DIE FOR VIRTUE
TO DIE FOR DUTY
TO DIE FOR LOVE

GO NOVELS
GO WITH IT
GO IT ALONE
GO ALL OUT
GO ALL IN
GO FULL CIRCLE

KINDRED SERIES
RAVEN
SWALLOW
CUCKOO
SWIFT
FALCON
FINCH

LOVE AGAINST THE ODDS STANDALONE COLLECTION
SWEET SEAS
HEIR'S AFFAIR
RESCUED
MAESTRO'S MUSE
GETTING TRICKY
THIRTEEN
REMEMBER WHEN...
RELUCTANT SUSPICION
XY FACTOR

EXILE
HIDE & SEEK
KISS CHASE

THE EXPLICIT SERIES
EXPLICIT INSTRUCTION
EXPLICIT DETAIL
EXPLICIT MEMORY

WRECK & RUIN
RUIN ME
RUIN HIM

MISTAKE DUET
MISTAKE ME NOT
SLEIGHT MISTAKE

NOTHING TO...
NOTHING TO HIDE
NOTHING TO LOSE
NOTHING TO DECLARE
NOTHING TO US
NOTHING TO SAY
NOTHING TO GAIN
NOTHING TO YOU
NOTHING TO THIS

THE BRANDED SERIES
BRANDED
SCARRED
MARKED

RISQUÉ & HARROW INTERTWINED
TAKE A RISK
FIGHTING FATE
RISK IT ALL
FIGHTING BACK
GAME OF RISK

FORBIDDEN PREQUEL DUET
ALL. ONLY.
ONLY YOURS

THE FORBIDDEN NOVELS
FORBIDDEN DESIRE
FORBIDDEN WANT
FORBIDDEN WISH
FORBIDDEN NEED

LOST & FOUND
LOST
FOUND

ONE

"PLEASE DON'T MAKE me do it, Daddy," Whisper Doherty begged her father who sat on the other side of his huge desk.

The piece was an almost-replica of the President's Resolute Desk. The difference being that the crest of their family was embossed on the front.

"I didn't bring you here for a debate," Cyrus Doherty stated, picking up a pen to begin writing on the page he'd been reading when she came in. "You will marry him on Friday."

"But Daddy… he's a psychopath!"

Her father didn't even crook a brow. "By all accounts, yes," Cyrus said, turning the paper over to write on the back. "Which is exactly why we need him. I won't allow the Byrne family to overtake us."

Three months ago, the ranks of both the Dohertys and the Byrnes had been decimated by a shoot-out at what was supposed to be a peaceful meet. The intention was for the families to discuss territory and the increase of skirmishes between the two sides.

The conversation never took place.

Whisper had been at her father's side when he got the call from her brother during the bloodbath. Listening to the horror almost moved her to tears. Being the only daughter of one of the country's most notorious crime bosses, she wasn't squeamish when it came to violence or depravity. She'd grown up seeing it all. Still, hearing cousins fall, her uncles, her brothers… it was stomach churning.

The Dohertys lost just as many as the Byrnes, which was the only saving grace. Near to a whole generation of both families, and those loyal to them, were gone.

The initial ordeal only took an hour. Neither side would let the other survivors leave. Their stubbornness, their feud, gave the cops enough time to surround the place and arrest whoever was left.

Since that fated day, both sides had struggled to maintain their operations. Every wise-guy on the street was in play and enjoyed the two families vying for their loyalty. The Dohertys and Byrnes needed numbers, needed allies, or they'd be picked off and lose what market share they had left.

Apparently, that was where Zaiden McDade came into the equation.

The McDades were in the same business as the Dohertys and the Byrnes. They rejected their invitation to the meet, so were the only family unscathed. Now instead of three families jockeying for the top spot, the McDades had leaped to prime position, in terms of numbers on the streets and influence.

Both the Byrnes and the Dohertys were guilty of trying to poach the McDades' top guys. Their lack of success wasn't much of a surprise given the McDades reputation. The only reason Whisper could figure that anyone would be so loyal to such a vicious family was if they were afraid for their lives. And that same vicious family was the one her father was proposing she hand herself over to.

Slamming a fist to the desk, Whisper lunged over it. "He'll beat me, Daddy," she hissed. "He'll beat me and rape me. Him and all his depraved, sick brothers."

Surging to his feet, Cyrus grabbed her wrist, yanking her so far over the desk that she ended up with a knee on the surface. "You will not fuck this up, Whisper! You let the man run his house," he snarled. "You are a Doherty. You will do what this family tells you to do. You will marry him. You will be his obedient wife!"

"I won't," she spat. "I won't marry him! How about that?"

Bowing to get in her face, Cyrus didn't display anything of the man who'd bounced her on his lap when she was a child. That man called her his precious princess. A lot of years had passed since then; a lot had changed.

"Then you deserve everything he does to you. They have manpower. I need their manpower. Joining forces with them will put us back on top… You are the price for victory… One I'm happy to pay."

Cyrus shoved her away with so much force that she stumbled backwards. If the guest chair hadn't been there to catch her, she'd have landed on her ass.

"I am not a bargaining chip."

Sinking into his seat, he leaned back, swinging the chair side to side. His laugh warmed the air. "Sweetheart, you're female… You're only worth to me is what I can sell you for, who I can sell you to. You've been a drain on my resources since the day you were born. It's time to pay the piper." The laugh became a kind of disdainful smile. "Do your duty or I'll slit your throat myself…" Picking up his pen again, he began writing. "Be at the City Clerk's Office Friday at three… wear white."

Shooting to her feet, Whisper wanted to argue with him, wanted to point blank refuse… But considering what her life would be after disobeying her father's orders kept her silent.

Cyrus would cut her off; she'd have no access to funds. Even if scraping some cash together before fleeing was a possibility, her family couldn't weather the embarrassment of her bolting against her father's wishes.

Whisper and her father were the only members of their immediate family left. Her brothers were gone. Well, she did have an uncle and a pair of cousins, but they'd never been closely involved in the family business. They'd never been trusted enough… necessity was in the process of changing that.

If she ran, the Dohertys would be decimated. After that, her father would make it his life's mission to track her down. As soon as he found her, he'd extract his payback in the most agonizing way possible.

Whisper was a Doherty and had always been loyal to her family. Always. It was in her blood to do what was best for the family.

The McDades might be despicable, but their hatred for the Dohertys was meager in comparison to their loathing for the Byrnes. Even though the idea of being betrothed to a McDade turned her stomach, she'd sacrifice anything if it meant not letting the Byrnes triumph.

It was conditioning. She knew it but couldn't fight it. Whisper, just like the Byrne and McDade children, was taught that their family was superior over the others. The exaggerated stories exchanged among their peers fed the animosity between the trio of families.

The McDades could sneak in and take over while they had the numbers, but their infrastructure wasn't as robust. This union, if she didn't fuck it up, would see a Doherty-McDade alliance that could create a new power monolith at the top of the food chain. They'd be bigger and stronger than ever before. Wasn't that worth her opening her legs for the scum of the earth?

Storming out of her father's echoing townhouse, Whisper missed the sound of her brothers and cousins charging the space. Once the place had been full, alive with the buzz of activity. Now it was quiet. Still.

They'd cut the number of household staff. Without boots on the ground to pedal product and manage venues, the Doherty finances had taken a hit. Beyond that, with most of their loyal associates either dead or in jail, they just didn't need to cater to as many people.

Marrying Zaiden McDade would mean living in the McDade house. Her father would be alone. But only for a while. The Dohertys weren't done yet. It was up to her to ensure there were no glitches on their return to power... That meant getting hitched to a man she'd been trained to believe was her enemy since before the word even had meaning.

TWO

THERE WAS NO out. All week the breath of Cyrus' henchman on the back of Whisper's neck reminded her of her invisible bonds. Said henchman had stepped in on Thursday when it came time to take her to the City Clerk's Office to sign for the marriage license.

She didn't see Zaiden. The ink of his signature was still wet when the sheet was presented to her. Whisper guessed he was close by, but didn't really care.

Once their names were dry, nothing could stop the inevitable.

So, just as her father commanded, Whisper ended up standing alone at the chapel inside of the City Clerk's Office Friday at three. Other couples sat around, waiting to be married. Couples who had been there first. In what she could only imagine was deference to the bride and groom's last names, no one minded stepping aside to give them priority.

Her father came up next to her. "Mom will be turning in her grave," Whisper murmured as he took her arm.

His hand paused on the way to the door handle. "Your mother was a good woman… one who knew her place was under her husband's command…" Turning a glare on her, Cyrus Doherty didn't leave any equivocation. "Make him happy, Whisper, and he will do what I tell him when I tell him. The fate of our family rests on you being a dutiful wife. You will do whatever it takes."

Whatever it takes. Those words rattled around in her mind while her father opened the door and took her inside. Whisper wasn't sure what she expected to find in there. Yet, it was a surprise to discover there were only three people present. They stood at the head of the room and none of them were the McDade parents.

Guessing that the man facing them was the officiant, Whisper took advantage of the opportunity to examine the other two males who stood with their backs to the room. One was shorter than the other. The top of his head only reached the taller one's shoulder.

Whisper figured the taller one was Zaiden. Every description of him mentioned his height and his jet black hair. Those locks were a mess, but matched the untucked shirt, scruffy jeans, and the heavy boots on his feet.

In her boat-neck ivory dress, Whisper's effort outmatched his, but she wasn't offended. If anything, it was a relief to learn he wasn't taking the wedding seriously. Her dress was a nod to her father's request; she'd avoided actually going with white. If Cyrus hadn't made the request, she'd likely have shown up in her usual Friday afternoon apparel: yoga pants and a sports bra.

The shorter guy peeked over his shoulder. As soon as he spied her scrutinizing him and his buddy, his attention sprang back to the front. Being close to a McDade, she wouldn't have expected him to be skittish. But he was shorter and less toned than she'd have expected too.

It was difficult to see Zaid's physique beyond the breadth of his capable shoulders and the vee of his torso to the narrowing of his hips. The shorter guy had love handles above the cinch of his tight belt and she'd seen a little extra weight in his face when he turned. It wasn't like the guy was overweight. Just an obvious contrast to the man at his side.

Her examination came to an abrupt end when she and Cyrus reached the front and the officiant started to talk. It wasn't a long drawn out ceremony; there were no sermons or hymns. It was business only.

Zaiden didn't turn to look at her, so she didn't look at him either. Not that it was easy to be sure what he was doing because, like the guy on his other side, she was no giant. All her peripheral vision picked up was the lack of movement in his body. It didn't flinch, which suggested he didn't register her.

Whisper thought they might get through the whole ceremony without acknowledging each other at all. But her luck wasn't that good. When the officiant asked Zaiden to recite his vows, the deep, growling voice that came from him filled her with chills that forced her body to react. Her baser instincts responded to him anyway.

Whisper couldn't remember the last time anything had made her afraid. Not that she was afraid. In fact, it was sort of impressive how the sinister tone of his drawling voice made every word sound like a threat rather than a promise.

He carried on just like that, saying whatever he had to without changing his tone or looking at her. Whisper didn't mind returning the latter favor on the occasions she was required to speak. She said only what was required and nothing else. Whatever impression that made on her groom, she couldn't care less.

The officiant produced rings. He placed them on the sheet in his hand like maybe he intended to say or do something with them. Zaiden didn't give him the chance. He grabbed the larger ring and shoved it onto his own finger, so she did the same with the smaller one. Apparently, they didn't have to say anything about that, which suited her fine. It was done. That was it.

Sweating and pale, the officiant was nervous. Somehow, it had taken Whisper the whole ceremony to notice. "You can kiss the bride," he said, his voice vibrating.

His hands were trembling, shaking the paper in his pale fingers. Whisper smiled. The man was terrified. It shouldn't really be a surprise. The guy at her side, her groom, was more than twice the size of the officiant, and her father was somewhere behind them.

He'd probably never presided over a marriage with

such potential to get him killed. Just one wrong word could be enough for either her father or her groom to order the officiant's family murdered… or at the very least maimed.

"We done?" Zaiden asked without kissing her, sounding unimpressed.

Whisper wasn't impressed either and had no desire to kiss him. The smart officiant wasn't going to push the issue. He backed away to show the paperwork on the table behind him.

"You… you both have to sign the—"

"Right," Zaiden said.

Taking her by surprise, Zaiden grabbed her upper arm and hauled her forward, throwing her in the direction of the table. The force gave Whisper no choice but to run the way he'd tossed her. With that momentum, her body kept going until she was bent over the hard surface, clutching the edge.

Whisper pushed up onto her palms. "Asshole," she muttered, snatching the pen from the officiant to scribble down her details. "What's that?"

Jabbing the pen toward the blank line at the end of her section, she looked at the officiant for an explanation.

Twisting around, he dipped his attention to where she was indicating. "Oh, that's a new feature. It allows couples to record their own words; like a sentimental phrase that means something to them or a tender wish for the future."

"Oh," she said, tilting her head to begin writing, reading her words as she recorded them for posterity. "Fuck you, asshole… good luck sucking your own cock."

Pleased with her addition, Whisper smiled at the officiant and raised her chin, pushing her shoulders back as she did. Ignoring the shock on his face was easy. Shocking people was a regular occurrence for her. Her sentiment probably didn't match what other people wrote on their marriage certificates, but she was proud of it.

"Ma'am, I—"

"You married, sir?" she asked, turning on her sultry side and drawing the pen to her lips. Swaying her hips, Whisper twisted her body toward his, ready to have some fun.

Raising her arm up, she locked her elbow, and let her arm sink down to rest straight on his shoulder. "You must get tired of working so long… and hard…"

Flirting was one of her favorite things to do, she considered it a hobby. Her desire to tease and play was probably rooted in her years of teenage rebellion. Back then, her father and brothers were dead against her showing any kind of sexuality. Never stopped her from doing it whenever she could, usually whenever they weren't around. As she'd got older, her interest in their presence or opinions had waned.

"Ma'am—"

"Shh," Whisper said, tossing the pen onto the table. Moving in, she got up close to rest the length of her finger on the shaking man's mouth. "All these men who stand before you every day…" With her finger still on his lips, she flattened her other hand on his torso and let it turn to slide south. "All these men get their happy ending…" Pouting, she forced herself even closer while pressing her palm against his groin, rubbing his dick through his slacks. "Where's your happy ending… Have you got an office…" Trailing her finger from his mouth to his belt, she slid the leather from its buckle. "Or would you like it right here."

"Whisper!" her father barked.

Rolling her eyes away from the stunned officiant, just a moment before her father seized her arm and yanked her away, Whisper groaned. "Daddy, I'm just having some fun."

He hauled her closer to hiss in her face. "That kind of fun could get a man killed. You're a married woman now."

Somehow she doubted he cared about the officiant's safety or her virtue. "Yeah? What does that matter?" she asked, admiring her manicure. "Are we going someplace to get drunk?" Peeking over her shoulder, she ignored the groom and his buddy who were just out of her field of vision. Her focus stayed on eyeing the officiant, running her tongue along her top lip as she did. "Or have I gotta find my own fun?"

"You are going to your wedding reception," her father said, tightening his grip and giving her a shake. "And you will behave yourself."

"Or what?" she snapped, jerking her arm down and

out of his grip. The kind of bruises that would leave were normal for her, she'd worn them most of her life. "No one said anything about a reception. I have plans later."

Grabbing her again, Cyrus hauled her up the aisle. At the other end of the room, by the door they'd first come through, he swung her around to slam her back against the wall. "Are you trying to get yourself killed?"

"Do you care?"

"Whisper," he growled, slapping his hand flat to the wall next to her head. Instinct made her flinch. Damn instinct. "You think I'm going to hit you?" With a shake, he seized her chin to force her attention back to him. "That's not my responsibility anymore, sweetheart. If you need to be taken in hand, it will be your husband's job… Tell me who you'd rather have disciplining you? Your father or the man you branded a psychopath?"

Gritting her teeth, she sucked in a breath. "If he touches me, I'll slice him open."

Easing back, Cyrus' eyes dropped for a moment. In the next breath, he lunged forward again, getting so close that his nose bumped hers. "You're carrying a weapon? On your wedding day? Are you fucking insane?"

"I'm a Doherty, Daddy," she sneered. "I haven't walked the streets unarmed in all my twenty-nine years… Momma used to hide her blade in my stroller… remember, Daddy?"

Shoving away from her, he put a foot of space between them. "For all the good it did her, she was still slayed by that bastard Byrne." He opened his hand to her. "Give it to me."

"No," she said.

There was a chance her new husband might have designs on what he'd like to do with their wedding night. Complying was her duty. Giving him what was left of her shredded virtue was her obligation. But there were some acts she'd never consent to. If he tried to take from her against her will, she'd take something precious of his in return… Something that would make it impossible for him to ever violate another woman.

"Whisper," he growled, but she remained defiant.

Her father's backhand was swift. Her head snapped to the side, but she felt nothing, not really. It wasn't like she'd never been on the receiving end of his wrath before. Tossing her hair away from her face, she brought her focus back to where it had been before.

"You should've just killed me," she murmured, sneering at him.

Sliding her shoulders down the wall to bring her leg up, she hooked the heel of her stiletto on the back of the wooden pew-like bench behind her father. Whisper curled her fingers around the end of her skirt to drag it up, revealing the sheathed knife strapped to her thigh and wrapped in a length of white silk.

"Festive," came a voice from the aisle beside them.

She rolled her head on the wall to see the shorter man from the altar. That was her first chance to get a good look at him. In his thirties, the man wasn't exactly smiling, but he wasn't scowling either. His attention was fixated on the weapon on her leg.

"Like what you see, baby?" she asked, shifting her foot from the back of the bench to his torso.

Her shoulders were still on the wall giving her an anchor point. Whisper raised her leg a little higher to bring the silk over her crotch into his view, which was exactly her plan. Her grip on the hem of her skirt remained firm to ensure it stayed high.

With heavy eyes, she maintained her focus on the man under her heel. Pushing it a little deeper into his gut made his mouth open, Whisper wanted more of a reaction than that. A shadow appeared behind him, putting an end to her toying. For a man of his size, Zaiden McDade moved quietly. Despite being aware of him, she did her best not to look over her prey's head.

"Stop this bullshit," Cyrus hissed. "Give me the knife, Whisper."

"Let her keep it," Zaiden said, startling both her father and the man under her shoe. "Anyone who can be taken down by a little girl deserves to go down."

Grabbing his lieutenant's shoulder, Zaiden pulled him away from her, sending her foot back to the floor with a thud. The two men vanished through the door without waiting.

Whisper boosted herself off the wall to straighten up. Swiping her hair from her face, looking at the door, she touched the cheek her father had struck. "He's got some damn nerve."

"He's not the only one," Cyrus said, snatching her shoulder to pull her through the door. "You're going to get yourself in check, Whisper. No more of your bullshit."

Those waiting in the hallway outside didn't dare look at her being dragged past them. Even the people who probably weren't from the area seemed to get the sense that it wasn't a moment to gawk or, God forbid, step in.

Not that she'd be averse to getting a little blood on her dress. Her father hauled her out to the street and threw her into a waiting limo that got moving the minute the door closed.

"Dragging the name of this family through the mud has always been a specialty of yours," he said. Her skirt had ridden up when she'd fallen face first into the back of the car, so she raised her hips to tug it down. "Your mother would be ashamed of you."

"No more ashamed than she'd be of you," she said, lifting and dropping into the seat to get comfortable. "You think this is what she'd want for any of us?"

"I think she would be disgusted that you dishonor your brothers' memory."

Losing Adan and Keegan had changed everything about their lives. Most of the time, her brothers found something to be on her case about. Despite that, there was no way she could deny they'd loved her, in their own way.

Both were hard men… or they had been. Their father had raised them both to believe that showing affection was a sign of weakness. The one thing none of the men were allowed to do was expose any vulnerability. Women were seen as weak just by their very nature. Whisper had fought against that ideology all her life, which was probably why she acted out. It wasn't easy to be noticed when you were considered the weakest member of the family, even if that was the Doherty family.

The Doherty legacy was a lot to live up to and it wasn't a role she'd coveted. Her brothers were expected to take over the family business. Whisper was a drain on resources, as her father often reminded her. Although she'd been in the bosom of the family, it had never fallen on her to prove her loyalty, not to the level of handing herself to the enemy.

Whisper opened the fridge to retrieve a bottle of champagne. "I married him, didn't I?" she said, filling a flute. "I did what I was told."

Her father seized her arm and tugged her around with such force that champagne sloshed onto the floor.

"You were told to make him happy," Cyrus hissed. "Finding out his wife is a slut will not make him happy."

"You don't have a damn clue what will make him happy," she said. Despite still being in her father's grip, Whisper turned her head to tip some alcohol into her mouth. "He didn't have a problem with what I was doing and, like you said, I'm his to discipline now, right?" His grip tightened. The pinch was obvious, its meaning was not. Wearing her own glare, she drew her lips away from the glass to pin it on him. "You put another bruise on me, Daddy, I'll go to the cops and tell them he put it there… What will that do for relations with the new in-laws?"

"I made this deal to show this family we are serious about an alliance… If I have to sedate you to hand you over, I will do it. You will behave. You will show respect and deference. You will *not* make a fool of me or your husband."

The vicious look in his eye didn't scare her, it disgusted her, but that didn't prevent her from returning it. "You hate that you have to rely on me."

"Yes," he spat. "You're a woman. You're weak and unreliable. I told your mother we should've drowned you at birth."

Hissing, she lunged at him. "And I told her she should've left you when we found you balls deep inside that hooker."

The next slap sent her onto the limo floor, scattering her champagne. Still, Whisper wouldn't relent. On a sharp inhale, she whipped around to glare at him. The power in that last hit was impressive given their restricted space. Practice really did make perfect; her father had always been quick and strong with his hands.

"It should've been you that day," he growled.

She breathed out a laugh. "There isn't a day that goes by that I don't wish it had been... Daddy."

Spitting out his title, she checked for blood on her lip and was pleased to find none. A speckling daze crossed her vision; Whisper damned him and his short fuse. Resenting him was only half the battle. Frustrating as it could be to exist only as an object for her father to despise, at least she'd always known where she stood with him.

For the first almost two thirds of her life, Whisper's mission was to make her father proud of her, to get his attention or some kind of recognition that she even existed.

That changed the day of her mother's funeral when she discovered him having sex with one of the servers at the wake. Her mother's body wasn't even cold in the ground, and he was enjoying himself in the first nubile body that crossed his path.

Her respect for him had dwindled almost daily since then. She'd known he cheated. Whisper didn't know a single man in their circle who was faithful. But to see her mother so disrespected did something. It twisted whatever optimism was left inside her, wringing it out until cynicism was all that remained.

THREE

WHISPER WAS STILL on the floor of the limo when it came to a halt.

Cyrus shifted in his seat. "Everything of yours has been packed up and shipped to the McDade house," her father said. "They own a townhouse in their neighborhood. You will go home with your husband tonight."

"I figured that out all on my own," she said, getting over the fog created by his hit.

The driver opened their door. Getting out of their way, he stepped aside; the move revealed a group of men loitering on the sidewalk. McDade men. Whisper didn't have to be a genius to know that. Behind them was a restaurant, a homey looking, unremarkable establishment that she couldn't remember ever visiting in the past.

The McDade men saw her too. Despite the passers-by and the noise of the vehicles on the street, she could tell that they'd stopped talking. Whisper wasn't interested in their conversation and couldn't have heard it anyway. Either they thought she had super hearing or their glaring was an attempt to intimidate her. Idiots. Being vigilant made sense, they didn't have trust. An enemy was at their door. On the other hand, if they thought they could scare her, she'd stick with her label:

idiots.

Cutting them some slack, Whisper considered that their silence might be something to do with seeing her sprawled on the floor of the car at her father's feet. They couldn't be shocked by the sight. The Dohertys treated their women with disdain and there was little chance the McDades didn't do exactly the same.

Her father got out of the car and snapped his fingers at her. All Whisper could do was climb onto the seat and drag her fingers through her hair. When they caught on the knots, she enjoyed the sting in her scalp. Causing herself pain was a million times more satisfying than letting her father have the pleasure. So much of her life was out of her control that she clung to any glimmer of it.

Cyrus bent to grab her arm and pulled her out of the car. The men she'd seen before were gone, so at least the ogling was over; there was some solace in that.

"This is a happy occasion," her father said, dragging her to the external stairs that led to the basement section of the restaurant. "Go in there, sit with your friends, and for God sake, behave… or you'll get us all killed."

Her father wasn't the type to wilt in any room or scenario. Cyrus Doherty was made of steel. That said, the shootout had shaken everyone up. Their family had never been more vulnerable and although she had no idea how long the possibility of the alliance had been in the mix, the reality of it was still in its infancy.

The McDades weren't going to put in much effort for the Dohertys until they proved their word was good. By going through with the wedding, Whisper had completed the first challenge. It definitely wouldn't be the last she'd have to endure.

At the bottom of the stairs was a wooden door with a small glazed section. Next to that was a large picture window adorned with gold lettering that declared the place "Kitty's."

"Inside," her father said, shoving her forward and grabbing the long brass handle to open the door in front of her.

Giving her no choice, Cyrus pushed her inside. The

rumble of conversation dwindled and died. As those present assessed the Doherty interlopers, Whisper scanned the space. The large dim room had a bar to the right at the back and an empty stage to the left. Four square pillars equidistance from each other supported the floor above.

Two long, busy tables, stood far from each other with all the pillars between them, separating the families. The table closest to the door was full of what appeared to be McDade family members. On the furthest right of the pillars the other table was occupied by people familiar to her.

In between, in the middle of the pillars was a chasm of space. Maybe it was supposed to be a dance floor? Whisper doubted it. The stage was empty and she couldn't hear a beat of music. More likely these two families just didn't want to mix with each other.

She turned her chin toward her shoulder. "Great start to your alliance, Daddy, huh?"

Believing the families would ever be able to trust each other was insanity. That was her wedding reception, meant to be a time when they were building trust, and the two sides couldn't even share a table. Urging her forward, her father took them past the end of the McDade table. Those around it turned to each other to mumble as she passed.

Yes, to them Whisper Doherty was a spectacle, but she couldn't complain. The McDade side would be just as fascinating to her faction. Her father pushed her around the Doherty table with an urgency that made her deliberately slow. Offering waves and smiles to those she was happiest to see, Whisper wouldn't be rushed. Unfortunately, there weren't many people on that list. Really it only consisted of her girlfriends. They'd been arranged on the far sides of her two cousins. The empty space between was apparently reserved for her. Her father forced her into the seat flanked by her cousins. The ones who would never have been invited to something like this pre-bloodbath.

With her back to the wall, Whisper was in the middle of the length of the table. Cyrus planted her there between Caelan and Miles, her Uncle Dallin's boys. The three had been promoted within the family since the shootout. Even without there being a discussion, Whisper knew her father resented the necessity of elevating his brother. Caelan and Miles loved their new positions of power, even if they were eager idiots sometimes.

Her girlfriends, Mariana and Paula had been put on either side of her cousins. Whisper would rather be sitting next to them, but the setup was no accident. Cyrus must have planned it. She couldn't flirt with her cousins. No doubt they'd been given instructions to stop her from making any kind of scene as well.

Caelan was talking over her to his brother. Despite not acknowledging her, he at least had the presence of mind to grab one of the bottles of champagne from the table to pour her some alcohol.

Drinking from her flute, ignoring her babbling cousin, Whisper already wanted a way out. As she wondered how long the farce would go on before people started to disperse, she glanced up, past those at her table. At the other table, the eyes of the man from the altar were on her.

He sat in the position that mirrored hers. His back was to the stage and despite the hubbub at his table, he didn't flinch. The shorter guy from the ceremony was at his side, talking, though probably not to his buddy because he wasn't paying attention. Scrutinizing the McDade table, she counted only one woman. The pillars did obscure some of her view, but Whisper couldn't recall seeing any other women during her initial scan from the threshold.

So, the McDades were a male clan, no shock there. Maybe the idea was to protect the females from her. Though Whisper didn't know the specifics, no doubt her reputation preceded her. The McDades probably shared accounts of her family, just as hers did of theirs. Though there was always a chance a feeble woman such as herself didn't feature in the tales.

Decoding his gaze at such a distance wasn't possible. Whether he was judging her or lusting after her, she was oblivious, and didn't much care that he was difficult to read. He was her husband, sure, but as far as she was concerned, they could maintain this same distance for the rest of their lives. Given his reputation for violence, if she was really lucky, widowhood may feature in her future. Hopefully sooner rather than later.

It was on the tip of Whisper's tongue to ask her cousins if that was an easy thing to set up when her father rose from his seat at the top of the table. He raised a glass and didn't do anything delicate like tap a spoon against the crystal. No, her Uncle Dallin took care of getting the room's attention by calling out.

"Shut it! The lot of you bastards!"

Well, so much for the ladies in the room. Mariana and Paula were used to her family, and if the woman at the other table was a McDade, she'd be used to the same kind of language.

In credit to the room, everyone did quiet down. No one drew a weapon or responded with offence, they just looked to her father on his feet with his glass aloft.

It lowered in time with the start of his speech. "This is a historic day…" Cyrus began.

Whisper smiled. Anything that reminded her of just how important her father believed himself to be brought a smile to her face. It was just so ludicrous. He was a man, like any other. Thinking himself a God didn't make him one. Though the element of irony in her silent mocking wasn't lost on her. For most of her life, she'd believed him to be one. There was probably still some corner of her psyche that thought it could be true.

"Our two families have been at war for too long," Cyrus continued. Whisper picked up her glass to drink, wishing for something stronger than champagne. "This union will bring us closer. We are one family now. Our interests are yours, and yours ours… Solidifying our alliance with this marriage will allow us to move forward. We will share our failures and our successes, which I'm sure will number many."

It wasn't exactly a typical father of the bride wedding reception speech. Whisper drained the last of her champagne and filled her glass with more. No one else at the table, or in the room, seemed to be drinking. She made her peace with her actions, figuring she had to catch up. The people at her reception might have been there for a while before the actual wedding party arrived. That was her excuse anyway.

"To the Dohertys and the McDades," Cyrus said and raised his glass to drink.

The rest of the room drank too. Conversation resumed as Cyrus sat down again. Whisper swept a hand around her glass and gasped in a breath. Before she could stand up, both her cousins grabbed a wrist each, pinning her hands to the table.

"Your father doesn't want you to speak," Caelan said, leaning in at her side. "He thought you might try it."

"It's my wedding," Whisper said. "I can do whatever I damn well please."

The internal door next to the bar opened and a procession of servers came out to begin distributing food. The moment for speeches was over. She turned a glare to her father who was returning her ire.

Already Whisper knew it was going to be a long night and she doubted that signaled anything positive for her future.

FOUR

FOOD WAS PLENTIFUL, Whisper wouldn't have expected anything less. By the time the meal was over, night was beginning to descend outside. The long window at the front of the building, by the entrance, was lit from the outside by the lanterns on the enclosed terrace at the bottom of the stairs. The external space was used by the smokers.

At least, the Dohertys went out the front. Every once in a while, a posse of McDades used the same door the servers had emerged from. Any time the door opened, she expected a burst of light that never came. Whatever was back there, it was no kitchen. With the pillar in the way, she couldn't see much, but couldn't say she really cared.

Cousin Miles had left his post to scurry up to the top of the table where he huddled with her father and his.

Mariana bounced onto his seat to get closer. "Why didn't you tell me about this?" her friend asked.

"I only found out this week," Whisper answered.

Paula leaned over Caelan who was typing into his phone and didn't seem to mind the skinny woman disregarding him. "You should've called us."

"What would you have said?" Whisper asked, realistic about her friends' capabilities and limits.

"We'd have said you don't love him," Mariana said. "How can you marry a man you don't love?"

"You don't understand," Whisper said, tipping the last mouthful of champagne from the nearest bottle into her glass.

"We do understand," Mariana said. "How can you say we don't?"

"You think love matters," Whisper said. "That's how I know you don't understand."

"He's attractive," Paula said, looking over at the McDade table, something Whisper had been trying to avoid since finding the groom leering at her. Caelan let his phone drop to the table. The positive words probably perturbed him. "Though I think I'd be too scared to… you know."

"You're too scared of your own shadow," Mariana said, slipping a hand under Whisper's to link their fingers. "You know what the Wild One's like with guys."

"Yeah, no worse than you," Whisper said, responding to her friend's use of her nickname. "Speaking of which, we should go out after this."

"Uh, you're not allowed to go out," Caelan said.

Whisper scoffed and reached over to take his whiskey. "Says who? It's Friday night. We always go out on a Friday."

"Yeah, and usually don't get home until Sunday… sometimes Monday morning," Mariana said, dropping her head onto her shoulder.

Whisper turned to kiss her friend's hair. Mariana was as wild as her when it came to their nights out. Paula was more subdued, that's what she liked to think anyway. Usually after a few drinks, Paula was almost more eager than them to party.

"Yeah, well, Cyrus said you're following Razer's rules now," Caelan said.

"Razer?" Paula asked. "Who's… who's Razer?"

"That's what they call Zaiden McDade," Caelan said, blinking at the three women as they turned their focus to him and drew in closer. "Do you have any idea who he is?"

"He's Whisper's husband," Mariana said, making Whisper smile. "What do you mean? Who is he?"

Whisper knew of his reputation for being vicious; details weren't that important to her.

"Burl McDade is the head of the family," Caelan said, looking over them to nod at the older man standing behind Zaiden's seat. The patriarch wasn't alone, a group that included his sons clustered around him, hanging on his every word. "He took power from his own father by slowly poisoning the man. Didn't even have the decency to do it quick; that man's death was torturous."

"That's horrible," Paula said, sickness in her expression.

Caelan scoffed. "That's nothing to what he did to his wife. Killed her while he was fucking her. Apparently, he did it 'cause she asked him to give up his favorite mistress. The mistress had threatened his wife's life, but that didn't matter to him. He killed her for questioning him."

"While he was…" Mariana trailed off and pulled herself closer to Whisper. "How did he kill her?"

"Did he strangle her? Smother her?" Paula asked.

The woman had an uncanny ability to appear both queasy and enthralled at the same time. Whisper had recognized Paula's ability to do it during the numerous times she recounted the tales of her brothers' exploits.

Making eye contact with each of them, Caelan shook his head. "Gouged out her eyes."

A disgusted chorus of "*ew*" went around their group, which probably drew the attention of others. The women were too intrigued to care.

"That doesn't kill you though," Mariana said. "Does it? You can live without your eyes."

"Does when you fuck the empty socket that's left."

Mariana and Paula made another sound of disgust.

Whisper sank back in her seat, away from the huddle. "That's not true."

"It's true," Caelan said, twisting toward her and nodding fast. "I swear on my mother's fucking life."

"Your mother's dead, Caelan," she said, tipping the rest of his whiskey into her mouth. "There's no way Burl killed his wife like that. Even if he did, it wasn't for asking a question. The woman gave him four sons; they must have been together a long time."

"Ten, fifteen years, I think, maybe," Caelan said in what was obviously a blind guess. "This was just after Doran was born… he's the youngest…" Turning around, he scanned the table opposite and nodded to the group Burl was commanding. "The one wearing the red tie. That's Doran, he's the one always fucking up. The Byrnes best friend and the one we're most worried about."

That made her sit to attention. "Byrnes friend?"

Any notion that the McDades were friendly with the Byrnes turned her stomach.

"Not really, just… when he fucks up, it benefits them," Caelan said. "See the problem with the McDades, they're known for being short tempered. Previous generations couldn't keep their guys out of prison… You know how they say serial killers are usually caught for something stupid? A broken taillight, that kind of thing." The women nodded. "McDades can run an operation probably better than any other family. They've got their network, women, drugs, all of it, they're in it, and they've got the guys to hide the money trails… But you piss off a McDade and he'll put a bullet in your head, witnesses be damned."

"Idiots," Mariana murmured. "Who does something like that?"

"They are idiots," Caelan said. "Some guys slights them, insults them, even in the tiniest way, and they blow a gasket… Doran's done a couple of short stretches in prison… and everyone knows about Score McDade. Only one who can manage to hold it together is Razer… Zaid."

Mariana stroked her arm. "Least you've got the calm one."

Caelan snorted. "That's not what I said. No fucking way. He doesn't murder guys 'cause he enjoys seeing them in pain. Word is the guy carries a straight razor on him at all times. He doesn't care about the insults; he isn't easily offended like that people say. But if his father sets him on someone, he'll track a mark down and literally carve pieces off the guy… It's sick. I've seen some of his skinning work, it would make you puke."

A guy who could be cool and methodical in his torture; that was something. A secret corner of Whisper heard Caelan's words as a challenge. She'd married the calm McDade, though that was a relative term given what Caelan was saying. But it sort of made her want to see how easy it would be to bring out his inner McDade.

"I don't know about Score McDade," Paula said. "Which one is he?"

Sitting up straighter, her friend bobbed left and right, trying to seek him out. "You won't see him over there. Score did time in Texas for murder."

"Did? Past tense?"

Caelan's nod was solemn; Whisper called bullshit. "The vic wasn't even dead, Biz set him up."

"Biz is Parker McDade," Mariana said, leaning against Paula. "Burl's number one son. His second in command."

"He set his own brother up for murder?"

"Who cares?" Mariana asked. "Zaiden is the one Whisper has to live with."

"Zaid," Caelan said. "Everyone around him calls him that... calling him Razer, unless you're part of their inner circle, usually leads to bloodshed."

"Is he violent to women?" Paula asked, the sweetheart really sounded concerned.

"They all are," Caelan asked.

"I heard he was a psycho."

Caelan was nodding. "He does most of the family dirty work, 'specially now Score's out the picture," he said and was more discreet about his next nod across the room. "The guy with the pocket square, that's Parker McDade, Biz, the oldest of the brothers. He's married to Nicole, the only woman at their table. He's all business."

"Who's the guy with him?" Whisper asked.

"With who?" Caelan asked, then seemed to notice her eyes were narrowed on the man standing next to Zaid. "Oh, that's Bosco... I don't know his story other than... well... like you see, he sticks to Razer like glue."

"I can't believe they call him Razor," Paula said on an

exaggerated shiver. "I get it's 'cause he carries a razor, but—"

"No, that's not why," Caelan said. "It's not with an O, it's with an E. When he was a kid, after his mom died, he set fire to everything, literally everything. He set fire to his family members' homes, his schools, cars, whatever. He turned into this crazy fire razer."

"Does he still do that?" Mariana asked. "Damn, that's scary…"

Caelan shrugged. "Don't know. Haven't heard about anything going up in smoke for a while, but… maybe. I think if he has to, he'll do whatever his father says."

"Sure 'cause gouging out his mother's eyes probably really showed him what his father was capable of," Mariana said, her lip curling to a sneer. "That's disgusting."

"You know they probably have stories about us too," Whisper said, glancing at Caelan, though her sentiment was meant for Mariana and Paula as well.

They weren't from crime families. Well, Paula wasn't. Not exactly. Her father was a lawyer with questionable ties. Mariana's uncle did work for the Dohertys.

"None of us ever gouged out a woman's eyes while we were fucking her," Caelan said.

"Says you," Whisper said. "I don't know what you men do while you're in bed with women. Don't forget two thirds of our family just died, Cae. I don't know about all of them, but I know Keegan had a sadistic streak, that's for goddamn sure."

"Not that sick."

Leaning back, she tried to seek out a clock… or some liquor. "What time is it?" Whisper asked.

"Seven thirty, maybe eight," Caelan said. "Why?"

Whisper took Mariana's hand, then sought out Paula's over Caelan. "We can go get ready at your place, Paula. Be at Scooby's by nine, maybe ten."

Paula was nodding. Mariana pushed out her chair, ready to go.

Caelan grabbed Whisper's arm before she could stand. "You can't leave. It's not allowed. Did Razer say you could go?"

"Razer hasn't said a damn word to me," Whisper said. "If he hasn't given me any instructions, how can I be expected to follow them? I'm not breaking any rules."

"Why do you want to leave?" Caelan asked, probably against revealing his concern. It was obvious, so she hoped he didn't think he was doing a good job of hiding his worry. It was a shame really. Her cousin had been charged with controlling her, which wasn't an easy feat. "Why not just stay and keep the peace?"

"How many reasons do you need? I don't have any money or a drink," she said. "There's no music or dancing… This place is a dud."

"You got that right," Mariana said. "I say we hit the clubs hard tonight."

"Agreed," Whisper said, pulling her friends to their feet.

Caelan didn't let her go, so he was forced to stand too. "Okay, hold on, how's this," he said, opening his arms in an attempt to block them against the table. "I'll buy you all liquor… and there's a jukebox in the corner. You can find something to dance to on there … right?"

The jukebox was on the wall beside the mysterious door used by staff and McDades. The dancefloor was on the McDades side of the room too, laid out in front of the still empty stage. In that dance space were a couple of groups of McDades. That family seemed to be against sitting at their table, whereas hers barely left their seats.

"I kinda want cake," Paula said.

Whisper smiled. "You're thinking we stop at The Creamery? See if Jimmy will feed us out the back door?"

Mariana squealed in delight and Paula laughed. "I like when he says we're like lost little kittens."

The Creamery was their favorite bakery in the city. While it would be closed at that time of day, they knew the owner. He was often there late preparing for the following day. Whenever they stopped by, he'd feed them no matter the time. Before or after, sometimes during, their night in their favorite club, which was just down the block from his premises.

"I think we should go to Santiago's first," Mariana said.

Paula laughed again, but it was Whisper who called their friend out. "You wanna fuck Santiago," she said. "That's why you want to go there."

Paula kept laughing. Mariana whimpered. "You got to do it. He's so hot… you're married! You can't keep him to yourself anymore."

Holding up her hands, Whisper didn't hide her smirk. "I never wanted to keep him all to myself… You know we're allowed to share guys unless we specifically claim exclusive rights."

"Which you've never done," Paula said.

"Thank you," Whisper said, presenting a flat hand to her friend. "Which I have never done. Thank God someone's paying attention."

Leaning in, Mariana teased. "Santiago only has eyes for you though… maybe someone should tell him he's a free agent."

"Oh, they all fall for her and you know it," Paula said.

"It's the danger," Whisper said, knowing that Paula's statement wasn't even close to true. "See half the guys in the city are too afraid to fuck me because they think my father will gut them… The other half want me as a trophy on their wall."

Pouting, Mariana hugged her arm and nuzzled in close. "And none of them see the true you, honey, do they?"

Whisper stroked Mariana's hair. "No, they don't. I'm so misunderstood."

Paula leaned past Caelan, a look of mischief in her eyes. "You guys should do that show thing you do," she whispered and actually covered her laugh with a hand.

Mariana lifted her head from Whisper's shoulder. "At her wedding reception?" she asked before turning an expression of glee on her. "Want me to say congratulations properly, girlie?"

Sliding her arms around Mariana, Whisper's eyes got heavy as she scooped her hands around her friend's ass. "Think it's only right, don't you?"

The women were practiced at teasing a room like

pros. Finding each other's mouths, they wasted no time. Kissing one way and then the other, they pressed closer and let their tongues touch in the ecstasy of a kiss that never meant more than the moment.

In nightclubs, they danced together like they were lovers. They knew how to work a pole and were no strangers to the podiums. Paula encouraged all the misbehaving, but usually ruined the mood with her giggling.

Mariana slid her hands up and down Whisper's back and into her hair, sampling her neck as Whisper's hands drifted to her friend's breasts. The move encouraged Mariana's mouth lower; together they sank against the wall.

"What the hell is this?" Miles' voice came from somewhere.

Whisper was more interested in bringing Mariana's mouth back to hers than she was in her cousins.

"I… I don't know," Caelan stuttered. "They just started—"

"Well, stop them," Miles said.

Mariana was yanked away. Without missing a beat, Whisper grabbed her friend and pulled her back to the kiss. Cupping her face and holding her close, she enjoyed the whimper of desire Mariana added for effect.

"It's just good fun," Paula said.

"He's fucking watching," Miles hissed. "This fucking shit is exactly what Cyrus didn't want. It's fucking bullshit."

Pulling away from the kiss, Whisper licked her lips, making a show of trying to regain her senses. Mariana stroked her hair and nuzzled her neck.

"You gotta swear so much, Miles?" Whisper asked. "It's distracting."

Her fizzing cousin bounded closer. "Good. I'm fucking glad. How you want your father to explain to your husband that he's married to a dyke?"

"I don't need anyone to explain anything to anyone," Whisper said, turning her head to sample Mariana's mouth again. "I'm a free spirit."

Mariana's lips trailed to her ear. "A hot spirit… Want to come back to mine?"

That would give them a good excuse to leave the reception to go get ready for the club.

"Paula, you wanna come fuck me and my girl? We'll eat you first, be real gentle."

"Mrs. McDade…"

It didn't even occur to Whisper that anyone was talking to her until Caelan and Miles parted. Someone was standing just behind them… Bosco.

"Aww," Mariana pouted. "Is he going to ruin our buzz?"

Whisper ran a hand through her hair and tipped up Mariana's chin to kiss her again. "No, baby, don't you worry about that. He just wants a better view. Isn't that right, Mr. Bosco?"

"Happy someone's told you who I am," Bosco said. "Means I don't have to explain who I'm speaking for when I tell you that it's time to leave."

"Time to…" Mariana made a sound of disappointment. Whisper straightened her friend up and pushed away from the wall. "I don't want to leave, Mr. Bosco. The party's just getting started… I'm sure your boss's dick can wait until after I satisfy my girl's pussy… Hasn't he ever heard the expression 'ladies first'?"

"He has," Bosco said, unruffled by her question. "But I've worked with him long enough to know that making him wait won't lead to anything good for you… Mrs. McDade."

A beating on her wedding night, was that what he was promising? What a welcome to the family. But she had to pick her battles. Whisper kissed Mariana and gave Paula a hug before opening her arms and letting them fall to her sides.

"Well, Mr. Bosco, what's he got in store for me?"

FIVE

NO ANSWER WAS FORTHCOMING. When Bosco gestured to the exit, Whisper glanced around to see who was gawking only to discover that Zaiden wasn't even in the room anymore. His absence led her to assume he'd be in the back of the car waiting at the curb. He wasn't. Bosco slotted her into the back, closed the door and then got in the front passenger side. With the privacy screen locked up, there was no way to demand answers.

Whisper wasn't bothered enough to make a fuss. Alone with the minibar, she poured herself a generous drink. Getting through as many of the bottles as she could was the plan. Unfortunately, she barely got to sip the first drink before the car drew to a halt.

They couldn't have driven more than a couple of blocks. Whisper peeked out the tinted windows to check if they were stopped at a light or stuck in traffic. Neither was true. They were actually ensconced in a shadowy residential street lined with narrow townhouses and tall trees. Whisper tried the door, but it didn't open. Damn, she cursed men for their need to control others. McDade men were shaping up to be exactly the same as Doherty ones. Just as Whisper expected.

After a boring wait, someone got out the front. She heard the door open, but didn't know who it was until Bosco appeared to open her door.

"I'm not a child," she said, climbing out, straightening her skirt.

"Really?" Bosco asked. "'Cause you seem like a brat to me."

"Good," she said. "That was exactly what I was going for."

Looking up at the building in front of them, she couldn't deny that it was pretty. With red brick and black accents, there was a gated stairway to the basement level. A wrought banister flanked the stoop that led to a grand black door.

"Welcome home, Mrs. McDade," Bosco said and gestured at the stairs.

"No one going to carry me over the threshold?"

In opposition to her tease, Whisper was actually quite happy about that. Being in anyone's arms, especially McDade affiliated arms, would make her edgy. Her aversion wasn't entirely about her in-laws. Relaxing with any man who did anything affectionate or sentimental was beyond her capability. She could handle just about anything else. Tenderness, intimacy, ridiculous sappy things like that made her feel weak and soft. Whisper resented anyone who even implied she was either.

"If I were you, I'd be glad it's quiet now," Bosco said, opening the front door. "It won't always be like this."

The parquet floor in the hallway wasn't easy to see in the dim light of the unilluminated hallway. In contrast to the shadows lurking around them, dull light shone from somewhere deeper inside the building. The stairs to the left would take them up or down. But the light came from the open double doors on the same wall as a long display unit to her right. The unit with its cabinets at the bottom and shelves above obscured her view. Whatever its origin, the illumination wasn't bright enough to be from an overhead light.

Her curiosity was piqued. "Am I getting a tour?"

"No," Bosco said, going to the bottom of the

ascending stairs. He swept an arm toward them. "Keep going all the way to the top."

"Like the princess in the tower," she muttered, but started up the stairs given that there was little else for her to do.

Bosco was a McDade, by blood or not. Because of that affiliation, there was a brief moment in which she considered taking him down. It was instinct… least that's what Whisper told herself. They were alone, far as she could tell, so would it be really that wrong to—

"The garden floor is at the very bottom of the house," he said, following in her wake, interrupting her speculation. "That's where you'll find the gym, breakfast room, kitchen, and dining room, as well as access to both the front and rear courtyards. Mr. McDade Senior's office and the living room are on that floor we just left. The rear deck overlooks the lower courtyard. From inside, that's accessed from Mr. McDade's office. I'd advise you to avoid going in there. His living space is on the second floor. We don't encroach on that either. He likes his privacy."

"You know people say that all the time," she said over her shoulder, still tramping up the stairs. "I've yet to meet a person who says they *don't* like their privacy."

Like she hadn't spoken, Bosco kept going. "The third floor is Mr. and Mrs. Parker McDade's suite. The fourth floor is where you'll sleep."

He finished his round-up just as they got to the top of the staircase. All the wood she'd seen so far was a warm shade of cherry red. The floors and doors matched, though with the doors in that hallway closed, no artificial light seeped in. All she could do was assume it was the same hue up there.

As her eyes adjusted, she counted three doors. One to the right, at what would be the front of the house. One straight ahead. To the left was a third, wider door. That was the one Bosco pointed at.

Going to open it, Whisper had no inclination of what she'd find on the other side. It was a bedroom. A large bedroom.

Decent was her first thought as she scanned around.

The huge bed stood against the right-hand wall. A long couch ran the width of the footboard at the end. It was one of those boudoir type pieces. Didn't look that comfortable, but she'd pick sleeping there over sharing the bed with a McDade.

"Bathroom's there," Bosco said, walking past her to point to a second door further along the wall from the one they'd entered. "Closet's to your left." Perpendicular to the entrance. That wasn't the only door on that wall either. The one further along was Bosco's next destination. Without going through it, he opened it up and gave it a push. "This is your room."

At first, she thought he meant the one they were standing in. The McDades generosity was a welcome surprise. With two tall narrow windows on the back wall and a thick carpet, it was a substantial, and clean, space.

Whisper should've known better.

He didn't mean the whole suite, he meant whatever was through the door he'd just opened. She only figured that out when he swept an arm across the threshold. That arm sweep seemed to be his thing. Maybe that was some kind of signal he used to sic Razer onto people.

Showing her into the adjoining room, Bosco reached around to turn on a light as she approached. Whisper entered to find it wasn't substantial, in fact, it was tiny.

With just one window and not so much as a dresser, she pushed out her lips while studying the twin width bed. "Hmm," she said. "Cozy."

"It's the nanny's room."

Well, that startled her. "The nanny…" she said, smirking. Wouldn't be natural for her to miss such an opportunity. "Guess we should've discussed fetishes before I said I do." Turning to Bosco, she exhaled. "Does he wear diapers too?"

Her guide didn't look at her, but the sound of his inhale was intriguing. "Mrs. McDade, you are in a precarious position… it's not a safe one either."

She shrugged. "I like trying new positions."

Bosco was a tough audience. "You'd be an idiot not to treat your status here with respect."

"I treat it with respect," she said, unable to muster much concern. "From my place in the nanny's room…" She sighed. "Guess it could be worse. I could be in his bed."

"Just because you're in a separate bed doesn't mean you'll be exempt from your marital duties," he said, reversing out. "Your things are in the closet. You are free to use the bathroom… Your husband will be home any minute." Sound from beyond the room brought a smile to his previously unamused lips. "That'll be him now."

For him to be home so soon after her and Bosco, whatever said "husband" had left their reception to do couldn't have taken long. It screamed power play. Did the McDades really think she'd be kowtowed by such an obvious maneuver? They were going to be surprised if they believed she was simpering. Maybe they'd confused her for the affable Madison Byrne.

If her so-called husband was already back, the time to change her outfit was limited. After Bosco strode from the room, Whisper went straight to the closet, which she discovered was about the same damn size as her fucking nanny's room.

Interior design affronts would have to wait. She needed to find something to change into. The first door she slid open revealed a rail of expensive suits. Definitely didn't belong to her. Closing it up, she tried the opposite side next. Behind that sliding door were her dresses, all hung up in neat rows. Turned out her things weren't just there, they'd been put away with care. Interesting.

Something behind her banged, snapping her out of her intrigue. Figuring it must have been the bedroom door, she froze, waiting to see what would happen next. Bosco had distracted Zaid for a minute, but not for long enough.

The closet door was open, so it didn't take long for him to find her. Whisper expected some acknowledgement, given they'd gone the whole day without speaking to each other. But he didn't say a word or even give her a chance to come up with something.

The oaf grabbed her arm to haul her out of the closet and across the bedroom. He hadn't even bothered to turn on a light. The only illumination came from the closet and nanny's room.

Whisper wasn't fighting him, but didn't appreciate being manhandled without so much as a hello. A guy had to earn that right. As a McDade, Zaid was starting from a position a hundred behind the others. The meathead.

He flung her to the floor in front of the couch at the end of the bed and started to unbuckle his jeans. She'd just risen to her knees and shoved her hair from her face when he pulled his cock out of his pants. Her mouth—which had been open, ready to release a barrage of outrage—clamped shut without uttering a word.

"Suck it," he growled.

All Whisper could do was blink at it, there above her in all its ample glory. "Fuck me," she breathed out.

"That comes later. I said suck it."

Shaking herself from her surprise, Whisper located her grit again. "And I say no," she said, clambering to her feet, yanking her shoes off as she rose. "Would you look at that thing? No way I'm putting it in my mouth… that's an injury waiting to happen, Buster. I'm all for a hung guy, but that's gotta be ten inches!" And he wasn't even hard yet. Tossing her shoes aside, she growled. "See what you did? You made me compliment you. I really didn't want to do that."

As she turned away, he grabbed the neck of her dress at her nape and hauled her back, pulling at both sides to rip the zipper right open.

With her jaw clenched, Whisper whirled around, grinding out a sound of frustration. "This is your goddamn seduction? No wonder you McDades have to blackmail women into bed. What the fuck?"

He lunged at her, but Whisper was quick and leaped back, holding up both hands.

"Take your goddamn clothes off… wife."

"Oh, well this is a great start to our marriage. Suck it and take your goddamn clothes off." Slipping one arm out of her dress, she fanned her face. "Am I blushing?"

Bearing his teeth, he growled at her. "Do what the fuck you're told, slut."

"Okay," she said, taking her other arm from its dress sleeve. Once her arms were free of the garment, she held it to her chest while presenting a forefinger. "I love dirty talk, love it. But I am not actually a slut. If we're using the word for effect, you know, to make things dirtier and hotter, we've got to build up to that. It's only allowed if I believe there's an underlying element of respect. '*Suck it*' as an opening gambit doesn't tell me you respect me."

"You talk too much."

"Maybe I'm trying to put off the inevitable," she said, opening a hand toward his groin. Looking at it again brought a scowl to her face. "I mean, my God, man, send the next girl a disclaimer with the proposal, huh?"

"I'm six four, what did you expect?"

Her brows rose. "I've gotta be honest, I didn't spend a lot of time considering your proportions. You're a McDade and I only laid eyes on you for the first time this afternoon."

Moving in closer, he seemed less frantic when he spoke again. "Let go of the dress."

The simple command stirred something in her belly. Like a weight gathering mass, it reached her chest and kept on spreading. Her fingers loosened. The material dropped first to her waist and after catching for just a moment it drifted off her hips and to the floor.

"Do you want my weapon?"

Whisper assumed he'd want her unarmed while she was so close to such a sensitive part of his anatomy. Apparently, she was right because he opened his hand in expectation. Reaching down, raising her knee as she did, her leg came into brief contact with his. Ignoring that contact, she kept her eyes on his as she unsheathed it and placed it on his open palm.

Her expectation was that he'd toss it aside. Instead, in a deft move, he flipped the blade toward her and flicked it up, slicing through the strip of material connecting her bra cups. They fell away from each other.

But he wasn't done. Grabbing the thin strap of silk at her hip in a loop, he used the knife to cut through it in a single move, then did the same on the other side. Her panties joined the pool of material already on the floor.

"Shit," she said, crossing her hands to cup her breasts.

Zaid put the knife in his teeth and laid his heavy palms on her shoulders to push the straps of her bra away. The entitlement of his touch somehow had the effect of loosening her hands to let him follow through.

He took the knife from his mouth. "No reason you should ever have clothes on in this room," he said, using the flat of the blade on the underside of her chin to force it up. "You're my wife. Your duty is to be groomed and prepped for me every minute of the day."

"For sex," she sneered.

Zaid bowed lower, though that didn't bring him even close to her level. "For whatever the fuck I want."

Throwing the knife to the bed, he forced her down onto the floor in front of the couch again. After waiting for a couple of breaths, presumably to ensure she wasn't going to get up, he dropped onto the couch and took his cock in hand.

This was what he wanted. He wanted head and she was his wife. Damnit. Whisper had figured there would be sexual duties and that she'd be prepared to handle them when the moment arose. Turned out that actually being faced with what arose was tougher than she expected.

Scooping a hand around the back of her head into her hair, he pulled her forward, stroking himself as he did. "Suck it."

"Yeah, okay, I know," she said, resisting his force. For all the good it did; the meathead was much stronger. Flattening her hands on his thighs, Whisper pushed back, clearing her throat and moistening her lips. Another grumble from her husband tested her patience, so she took her hand to his. "Give it to me."

His hand slid away, leaving his cock in her grip, giving her a chance to learn what she was dealing with. Sliding her fist up and down, she wasn't encouraged by its length and girth. It was nothing like she was used to dealing with.

But, as was her luck, the situation wasn't going anywhere. So while reminding herself that she'd given head a bunch of times, Whisper gathered her courage and opened her mouth. It had been her intention to just suck him in and see how far he'd go. Instead she hesitated and wasted some time flicking her tongue over his head, circling it, licking, tasting.

"Wife—"

"Okay, goddamnit, I'm doing it."

Closing her eyes, Whisper took the plunge. Sucking him hard into her mouth, she dragged him in as far as he'd go. Of course, he hit her gag reflex, so she made a horrible sound and immediately pulled back.

It didn't help matters when she peeked up to find him smirking at her. "Suck it," he mouthed.

In reply, she narrowed her eyes in a glare.

Working her hand over him, Whisper hated that he got so hard. His cock was like a concrete column; a monolith that she was supposed to scale and couldn't begin to mount. As soon as that word popped into her head, she immediately chased it away.

Having him in her mouth was bad enough. If the meathead McDade tried to put it anywhere else inside her five two frame that barely reached a hundred pounds, he'd likely split her down the middle.

Determined not to give him the same satisfaction again, she squeezed him tight and shifted his dick out of the way to give her a shot at sucking his balls. He'd only said "it" and hadn't actually stated what she should suck. The more time she spent working his shaft in her fist, the less time she had to worry about how deep she could take him.

The reprieve didn't last. The meathead grabbed a handful of her hair to pull her away. Apparently, he'd figured out her game. Closing his hand over hers, he forced his dick between her lips again and used his grip on her hair to work her mouth over him.

On the plus side, he didn't seem to mind, or notice, that she was using her hand as a chaser. Her mouth only had to advance so far while her hand worked fast near his base.

"Look at me," he grumbled.

Opening her eyes, she blinked them up at him. Registering how heavy and satisfied his lazy gaze was gave her another shot of that odd sensation in her gut.

"You're good at sucking cock, Peanut," he said, pushing deep into her mouth and sliding out slow while she worked to keep up the pace, hoping he'd go off soon. "Look at the precious little Doherty Princess with those sassy cherry lips wrapped around my cock..." His smirk became something close to a sneer. "Who's your daddy now?"

That suggestion almost made her gag again. All of a sudden, the meathead jerked her hand away and surged up, forcing himself into her throat with both hands buried in her hair.

Even in spite of her struggling and the sound of her gagging, he pushed himself into her throat and held her face firm to his groin while he came inside her. Half a minute of nothing reverberated before he yanked her away and tossed her to the floor.

"You're gonna do that every night," he said, breathing out, then resting for another few seconds before tucking himself back into his pants. "And in the morning too... you need to practice 'til you get it right."

Whisper didn't have to ask herself what kind of an asshole would say that to a woman after she'd just given head. The meathead was a McDade; that was all the explanation she needed.

He stood as she sat up and crossed her legs, pulling her ankles to her body and laying her hands over them.

"You sleep naked and never close that door." He nodded toward the nanny room. "If I close it, you don't open it. I don't care what side of it you're on. It doesn't open until I open it."

"You're a real fucker," she said, her focus on the couch.

"I'm your husband, Peanut. That makes you my possession. Mine to control," he said, heading for the door. "I'm going out. Go to bed, you won't leave this suite until breakfast."

He went out without waiting for a response. A frustrated breath was about to leave her throat, but the sound of a click dammed it. Whipping around, she stared at the door for a minute before clambering up to rush over in a half-crawl, half-crouch. Grabbing the handle, she gave it a tug. It didn't move.

He'd locked it.

Fuck.

He was an asshole; she was trapped.

So much for trust in a marriage.

SIX

"THE GUY IS A MANIAC!" Whisper protested the moment the bedroom door was opened the following day. It wasn't opened by the man who'd locked it. No, course not, why face her in the light of day? Bosco was the unfortunate one standing there receiving her wrath. "There's no lock on this side. What kind of a lock doesn't go all the way through the door?"

Bosco narrowed an eye. "The kind that doesn't want to be picked from the inside?"

Snatching her purse, she shoved past him to storm toward the stairs. "You came just in time. Three more minutes and I was kicking that fucker in."

"You're a hundred pounds soaking wet," he said with a smirk in his voice. "How the hell are you going to get through a solid wood door?"

She tossed her reply over her shoulder. "Oh, believe me, I have my ways."

"You're going all the way down to the basement."

"I don't think so, buddy. Your hospitality has been swell and all, but I've got an appointment with Fuck You City and I'd hate to be late."

Swinging herself around the banister on the lower

floor, Whisper expected a clear path to the front door. Instead, she ran smack bang into a tall, hard body. Leaping away, she threw her head back to find Doran McDade peering down at her.

While he examined her, he spoke to the man still descending behind her. "You know if I saw any other guy coming down the stairs with my brother's wife, I'd have cause to put a bullet in him."

"I've done every task your brother's ever set me," Bosco said. "But we both know fucking his wife won't ever be on that list."

Still peering at her like she was a science experiment, Doran didn't hide his perusal. "Didn't think he came home last night."

"He didn't," Bosco said.

One side of Doran's mouth sloped up. "So, you haven't had your morning dose of McDade, sweetheart? Let's go upstairs and fix that, huh?"

"No, thanks," Whisper said, straightening her arm that was still connected to the newel post. "Think I got a double dose last night. I'm good for a while."

The other side of Doran's mouth twitched. Rather than respond to her, he looked over her head at Bosco. "That was a good answer."

"I've been practicing my whole life," she said, kind of pissed that he was ignoring her, though McDades being rude wasn't a surprise. "Just in case an asshole was arrogant enough to proposition me the day after my wedding."

Doran didn't care about her sass and kept his focus on Bosco. "Where was he anyway?"

"He was at... you know."

"Oh," Doran said on a blink of surprise. "Thought that was over."

Stepping aside, Whisper remained on the bottom stair. Even with the extra boost to her height, she still had to tip her head back to see both of them. "You know, you don't have to talk in code about his girlfriends. I don't care where he sleeps or who he fucks. Only thing I care about is not being locked in all night."

Doran's smirk grew. "He locked her in?"

"Yes," Whisper spat out. "He locked her in and she didn't like it. Now if you don't mind getting the hell out of my way, I have my own boyfriends to service."

"I don't think so," Doran said and did move, but only to completely block her route to the front door. "Breakfast room for you."

"My boyfriend has better breakfast," she said as he took her by the shoulders to direct her toward the descending stairs. "Every day he gives me a hearty shot of protein, right down the gullet, wakes me right up."

At the bottom of the stairs, Doran gripped her tighter to pull her back and mumble above her ear. "Only protein you'll have in your gullet is McDade protein, Hot Wheels. McDade men don't let their women cheat."

"Or ask questions," she said. "Yeah, I've heard a lot about McDade men."

He pushed her toward the back of the house into a light airy space.

There was a booth to the right and a sort of breakfast bar with stools straight ahead. Beyond that was a massive kitchen with a central island. Past the kitchen were a couple of equally spaced columns and a large dining table. Most of the end wall was glazed, so she could see light and greenery in the rear courtyard Bosco had referred to the previous night.

Doran kept shoving at her until she got to the dining table. The woman from the McDade reception table was seated there alone, surrounded by a table full of breakfast goodies. Caelan had identified her as Nicole McDade, Parker's wife. She was leafing through a hefty pile of glossy magazines with her legs crossed away from the table. Her position was definitely designed to ensure her long tanned pins were on show to all. That would be why she chose to wear the micro-mini, but classy, shirt dress. She toyed with a diamond earring and glanced up to check who was approaching. Nicole seemed to fixate on her brother-in-law, their brother-in-law actually, who was coercing Whisper forward with jabs and shoves.

"Oh, Doran," Nicole said, her lip curling in disgust. "Do you have to touch it? God only knows where it's been."

It? At first, Whisper didn't put it together that Nicole was talking about her. She only figured it out after Doran pushed her down into a chair at the table and Nicole twisted her legs away while deepening her sneer.

"*It* was trying to speed on out of here. Had to steer it back inside," Doran said, dropping into a seat a couple of places up from her.

"It's disgusting," Nicole said, without disguising her repulsed perusal. "Do we have to keep it in the house? Poor Razer, the things he does for this family." Whisper's assessment of the beauty included logging the note of hope in her next question. "Is he home?"

"Zay? No, he's out at…"

"Oh, right," Nicole said, licking a finger to drag a page of her magazine across to reveal another, then she frowned. "I thought that was over."

"When is it ever," Doran said, reaching across the table to snag a bagel.

Nicole turned up the dial on her next glare. "What are you going to do with it all day? You can't leave it here. Daddy won't have that. Shouldn't we get a pen for it or something?"

Did Nicole call her father-in-law daddy?

Whisper smiled and put her purse on the table. "Should I call him Daddy too?"

"I don't think it should call him anything," Nicole said, answering her while ignoring her completely, which was quite a skill. "I don't think it should be allowed to address any of us directly."

"Whisper is family now," Bosco said, coming through the pillars carrying two cups of coffee. "She's Zay's wife."

"It's as much family as you are, Bos," Nicole said, spitting out a scoff of horror when Bosco put one of the coffee's down at Whisper's place.

It surprised Whisper too. But she was too drawn in by the intoxicating scent of the steam to question him. Grabbing the mug, she gulped the hot liquid, almost burning her tongue. With that little piece of java satisfaction warming her, Whisper drew her heels up onto the edge of the seat.

Keeping the drink close, she hugged the cup in both hands on top of her knees.

"And we all know how you feel about me, Nic," Bos said, going around to sit at the opposite side of the table. "You'll be pleased to hear you're on Doherty duty today."

Nicole sat up straight. "Uh, excuse me?"

"You're taking her with you today. She has an appointment…" Bosco retrieved a card from his breast pocket and slid it across the table to her.

Parting her knees, Whisper leaned across to take the card. When she read it, her jaw swung loose. "The sexual health clinic?"

Bosco shrugged, but Nicole laughed. "I don't blame him for wanting to get it checked out." Shaking her body, she exaggerated her shudder. "God, just the idea of it is enough to make me want to puke."

Whisper's outrage was the inverse of Nicole's. Despite their opposing views, Whisper slanted Nicole's way, keeping her attention on the card. "I don't disagree with you."

"You have some nerve saying that in this house," Nicole blustered. "You have no idea how lucky you are to be in your position. Raze is a catch!"

"If you want him, I'll loan him out to you for free. In fact, why don't you just keep him? You love the McDades so much, two for the price of one is a steal." She tossed the card across the table at Bosco. "I'm not going. If he thinks I'm diseased, so be it, he can keep his dick to himself. No problemo."

"Wait," Doran said. "Does that mean he didn't fuck her last night?"

"He fucked my face if that counts," Whisper said, gulping her coffee. "There's no way I am going to some McDade quack. He'll poke and prod at me then make up some excuse for your buddy to back out of this."

Talking to Bosco was easier than talking to the other two, at least he'd never referred to her as a thing.

"Most STIs are curable these days," Bosco said. "And from what I saw yesterday, you wouldn't be averse to finding a way out of this deal yourself."

The McDades backing out would make her life easier. That way she'd be off the hook with her father… providing he didn't blame her for screwing it up. But what would that mean for the Doherty machine?

Whisper had always been on the periphery, never important enough to do more than just menial jobs for the family. Things were different since… Without her brothers around, she must have ascended a few rungs. Maybe? Her father had never said it, would never consent to it, but with her being the only descendant he had left, who was next in line? It couldn't be her Uncle Dallin; he'd get about as much support from Cyrus as she would. Her cousins, Caelan and Miles, were too incompetent to run it well. Did that mean when her father died that there would be a Doherty civil war with everyone trying to wrest control?

Doran's voice snapped her out of her daze. "Well, is there?"

All three people around the table were fixated on her. "Is there what?"

"A chance you might be pregnant," Bosco said.

"There's a pill you can take for that now," Nicole said, flicking over a page of her magazine. "I heard it can make women violently ill…" Turning another page, she smiled. "I say we give her two or three, see if she can take it."

"A pill for what?"

"An abortion pill," Nicole said like it was nothing.

Whisper's chin came up slowly. Bosco had no decipherable reaction.

Doran was her last hope, so she twisted to look at him. "I never thought to ask," she said, clutching her cup in one hand while she scratched the back of her ear with a manicured nail. "But you McDades are Irish Catholic, right?"

"Irish, yeah," Doran said and smiled. "Not so much of the Catholic these days."

"Burl still goes to mass," Bosco said.

"Yeah, but he's the only one."

Whisper extended her thumb and jabbed the air in Nicole's direction. "Did she really just say the word 'abortion' to me?"

Bosco folded his forearms on the table to lean closer. "If you're devout, you can't use birth control either, can you?"

"Of course I use birth control," she said, rolling her eyes and letting her feet slide to the floor. "That's just good sense. But if I got pregnant, I couldn't… I just couldn't."

Bosco's brows rose. "What if you were carrying a McDade baby?" Whisper hadn't thought to ask if she was expected to reproduce with the Neanderthal who'd locked her up last night. "What if it was a Byrne baby?"

That changed the whole hue of her pondering. Hit by rage, Whisper dropped her cup to the table, squeezing it tight in her hand. "That's not funny."

"He's not trying to be funny," Doran said. "And he's got a point, what if you were pregnant with a Byrne baby? You just said you wouldn't abort."

Recognizing that getting a reaction was what they wanted, Whisper drew on all her reserves to maintain her composure. She sank back in the chair to draw her heels up to the seat again.

"I wouldn't have to," she said, doing her best to be casual about sipping her coffee. What she really wanted to do was launch it against the opposite wall. The pressure of her anger needed a vent. Even the suggestion she'd let one of those animals touch her body tempted her to seek out a weapon.

"Why not?"

"Because my father would slit me open and let me bleed out before he'd ever let me come to term."

"He'd kill you?" Bosco asked, narrowing his eyes to peer closer. "His own kin? Even if this baby was a product of rape? Which I'd guess it would have to be if your reaction to the Byrne name is any indication how you feel about them."

"If it wasn't rape, her husband would do the slaying," Nicole said and licked her fingertips again. "McDade men don't like their women to cheat."

"Neither do Doherty men," Whisper said. "Wasn't a double standard I paid attention to when they said it either."

Nicole's face was turned down, so there was a chance Whisper read it wrong, but she was certain that for a fraction of a second, a quirk of a smile touched Nicole's mouth. Filing that tidbit away, Whisper wondered if Parker knew his wife stepped out on him. There was no way that reaction could mean anything else.

"Doran, what are you doing down here?" a voice boomed from the other end of the room, somewhere around the bottom of the staircase. "You have a meeting upstairs."

The voice was too mature to be Parker, so she'd guess it was Burl. If it was Parker, he'd probably have come to say good morning to his wife. But she didn't know the dynamics yet or what kind of marriage they had. For all she knew, they hated each other.

"Now? Are they here?" Doran jumped to his feet, tossing the last bite of his bagel down. "On my way." He put a hand on the back of Whisper's chair, but leaned down to kiss Nicole who tipped her cheek up for him. "You good, babe?"

Nicole rotated her hand in an absent wave and caught a tendril of hair as she let it droop. That seemed to be enough of an answer for Doran who turned to hightail it in the direction of the voice.

"You better get ready, Nicole," Bosco said.

"Are you giving me orders, Toad? How do you think my husband will feel about that?"

"I don't know. How do you think Razer will feel about you referring to his wife as an object all morning?"

Unfazed, Nicole sighed. "He knows all Dohertys are sub-human."

Whisper grinned. "You know, I thought the McDades were rude and undisciplined. Now I've moved in, I find out you're disciplined in your rudeness. Least I was half right." She took a mouthful of coffee. "But I can't be offended. In fact, I encourage all of you to talk about this in front of Zaid as much as possible."

Nicole sighed again. "Nobody calls him Zaid… though I suppose you probably should… or Mr. McDade… or lord and master, I don't know."

"Thanks for the suggestions," Whisper said. "I have plenty of my own to try out."

Most of her suggestions started with curse words… ended with them too, but she wasn't short of ideas.

Nicole closed her magazine and twisted around to stretch herself out before rising to her feet on a long exhale. "I suppose if I must take the mutt to the vet, I should get moving… She better be riding up front… or in the trunk. I won't sit with her."

"Don't worry about that," Whisper said and put her cup down to hop to her feet, blocking Nicole's way. "I'll just sprout my devil Doherty wings and fly…" Though Nicole crooked an unimpressed brow, there was enough hesitation in her eye to reveal a simple truth. Sniffing out weakness was in Doherty blood. Relishing her discovery, Whisper smiled and tsked. "Oh, Mrs. McDade, your husband never taught you how to defend yourself… did he?" Resting a hand on the back of her chair, Whisper cocked a hip and raised her other hand to drum her nails against it. "You married into crime… right?"

Sliding her hand from her hip down the line of her thigh, she gathered her skirt out of the way. Whipping her knife from its sheath in a flash, Whisper thrust Nicole against the wall with one sure forearm.

"Bosco!" Nicole squealed in fright.

"Whisper!" he called.

Despite the sound of him darting around the table, she didn't retreat. In fact, she leaned in closer, pushing herself against the tense, rigid Nicole whose wide eyes reeked of fear. Parting her lips, Whisper licked the blade until the end nicked the tip of her tongue. The familiar metallic taste of blood heightened all of her senses. Nicole's eyes couldn't get any bigger, but her breathing grew faster and shallower.

Whisper leaned in close. "How fast can your heart beat for me, Sweet Nicki?"

Pushing her mouth over Nicole's, Whisper anticipated the instant the frozen woman was going to gasp. She used the opportunity to push her tongue into the beauty's mouth to share the taste of her blood.

Bosco grabbed her shoulder to haul her back and put himself between them. "Whisper," he hissed.

Whisper laughed and held up her hands. "Just a little

fun," she said, wiping blood from her lip and sheathing her knife.

Nicole spat on the floor in the midst of her huffing and puffing. Eventually, she worked herself into a full wail and opened her mouth to scream. As Nicole ran away in floods of tears, Whisper laughed.

"Did you have to do that?" Bosco asked, folding his arms.

Whisper had trouble flattening her smile. "I take back all the mean things I said. This family is a lot of fun. I'm bringing my knuckledusters to dinner."

Raising her hands, she wiggled her fingers near his face.

Unimpressed, he leaned away. "As you pointed out, Nicole is not from a family who practices that kind of stuff."

"Are you kidding? I don't think I ever left the dinner table without a new bruise or shedding a little blood..." Losing her smile, concern hit her. "You guys have trained her, right? She's vulnerable on the street. Her name makes her vulnerable... Shit, I can't believe I have to say that to you. The McDades are slow on the uptake."

"That's not my department," he said, pushing what had been Nicole's chair under the table.

"But you work for Zaid who—"

"Not his department either," Bosco said. "One man doesn't tell another what to do with his own wife."

Whisper shoved her own chair out of the way as she started to turn. "I'm going to beat on her."

Bosco grabbed her arm to haul her back. "What? What the hell? Why would—"

"You'd rather I do it than some fuck on the street who won't know when to stop," Whisper said. "You wanna see how fast Parker starts her training after I'm done with her?"

To his credit, Bosco grew solemn. "You wanna see how fast he beats on you if you lay a hand on his wife?"

She grinned. "You think I've never taken a beating before? Shit, Bosco, I've been in intensive care four times! Never stopped me from sassing my family, did it?"

"It doesn't work like that here," he said, clutching her arm tighter when she attempted to withdraw. "If you hurt Nic, and Parker hurts you, then Zay will have to take it up with his brother and—"

"I don't need him fighting any battles for me. If Parker wants a fight, I'll give him a fight."

"God, you don't know when to stop, do you? You won't be satisfied until you kill yourself or everyone around you."

"That's kinda the idea," she said. "Be the strongest. The smartest. The quickest. I'll never be the biggest; I know how to fight dirty to get what I want."

"I don't doubt it," he said. "But be careful around here… It's more complicated than you think."

Taking Bosco's face between her palms, she gave him a squeeze and then patted his cheek. "This is my life too, Bosy-baby. I know all about the jockeying and the deceptions and the fierce loyalty… I'm no rookie. I have been trained."

"Then use that to protect her if she can't protect herself," Bosco said. "Because like it or not, you're a McDade now."

Like she needed to be reminded of that fact.

Releasing some of her tension, Whisper stepped aside. "Fine, go tell her I'm terribly sorry. I'll travel in the trunk… I'll even buy her lunch."

"With what?" Bosco asked, going past her to the kitchen. Whisper followed behind him, grabbing her purse as she went. Opening a drawer in the center island, he produced a bunch of things. "Cell phone. Keys. Credit cards."

"For real?" she asked, picking up the credit cards. Her excitement chilled when she read the name Whisper McDade on them. "Really?"

That led to him pulling out a stack of paperwork and handing her a pen. "Time to practice your new autograph."

"You guys don't mess around, do you?" she asked, irritated, though what else did she expect? Whisper signed a bunch of name change forms, but paused when she registered what was beneath her pen after he turned the next page. "This is life insurance."

"Yep."

Narrowing a glare on him, she put a fist to her hip. "Did you think you could just sneak it in and I wouldn't notice?"

"No," he said and pushed away the sheets she'd already signed to make space. Bosco spread out the pile that were left. "There are six policies."

"Six?" she asked, her eyes about leaping from her head. "You think I'm nuts?"

Laying a hand on them, Bosco showed no shame. "Three for you. Three for him."

"Him?"

"Your husband," Bosco said, resting a hip on the island. "He doesn't trust you and you don't trust him. Understandable. But your fathers think this is going to benefit both families. Let's not bullshit each other, Whisper. This is going to get worse before it gets better, for both sides. As soon as the Byrnes hear about this, that it actually happened, they're going to be on the warpath. That doesn't leave us much time to come to terms with our new reality. You hate the McDades. We get it. We're not that wild about the Dohertys… The one thing we both hate more than each other is the Byrnes… So, are you going to help us stand up against them or you want to hand them a victory with your fucking around?"

Life insurance. Her father probably had policies on her; he'd had them on his sons. As Whisper signed the forms, she thought about how she was worth more to the men in her life dead than alive. Her hope was that she didn't come to regret the ink she was laying on the paper.

SEVEN

AFTER WHISPER WAS DONE with the paperwork and had stowed the wares in her purse, Bosco told her to stay put in the kitchen and wait. When she asked why, he glared and told her he was going to try talking Nicole down from her, probably justified, tantrum.

She didn't do well with staying put. Bosco went upstairs and Whisper began to count, she got all the way to seven before beginning to move. Creeping along to check out the gym at the front of the house on the same floor as the kitchen, Whisper remained as near to the kitchen as possible for even longer.

A good minute went by with her just loitering at the foot of the stairs. Really, she figured, it made sense to be on the same floor as the front door. They'd need to use it to leave, so going up one floor was her helping them out. Least that's the excuse she planned to use if anyone questioned her.

No one crossed her path. The front door was tempting, but so were the double doors that had tried to lure her with their light the previous night. Putting her purse on the display case opposite the stairs, she read the spines of the books on the shelves and admired the knickknacks, moving sideways up the hallway, edging closer to the open double doors. Ensuring no one was around, she sidled into the living room. The floors and sleek décor were beautiful. The warm space managed to be homey while maintaining its modern, masculine appeal.

All she'd wanted to do was snoop. Whisper didn't expect to hear voices carrying from the back of the house. The narrower double doors at the head of the living room were just slightly open. The strip of light stimulated her speculation. The back of the lower floor was glazed, that light suggested this floor could be the same.

Recalling Bosco's audio tour, she guessed Burl McDade's office was on the other side of those doors. Inching toward them, she went to the dresser just next to the doors, pretending to admire the statue in the middle while actually listening in.

"…it will take considerable effort," said the voice responsible for calling Doran that morning: Burl McDade.

"Yes, it will," her own father said. Whisper's interest increased. Her father, in McDade territory? Hell must have frozen over. "You knew this was not going to be an easy task… It is the largest operation either of our families have ever undertaken… But it will be worth it; it'll unite us as the strongest force on the east coast. Perhaps in the country."

"Let's not get ahead of ourselves," another male said. Since it wasn't Doran or Zaid or any Doherty, she guessed it was Parker. "We want to be careful, plan this right… And we need to know you're holding up your end of the deal before we commit ourselves."

"Before you commit yourselves?" Cyrus Doherty said. "I gave you my only daughter. That should demonstrate the lengths I will go to… Doesn't that prove I can be trusted?"

"The deal was she became a McDade," Doran said. "You might be willing to hand her over, but if she's not willing to follow through and commit to us…"

"My daughter is headstrong," Cyrus said. "I won't deny that she can be difficult. But she will do what is in the best interests of her family… and we are all family now."

"She doesn't get that," Doran said.

"Doran's right," Parker said. "Whether you're

trustworthy or not doesn't matter. Your daughter's the one in our bunker. Until we trust her, there's nothing we can commit to you—"

"Now wait a minute—"

"It's rude to eavesdrop."

On hearing the voice behind her, Whisper whirled around on instinct to lash out at whoever was there. Her hand was sure in its path, but it was easily halted by a bigger, stronger counterpart. Looking up at the solid form blocking out the light, she only hissed upon registering Zaid was the one scowling down at her.

"It's rude to sneak up on people," she said and tried to yank her hand back. The meathead didn't let it go. "And it's rude to lock people up too. I spent all damn night locked in that bedroom."

But there was no apology. His focus was trained on her wrist caught in the circle of his long-fingered hand. He raised it up high until her arm was almost straight.

"Delicate bones… wonder how little force it would take to crush them."

"Not half as much force as it would take for me to crush your balls in my teeth next time they're in my mouth," she said, setting a smug smile on him. The longer they stood there, the more her impatience rose. Whisper sighed. "Break it or let it go, husband. I hate a man who hesitates."

"Yeah?"

His narrowing gaze slid around to hers. Gradually, his grip began to tighten. As it did, a heat of gratification infused through her. Finally, someone in the damn McDade house who was more than just talk.

One corner of her mouth curled. She was waiting for his grip to creep past comfortable. Just past… On the threshold of her pain boundary, Whisper bent her knees to jump up. Using his own strength as a lever against him, she threw both legs around his arm and pulled down. As she flipped upside down, she swung out to thrust a fist between his legs, around to the back of his knee. One swift punch was all it took to buckle his leg.

He went down onto one knee at the same time she

landed on the floor flat on her back. Immediately Whisper did a backward roll to spring up in a crouch facing him. With her chin down, she smiled, enjoying the flame of surprise in his probing eyes.

"Interesting," he murmured.

"Mm hmm," she responded. "You'll always be stronger than me… but don't ever expect me to go down without a fight."

Standing up, he extended a hand to her. "Doherty." Slapping her hand into his, she let him pull her onto her feet. "Why are you listening in to a private conversation?"

"I'm waiting for my date," she said, her focus bouncing upward. "Just so you know, those pesky diseases you're worried about floating around in my blood? Yeah, they're floating around in Pretty Nicki's blood now too."

"She hates being called Nicki."

Playing it coy, Whisper pouted without hiding her mischief. "I figured."

No one had to tell her. Just the fact that no one used the shortened version of the name was enough of a tell for her.

Sealing his lips until they thinned, Zaid inhaled through his nose as his eyes move to the side. Although he was doing a semi good job of acting displeased, he was definitely faking it. The irritation wasn't real and she couldn't see a glimmer of genuine anger either. Pissing people off was something she was usually fantastic at. This time, she'd missed her target, but, for some reason, he didn't want her to know that.

"What did you do to her?" he asked.

Sliding one foot closer to him, she glided nearer until she could skim her knee up the outside of his leg. The fabric of her skirt drifted up her thigh the higher her leg went.

"Come closer, husband," she purred. "I'll show you."

When the sheath of her blade became visible, his gaze dropped. "You cut her."

"Uh-uh," she said, shaking her hair away from her face. "Why would I let her have all the fun?"

His awareness cooled in the time it took his eyes to

find hers again. "Flirting is your shield."

Whisper shrugged. "I prefer to think of it like a hobby," she said. "If I don't practice, I might never get good enough to play in the big leagues."

Zaid began to move, and not slow either. His long legs were capable of eating up the floor. In the momentum of his stride, he scooped her up and dipped to slide an arm around her, plucking her off her feet. Carrying her for just a step, he dropped her onto the dresser next to the statue she'd been fake admiring before he startled her.

Snatching both her wrists, he stretched her arms over her head to pin them against the wall. "You're in the big leagues now, Peanut," he growled, crouching lower.

"Careful, husband," she murmured, arching her upper body toward him. "I could be a dirty, dirty girl… Don't want to get too close without a note from your doctor." Kicking off her shoe, she folded her leg against her body to press her toes against his fly. Just because he'd captured her arms didn't mean Whisper was helpless, as she proved by sliding her toes up and down, stimulating him. "I'm not really in the mood for practice right now, Coach."

Pushing his hips against her foot, he showed he wasn't going to bow down or break. Something about his determination fired hers. Most people were either too afraid or became putty when she played with them. Zaid pushed back; unexpected, yet invigorating. She liked it. A slap or a sexual demand would've been expected, instead, he was… teasing her.

"You're in the mood for whatever I say you're in the mood for, wife."

Thrusting both her wrists together to hold them in place with just one hand, he freed his other. It slid down the sensitive flesh of her inner arm from her forearm to her breast. Pressing his palm against her, his fingers curled to squeeze her hard.

The spirit of a gratified laugh caught in the back of her throat when he bowed to drag his teeth down the swell of her breast, into her cleavage.

The only way she could hide the reaction of her

hormones was with disdain. "Our fathers are in the next room, your brothers too. Is this any way to respect your wife in company?"

His mouth stayed in her cleavage. "You didn't give a damn about modesty at the reception yesterday." When she was making out with Mariana. "Or at the wedding with the guy who married us."

No, that was true. Learning that he'd noticed both was interesting. It was on the tip of Whisper's tongue to announce those instances didn't count because they weren't real. Except the thought brought her up short. Did that mean this was real?

Fighting to get her wrists out of his grip caused him to squeeze her harder. "Zaid," she said, struggling against his hold.

Somehow he read the truth that she actually liked that he pushed her. Either that or he just didn't care about her writhing. Whichever it was, he took her mention of his name as encouragement. He sucked her breast harder, clamping his hand over her mouth as he did, probably to silence her so she wouldn't rouse the men in the next room.

But Whisper wasn't trying to encourage him. Murmuring his name was an accident, it wasn't like she was caught up in feeling good. Actually, if she was honest, she felt more than a little ill. Not because he didn't feel good, but because he did. Damn her, she was enjoying his tongue. Enjoying the curl of it on her flesh and the way it trailed down to the line where her bra cup cut across the mound he was pleasuring.

His tongue began to insinuate its way between the fabric and her skin to snake closer to her nipple. The drag of a door being opened made him straighten up.

Hauling her off the dresser, Zaid put her in front of himself. He didn't go so far as to let their bodies touch, though Whisper couldn't really figure out what he was up to because she was still trying to find her balance. Her father and Burl McDade came out of the office with Parker and Doran behind them. The sight of the men shifted her gear from bewildered to brazen.

Either the men hadn't expected to see the newlyweds, or the meeting hadn't ended well. All of them were scowling. That didn't prevent them from stopping to examine the couple. Her father looked her up and down like they were strangers rather than blood. Sure, he wasn't her biggest fan, especially of late, but she didn't think such loathing in his expression was warranted.

Even doing everything she was told couldn't win her his approval. "A whole night and they haven't killed me yet, Daddy," she said, opening her arms.

"It's early," Zaid grumbled from behind her.

Whisper chose to ignore him. "And, you'll be so proud, I think I made a friend today too," she said, raising a triumphant forefinger, not honestly expecting his praise. "Parker's wife is extremely friendly... and she tastes like strawberries."

She just couldn't help herself. Bosco was right. If she wasn't sassing or shocking, Whisper didn't know what to do with herself.

"Whisper," Cyrus hissed. "Have you hurt anyone?"

"No," she said quickly, then second guessed herself. Her chin went one way and her eyes the other. "Maybe... Does myself count?"

"No, I don't give a damn what you do to yourself," he said and lunged forward to grab her arm. He hauled her away from the McDades to drag her into the hallway. "You better not be fucking this up."

"I'm not," she said, rushing along in his wake, which wasn't that easy in only one shoe. "Not on purpose."

"You're being you," he said, whipping her around to face him when they reached the front door. "You have to stop that."

"How do I stop being me?"

Cyrus took his coat from a stand by the door and pulled it on. "You will stop your stupidity and play the dutiful wife like you were told."

Tugging on his lapels to straighten them, he only let go to seize her wrist and twist her arm further than it should go. Despite him squeezing her hard, Whisper tried to turn to counter his assault, but he pushed her back, blocking her in.

"Ah," she squeaked, bending under the pressure he put on her shoulder.

It buckled her knees, but he grabbed her throat and pulled her back up, forcing her further against the wall by the door.

"You have forty-eight hours. If you don't make progress, *I'll* terminate the arrangement."

Didn't take a genius to know that translated into him terminating her.

"Daddy," she said, gritting her teeth together so hard that her jaw began to ache. "You're gonna break my arm."

"I'll break more than that if you fuck this up for us," he said, stepping back to shove her aside, giving her arm one final yank as he released it.

The pain in her shoulder shot to the back of her neck. As he backed away, her mouth opened in a silent yelp, no way she'd dare let a sound out. It was only then that she noticed Zaid in her peripheral vision, standing at the other end of the hallway.

Her father didn't see him, thank God. He went to the door and opened it to slam out of the building. Left there, she sank against the wall, her hand resting on the ache in her shoulder.

"You don't fight him," he said, his voice as deep and menacing as ever.

Even though her arm felt like it was about to combust or drop off, Whisper smiled and forced herself to stand up straight. "After dealing with me for twenty-nine years, I deserve everything he gives me. He's my father."

Zaid came just a couple of steps closer to put her stray shoe on the dresser near her purse. "I'm your husband."

"You want to beat me?" she asked, strutting away from the wall. Even although it still hurt like a motherfucker, Whisper made herself let go of her limp arm to retrieve her shoe. "You want to break my arm and hurt me?" She dropped the shoe to the floor and righted it with her toes while slipping it on. In the second she picked up her purse, movement registered in her peripheral vision. Bosco was coming down the stairs. "Deal with my crap for twenty-nine years, then I'll let you do whatever you want to me, husband."

Broadening her smile, she pivoted to show only positive exuberance when Bosco reached the foot of the stairs with Nicole just behind him.

"Nicole has agreed to let bygones be bygones," Bosco said, giving her the eye like achieving that hadn't been an easy task.

With the high-maintenance Nicole, Whisper could believe it. "Would it make her feel better to hit me in the face?"

Bosco tilted his head. "Probably couldn't hurt."

"Not you anyway," Whisper said, stepping closer while raising her chin. She put a hand on Bosco's torso to ease him aside. "Hit me, Pretty Nicki."

Nicole gaped, and glanced from Bosco to Zaid who, no doubt, still loitered by the living room doors. "I… I… what?"

"Hit me in the face," Whisper said. "Give it your best shot."

Bosco smirked. "This sure is interesting," he said and looked beyond her. "Should I get the jello and bikinis?"

"This is a limited time offer, Nicki, so if—"

Nicole brought her hand across Whisper's cheek in a fast slap. It wasn't the hardest she'd ever received, but wasn't bad for a first try. Touching the sting in her face, Whisper noticed horrified anticipation spread on Nicole's expression like she expected her new sister-in-law to launch herself. Rather than satisfy that anticipation, Whisper smiled.

"Wow," Bosco said.

"Not bad," Whisper said, reaching for Nicole's hand to raise it up. "But you deliver the power from—" Bosco cleared his throat, reminding her of what he'd said downstairs. "Right… right. Sure." She let Nicole go and smiled again. "Shall we go and check if I'm diseased so my lord and master can fuck with confidence?"

Playing the dutiful wife wasn't really in her DNA, but she could vamp with the best of them. Nicole was going to be a thorn in her side. Whisper didn't excel with delicate people.

Looking on the bright side, at least there was one person in the house she'd be able to take down in a fight.

Problem was, every one of the McDade men would probably die for Nicole. Pretty Nicki had chosen to be a part of the family after being selected by one of the McDade brothers. Whisper was nobody's choice. That made her vulnerable.

Hateful though it was, her existence there was about survival. If she fucked her marriage up, her father would kill her, and the Doherty family would go down. Whisper wasn't sure which was worse. While she lived within the four walls provided by the McDades, she was vulnerable. Acknowledging that truth led to her making a vow to get out of those four walls as often as possible.

That day it would be the doctors and the salon and shopping with Nicki. The night would probably involve another wrangling of the monster.

Whisper was quick and shrewd, she'd learn how to get herself out in the open air. Out there in the world, she could be herself again.

EIGHT

SUNDAY WAS ONE of her favorite days of the week. Part of Whisper's usual routine required her to laze in bed for as long as possible. On that particular day, her lazing was interrupted by her husband whistling from the next room. He'd summoned her the same way on the Saturday night. Meathead.

Doing her duty, she dragged herself from her nanny bed and went through to the master's. Just for long enough to practice her head giving skills. Once he was done, he literally kicked her out of bed, using his foot to push her away from his body to the edge of the bed, sending her to the floor.

Whisper didn't care. She dragged herself back to her own bed and went back to sleep.

By the time she woke up, Zaid was gone. That worked just perfect because it gave her the chance to soak in the tub and go through her exfoliating and moisturizing ritual. The spa people had done the same thing the previous day too, but Whisper didn't think anyone could ever exfoliate too much... not on the McDade's dime anyway. It just so happened she was using all the expensive product she'd loaded herself up with on her day out with Pretty Nicki.

No one was in the kitchen when she went down

around lunchtime. Seeing a prime opportunity to get a breather, she decided to go out for coffee. After the insanity of the last few days, having time to herself was a welcome change of pace. The cherry on her cake involved melting her McDade plastic through the afternoon before meeting up with her girls for dinner.

They were on their third cocktail and hadn't quite got to ordering food yet, but there were menus on the table, which was a start.

"You haven't had sex with him?" Mariana asked, her hands clutched near her chest as she bowed over the table. "You… you haven't had sex with your husband?"

"Oral," Whisper said, picking up the menus to hand one to Paula at her side. Mariana ignored the menu even when it was being waved in her face. "Lots and lots of oral."

Mariana put a hand on the menu to slap it down to the tabletop. "Is he any good at it?"

"For him," Whisper said, scanning her menu. "Lots and lots of oral for him."

"He hasn't returned the favor?" Mariana asked and sat up straight, her mouth open in outrage. "That's… oh my God, that's so rude!"

Smiling, she glanced over her menu. "Maybe he's just no good at it."

"How are his hands? He's tall, right? He's got to be good at—"

"Hasn't done that either," Whisper said. "I think he likes my boobs."

Mariana spat out her disgust. "Uh, I hate guys like that. Guys that drool all over your chest and tug on your nipples like they're supposed to come off. Ugh, it's horrible."

It was so great that she didn't have to worry about concealing her amusement. For the first time that weekend, Whisper could be herself without the requirement to apologize or justify herself.

"Is he a good kisser?" Paula asked. "I always think a good kiss can erase a whole bunch of sins, you know?"

Mariana's eyes widened in hope and she nodded, begging for the answer. Expectation radiated from both of her girlfriends as she lowered her menu wearing a frown.

"You know…" Whisper started. "I don't think we've done that either."

Mariana threw up her hands. "So all you've done all weekend is suck his dick? Are you kidding me?" she exclaimed. "I disown you. That's it. No way you can be a friend of mine if you put up with that kind of bullshit."

Whisper laughed. "What do you want me to do? Demand that he eat my pussy?"

"Why not?" Mariana squawked. "He obviously has no qualms about demanding what he wants… Come to think of it, why the hell haven't you? You have never, ever been shy with a guy in the past. Not ever! If any guy thought about leaving you hanging, you'd *never* go back for seconds."

"This is different; he's my husband," Whisper said, raising a hand to the server to call him over. Ordering a bunch of sharing food, she figured everyone would find something they liked. Just for good measure, they ordered another round of cocktails too. "Don't worry, tonight's on Zay."

"Oh, it's Zay, is it?" Mariana asked, nodding at Paula.

Whisper just shook her head. "No one calls him Zaid… as I keep being told," she muttered.

Saying the shorter shortened version was quicker anyway. The less time a McDade name spent on her tongue, the better.

"I think it's shocking he's expecting you to do all the work," Mariana said. "I'd kick him out of bed tonight."

"We don't share a bed either," she said, picking up her Cosmopolitan. "I sleep in the nanny's room; it adjoins his bedroom."

Her friends made eye contact and blinked at each other. After a second, they burst out laughing.

"Oh my God," Mariana said. "Why does he need a nanny's room?"

Whisper shrugged. "Who knows?"

"We need to get you laid, girl," Mariana said.

Her purse began to vibrate against her hip, so Whisper slid her hand inside to retrieve her cellphone. The caller had never rung before, yet the phone identified who it was. Someone else must have pre-programmed the device because there was no way she'd saved any number under the single word that flashed on her screen: "Husband."

"Excuse me," she said, answering the phone and raising it to her ear. "I apologize, the person you are trying to contact is unavailable to suck it at this time…" Her friends began to laugh, but she held up a finger to quiet them. "However, if you happen to be from Nantucket, you should be able to handle the task on your own. Thank you for calling."

"Where are you?" came his deep, monotone voice that didn't display an iota of acknowledgement that she'd even spoken.

"Out. Where are you?" she asked, picking a skinny straw from the holder at the end of the table to dip it in her drink.

"You need to come home."

Whisper ducked to take the straw between her lips. "I don't need to do a damn thing, husband," she said, sucking up as much of her drink as she could when she saw her server coming over with their double round. "I plan to stay out very late, drink lots and lots of alcohol, and dance until I can't stand up… I may or may not pass out in some random man's apartment before or after I do or don't have sex with him… Whatever happens, I plan to have no memory of any of it tomorrow."

"There's a car outside Santiago's," he said. "Go outside. Get in it."

"Are you kidding?" she asked. Sitting up straight to look over the back of the booth toward the large windows on either side of the door, it didn't take long to spy the limo waiting outside. "Are you fucking kidding me?" He didn't respond; Whisper scowled at the table. "So your question was just bullshit?"

"We can track your phone."

"Well, no shit, I know that now," she said. "You can bet your ass I won't ever bring this with me anywhere I go ever again… Why do I have to—"

"Everyone eats dinner together on a Sunday.

Everyone."

Their food hadn't come yet and she was hungry. Those concerns were secondary to a more pressing issue.

Whisper felt it was only right that she be honest about why it probably wouldn't be the best of ideas for her to join the weekly family meal.

"Husband," she said, sort of wincing and raising her attention to her friends in hope of a little moral support. "I don't think that I'd be very good company right now."

"Why not?" he asked, his voice flat.

"It's possible I've drunk a considerable amount of alcohol," she said, attempting to catch her straw between her teeth. It slipped away when her friend's laughter caused her to laugh too. Whisper waved a hand at them. "Shh. Shh!"

"You think I can't keep you in check?"

The grumble of his confidence carried down the line to quake her insides. "I think if you try, I'll just want to rebel more," she said, holding the straw in her teeth and finishing the drink before gesturing for another. "I'm just being honest, husband. I'm a brat. You married a brat. Who likes to push, and tease, and fuck…" Sitting up straight, she recalled Mariana's question. "How come you've never kissed me?"

"You're a Doherty and a brat," he said. "Why would I want to kiss you?"

Dropping a flat hand onto the table, her head fell back as she groaned. "Oh my God."

The sound may have come across as annoyance or impatience, but the terrifying truth was much worse than either of those… she liked it. Whisper liked that they acted as though they repulsed each other. In every way, they should. Although she acted inconvenienced when he summoned her to do him a favor, there was something hot about being commanded.

Maybe it shouldn't be a shock. She'd been under the influence of powerful men all her life after all, surrounded by them since birth. The truth was, if a man wasn't willing to be firm with her, she was going to walk all over him. Whisper played more than she should. She could take life seriously, but that outlook had only one end: a short drop and a sudden stop.

The daughter of the city's biggest crime boss, as he had at least once been, couldn't go through life taking every second seriously. Danger and violence had peppered her life. The best way to handle all the tragedy and terror was to have fun while life lasted. At the end of the day, Whisper was under no illusions that there was any hope she'd die an old woman, in her safe, cozy bed.

"Za—"

"Get up, out of the booth, and get your ass in the car… If you don't, we'll come for you… and you don't want the McDades coming for you in force."

Maybe she did. For a few seconds, Whisper's mind wandered, picturing how that would go down. Zaid coming in with a posse of his men, guns drawn, fists raised, knocking down anyone who got in their way… Her husband crossing the room to drag her out… maybe by her hair.

The line disconnected to a droning sound that pulled her from the daydream. Breathing out, Whisper slid the phone back into her purse and hooked her hands onto the front of the table.

"What?" Mariana asked. "What is it?"

She whimpered. "I think I'm in trouble."

Mariana was again leaning over the table as Paula swayed closer. "What?" Paula asked. "Did he threaten to hurt you?"

A shudder of unwelcome arousal wracked her.

Whisper closed her eyes and covered her face with both hands. "I think if he did, I would like it," she said and slid her hands down enough to peek at her friends over the top of her fingertips. "I think I'm attracted to my husband."

Paula's mouth opened, but that was as much of a response as she could come up with.

Mariana licked her lips, pulling one into her mouth before scoffing out a laugh. "Oh my God," she said. "I think you're the first woman who's ever said that as a bad thing."

"You're married to him," Paula said. "You have to be attracted to him."

Sitting up straight, Whisper took Paula's hand across the table. "He's a McDade, Paula, honey… They're scum."

"Isn't that what they say about you?" Paula asked.

"It's not like that, it's not like…" Opening the hand that wasn't holding Paula's, Whisper tried to find the explanation. Coming up with the best way to make her point wasn't easy, so she looked to Mariana. "Wanna help me out?"

"I think he's hot," Mariana said, picking up her drink. "I would definitely do your husband… I'm not even sure what my affiliation with your family is anymore…" She frowned at nothing and took a drink. "I've always been loyal to the Dohertys, but… aren't the McDades the Dohertys now? I mean… aren't you one and the same? Wasn't that the point of you getting married?"

"It's a lifetime of conditioning," Whisper said. "My sister-in-law calls me an *it*… or she did until I sliced open my tongue and kissed her."

Mariana grinned while Paula squeaked. "Can I see?"

Whisper waved her away. "It was just a tiny cut, it's gone now. It's not like I gashed myself open. She just has no sense of humor."

"You are a little off the wall sometimes," Paula said.

"She called me *It*," Whisper said. "You're lucky I only cut myself… I have a reputation to maintain."

"You've never been the most violent Doherty."

"No," she said, her attention drifting to her drink. "Not until the majority of us died anyway…" Glancing at her friends, she wasn't surprised to see their somber expressions. "Don't I have to be a little bit more insane now to uphold the family name? These stories, they make or break a family. True or not, we have to be insane. We have to be violent. We have to instill fear and curiosity and trepidation… Without Keegan and Adan, who are we supposed to rely on? Caelan? Miles? The worst thing he ever did was snap the heads off my dolls as a child… Keegan would set them on fire… Adan would strap them to bricks and toss them in the river…"

Mariana smiled. "What would you do?"

"Dismember them and slice the lengths in half," she said, tossing another mouthful of her drink into her throat. "I better go before he sends Bosco."

Grabbing her purse, Whisper shimmied down the

seat. "You guys have fun." Taking a credit card from her purse, she tossed it on the table. "Compliments of the McDades."

Leaving the bar left her feeling sick and sad, two of her least favorite things. Her father's clock meant time was running out. If she didn't show progress with the McDades in the next day or so, Whisper might be joining the brothers she missed so much.

***

"YOU LED ME to believe you were going to be wild and uncontrollable."

In Kitty's that night, the family table was central, between the columns in the space that had been vacant during their reception. Sitting next to Zaid, Whisper held the weight of her head on her hand that was plastered to her cheek.

The limo hadn't taken her back to the house. The family meal was at Kitty's, which made sense because there were more than just immediate McDades there. Two other tables stood parallel to theirs, front and back. Doran sat at the head of one of the other tables. Burl sat at the head of their table with Parker and Zaid at each side of him, their dutiful wives next to them.

There had to be thirty McDades in the room, maybe more. Whisper hadn't lifted her head for long enough to count.

"I'm tired," she murmured, drawing a fingertip over the edge of her napkin that was flat on the table.

Dinner was done and the drinking had begun. It was late. Her subdued mood was nothing to do with exhaustion. The conversation she'd had with her girls earlier still rattled around in her mind.

"I don't believe you."

Just the words were enough to make her raise her head. When Whisper turned toward him and saw how intent he was on her, she froze under his gaze. The rest of the room was alive with noise and joviality. There was music and laughter. Without the Dohertys in the room, the McDades knew how to relax and have a good time.

It was just a shame that Whisper wasn't in the mood.

"Your family aren't scum," she murmured.

The shiver of numbness across her shoulders suggested her brothers were turning in their graves.

Zaid didn't respond to her words, he just kept on looking right through her. "What do you need?" he asked. "Tell me and you'll get it."

Although there were no outward signs of it, Whisper could almost feel his desire to help her, or maybe it was a desire to fix her. Fixing her would solve a lot of his problems. Like how inconvenient it would be if she was melancholy later when he wanted his cock sucked.

For a minute, the thought of asking for a kiss flitted through her thoughts. She wouldn't do it. Wouldn't ever be able to do it. Risking any chance that it might mean something to either of them wasn't worth it. In her current mood, Whisper was already vulnerable. If she asked him to screw her, she'd end up doing something insane like crying. That was something she'd never done in front of another person in her entire life.

Pushing herself a little further his way, Whisper licked her lips. "I want them to burn," she whispered. "I want you to help me burn their house down."

"The Byrnes?" She nodded. Touching the corner of her mouth with a fingertip, he trailed it to her chin. "Peanut, I thought you'd never ask."

He surged to his feet so suddenly that she gasped. Zaid gave Parker and his father a nod, which brought them both to their feet too. After gathering Doran and one or two others, the men went to a table next to the stage. It had been occupied, until those sitting at it saw who was coming. They bolted fast when Zaid and his group approached.

Whisper was still watching them when someone dropped into the seat next to hers.

"What's going on?" Nicole asked, probably watching the group too.

"I think I... showed him trust... or maybe gained his..."

Enough of it to appease her father anyway. Whisper didn't know exactly what was going on over there. But she'd bet they weren't making Christmas plans.

All weekend she'd been thinking of ways to provoke the McDades into holding up their end of the deal. That was what her father wanted. Even in the moments she believed progress was possible, it was never with Zaid. Doran was the only one of the brothers who'd spoken to her. Even then, he seemed more interested in making sure Nicole was happy than forming any kind of connection to anyone else.

Bosco was the only McDade who treated her as anything even resembling a friend. They weren't buddies. They didn't sit and chat or seek each other out. The bar was low, but when it came to treating her as a human being, he got highest marks.

Watching her husband at the table with his father and brothers, Whisper began to feel like a part of the family. Even if it didn't last, the illusion of it was seductive. All she'd had to do was ask. That was her position in the McDade family. As a wife to one of the heirs, it didn't matter if she was loved or even liked. Zaid's response to her question was the greatest show of respect she'd experienced yet.

Whisper wanted something, so she'd asked her husband for it. Without question, he'd granted her request. No fuss. No begging. Just… done.

NINE

WHISPER COULDN'T REMEMBER ever being so excited about a night out in her life. It was typical for her and the girls to go out on a Friday. She always looked forward to it but never to such a high degree.

Working late on Friday was the norm for her too. Whisper had her routine down. She started work late, came home late, and went out to party late. And that was fine; they weren't refused entry anywhere no matter what time they showed up.

Getting ready with a bottle of wine at her side was usual too. In the closet, admiring herself in the vanity mirror, Whisper finished with her lip-gloss, signaling it was time to leave. At midnight, her girlfriends would be waiting for her at the back door of Scooby's.

A sudden bang from the bedroom startled her. Tossing her lip-gloss onto the vanity, she left the closet to investigate. Zaid was in the bedroom peeling off his jacket.

"What are you doing—" Her words died in her throat when he turned to reveal blood on his chin and forehead. "Oh my God, what happened?"

"Intercepted a little product handover," he said, without objecting when she pushed him to the bed. "No big deal."

"Product handover," she said, dropping to her knees to unlace his boots and pull them off. "Drugs… whose drugs… because whoever it was, they didn't hand them over willingly."

When his boots were off, she scooped an arm under his legs indicating he should raise them to the bed. He took the hint and shifted back to lean on the headboard.

"Oh God," she said again, climbing onto the bed on her knees by his side to inspect the cut on his head and the gashes on his knuckles. "Stay here."

Running into the bathroom, she filled a basin with warm water and grabbed medical supplies from under the sink along with a clean wash cloth. Taking everything to the nightstand, she climbed onto the bed again.

Kneeling next to him, Whisper held his chin to begin cleaning the cut on his head. "You could've been killed, you know," she said, ignoring his hiss. He tried to pull away, but her grip on his chin didn't let him get far. The antiseptic wipes were next and he wouldn't like those any better. "People carry guns out there."

"We carry guns," he said, trying to pull away again.

Grabbing his tee-shirt in her fists, she climbed over to straddle his lap and clutched his face tighter. The blood on his chin just wiped off. That meant it was someone else's, which was good… or was it? Her sense of relief was unexpected.

His black tee-shirt made it difficult to see if he had other injuries.

Whisper took the hem and raised it up. "Were you hit?"

He sat up to let her pull his tee-shirt off over his head. Once it was on the floor, she could examine his body. Quickly, Whisper figured out that might not have been the best of ideas. She'd never been as close to him. Not in that position. His impressive physique begged her fingers to explore.

Her mouth began to water. His broad shoulders and solid arms had been obvious to her since day one. His tee-shirts strained around his muscles; it wasn't like she'd been completely oblivious to his remarkable form. Once or twice, while blowing him, she'd even gotten a peek at his abs. But it was only in that moment she realized he was either clothed or at least in a tee-shirt every time he got oral. He slept in the tee-shirt from what she could tell. Though why he'd do that when he had such an incredible stature to show off, Whisper had no idea.

"Why are you all dressed up?" he asked, a scowl on his face, which she only saw when she snapped out of her daze.

"I'm going out," she said, leaning in to touch the cut on his head. No matter how tempting it was, she wouldn't let her body touch his. "Did you fall down? Hit your head?"

"No," he said. "Where do you think you're going at midnight?"

"Out," she said, leaning over to the nightstand to retrieve the butterfly stitches. "Do you know what day of the week it is?"

"Friday if it's still before midnight. Where are you going at midnight?"

For some reason, the time seemed relevant to him. "To a club," she said. "Do you know who I am?"

"You're Peanut."

Though he was in a grump, as always, he made her smile. Whisper peeled one of the butterfly stitches from its backing and leaned in to position it in the right way.

"Hold my waist," she said, because her body resting on his wouldn't help any injuries he might have. He did as she said and she put the stitch on before returning her focus to the pack. "You never use my name."

"That's 'cause I don't know your name, Doherty."

"My first name," she said, concentrating on placing another stitch. "You never use it."

"You have a stupid name."

Her grin widened, but just for a moment. Whisper resorted to outrage. "I do not!" Easing back to meet his eye, she let some of her amusement show. "What a terrible thing to say to your wife."

"My wife has a stupid name," he said. "Why would I

want to use your name when it sounds like a command?"

"Whisper?" she asked, tilting her head. "You like giving me commands. You do it enough."

"Yeah, 'cept I don't want you to whisper. I want to make you scream."

Though he wasn't explicit, she got the impression he wasn't talking about pain. Zaid was forceful about what he wanted when she had her mouth around him. But she had to be fair and acknowledge that he had never raised his hands to her… not yet anyway.

"Scream," she murmured, leaning a little closer. His grip on her waist tightened, but it allowed her to get nearer. "How would you do that, husband?"

Moving in, she could taste his breath and thought they might break the boundary neither had stated, but both seemed to respect.

"Razer?"

The female voice from the doorway interrupted them. Whisper pulled back to see Nicole was in their bedroom doorway.

"Nicole, what is it?" Zaid asked, his voice deep and commanding again, not at all like the man who'd just been bonding with her.

"Doran's bleeding pretty bad and we've got some guys bleeding in the kitchen."

"I'll go," Whisper said when Zaid began to lift her from his lap. Picking up one of the ice-packs, she snapped it and handed it over to him. "Hold it to your head with your knuckles, it will soothe the swelling on both at the same time. I'll come back to check you didn't break any bones later. I'll have to wake you to check for concussion anyway."

"Wake me?" he barked. "I'm not going to sleep."

On her feet, Whisper pushed on his shoulders when he tried to get up. "Please. If it looks like Doran is in trouble, I'll come get you, I promise… otherwise, all you'll do is increase his chance of infection." Smiling, she smoothed a hand across his forehead. "Please lie down, baby." Something flashed in his eyes. Her use of the endearment surprised her as much as it did him, but she kept stroking his hair until he relaxed. "Please."

When he gave in and lay down, she smiled and bowed to kiss his forehead. That was as much as he'd get until she saw to everyone else. Whisper whirled around to start toward Nicole.

"Can you… handle this?" Nicole asked as they went down the stairs. "There's a few of them."

Whisper just smiled. "I've been patching up thugs since I was in diapers… Bring me warm, clean water, and all the medical supplies you have… it could be a long night."

***

WRONG WASN'T EXACTLY the right word; she hadn't been wrong. It just so happened Whisper underestimated what would be needed. Those worst off were put on cots in the living room. The scene was bad, but not as dire as it could have been. Most of the guys were just stealing a chance to be in the McDade home. They wouldn't get many opportunities to hang out there; they took what they could get.

Doran looked worse than he was. He'd been sliced, but the cut wasn't deep enough to penetrate the abdominal muscle, so it was fine.

The number of guys needing care had been a surprise, sure. The bigger surprise was witnessing Dohertys mixed with McDades. Apparently, they'd been fighting shoulder to shoulder, muscling in on a large Byrne shipment. Needless to say, the Byrnes hadn't wanted to part with it and the McDade-Doherty side didn't ask for permission to take it.

Their makeshift med-bay was manic. Cleaning wounds, changing dressings, and icing bruises, Whisper didn't get much time to stop and think. Yet, every once in a while she'd take note of the mission's bonding effect on both crews.

Her father had ordered his men into the fray with the McDades. Caelan and Miles had apparently been there too, though they hadn't come back to the McDade home. Whether that meant they weren't injured or they were cared for elsewhere, she didn't know. The suspicions of those who were there eased. As the hours past, each side became less dubious.

By the Sunday night when everyone was being tossed out, they were making plans to meet and help each other out with other jobs.

Even those who were unsure came to her to ask about the rules. All Whisper kept reinforcing was that they were family now. True or not, her father couldn't keep saying those words and not expect others to repeat them. As far as she knew, the whole damn point of the wedding was to prove they believed the sentiment.

Parker closed the front door on the last group of guys and actually smiled at her as he passed by to head into the living room where his father and wife were.

Spinning around, Whisper darted up the stairs as quickly as she could. Reaching the top and running straight into Zaid's room, she found him sitting on the bed tying his boots while Bosco stood beside him.

"Ready for the McDade grill?"

Because Doran was still recuperating and everyone had basically spent the weekend together anyway, Burl decided they were going to barbecue in the rear courtyard. The commotion the house had endured since Friday night led him to declare only immediate family were allowed. That basically meant those who lived in the house.

"I will be in a minute," she said, unzipping her dress and kicking off her shoes. "I need to stand under the shower a minute and change my clothes." Whisper went into her room to snag a hair tie from her nightstand so she could pull her hair up into a messy chignon off her neck. "I have blood, and sweat, and pus, and God knows what else all over me. It's been a day."

"You did good this weekend!" Bosco called through to her room.

Pushing the straps of her dress down, Whisper let it fall and grabbed the clasp of her bra as she departed her bedroom. "Thanks," she said, crossing Zaid's bedroom, a bobby pin in her teeth.

Slipping her bra from her arms, she didn't think anything of tossing it aside until Bosco whirled around to face away.

Zaid leaped to his feet. "Whisper!" he exclaimed.

"Guess I know how to get you to say my name now," she said, sliding the bobby pin into her hair to hold up the loose wisps and her bangs. Standing in the bathroom doorway, she looked right at him as she hooked her thumbs into her panties to shimmy out of them. "You told me I should always be naked, husband, I'm naked." She blew him a kiss. "Aren't I a good wife?"

Zaid still wasn't used to her aggravating ways, but she couldn't change them. Whisper liked to be playful. In time, he'd become accustomed to her… or he'd throttle her. Could go either way.

TEN

SITTING OUT IN the back courtyard the following Sunday, with her girls and their pitcher of margaritas, Whisper was adjusting her life to fit into the McDade routine.

The trio had missed their Friday night out again that week. It wasn't her fault that time, or even the McDades fault. Paula had met herself a special man the previous week while Whisper had been patching up the walking wounded. Even though she hadn't made the party, Mariana and Paula had gone out together. In the club, Paula had caught herself a live one.

At least, that's what they'd thought. Paula showed up to the arranged date two days ago, on Friday, excited, looking forward to her night. And the stupid guy had left her sitting in a bar for hours before texting to reschedule for the next night, Saturday.

The fact that Paula was sitting at the patio table, red-faced and blubbering was evidence that the Saturday hadn't exactly gone to plan either.

Mariana was leaning back in her chair looking up at the building while Whisper topped off their glasses.

"It seems bigger than your dad's place," Mariana said, adjusting her shades.

"It's four feet wider," Whisper said, glancing at her admiring friend. "Doran told me, like he'd actually figured it out… Guess he's obsessed with size…" Her mind wandered in a salacious direction, as it so often did. "Don't know why he'd be worried if he's anything like his brother."

Paula opened her mouth to begin crying again. Mariana, who was on the opposite side of the table, leaned over to take her hand. Having finished pouring duty, Whisper twisted around to face Paula's way. She draped her legs over the arm of her own chair to rest her crossed calves on the arm of the patio chair next to hers.

"Oh, honey, don't cry about that," Whisper said. "The asshole who stood you up probably has a weenie pencil dick. That's probably why he didn't show up…" Picking up her glass, she swung it around to her lips. "Was a lucky escape, no woman wants to be with a guy like that."

"With a guy who has a weenie pencil dick?" Mariana asked, wearing a grin. "No, she doesn't." Her smile dropped in an instant and she sat upright. Mariana's sudden switch to instant terror caught Whisper's concern, so she followed her friend's line of sight over the back of her chair into the house. "Oh my God, should we leave?"

Three men were walking through the kitchen, past the pillars into the dining space. Zaid, Doran, and Bosco. All three were intent on their path to the back courtyard, though she had no idea if they'd seen her and her friends seated out there or not.

"No, we're good for a while."

Mariana leaned over the table just as the men emerged from the house. "But are we allowed to be here?"

Whisper turned a reassuring smile to her friend and saw Paula was peeking over the top of her balled-up Kleenex. "You're not a threat to McDade security… not more than I am."

"Mrs. D," Bosco said, coming over and ruffling her hair while Doran dropped into a seat at the end of the table.

Zaid put a hand on her shoulder.

Sensing his question, Whisper laid her hand over his. "They know about dinner. They'll go before it's time for us to leave."

She'd made the choice to bring her girls back to the house, knowing she'd eventually have to duck out for dinner. Having them there meant they could enjoy each other without worrying about a repeat of two Sundays ago.

Appeased, Zaid took his hand back. He went to the chair her legs were draped on and hooked an arm under them to raise them just enough to let himself sink into the seat. After resting her legs on the arm again, he reached over to take her glass from her hand. Watching him drink from it gave her a weird sort of satisfaction.

Shaking that off, Whisper returned her focus to her friends. "What's his number?" she asked. Paula and Mariana were gaping at Zaid and didn't seem to register the question. Crunching up a little, she snapped her fingers near him to get her friends' attention back. "Pencil Dick, what's his number?"

"I… it's in my phone," Paula said.

"Give it to Bosco," she said, pointing at the man sinking into the chair at the opposite end of the table from Doran.

"Why do I want Pencil Dick's number?" Bosco asked, but raised his hips to take his phone from his back pocket anyway. "Who is Pencil Dick?"

"You want it because my phone is on the kitchen counter," Whisper said, glancing that way. As she turned her head back toward the table, Zaid leaned over and put a finger under her chin. When he tipped her head toward the light, she guessed he'd seen the bruise on her forehead. "Oh, yeah, I had lunch with Cyrus."

"Didn't duck fast enough?" Bosco asked her, scrolling through his phone.

"Too fast," she said. "Head-butted the table… saw stars for a minute. He didn't like that he missed. But…" She scratched her fingers into her hair at her crown. "You can't see bruises on my scalp, so that's something." Zaid was still peering. Whisper didn't like the intensity of his scrutiny, so she pushed his arm down. "I'll put concealer on before we go out. I promise no one will think you're knocking me around." She grinned. "Though it wouldn't hurt the rep, I guess."

"I want to hear more about Pencil Dick," Doran said. "Who is he?"

"Some guy who stood Paula up two nights in a row," Whisper said. Paula yelped. "It's okay. Doran doesn't think any less of you for that guy being an asshole… or if he does, that just proves he's an asshole too."

She smiled at Doran who just glared. "I remember a time when you were scared of us, Whis."

"I was never scared of you, honey. I'm just really good at faking it."

Doran's gaze shifted past her. "You gonna take that from your wife, brother?"

"Don't think faking it with you is the same thing as faking it for her husband," Bosco said.

Whisper wasn't sure that Zaid was listening, he was scooping ice from their glass onto the napkin he'd pulled to the edge of the table. She was watching him, thinking that she hadn't had to fake anything with her husband. Not because he was so good at pleasing her, but because he'd never tried. He'd never used that mouth on her, anywhere except her breasts. Even then, he hadn't given them much attention. Those hands had never been between her thighs, his tongue—

After putting the glass on the table, he grabbed her wrist to pull her forward, so her upper body was folded over her legs. He slapped the ice filled napkin to her bruise.

That he even tried to show any care was enough to make her smile. "It's probably too late for that," she said, earning herself a growl with his glare. "But thank you, baby."

Curling her fingers around his, she held the ice to her head. Taking her turn, Whisper touched the bruise above his brow that was fading. The cut within it was still healing.

"Don't fuss," he grumbled and swatted her hand away to sit back, snatching up the margarita glass as he went.

Wouldn't do much for his rep to have his wife fawning over his boo boo.

"We don't know that he has a pencil dick," Mariana said. "We're just assuming for compassion sake."

Doran's smile was obvious in his voice. "Compassion to who? Not the guy."

"To Paula," Whisper said. "The guy is a jerk. He made two dates with her and didn't show for either."

"We assume, for compassion sake…" Mariana said, finding her voice though there was still trepidation in it. "That our friend isn't missing out on much."

Bosco laughed. "So you gave the guy a pencil dick? Ouch."

Whisper waved at the table and kept her attention on Paula while leaning over to take her glass from Zaid. "Give Bosco his number and I'll find out exactly how he's hung for you." Both Mariana and Paula looked at Zaid. Grinning, Whisper didn't even bother to check her husband's reaction. "I don't have to fuck him to feel him up. Besides, Zay doesn't care."

"Might be difficult given that he doesn't show up when he makes dates," Mariana said.

"Who said anything about making a date?" Whisper asked. "We can get his address from his phone number. Right, Bosco?"

"Probably," Bosco said.

Topping off the glass, she gave him the sultry eye. "The Dohertys could do it."

"The Dohertys can't tell their ass from their elbow at the minute," Doran said. Whisper handed off the glass to Zaid, while taking her focus to Doran. "Won't apologize for telling the truth."

"You don't apologize anyway," Whisper said and put the ice on the table to grab up the empty pitcher. "We have time for one more refill."

Leaving her seat, she went into the house and through the dining room to the kitchen. Most things were still out, so she began to mix up the fresh batch of margaritas.

She was slicing into a lime when a pair of hands slid onto her shoulders, startling her. Peeking over her shoulder, Whisper found Zaid peering down at her.

"Tell me and you'll get it," he said.

Holding up the knife, she kept her lime balanced in the other. "I'm holding a knife, Zay," she said, returning to her quartering. "You shouldn't sneak up on me when I'm holding a knife. I might accidently cut something off that could be of use to both of us one day… Why is Doran in such a good mood?"

"We made a profit," Zaid said. "A good profit."

She smiled and stirred, picking up another lime to quarter it. "I love the taste of lime, don't you?" Raising it over her shoulder, she offered it to him without bothering to look his way. "Suck it." The joke was unintentional, but Whisper appreciated it anyway. "Ha, you see what happened there?"

Taking her wrist, he raised it higher and sank his teeth into the fruit. The juice trickled down her hand, over Zaid's grip to her arm. He bent his knees to catch a drip on her skin with the tip of his tongue. Running it up the delicate flesh of her wrist and between her moist fingers, he took his time about tormenting her.

Whisper stopped what she was doing with the fresh glasses and the salt when her eyes closed. That was the most contact she'd ever had with his tongue. It felt good. Damn good. Strong and sure, he varied his pressure, being softer with the sensitive crevices and harder on the edges.

After two weeks as his wife, Whisper was used to the way his dick felt in her mouth. She'd even learned a few tricks that he seemed to enjoy when she blew him morning and night. But she hadn't learned anything about the way he liked to kiss or the weight of his body on hers. She didn't know what he felt like in her most intimate space. He'd never even given her the pleasure of his teasing fingers.

At first, she hadn't minded or given it much thought. But as the days passed and she became more used to having him around, her curiosity increased… and so did her yearning.

Pushing everything out of the way, Whisper spun around and jumped up to sit on the counter, quickly coiling her legs around his when he began to back away.

"No," he said before she opened her mouth.

"I'm your wife," she said, sliding the leather of his belt from its buckle and bowing forward to accentuate her cleavage. "God won't frown on you fucking your wife."

That made his brow arch. "Peanut… you astound me," he murmured, opening his fingers to comb them through her hair, pushing it back behind her ear.

He didn't look astounded, he looked as indifferent as ever. "I think that's cause for celebration, don't you?"

Zaid didn't stop her from unbuttoning his pants, though he seemed more interested in his fingers in her hair than what her hand was doing to his dick. His body was paying attention though, as always, his cock hardened for her fast.

"You ever say no to a guy?"

"For sex?" she asked, rubbing in long, slow strokes. "I'd say no to any Byrne who asked… and any McDade too before I married you."

"You saying yes now?"

Loosening her legs from his, Whisper parted her own wide. "Open for business, husband."

"Why? Because we're here and you're horny?"

Letting her lips curl, she boosted a little higher. "Is there another reason?" she asked, but was surprised to feel him withdraw. "Hey." Letting go of his dick, she took hold of his ribs instead. "I haven't had an orgasm for two damn weeks, more than two weeks. I think I've been more than patient."

Zaid just shook his head and stepped back to fasten his pants again. "You're not ready."

"Not…" Her reaction to that insult fired her up and not in a warm, sexy way. "Are you fucking kidding? I service you every damn night, and every damn morning. I haven't objected or rejected you, not once."

"You don't like doing it."

"Blowing you?" she asked, feeling a little ridiculous when her hands went to her hips because she was still on the counter. Sitting up there gave her more height than she'd have on her feet, so Whisper stayed put. "I would relish sucking your dick every hour, on the hour for the rest of my life, if I didn't get the impression it was all going through the motions for you."

His brow came down hard and fast. "What? I come every damn time."

"Yeah, I know, but why wouldn't you? You've got a woman's mouth on your cock, of course you come. But you couldn't care less whose mouth it was. There's nothing special about it. It's a physical release, that's all. I just don't get why I'm not allowed one too."

"If it's such a chore for both of us, why do we do it?"

"You tell me, husband," she said. "You're the one who demands it."

"Why wouldn't I take it? You've never said no."

Spitting that truth at her gave Whisper a new perspective. Her defiant nature curled her hands around the edge of the counter. She leaned toward him, her eyes sure and wide when they locked onto his.

Deliberately, Whisper accentuated the word, "No."

Every second of silence that passed heated the tension. Whisper could actually feel it. The crackle of his simmering interest had always been there to some degree, now it was rising to a boil that she suddenly felt unable to control.

When his hand rose from his side on route to her knee, she batted it away and twisted to get further out of his reach. The sound of his nasal inhale gave Whisper a rush. He provoked a sense of power like she'd never before experienced.

"Didn't you hear me say no, jerk?"

Lunging forward, he grabbed the counter on either side of her thighs and surged over her, forcing her to slant back. "Open your fucking mouth," he hissed and tried to dive down for a kiss.

Whisper twisted away fast, leaning even further back. "No way," she said, peeking around at him. Tipping up her chin, she curled her leg around his again, running her heel up the back of his thigh. "Tell me I'm pretty." Zaid bared his teeth and hissed at her. A satisfied smile rose on her lips. She'd never seen that kind of heat in his eyes. Nothing even close. She'd had his dick in her mouth and watched his every nuance as she brought him to climax. Even in those times, she'd never seen him want her like he did right there, right in that second. "Tell me I'm pretty and take me to dinner…" Resting a hand on his shoulder, she let it slide down his chest as she pressured him back, touching her lips to his ear as she eased up. "And maybe there will be a reward in it for you, husband." She drew back just enough to let her mouth dance in front of his, their drowsy eyes almost as close. "But I doubt it…"

With her lips parted in a pout, Whisper thrust her hips against him, pushing him away from the counter so she could slide down onto her feet. Turning her back to him, she grabbed her pitcher and sashayed out to the courtyard. Her husband liked games. That was good to know. Very good to know.

ELEVEN

WHISPER SPENT MOST of dinner that Sunday fighting to keep Zaid's hands out of her skirt beneath the table. Even when she stood up, he wasn't shy about sliding a hand up the back of her thigh to grab and grope her ass. At bedtime, her refusal to give him head gave her a glimpse of what astounded really looked like.

After that moment of shock, like he couldn't believe she was actually refusing for real, his lips curled. Pride shone through his feral smile, flooding her system with a potent shot of adrenaline. Fueled by that power, she almost ran over to his bed to launch herself on top of him.

But Whisper stayed strong and swayed her tush into her room, blowing him a kiss over her shoulder before disappearing from his view.

The whole next week ended up being much of the same. Playing the tease was an enlivening change to playing the flirt. In standard play, Whisper wouldn't tease cock; she'd always been interested or not interested. Teasing her husband wasn't standard play. Zaid was teaching her the virtue of saying no even when she was interested.

Another bonus of their new dynamic meant that instead of waiting, she got her orgasm… though it was at her own hand.

With the door between their bedrooms open, she'd decided to take her playing to another level by pleasuring herself… and not being discreet about it. About halfway through, her eyes had opened just a sliver. And there he was, propped on the doorframe, watching her through the darkness. If he'd expected her to stop or be embarrassed, she disappointed him. Whisper kept on going until she came hard and loud.

That became their new routine. It thrilled her far more than their original dynamic.

Whisper was still thinking about the night ahead and how eager she was to tease her husband when she ran up the external stairs to go inside. Her last client had cancelled his training session at the gym. Being home that early on a Wednesday wasn't usual, but she'd decided to get back to the McDade house to enjoy some time in the tub before Zaid appeared. Whisper was never exactly sure when he'd be home, but she'd be ready whenever he showed.

Sometimes he was home when she got back from work at the gym. More often than not, it was dark before they saw each other. That meant fending for herself most nights at dinner time. She'd eat with Nicole or by herself in the kitchen or courtyard.

Despite wanting to see him, Whisper didn't mind if her husband was late. His tardiness supplied her a great excuse to give him the evil eye and act even more unimpressed. Those were the times she came hardest as he watched from the doorway.

Preoccupied by thoughts of her husband's heated gaze, Whisper was about to swing herself around the banister to run up the stairs when something at the back of the house clattered. Startled to a stop, she forgot all about sex and dipped a hand into the purse hanging across her body to pull out her cellphone.

Creeping in the direction of the sound, she caught glimpses down at her phone as she scrolled through the numbers to stop on Zaid's. With her thumb hovering over the call button, she kept going forward. If it was nothing, then there was no need to call and disturb whatever he was doing like she was a frightened rabbit. But if someone was there who shouldn't be, she'd find a way to delay them long enough for the cavalry to arrive… At the very least she'd get close enough to lay eyes on the fucker.

The living room was clear, but she expected that. The clatter had come from deeper in the house, further to the rear. The stairs to the back terrace led into Burl's office. Someone could've snuck in the there.

Tiptoeing to the slightly ajar office doors, Whisper's thumb drifted away from its poised place. As she got closer, the noises took shape, becoming easier to identify. Whoever was back there was no intruder. They were welcome, very welcome… in a definite carnal way.

The feminine pants and squeals were punctuated by the slapping of flesh and deep male grunts. Never shy, Whisper was curious enough about who might be fucking in the middle of the afternoon in Burl's office to peek through the crack between the sliding doors.

What she saw shocked her through to her core. What was intended to be a naughty voyeuristic moment changed to something far more sinister in a snap.

Whisper could have retreated; that would've been the smart course. But something drove her forward. Maybe it was the sight of something so wrong. Like her father fucking the server at her mom's wake. Some things were just so wrong that they shouldn't go by unrecognized.

Shoving open the doors, she strode in and stopped.

Burl's shirt was only part open. He hadn't even removed his pants, though they were definitely open. That was how he thrust himself into the naked woman bent over his desk, jolting her every time he surged forward.

Burl raised his attention, but finished his advance as Nicole lifted her head. Both spied Whisper standing there, a few feet inside the room. Although it only took half a second for the couple to notice they'd been discovered, the image was so disturbing, it burned itself onto her eyeballs and seemed to drag forever.

"Whisper!" Nicole wailed, grabbing at her chest,

though she had nothing to cover herself with.

Whisper folded her arms, happy to stick around and ensure there was no mistaking what was going on. Nicole stood up so fast that Burl had no time to react. The woman's head came into fast contact with her lover's chin. Burl cried out and clutched his face, staggering back a step and disengaging from Nicole, who was frantic in her hunt for a way to cover herself up.

The modesty seemed crazy and misplaced. They'd spent days in the beauty parlor together and seen just about every part of each other there was to see.

"Hello, Pretty Nicki," Whisper said. "Nice day for it."

Turning around, she started out of the room figuring there wasn't anything that the couple could say to justify their actions. That didn't stop Nicole from chasing after her. She caught up just as Whisper reached the bottom of the stairs.

Nicole still wasn't clothed. She clutched her dress to the front of her body, holding it to her chest and her crotch.

"Oh, Whisper!" she called. Whisper started up the stairs without hesitating. "Whisper, please wait!"

"Wait," Whisper said over her shoulder without slowing down. "Why? Is it my turn with Daddy next? I'll pass, thanks."

"Whisper!"

Grabbing her arm on the landing, Nicole tugged on her. Whisper whirled fast, her fist pulled high, ready to strike. Nicole's gasp gave her a second to assess the situation. Registering the stairs behind her could-be victim, Whisper exhaled. If she hit Nicole, as she wanted to, the woman would tumble back down the stairs. The last thing she wanted was for her sister-in-law to break her neck before her husband found out what kind of a harlot she was.

Taking her frustration out on the banister, Whisper slammed her fist into it hard. A shot of pain blasted through her arm, but she ignored it to point in the woman's face with her other hand.

"I knew you were screwing around. I knew it," she hissed, getting up close to Nicole, forcing her to clutch at the banister to keep her balance. "I didn't give a fuck when I thought you were doing it outside the family. That would be none of my business. But this… it's sick."

Turning around, she started along the landing, heading to the next set of stairs.

"Please! Please, Whisper! You don't understand! It's not what it looks like."

The woman's pleading shouldn't make a damn sight bit of difference. Yet, it enflamed her infuriation. She was filled by a heated sense of betrayal that was probably completely inappropriate. Just the idea that Nicole thought she could argue her way out of it made Whisper spin again when she got to the bottom of the next set of stairs.

"What? I can't wait to hear how our father-in-law's dick in your pussy is not what it looks like. Go. Please. Explain." She faux gasped, crossing her hands on her cleavage. "Oh my God, was he raping you? 'Cause if I was being raped, I wouldn't be pushing back and whispering little moans of satisfaction."

"Parker and I can't have kids," Nicole said in a rush. "I… I don't know why. I… I went to get all the tests and it's not me. I… I'm ovulating, my system is fine, but he… he won't listen… He won't go for the tests."

Smiling, Whisper wasn't impressed. "Oh, and one McDade's spunk is the same as another's? I can't wait until you tell Zay it's his turn to take a swing…" Leaning forward, she stage whispered, "Word of warning, he's hung bigger than Daddy, so you might want to take a deep breath before he slides on home."

Losing her contrition, Nicole huffed in anger. "This is just what you wanted, isn't it? To ruin this family! You Doherty—"

"You're doing the ruining yourself," Whisper argued back. "You can't fuck your husband's father and think that it's going to end well!"

"If you tell Parker—"

"Parker? Why would I tell him?" she asked, sneering at Nicole in her shame. "I'm going to tell my husband… because unlike you, I respect my husband. I wouldn't dream of keeping something like this a secret from him."

Continuing up the stairs, it hit Whisper that despite their numerous mistakes, she and Zaid had actually made a lot of headway. At the beginning of their marriage, she believed the name McDade was synonymous with scum and psychopaths. Yet, the truth was, she had more freedom as a McDade than her father had ever afforded her.

Sure, Cyrus had never cared about her social life or her opinions enough to argue with her. Why would he? His word was law in their home. Even in her attempts to rebel, she'd always eventually bowed to his will. In the McDade house, she could breathe and wasn't on edge, waiting for the next hit to come.

Being wild with men and partying was a way of escaping the house, liberating herself from her father's decree that she should be seen and not heard. The only task he ever set to her was cooking for the family when his housekeeper wasn't in. Whisper was terrible at it and at serving, yet, it always fell to her. Her father enjoyed casting her as the weak victim in his old fashioned regime.

Whisper didn't feel like a victim in the McDade house. The resentment she'd built up towards her father, from growing up as a child right through to her adult life, wasn't present inside McDade walls. There Whisper could just be a woman living her life, without worrying she might end up with a black eye or a fracture because someone was having a bad day.

McDade men were tough. They could be cutting and cruel, but none of them had ever raised a hand to her. Maybe it would be different if she were in the field with them. Their apathy probably had something to do with the fact that none of them cared enough about her to argue with her. She'd never injected herself into their family politics either. At least she hadn't until walking in to find the patriarch inside his daughter-in-law.

Whisper went to her room and closed the door, despising for the first time that it couldn't be locked from the inside. After some pondering, she resolved to wait until Zaid came home. No one pursued her into the suite, so she got to soak in the tub. It might not be as relaxing as she'd hoped, but at least the door locked, assuring her peace.

The Dohertys were fucked up. Neither of her brothers ever married, so there was no way to know if this situation could've arisen in their ranks. Her father was a short-tempered tyrant, quick with his fists, and slow with his contrition… No, that was a lie, she'd never heard him apologize in her entire life. Cyrus Doherty was slow to consider alternatives to violence.

Facing her own naivety was sickening. Whisper liked to think she understood the way of the world and grasped that everyone was capable of anything. But if that was true, she wouldn't be so repulsed by Burl and Nicole's affair. Facing that truth meant accepting that the thing she despised most about her father, his lack of loyalty to the women in his life, wasn't only a Doherty trait.

Grinding her teeth as she slid into the water that was supposed to cleanse her, Whisper's skin crawled with disgust. For a minute there, just a minute, she'd let herself think that maybe all men weren't the same. That maybe, just maybe, it might be okay to trust one with her heart.

She'd never done it before. Had always vowed not to turn into her mother. Whisper wouldn't let herself fall in love and wouldn't be blind to how a man could ruin her. Her decision to remain independent and never trust a man had been made in her adolescence. No one, no man, ever tempted her to reconsider that position.

Yet, in the previous almost three weeks since her marriage to Zaid, something in her subconscious had contemplated shifting. Their push and pull, the draw seemed to be tangling them together, and the possibility of more, for a brief moment, had intrigued her.

Now, in a position she hadn't coveted, her thoughts were all over the place. If she told her husband the truth, the McDade family could combust. But if she lied, there would never be any chance of trust between them. Whisper couldn't ask for his trust while being dishonest with him.

Trouble was, it wouldn't be a truth Zaid wanted to hear. Her position there was already precarious. Telling the truth could mean inviting more trouble.

Sighing, Whisper slid under the water. Just as life seemed to be getting easier, it went and got a whole lot more complicated in a hurry.

***

THE DECISION WAS TAKEN from her hands. That night anyway. None of the McDade men came home. Zaid, Parker, and Doran stayed out all night, Bosco too. Whisper wasn't stupid enough to believe that was any kind of mistake or coincidence.

Her suspicion was confirmed when Nicole didn't appear in the kitchen the next morning. While she was pouring her coffee, Whisper felt someone approach and glanced back to see Burl stopping by the end of the breakfast bar.

"My sons have been waiting for you to make your move," Burl said. She went back to pouring her coffee. "All of the McDades have."

"Let me guess, if I tell them what I saw and start a McDade civil war, everyone will blame me."

"Something like that."

"Except I'm not the one banging my son's wife," she said, turning around and resting against the counter as she blew steam from the top of her cup. "If like you say, none of them ever gave me a chance, then you've just confirmed what I should do, I have nothing to lose… Why shouldn't I tell the truth?"

"Because I've seen the way you look at my boy," he said, so sure of himself that upholding her façade of indifference became more challenging. "There was a disconnect between you after you were first married. Something's changing between you… I assume he started fucking you."

Tilting her head, she pouted. "Disappointed you didn't get there first?"

Sliding one foot forward and then the other, coasting toward her, Burl didn't lose an ounce of his confidence. Whisper put her cup down then rested both hands on the counter at either side of her. Keeping her attention trained to his, she slid one hand backwards toward the knife block.

"If I'd wanted you, Doherty, I'd have told your father to give you to me," he said, pushing himself close to her. "But now that you're here… and we're alone…"

Grabbing a knife from the block, she flipped it around. With the handle in her fist and the back edge of the blade resting horizontally along her wrist, she had solid support to thrust it up to his throat. Maintaining pressure with her arm, Whisper ignored the line of blood that seeped onto the blade.

"I am not my father's to give anymore," she said, deepening her voice to a growl. "You want use of this body, you negotiate with my husband. If he dares think to give you rights, I'll slaughter every McDade where they stand."

Stepping back, Burl's sneer only grew when he touched his throat to see the blood. "You tell him and what happens next? Think about it, Doherty! Think about what happens to your fucking family too!"

Storming across to the counter, he grabbed a napkin to press it against his cut. It may have been deeper than she'd realized, but certainly wasn't life threatening.

"You can't fuck another man's wife and get away with it," she argued, understanding this was more than an intellectual argument.

"I'm doing what I'm doing *for* my son and for the good of this family."

She wanted to throw the knife at him, but settled for tossing it onto the counter. "Oh, don't give me that shit," she said. "Nicole tried it yesterday and it's crap. Yeah, you're such a martyr."

"I have fathered children. I am capable of giving her what she wants, and ensuring the future of this family."

"You know, I wouldn't have so much of a problem with that if it was all out in the open, and you know, done properly. There are clinics who specialize in this stuff, and you have younger, far more virile members of this family who could do the deed… 'Cept, of course, in that scenario no one has to fuck the peppy little twenty-something other than her husband. She says Parker won't go to a clinic, maybe you should work on that, instead of—"

"We wouldn't take that shame. The embarrassment of the world knowing a McDade can't impregnate his woman."

Breathing out her disbelief in an almost laugh, she propped a hand on the counter. "Male pride knows no limit, does it? Much better the world should find out Parker's wife needs to get hers from the patriarch. Really?" Still pressuring the wound on his neck, Burl began to approach. "That might do something for your ego, but what does it do for his? And what happens to this family after you're dead in the ground and he has to take over? You don't think this shit will follow him forever? 'Oh, yeah, look there goes the guy who needed *Daddy* to do his duty for him'."

The swift stroke of Burl's backhand was so abrupt, it forced her head to snap around. Whisper didn't feel any pain. The attempt wasn't as strong as the practiced slap she was used to getting from her father. Pushing out her lips, she closed her eyes and exhaled.

"You watch your mouth, Doherty," he barked.

"What else would you like to do to me, Daddy?" she growled, bringing her attention back to him slowly. Turned out Nicole was right, she should be calling the McDade patriarch by the same title she used for her biological father. They weren't so different after all. "Will you spank me if I'm naughty? Is that how it started with Nicole?"

Snatching her face, he pulled her close. "If you tell him, if you tell anyone, I will make you and every Doherty that ever breathed regret every heartbeat."

"There aren't that many of us left," she said.

Facing the truth of the family she'd married into, Whisper despised herself for being disappointed to learn they were just like hers. Reality was numbing. This was life. This was the truth of the world. There was no alternative. She'd been a fool to entertain the notion there might be something more.

"Making it that much easier for me to decimate what's left of your pathetic ranks… I wonder what Rick Byrne would say if I called him up and asked if he wanted to make a deal."

Forging a deal with Byrne would ensure her demise. Her father would kill her before Burl ever got the chance.

Oh, how she wanted to assert that she was going to tell Zaid anyway... Whisper wished their trust was so strong that she could have the confidence to tell her husband without it resulting in him hating her.

She doubted he'd even hear her out.

The last couple of days had proven that she didn't know as much as she thought. That definitely extended into her opinions of people and their capabilities.

Burl McDade had her over a barrel. Even although he was the one doing something wrong and the one who'd been caught red-handed, he wouldn't suffer. As was always the way, men got away with their antics and women paid the price for them.

Leaning back, she thrust forward to spit in his face. "Threaten me again or ask me to cover for your depravity just once and I'll sky-write it, McDade."

Stalking off, she deliberately shoulder barged him aside as she passed. Nowhere was safe or sacred. Whisper went upstairs and out the front door, pleased to get out of that damn house. If only she could just keep on walking and rid herself of all of this forever.

Life always surprised her. As of yet, none of its hits were positive. Life as a McDade was no different to that as a Doherty. If nothing else, her experience helped her decision to forget about the new and return to the old. The habits some called destructive had kept her sane... or as sane as she ever wanted to be.

TWELVE

THE FOLLOWING NIGHT, Whisper was on her way down the stairs just as the McDade brothers came in through the front door. Nicole and Burl had been there to greet them. After the initial jeering about why they were getting a welcome party, someone noticed the cut on Burl's throat and the mood became more sinister.

The boys questioned their father on who'd gotten close enough, and had the balls, to come for him.   Burl shrugged it off, swearing never to let *her* get that close again. That changed the mood. The men crowed about their father's prowess assuming one of the patriarch's mistresses had gotten kinky.

It sickened her.

When Whisper got to the bottom of the stairs, Zaid tried to make eye contact, but she ignored him. She tried to ignore all of them and headed for the door. Bosco said her name, probably under Zaid's instruction; the two men had a silent language she didn't speak. Although she'd paused with her hand on the front door handle, Burl had told his boys to let her go.

Let her go. Yeah, that's what he wanted, for her to go and never come back. If Whisper had even an inclination that might be possible, she'd probably do it. But where would fleeing get her? Just like that brief moment in her father's office, before her marriage, when she'd considered running, it didn't take long to conclude that escaping would be hopeless.

Pleased to be out and away from her troubles, Whisper's girlfriends were on hand to offer her all the support she needed. Support? Yes. Advice? No. She couldn't tell her girls what had happened that week. Revealing the secret Burl had threatened to kill to protect would endanger them.

So she just threw herself into the mood of the club and forgot her troubles. That was the first Friday night she'd managed to make it out since her wedding. It felt good to be at Scooby's, back in the swing of what had been her life for so long.

She drank and danced and made out with every man who put the moves on her. Whisper hadn't been insane enough to bring her phone with her, so there was no way anyone could track her. She could be the twisted her that she recognized.

The last thing she wanted to worry about was reality. Whether her girls noticed her need for oblivion or not, she wasn't sure. Any time they commented on her being the Wild One of old, she'd say something about living life to the max and missing her usual way of life.

On the dark dance floor, she was wrapped around a man who'd picked her up at the bar while she was waiting for another drink. They never got to the drink. He'd led her out onto the floor and pulled her into his arms, forcing their bodies together.

A minute later, they were kissing and she was drowning in the heady void of numb debauchery. There were no Dohertys there, no McDades, just a man and a woman, strangers in a smoke filled club, surrounded by writhing bodies and flashing lights. Anonymous, unidentifiable people with no past, no future, and no present.

He wasn't even that good a kisser. She wasn't even sure if she was attracted to him. There was no burn of desire or urgency of need. Whisper just wanted to be this person, the one who got validation in the knowledge that someone in the world wanted her, even if it was just for this minute.

Letting her arms fall from his neck, she found his hand in the dark. The music was too loud to say anything, but when she side-nodded and began to walk backwards, his grin spread. His glee betrayed that he'd caught her drift.

Scooby's had been her haunt since she was a teenager. It wasn't like anyone was ever going to card her, so she'd been able to get in and drink since well before it was legal in most countries. Her loyalty to the club also gave her insider knowledge on the layout.

Leaving the pound of the music behind, she led him out of the main club and down the corridor to a stairwell she knew had a fire exit at the bottom. They pushed out into an alley and she dragged him along, deeper into the shadows.

Whisper didn't say anything, she put her back to the wall and pulled him to her. Whoever he was, he didn't ask any questions, which was probably just as well for him. She was in no mood to talk and definitely didn't want to get to know him.

After a brief kiss, she tipped up her chin to let him sink lower to kiss her neck. His hands slid up her body and cupped her breasts, squeezing and fondling her. Closing her eyes tight, Whisper tried to enjoy the need of his hot breath coming in short pants against her cleavage.

Men could get away with this kind of behavior. Her father. Her brothers. Burl McDade. They could do this without giving it a second thought. All she was doing was embracing the way the world truly was. Yet, for some infuriating reason, she had to keep repeating the names of those men in her head and reminding herself of the disgusting things they'd done to their loved ones.

When whoever he was crouched lower and touched the outside of her thigh to drag up her skirt, she pushed at his shoulders. Even the memory of her father fucking the server at her mother's wake wasn't working to justify her behavior.

Whisper couldn't explain why her strength of feeling was so extreme. Suddenly, it just felt wrong.

"No," she said. He didn't seem to hear her and kept pulling at her skirt. "No, I don't want to do this."

"It's okay," he mumbled, pressing his mouth into her

breast as he tried to squash his hand between her thighs.

Whisper kept them clamped shut. "No," she said, shoving and struggling against him pushing back. "I can't... I'm married."

Her wedding ring was in her room at the McDade house, which just made her feel all the more sick. Had she known she was going to do this? Didn't that make her just as bad as the rest of the bastards she couldn't stomach looking at? How could anyone ever think infidelity felt good? She had no idea.

"I don't care," he said. "I don't give a fuck about your husband. God, you're so hot, just let me fuck you."

The groan of want in his voice should've been enough to make her feel good. It didn't. It made her question his sanity and just how far he'd go even against her wishes. In her work at the gym, Whisper labored to build up her strength, but there was only so much her frame could take. Unfortunately, her type, like this guy, were strong enough to overpower her, especially when they were hot and turned on and possibly drunk or high.

Giving in wasn't part of her nature. "No," she said. The more she tried to push him away, the harder he pushed back against her, forcing her into the wall. Damn it, she should've known better than to put herself in such a position. If he managed to take what he wanted, it would serve her right for being such an idiot. "No! I said no! Take your fucking hands off me! I'm married!"

She might have heard the shot before the guy buckled, but it was silenced, so it took her a second to identify the very specific sound. The pressure was suddenly gone. The guy was on the ground at her feet, yelping and writhing, holding the side of his knee, which appeared to be bleeding. Curious, Whisper's head tilted in fascination. The dark stain spreading on his pale slacks mesmerized her.

"Fuck," he yelped. "Fuck! You're married to Razer McDade!"

The sound of his alias startled her. "How do you know that?"

"Peanut," came the drawl that made her turn.

He was only ten feet away, so she had no idea how she'd missed him. Maybe the alcohol and the sight of the man who'd been groping her thrashing around on the ground had fogged her brain too much to be aware of anything.

"You bitch!"

Another shot blasted and the guy screamed while grabbing for the other knee. As Zaid came up to stand next to the guy, Whisper noticed the gun in his loose hand. Her husband raised it from his side, just enough to aim at the whimpering, struggling guy's torso.

"Between the eyes or between the balls," he asked, though she wasn't sure who he was asking.

His gun moved up and then down in a pendulous action that suggested he was pondering which to aim for.

"Please," the guy begged. "Please, I didn't know."

"Yeah," Zaid drawled in what was barely a murmur.

Sliding his hand into his pocket, he kept the gun on the guy while retrieving something from his jeans. Raising his middle finger, Zaid flipped her the bird while showing something of hers encircling the top of his digit.

Her wedding ring.

Gratitude speared her. She grabbed for his hand, overjoyed to see the platinum band. Wrapping both hands around his fist, Whisper drew Zaid's finger down and parted her lips to take it into her mouth. Sucking the ring from his finger, she caught it on the point of her tongue, and kept on going to draw his digit deeper against her tongue.

His heavy gaze slid around to her. She sucked his finger free of her lips to show him where she'd caught the ring. Pressing the end of her ring finger to her tongue, she slid it back onto her finger and moseyed closer to him.

Something about him being there changed her mood. No longer alarmed or concerned, Whisper lost all sense of being in any danger. That was even in spite of the armed man who had every right to be mad at her. No, suddenly everything was okay. She couldn't explain it. Just Zaid being there made everything better.

Stepping in front of her husband, who had a gun in his hand, aimed at the guy crying and whining on the ground, she laid her hands on him. The guy was bleeding out and had just been shot in both knees. The sound of his distress didn't irritate her. All she could feel was aroused by the man who'd somehow found her in exactly the moment she needed him.

Whisper couldn't decipher the whites of his eyes, his brows were so low and obvious tension radiated from him. Tension she could do something about. Flattening her hand on his fly, she rubbed him through his jeans.

"Baby," she purred, pushing her chest into him. "Mmm, my baby."

"Suck it," he said.

Whisper blinked, parting her lips in a slow smile. "No," she whispered.

Never in her life had she wanted to blow a guy more. She had no idea how he'd found her or why he'd come swooping in to stake his claim. No man had ever done that. Sure, she'd never been in a relationship for more than twenty minutes before; but she'd never understood why possessive men were a turn on… Not until her husband showed up and put a bullet in the man who'd been kissing her.

Snatching her arm, Zaid rushed her back against the wall and dropped the gun onto the dumpster at their side. She didn't know what he was going to do, didn't know what to expect. With her palms flat on the walls at her side, Whisper could barely contain the beating of her frantic heart and the throb of her pulse wracking through every atom in her body.

Zaid was there. Her husband had come to claim her. He wasn't beating her. Wasn't screaming or punishing her, he was just looking at her with deep brown eyes so intense she could feel their every flicker.

Not that they went far. He fixated on her eyes, locked onto them, ensnaring her in the tractor beam of his gaze, giving her no chance to see anything else. Even the sound of the victim on the ground faded away to be replaced by the hum of her blood rushing through her ears. Whisper blocked out the world, everything except him.

It could have been her imagination, but the beat of the music seemed to be vibrating through the wall of the club at her back. It amplified her need, making it harder for her to draw in a breath. The combined effect of so many sensations threatened to buckle her legs and send her to the ground.

Zaid had other ideas. "You need to learn some respect," he growled, slapping his palms onto the wall and bowing lower to get in close to her face.

Whisper tilted her defiant chin higher, hoping that maybe the temptation of her mouth would be enough to draw him in for a kiss. "Make me," she whispered. "Jerk."

Loosening his belt took seconds, his buttons were opened with a single pull. She expected him to force her down to her knees to do as he'd asked. Although Whisper planned to object a little, she'd give it her all after relenting.

"I am your goddamn husband."

Zaid didn't wrestle her to the ground. Instead he crouched to hook a hand around the back of each of her legs and stood straight, picking her off her feet. The idea, just the notion that he might take her, fulfil her there in such a savage way excited her. So much so that when her teeth dug into her lip, she tasted a hint of blood.

Dragging his hands higher, he drove a forearm under her ass to support her while at the same time scooping the crotch of her panties aside.

"Don't you dare fuck me," she murmured.

Zaid closed his eyes in a slow blink. The moment they opened to hers again, he shoved his hips forward, impaling her on the thick length of his demanding cock.

The sting of him stretching her, clenched her teeth in a hiss. At the same time, in contradiction, her body arched to his begging for more.

"You will respect me, Peanut," he hissed. "You will learn your place is at the end of this cock."

Oh, she was trying to fight the need, but she wanted it. Damn her for wanting it so bad.

"Asshole," she said, smacking his shoulders before grabbing both to pull herself higher.

He surged forward, forcing her to take more of him, way before she was ready. The pain and shock and desire and need all clashed together. Zaid wanted her, she could feel it, and not just because he wasn't a gentle guy. The bulk of his hard dick wasn't patient and kept pushing harder, stabbing itself into her, demanding more. He retreated slow and then plunged in so hard that she cried out. The sinister curl of satisfaction shone from his eyes.

Whisper grabbed for his neck, digging her nails in deep. "You prick… You're a fucking asshole."

"That's right, Peanut," he said, pumping himself into her. "Feel it. Hate it 'cause you love it."

She did love it; hate couldn't be further from her mind. Whisper had never been filled like this. She loved every aching second of him driving himself into her, forcing her to take him so he could be satisfied inside her.

"Husband," she groaned, thrusting her hips to match the pace of his as the rollercoaster of orgasm began to rush through her body. "Oh, fuck, husband! Fuck!"

Just at the very second climax was about to hit her, he stopped. Embedded all the way inside her, he squashed her pelvis between his and the wall, holding himself within her.

"Did I give you permission to come, wife?" he mumbled, his mouth in her hair, his breathing ragged.

She smacked his torso. Her hips wouldn't stop moving. Her body was working of its own volition on instinct. Chewing her lip and moaning at the intense sensation of his girth occupying her, she didn't even care that the concrete behind her was biting into her back. Whisper tried not to whimper because her little mews of yearning betrayed just how much he was affecting her. Showing any vulnerability would be a mistake. She tried clenching her jaw, but a whine of need managed to squeak its way from her throat.

Grabbing a handful of her hair, he yanked her head back to glare down at her. "What's your name, Peanut?"

So that was what he wanted?

Limp and almost blind with her need, her lips curled in a lazy smile, drugged by the ecstasy of their union. "Whisper McDade."

One side of his mouth lifted too, not much, but just enough to let her know she'd given him the right answer. "That's right, Peanut. You're a McDade. My McDade," he drawled and pulled back his hips until just the head of his cock was inside her. "Now you can come."

In one slamming advance, he filled her up beyond her limit, pushing her into an ocean of orgasm that seemed to go on for days and yet be over too quickly. Still panting and purring over her own release, she almost missed his and couldn't think straight enough to hold her own weight when he put her on her feet.

Whisper grabbed for him to steady herself. Zaid put an arm around her to hold her upright while using the other to pick up the gun.

"Want me to kill him?" he murmured.

Although it was what she wanted, Whisper couldn't drift on the warmth of the aftershocks still wracking her body, not all night anyway. She told herself to get with it and serve her husband. Tucking him away with care, she fastened his pants for him. The guy was armed and holding her up, so he couldn't do it himself.

"And risk losing you to prison for a loser like that?" she asked, coiling an arm around his torso to hold herself against him. "No, let him suffer. He won't touch me again, and if he utters a word of what happened here tonight, or how he got injured…" Letting Zaid go, she went to the man rocking on his back on the ground, and put a foot to his hip to roll him over. Snagging his wallet from his pocket, she retrieved his ID. She tucked the card in Zaid's pocket and wiped down the wallet before tossing it in the dumpster. "We'll know where to find him… and I say we go for the balls first… but a bullet would be too kind."

Zaid hooked an arm around her neck and turned them to the mouth of the alley to guide her away. The guy would find help, he'd have to or he'd eventually bleed out. He wouldn't say anything about who'd put the bullets in him, not unless he wanted two notorious families to finish the job they'd started.

THIRTEEN

HER HUSBAND RODE a motorcycle. Whisper didn't know how she'd missed that. It put into perspective why he never travelled anywhere with her in a limo. He preferred going fast, weaving in and out of traffic, basically ignoring the rules that applied to everyone else. Whisper couldn't say she was averse to that attitude.

Maybe she read him wrong, but when they got back to the house, it seemed as though he tried to push her toward his bed. If he did, Whisper didn't take the hint and chose to go through to the nanny's room instead.

Their alley sex at least had the effect of helping her to sleep well. The next day, even her time at the spa was tolerable, though that may have been because it went by without Nicole, who never appeared.

Afterwards, Whisper's plan was to go home and change, then find some quiet corner restaurant to eat in. Something close to home that gave her the option of walking only just as far as she wanted to… and getting as drunk as possible.

Whisper didn't expect to go into the bedroom to find Zaid standing in the middle of it, typing something into a cellphone.

They looked at each other. Neither spoke, so she left him there to go into the closet.

"Peanut," he said, obviously deciding that there was something to be said after all. "Come out here."

"If this is about last night, I'd rather not," she called out, stripping off her clothes. "Don't worry, I still respect you, but I probably won't be calling." Whisper was still silently snickering at her own joke when she turned to discover him leaning on the enclosed vanity at the end of the closet closest to the door. "I'm gonna get you a bell. Shit, Zay."

"Peanut—"

"Look, it's not that the sex wasn't great. It was great. You know that it was and, hey, you're hung like a carnival donkey, so no complaints there."

Sauntering toward him, she wasn't surprised when he swung round to pin her back to the vanity. "Peanut—"

"You're the only person in the world who can make that word sound like a threat, you know?" she said, laying her hand on his ribs to give him a pat. "Let's just leave it alone, Zay, huh?"

For some reason she couldn't fathom, looking him in the eye was a struggle. She could only peek up at him for the shortest of seconds.

"I was right," he said after her chin fell again. "You weren't ready."

"Yep, that's right. Not ready."

Although she expected him to back off, he didn't.

Zaid drew in a long breath through his nose before speaking. "Three years ago, we were having a problem with a couple of our dealers skimming. We didn't know which team it was and didn't want to punish the wrong guy."

Punish translated to kill. Whisper knew what the Dohertys did to underlings who stole from the family. It wasn't rap their knuckles. "I don't—"

"Bos and me were holed up in a vacant apartment watching a couple of corners." The tale would be fascinating if she had the slightest inclination why he was telling it. Though given that this was the most he'd ever actually said to her at one time, Whisper stayed quiet. "We were looking out… Not much was happening, the street was quiet, our dealers had gone to transact in an alley with a couple of working girls… Last thing we expected was to see Keegan Doherty on our turf."

That changed the hue of her curiosity. Her interest sprang up, tightening her muscles. "Keegan?"

"Yeah," he said, tilting his head as his fingertips grazed a tendril of her hair by her temple. "He was with this babe, not one of ours, least not that we could tell at first. It was dark and they were on the opposite sidewalk."

For a minute, Zaid just watched his fingers moving in her hair.

Whisper wasn't patient enough for suspense. "What happened?"

"Don't know if he recognized the Doherty or not, but one of ours moved in on Keegan and this babe. He had a knife, but that didn't faze the babe. Minute she saw him coming, she went in, matching him step for step, moving ahead of Keegan. In one move, she took the knife from our guy, grabbed him by the balls and sent him down to his knees. Keegan didn't bother to get within ten feet of them, he knew she had it. With the knife to his throat in one hand and his balls in the other, she bowed to say something right into the guy's ear… Then she tossed him to the sidewalk and stepped over him, reaching back for her brother's hand."

Clarity parted her lips. "Her brother." He nodded. "Me? It was me." He nodded again. "I don't even remember that."

"Shame," he said. "I always wondered what you said to him."

Her attention drifted to the side and she smiled. "I always say the same thing to pricks like that who come at me. I tell them when they see the Dohertys coming they should kneel and pray we let them take another breath." Zaid didn't say anything else and let her just process the story. It didn't take long for her eyes to narrow. "But, wait, that was… you said that was three years ago."

"Yeah."

Looking up at him, she didn't know what to feel.

"How do you remember that? What made you remember it now?"

"I've never forgotten it," he said. "I know I'm ready. I came to terms with how I felt about my Doherty a long time ago, Peanut."

"Your… your Doherty?"

"Fucking you was never going to be enough. I want your vulnerability… Before I get that, I have to teach you respect."

He'd said that last night. The reminder caused her attention to spring up to him.

His expression didn't change, so Whisper doubted he was having the same memory. "I do respect you," she said, though she couldn't blame him for believing otherwise after the way she'd acted the previous night.

Zaid shook his head. "Not me," he said. "You have to learn how to respect you before you can give me what I want from you."

Stunned, she didn't even know what to say or how he wanted her to react. Whisper was still trying to process when he eased back to turn her around. Maybe now he'd shocked her into static silence, he thought she'd just bend over for him.

He slid one hand along the vanity in front of her while the other brushed the scrapes on her lower back. They were the irritated marks left by the nightclub wall during their session last night.

"Doesn't hurt," Whisper said, not sure she liked the tenderness in his touch.

Given what he'd revealed, his compassion could just be something conjured in her head. True or not, she felt the need to pull away. She understood then why he'd put the hand on the vanity. When Whisper tried to move, he flattened his hand on her abdomen, holding her still, preventing her retreat.

"None of them are deep."

"That's a shame," she said, arching her ass back. Getting out of his physical hold wasn't possible, but her arsenal wasn't empty. Reaching around to snag his wrist at her lower back, she guided it around her hip, directing his hand low. "I like it deep."

His fingertips brushed the top of her pussy. Whisper held her breath in anticipation of the moment he'd take over and give her what she craved. Letting herself breathe when he curled his form over the top of hers, she expected his touch. Instead, the only sensation she got was the warmth of his breath on the top of her ear.

"No," he exhaled and drew his hand out of her grip to give her ass a quick squeeze before turning and leaving the closet.

Once again, she'd been left unsatisfied.

But at least that time, he'd given her mind something. He'd known who she was three years ago. A single incident that she couldn't even remember had lodged in his memory and somehow awakened it.

Whisper had never given a lot of thought to why Zaid married her. His story changed that. She should have considered there was no reason for him to be her husband over the likes of Doran or anyone else loyal to their family. The McDades wanted a promise from the Dohertys, a sign that they were serious about the alliance, and she had been the price.

But who had set it?

FOURTEEN

SUNDAY WAS SUPPOSED to be dinner, but it was a birthday of one of the McDade cousin's. Whisper wasn't sure which one. The ongoing party meant Kitty's was jumping by the time they got there. Instead of their usual sit down meal, a buffet was laid out on a table along one of the walls. The rest of the place was filled with circular tables occupied by more people than she'd ever seen there.

The night was drawing on. Whisper was getting bored, which could have something to do with the fact that she'd been sitting alone at the bar for over two hours. It wasn't any surprise that no one wanted to be seen talking to the only Doherty in the room. Most of the partygoers dripped with disdain whenever they looked her way. When she stared at them, they drew their eyes away like they'd just witnessed her kicking a puppy.

Nicole was the center of attention at one of the tables. Everyone seemed eager to please the primary McDade wife. Whisper wasn't even offended by their love for her, she wasn't willing to pay the price it took to get that kind of adoration. Nicole could keep it.

She didn't have a clue where her husband or in-laws were and had given up caring. Though she noticed Bosco appearing from the mysterious door at the end of the bar, Whisper did nothing to attract his attention. He scanned the room and seemed to find what he was looking for when his gaze landed on her.

It was nice that he smiled on his walk toward her. Whisper didn't hazard a return of the expression. She didn't react at all. Her elbow slid further across the bar, taking her closer to it. Her hand was on her temple propping her up while the other stayed around her wine glass.

"How you doing, Mrs. D?" Bosco asked when he came up to lean on the bar beside her.

"Bored," she said, rising just enough to tip some wine into her mouth. "Want to have sex?"

His smile broadened to reach his eyes. "Man, you know how to flatter a guy," he said. "But no thanks… You need anything?"

"He sent you to check I'm behaving, didn't he?" she asked. "Well, you can report that I have no interest in tossing my carcass into this particular pit of coyotes."

"Ouch, and here I thought you were getting over your McDade prejudice."

Looking past him, she returned the sneers that were being tossed her way. "Look at them," she grumbled. "I'm like an amoeba."

"Think it would be any different for Zaid at a Doherty event?"

Back in the day, no. Though he'd probably at least get some action. One of her brothers or cousins would get drunk enough to say something and a brawl would breakout. Pouring the last of her wine into her mouth, she held a finger up to the bartender, and pointed at her glass.

After the acknowledgement of her order, Whisper slapped a hand on the bar and pushed herself up straight. "I am going to drink one more glass of wine and then I am climbing my ass up onto this bar to do my strip tease routine."

"You think that would go down well with the in-laws?"

She pushed the empty glass away, still endeavoring to enjoy the buzz of alcohol humming through her. "My marriage is pretty definitely doomed anyway, Bos. So, you know, I figure I should suit myself."

The bartender brought over her wine. Whisper wasn't slow in grabbing it up to gulp it down.

With her mouth still on the glass, her eyes slid to the side when Bosco lowered onto the stool next to hers. "Doomed? Why is it doomed?"

Putting her glass down, Whisper let her other arm flop beside it. "Yeah, the Doherty and the McDade live happily ever after, that sounds likely," she said, scoffing out a disbelieving laugh. "He wants something I don't have." Standing her index finger up on the bar, she raised it to drop it down, hammering home her point. "I don't have it." Whisper kept prodding her finger into the bar. "I don't have it." Twisting around, she slapped both hands to Bosco's thighs. "I don't have it, Bosco. I can't give him it if I don't have it, right?"

There was something almost pitying in his eyes. Whisper wouldn't let herself acknowledge it, even when he brushed her hair away from her face.

"What does he want, Mrs. D?"

Her vulnerability or for her to have self-respect; she was fast learning the latter didn't run through her veins. Some people were just incapable. That's what Whisper told herself anyway.

Rather than answer Bosco, she sat straighter to peek left and right over each of his shoulders. "Where the hell is he anyway? If he wants to check I'm being good, why isn't he here monitoring me himself?"

"He's in the back."

"The back," she said, taking another mouthful of wine then discarding the glass to jump off her stool. "What's in the back? Doherty men do that too, pisses me off."

Starting past him, she headed toward the mysterious door he'd come through.

"Women aren't allowed back there," Bosco said, almost frantic in his speech as he hurried along at her side. "Whis—"

"Women aren't allowed, huh?" she asked, just as two

young, barely dressed women traipsed through the door she was aiming for.

"They're going to the restroom," he said.

Without slowing, they followed the sinful sirens who carried on past the ladies' room and the men's too. Casting a look over her shoulder, Whisper didn't hide her glare. The two women kept on going, ignoring the open door at the very end of the corridor. From what she could make out, there was a courtyard back there. Interesting. The building was far deeper than she'd realized.

The women swung a right and flounced into a room that would be parallel to the main space at the front of Kitty's. The new room wasn't as crowded as the one she'd left, though it was darker. At a guess, she'd say back there was by invitation only.

Another bar backed onto the one she'd been propping up all night. The space stretched beyond the length of that bar. The room then opened out and took a perpendicular turn, making it an L-shape.

People watched her progress, but Whisper wasn't interested in the men in the velvet booths or their card games. Passing the bar, she looked down the length of the room, which stretched all the way to the front of the building, though she didn't see any windows.

What she did see was her husband on a long couch, surrounded by other men, including his brothers, in a corner set up like a slick lounge. But it wasn't the men she zeroed in on. No, that right was reserved for the blonde woman in the white dress straddling Zaid's lap.

Fixating on her, Whisper let her rage grow from a simmer.

"Whisper," Bosco said, probably noticing exactly what she'd locked onto.

Setting the couple in her sights, she strode on, ignoring every person she passed and the pulse of the music that masked their likely judgement. The element of surprise was on her side. Approaching, she seethed at the sight of the woman's long blonde curls cascading almost all the way to her ass. Blondie's svelte form moved back and forth, grinding into what was supposed to belong to Whisper.

Picking up her pace, Whisper crouched as she advanced, sliding a hand up the outside of her thigh and beneath her skirt. In a practiced move, she slipped her blade from its sheath and tightened her fist around the grip.

Before anyone saw her coming, she plunged her fingers into the blonde's lush locks to take a hearty handful. Blondie screeched and threw both hands back to clutch for the digits causing her instant pain. With her sharp nails digging deep into the blonde's scalp, Whisper swung her knife around to the woman's throat.

Jerking the beauty's head back to an uncomfortable angle, Whisper lowered her lips to the woman's ear. "That's *my* ride," she murmured without looking at the man beneath the panting babe. "Move."

Dragging the woman backward, Whisper gave her no option except to leave Zaid's lap. Hauling her across the floor, Whisper's knife hand dropped to her side as she turned to parade back the way she'd come. The blonde was in a stooped crouch, scrambling to keep up, losing her footing while still clutching at Whisper's hand in her hair.

Her destination was the largest space, where the two perpendicular sections of the room met. The area with the biggest audience. The more witnesses, the better. Whisper stopped, but swung the woman around hard, throwing her forward onto the floor, letting go of her hair so she skidded along before coming to a stop. Whimpering and grasping at her matted hair, Blondie just sat there, blubbering.

Walking around her in a wide circle, Whisper wasn't shy about kicking anything that got in her way out of her path. She didn't care about making a spectacle of herself. This was important. She didn't even care if she was embarrassing her husband.

The display would prove to everyone in the room, male and female, that the Dohertys weren't fools. Though that didn't matter to her as much as sending a clear message to anyone else who might think about screwing with her husband.

To her credit, Blondie kept her chin down, showing

her submission. Every few seconds, she glanced up to check what Whisper was doing whenever she wandered into her field of vision. Whether the woman was a pro or not, Whisper didn't know or care. With her nose for weakness, what screamed to her was the blonde's ineptitude. Blondie wasn't much better than Nicole in terms of her ability to stand up for herself.

Pausing in her circling, Whisper bent her elbow and threw her knife down so hard that it embedded itself in the floor between the blonde's legs. The sprawled woman wasn't the only one to yelp and jump at the abrupt move. The whole room was on tenterhooks, enthralled by the show.

Whisper didn't care about them; the blonde was her only focus. "Pick it up," she murmured. The beauty just sat there shaking and sniveling. The pathetic display fired Whisper's disdain. "Pick it up!"

Screaming at the woman startled her into action. She took her time about pushing her weight from her hands to shift them to the hilt. On those first feeble attempts, she couldn't get it out of the floor. Blondie moved onto her knees to use both hands. Eventually, using all of her strength, the beauty managed to pull it out of the floor.

Whisper let a sinister condescending laugh slip from her lips. "If you can't handle that, what made you think you could handle my husband?"

Once the woman held the knife in two shaking hands, Whisper crouched in front of her and held up her hand to point at her occupied ring finger. "You did know he was married, didn't you? You knew that's what that meant, didn't you?" Nothing from the meek, sniffling woman who was barely managing to hold the knife. Whisper screamed in her face. "Didn't you?"

"Yes," the woman cried. "Yes! I'm sorry."

"No, no, sweetheart," Whisper said, stroking both palms onto the woman's face to push her hair from her wet eyes. "We're past the apology now. We're onto the 'only one of us leaves this room alive' part." The blonde opened her mouth in a desperate wail that was almost a howl. Leaning forward, Whisper sank her fingers into the blonde's hair, with more care than before, and eased her forward to press a kiss to her forehead. "Don't worry, babe, you got the head start and I'm gonna give you an advantage." Still holding the woman's head, she leaned back. "You with me?" When Whisper got no response, she gave the woman a hard shake. "You with me?"

"Yes," the blonde cried. "Yes, I am!"

"Good," Whisper said, and jabbed a finger to the back of her own neck. "You're not strong enough for a spinal cord strike, but—hey…" When the woman closed her eyes to lose herself to the crying, Whisper gave her another shake. "Hey, keep listening. Eyes open, this is your only fighting chance, Blondie." Whisper pointed to her throat. "Carotid." Picking up the blonde's hand, she showed her where to aim the knife. "Stab and yank. Don't slash. This is not a movie." She showed the blonde the action, but the woman's arms were a dead weight and didn't seem to be in it. "You paying attention?"

"Yes," Blondie said. "But please… please, Mrs. McDade—"

Whisper smiled. "That's right… that's my name… Shame you couldn't have remembered that ten minutes ago… Next!" The loud exclamation made the blonde jump. Whisper raised her arm to touch another weak point. "Axillary. Easy in a dress like this. Forget the aorta, you'll never miss the ribs and it's too easy to block. Fun one…" Sliding a hand up the blonde's leg, she felt the woman shiver in fear as her aggressor's fingertips went under her skirt. "Femoral." Whisper's fingers touched the smooth seam of Blondie's leg and watched more tears cascade down the woman's face before leaning in. "Not sure you'd hit that either, but it's in a fun place, right?"

"Please," the blonde whimpered.

Whisper bounced to her feet. "All else fails, stab for the back of the knee. You won't fail to hit something vulnerable there." Backing away a couple of steps, she opened her arms. "On your feet, blondie." The woman continued to quake and cry. "On your fucking feet!"

A quivering, shaking mess, the blonde tried her best

to rise onto her feet. Disappointment sickened Whisper.

"Please," Blondie groveled again.

"You want to ride married men? Size up the wife's capabilities first, now…" She raised her arms higher. "Widen your stance, set your feet, and take your shot."

The room around them hung on pause. Almost every breath was audible. Blocking them out, Whisper focused on the blonde, waiting to see if the woman would defend herself.

"Please, Mrs. McDade. Please, I'm sorry. I didn't—I won't—"

"Five seconds, take your shot or I end this," Whisper said, without any emotion in her voice in contrast to the sobbing mess of the blonde.

"Please, Mrs. McDade—please—"

"Five, four—"

"Please!"

"Three, two…"

With a clumsy start, the blonde rushed forward, blade high, pointed at Whisper's throat. The angle would be okay, except Whisper didn't let it get anywhere close to her. Sweeping her arm one way to block the blade and push it aside, she slid her hand down the blonde's arm to take the blade from her weak hands. Whisper moved her leg in a similar arc at the same time, but the opposite way, taking Blondie's legs out from under her, sending her to the floor.

Catching her arm to direct the blonde's fall, Whisper twisted the woman's arm up her back and dropped onto her, setting a knee on her spine, trapping the woman's twisted arm under the strength of her knee. Her other foot stood on Blondie's hand to immobilize the prey and stabilize herself.

Bowing over her, Whisper used the tip of the blade to brush the glossy hair from the back of her victim's neck. She bent forward. "You're not strong enough," she said, pressing the point of her knife into the soft skin over Blondie's vulnerable vertebrae. "But I am."

Locking the handle of the knife in both hands, Whisper inhaled as she raised it high above her head ready to drive the blade down into the blonde's spine with all her strength.

Just as her arms reached their highest point, a hand smacked onto her wrist, locking her in the stretched position. Tipping her head back, she wasn't surprised to see Zaid standing behind her, holding her wrist.

"Peanut," he said in that dull, warning tone.

"Almost done."

Her husband didn't flinch. "You're done."

With the hand he didn't have locked onto her, he rolled each of his fingers around the weapon in her hand. Without him asking, she loosened her grip, surrendering it to her husband. Then with a yank, he hauled her onto her feet and bent down to drag up her skirt to slide the blade back into its sheath.

FIFTEEN

THE BLONDE BEGAN to wail. Ignoring that mess, Whisper kept her focus faithful on her husband who burned his gaze into her for another ten seconds before spinning around to march away. Dragging her along behind him, Zaid forced her to hurry, pulling her against his back.

They got into the corridor. Rather than return her to the front of Kitty's, he led her out the back. They went through an exterior courtyard that had a few others in it, and up a set of stairs to an alleyway.

Her shoulder was beginning to ache as they strode to the street, but Whisper let him keep tugging her along. Half a block later, he stopped and whipped her around in front of him.

Tossing her hair back from her face, she exhaled a deep breath. For just a second, she studied him, appreciating him up close before turning around to walk away. Whisper wasn't really sure where she was going. Unless she wanted to take a beating, her father's was out. It was further than she wanted to go anyway.

Mariana's was closest. Her friend might not be home, but Whisper didn't mind picking a lock to let herself in.

"Where are you going?"

Glancing back, Whisper figured she should have guessed that her husband would follow her, or at least ask questions. But she wasn't going to slow down just because he was hot on her heels.

"Mariana's," she answered. "Her apartment's not far. If she's home, we'll probably go out. You know, I never realized just how deep in McDade territory her place is... I should talk to her about that."

Grabbing her shoulder, Zaid pulled her around and to a halt. "You want to tell me what the fuck that was in there?"

"Fun," she said on a shrug.

"'Cause you don't really care who I fuck."

Whisper bobbed her head. "I was mad. I was. I won't deny it. I didn't like seeing her... on you," she said. A quiver of disgust went through her, accepting reality was testing her again. "But you're a guy, so... I guess it's your right to go around trying to stick it in as many women as you can. So long as you understand that every time I witness it, whatever I do to your whores is on you. That's *my* right."

He grabbed hold of her again when she tried to back away. This time he picked her up to set her feet on the low wall around the building beside them. The wall was just a foot off the ground and served as a plinth for the railings set in it. Hooking her arms around the spikes at the top, Whisper settled against the railings.

Zaid took the next spike along from each of her hands in a fist to bow over her. "Get mad, Peanut," he murmured.

"No," she said, doing her best to hold onto her composure. To avoid his gaze, she picked some invisible lint from his shoulder. "There's no reason I should expect anything different from you than I have from every other man I've ever known."

"Forget you had another guy between your thighs not so long ago yourself?"

Grinning, she pushed back on the railings. "What's good for the goose is good for the gander."

"So we just fuck around on each other, that's it?"

"Was your parents' marriage any different?"

The question hardened his brow.

Letting go of the railings, he rose to his full height. "My father murdered my mother for fucking around on him."

Apparently, there was at least some truth to the rumor. The murder anyway, even if the reason wasn't accurate.

Lifting her leg to his hip, Whisper hooked it around his ass. "You know where to find my blade… Don't think you need lessons on how to use it."

"In a choice between death or screwing around, you'd pick death?"

"Over living in hypocrisy, yes," she said. "I never knew the woman, but I guarantee your mother was no fool. She knew how your father treated her."

His head tilted. "How do you know how he treated her?"

Her leg fell from his thigh. Whisper stood on her own two feet again. "Because I'm not an idiot," she said. "I've never known a marriage, or relationship, where it didn't happen. Did you?"

His lack of response was enough of an answer. He swayed forward to catch the railings again, bringing himself so near to her that when she pushed back, the pressure of one of the railing spikes dug in deep between her shoulder blades.

"My mother died for fucking around," he said. "What my father didn't see was that he drove her to it." For a woman so sure she knew the world, Whisper didn't often experience shock. But that confession dumbfounded her. Through his vehemence, she read regret in his gaze. Regret so real, she couldn't look away from it. "By the time it happened, she was broken, damaged. He was the one responsible for making her feel like less than what she was. He did treat her bad. He made her feel like less than him, like she should be grateful for him. He screwed around, disappeared for days. Fucked her and ignored her."

"She had no self-respect," she murmured the words.

"Right," he said. "No self-esteem, and she put up with it for years. Over a decade. By the time her lover came along and showed her that she was worth something… Shit, Peanut, you think it was her fault that she wanted to keep feeling that way?"

"No," she breathed, her focus dropping to the sidewalk next to them.

Thinking of Burl and what he was doing with his son's wife, Whisper's sense of injustice flared brighter. The man had killed his own wife for stepping out on him, but now he was tempting his son's wife to do the same thing. The excuses were bullshit. Burl was fucking Nicole because he wanted to. What did he expect to happen when Parker found out?

Clearly, the sons had forgiven their father for what he'd done to their mother. Did he expect the sons would do the same when they discovered the truth about Nicole? What did that mean for the naïve idiot? Was Nicole going to be a sacrificial lamb? Cast out or killed as the traitorous temptress?

"Where is your mind, Peanut?" Zaid asked, his voice softer than she'd ever heard it.

"Why don't you beat me?" she asked, resting a hand on his sturdy upper arm.

"Do you want me to?" he asked. Without thinking, her head shook. "But you always assumed that your husband would."

"I'd deserve it," she said, watching her hand on the dark leather of his jacket. "After what I did."

"I want to understand you, Whis. I know you play the whore; I want to know why you do that. Why do you use sex to push people away?" Raising her shoulders in a shrug, she didn't trust herself to speak. "I know you went into that alley with that guy. I know what was in your mind when you did. What you planned to do. But you know what I heard? I heard you say no." Surprised that was where he put his emphasis, her eyes leaped to his. "What you were doing out there wasn't about sex." Slowly, her head began to move in a shake. "Tell me and you'll get it."

That was what he said whenever he was ready to give her what she needed. Maybe he was always ready because he never seemed to hesitate when saying it. It was almost like he just wanted to receive instructions and whatever she said, he'd comply with. The power he'd instilled in her began to simmer again, but Whisper wasn't sure she liked it anymore.

With that power came an expectation, a hope that maybe she could trust him, that maybe he could be her anomaly.

"When we got married…" she started. "When we got married, I didn't think it would be anything like this."

"What did you think it would be?"

"I… I don't know, I guess I thought it was just like a checkbox. Your family wanted something from ours and I was up at bat, you know? I had to go to the clerk's office, say some words, sign a piece of paper, and that would be it. I figured you would want the same as me. That our lives wouldn't change much, we'd just carry on as before except we'd live in the same house… I knew I'd have to fuck you, but I've had men do all sorts of shit to me…" Her gaze dropped again. "You learn to switch that part of yourself off."

"I don't want you off when I touch you," he said.

Whisper didn't know what was more surprising about the man her husband was turning out to be: that he really thought these things or that he was sharing them with her.

Standing there on that wall, looking into him, Whisper realized that she was feeling something. Something she'd never felt standing in front of a man before. She had to shut it down. Fast.

Beyond her own aversion, Whisper could never trust her husband because she could never ask him to trust her. As long as she was hiding the truth from him, there was no room for feelings of any sort.

"My father fucked around on my mom," she said. "My whole life there were always other women. Didn't stop me from idolizing my dad. I think there was a part of me that resented her. I don't know if I thought she was pathetic or if I blamed her for not giving my father what he needed. We were never close and my father could do no wrong. I… I never liked the other women, any of them. Guess I was always afraid one of them would take him away from us…" She inhaled. "Looking back now, I sorta wish they had."

"You don't still idolize him?"

It sickened her that he could even ask. "The day of her funeral I walked in on him doing some twenty-something year old server and I don't know, I just… just the sight of it made me ill. Sure, it was my dad screwing a woman probably not much older than me, but… Suddenly I just got it, I understood what my mother had endured. She was faithful to him every minute, and dad used her death as a way to stoke the fire of our war with the Byrne's. But I…" Narrowing her eyes, she peered into him. "If he loved her, as much as he wanted everyone to think when he talked about Byrne taking her from him, how could he do that to her memory on the day we were laying her to rest?"

"I don't know, Peanut." Opening his hand on her face, he rested it on her cheek over her hair. "Neither of our fathers are saints."

"None of us are. But you're right, it's about respect. He didn't respect her. She endured that way of life, feeling like some kind of sub-species and paid the ultimate price for his choices… I promised myself I would never live like that. Never… That's why I never had a relationship or made a commitment. If I ever felt like any fuck buddy was even getting close to asking for one, I ran out of his place like his bed was on fire and never went back."

Leaning further forward, he propped his chin on the top of her head. "And then you married me."

Going from no commitment ever to the deepest commitment for life sounded like a leap. Whisper understood why it wouldn't make sense to him.

"It wasn't like that," she said, pressing a hand to his chest to urge him back again. "I didn't know you even knew who I was. I wasn't marrying you; I was marrying an anonymous McDade…" Conceding a half-nod, half-shrug, she admitted. "Okay, I know that sentence doesn't exactly make sense. But, I mean, all I knew was your reputation, some whispers of stories I'd heard. I know most of that shit is exaggerated, so I didn't have any idea who you were."

"I've been watching you for a while."

"Yeah, three years apparently," she said. "Why the

hell didn't you just come up to me in a club or something?"

"You've got some sense of humor," he said. "Keegan wouldn't have gone for that."

"You weren't afraid of my brother," she said.

Though Whisper had to admit Zaid wouldn't have been dealing with just one Doherty. If he'd thought to take what he wanted from her, all the Dohertys could've gone for him. If she'd known who he was, Whisper would never have given it willingly. He could've lied about his identity, but that would've only held up if, A) no one else in the club knew he was a McDade, and B) he wanted nothing more than a one night stand.

"I already told you that fucking you wouldn't have been enough," he said. "That first time I saw you, I wanted your fire. I had never seen a woman face danger like that head on, not while there was a guy she trusted at her side."

"My brothers and I were always fighting," she said, pushing his hand away from her face because it was starting to feel too warm and familiar. "I never knew on any given day if they were going to be fighting at my side or against me, so I had to learn to defend myself… Doesn't always work…" She smiled. "Sometimes I get in over my head with a guy who's stronger than me, but I always pick myself up."

If Zaid hadn't swooped into the alley to blow out the guy's kneecaps, and he'd taken what he wanted, she'd still have brushed herself off and carried on. It was what she always did.

"You've never been able to trust anyone completely," he said. "I saw how you were with your brothers. I've seen you with your father… I've seen you with guys." The reality of being watched for three years was beginning to sink in. "But I've seen you with your girls too, how you relax with them, how protective you are…"

"They don't understand," she said, a frown leaping to her expression of its own volition. "They don't know what this life is like."

"I understand," he said and tried to touch her face again.

Whisper ducked out of the way and shoved at him, leaping off the wall to get away from the cocoon of his arms.

He didn't understand. He thought he did. He thought he had it figured out. Zaid had watched her from afar assuming that he'd never be able to have her. When the opportunity to own her had presented itself, he'd taken it.

Whisper didn't know what he'd expected would happen. If he thought they were going to build trust and fall in love then he was more naïve than she could ever have imagined. One day, whether it was in a week or a decade, the truth of what Burl and Nicole had done, or were doing, was going to come out.

Her knowledge of it would come out too. Putting her likely death aside, whatever she'd let herself feel or build with Zaid until that point would be blown apart. Either she'd be the one to tell him and he'd blame her for sharing the news that would destroy his family, or he would feel betrayed. Why shouldn't he when she'd lied to him since basically the beginning of their marriage?

Something touched her shoulder. Whisper reacted by spinning around and smacking it away. "Look, I know you think this is… something, that I'm… something. But I'm not…" She held up her hands in surrender. "I'm not, Zaid. I'm sorry. You think we're cut from the same cloth because our families are in the same trade and we lost our mothers because our fathers are assholes. But the truth is…" Making herself smile, she began to retreat. "I'm not that deep. I like cock. I like booze. I like partying… I don't like romance and all that soppy shit. I don't want hugs and spooning on a Sunday and all that crap… You want to fuck? You know where to find me. Otherwise, let's just keep our distance."

Turning around to walk away from him, Whisper swallowed hard to contain the emotion threatening to bubble up. Damn, it was insane. It didn't matter that he was her husband and it was supposed to mean something when they fought or connected, she didn't want it to mean something.

The marriage was supposed to be a formality, Whisper hadn't expected to feel. Zaid was making her feel and she didn't like it.

She'd heard the songs and seen the movies where love was this happy, cheery thing. Those in it were supposed to be filled with optimism and strength. Nausea was the only thing filling Whisper. She felt alone and vulnerable, things she despised. Probably things that her mother had felt any time she had to face the kind of man her husband was.

Except, despite his reputation and capabilities, Zaid wasn't the one causing the problem. He wasn't the despicable human being treating his partner with disrespect, she was. Whisper was the despicable human being in their marriage. It didn't matter who was cheating on the other when there was no honesty.

Her secret had the potential to ruin his family. There would be no coming back from that. Whisper was the last in, so she'd be the first out. That was the way it went. Beyond the certainty that her father would end her life for messing up his alliance with the McDades, Whisper was more unsettled by the idea of losing Zaid.

Bosco had become a friend. Sometimes she thought even Doran was warming to her. Parker was always out or away, she'd barely seen him with Nicole, so she didn't have much of a relationship with him. For the first time, she wondered if that was part of Burl's plan. If his son was away, he couldn't impregnate his wife, and the patriarch would have a clear shot at the lonely Nicole.

That didn't matter, it wasn't her business. Whisper had made none of the decisions, but was bearing the burden of them. Her marriage was doomed, just like she'd said to Bosco. The fuse was lit, she just had no idea how long it would burn before the bomb went off.

SIXTEEN

THE BOMB WASN'T GOING to wait a decade. After avoiding each other for over two weeks, she and Zaid had managed to find a rhythm that involved not saying much to each other beyond what was absolutely necessary.

Sometimes it was hard and she wanted to play with him or tease and seduce him. But every time they came to the crucial moment when she'd have to follow through, Whisper backed down. Playing with him meant bonding with him, meant risking more of her heart that was already tugging her toward him.

He was a hard man, but not a hard man to care about. Whisper wasn't sure she'd ever even cared for her brothers and cousins the way she found herself caring for her husband.

At dinners in Kitty's or at home in the courtyard when the family were grilling, she liked his easy touches. None of them were sexual as they had once been, yet they could set her alight.

He'd drink from her glass or eat from her plate. He'd rest a hand on her leg when she had them stretched out somewhere or he'd lay a hand on hers without even looking at her. Every time his skin made contact with hers, she'd begin to tingle.

It was an odd way to live. To be attracted to your husband but not allow yourself to feel for him. Still, that was her life and she had to make the best of it.

The Thursday had started like any other, with her sneaking into the shower early and leaving for work before Zaid was awake. She'd come back to the McDade house early after starting her day early and spent some time reading in her bedroom.

Feeling peckish, Whisper decided to descend the stairs, as she'd done many times, to poke around and see what could be scavenged for dinner. Her mind was preoccupied by the book she wanted to get back to, so it took a few extra seconds to hear the two male voices by the front door. After she did, Whisper slowed to a stop on the stairs.

"I'll talk to Doran about it when we get back," Burl said.

She could hear him putting on his jacket, which made sense because he and Parker were both supposed to be going away that weekend. Whisper actually thought they were gone already, which was why she hadn't minded heading for the kitchen with enthusiasm. She got her explanation as to why they were still there after hearing the front door open. The whoosh of crisp, cool air rushed up to her from the outside.

"Damn car still isn't here," Parker said. "I hate amateurs." There was a pause. Whisper decided to wait, she didn't want to talk to either man, much less both of them together. "Zaid will be a problem, even if you can convince Doran."

"He won't be a problem," Burl said. "They'll both do what's best for the family."

"You're ignoring how Zaid feels about Whisper. He's obsessed, he won't give her up."

Pulling herself closer to the banister, Whisper made herself as small as she could.

"I make the decisions for this family," Burl said. "I don't like this alliance with the Dohertys. It's not working out."

"And you think the Byrnes will be better? I'm damn pleased I was already married when you started this shit. Was it Rick Byrne's choice or yours to match Doran to Madison?"

Madison Byrne was Rick Byrne's daughter. The only daughter, much like Whisper in her family. Though she and Madison were nothing alike. They'd come across each other several times over the years and were around the same age. But their conditioned hatred was too deep to allow either woman to really see the other.

"Doran loves a pretty face and there's none prettier than Madison."

That was true, even Whisper agreed with that. The beauty was five feet ten inches tall too, much better suited to the McDade boys who were all over six feet.

"But marriage? It's hasty. You did it with Zaid and Whisper and now you're saying it hasn't worked out. Why do you think Doran and Madison will be different?"

"Because Madison wants this to work. She wants this alliance to happen. She's much better suited to this family."

Her mind was racing at a thousand miles a minute. Parker's probably was too because for the longest time, he didn't say a word.

"This isn't… Whisper didn't do something, did she? If you know something Zaid should know—"

"I don't have to justify my decisions to anyone. I make them and you boys carry them out. That's it. End of story."

He could accuse Whisper of doing something terrible, but there would be no logic in it. He wanted her out of the family as quickly and quietly as possible. Burl wouldn't care what her own family did to her afterwards.

But if he made an enemy of her by dragging her through the mud while at the same time ruining her marriage, he'd give her even less to lose. After that, Whisper could do as she'd promised and tell the truth to anyone who'd listen… and even those who didn't want to, like Zaid.

"I'm sorry. You're right," Parker said.

If she thought about the context of Parker's deference, his attitude would baffle her. Sure, Burl was the head of the family, but he was also more than two decades older than the fitter man who'd just been kowtowed. They lived an obscure life at this end of the social spectrum.

"I want rid of that woman no matter the cost. I want the Dohertys out of our lives. Doran will marry Madison Byrne and we will stand with them to eradicate any trace of every Doherty from this city."

"Zaid will fall in line," Parker said. "You make the law around here."

"There's the car. Take care of him as soon as we get to the airport."

Noise of movement carried to her. After the front door closed, Whisper turned around to dart back upstairs as fast as she could. The pair of men would be gone for the weekend. They wouldn't be back until at least Monday, which gave her a chance at a head start.

Hurrying into the bedroom, she didn't loiter and went straight into the closet to begin packing. Keeping the clothes to a minimum, Whisper selected a few outfits that would cover as many eventualities as possible and packed every piece of jewelry she owned.

Pulling her cellphone and all the cards from her wallet, she left them on Zaid's vanity diagonally opposite hers. For a second, she considered opening the drawers beneath the mirror to see if he had anything she could hock. The idea of stealing from him turned her stomach and it would make her traceable too.

There was a slim chance her own jewelry could be traced as well… her father probably had pictures for the insurance. So she decided to go to the pawn shop before leaving the city. That way, she wouldn't leave a trail across the country for anyone to follow.

"What are you doing?"

Whisper hadn't heard Zaid coming in, but she'd gotten sort of used to his creeping. "I thought you went out before your father left."

"I was in the gym," he said. She guessed that was the reason for his damp hair, fresh tee-shirt and shorts. "I said goodbye and then went to workout. And I asked you a question, what are you doing?"

"I, my friend, am outta here," she said, having been

caught there was no point in lying. Holding up her hand, she examined her wedding ring. "I don't know why, but I feel weird about hocking this so…"

Pulling off her wedding band, she put it on his vanity with the other things then grabbed her bag from the central bench to head for the door.

Zaid blocked her way. "You think I'm gonna let you walk out of here?"

"I think you can try to stop me, but you know how persistent I am. If you tie me down, you'll only be doing their work for them and…" She paused before her admission. "It sounds stupid, but I want to remember you like this, with concern in your voice. I don't want to have to sit still while you cut me down."

The next time Whisper tried to pass him, he grabbed her bag from her hand and hurled it to the other end of the closet.

"Would you stop with the bullshit and trust me?" he demanded. "What's going on?"

Laying a hand on his chest, she knew staying calm made more sense than losing it. Her bag was lost, her financial escape plan with it. If she went back to get it, he'd only take it from her again. Whatever happened, her concentration had to remain on getting out of the house. After that, she'd find a way to make it. Anything was better than sitting there waiting for her demise.

"This one I can't tell you," she said.

"You can tell me anything," he said, reaching for her face.

On reflex, she ducked back, away from his hand. "No, I can't."

"You're in trouble."

That almost made her laugh, but she did her best to contain herself. "Yeah."

"You think someone is coming for you."

"I know they are," she said, pressing her hand a little deeper into him, regretting all the time she didn't have left to be near to him.

"Then trust your family to protect you. That's why

we're here. That's why we're a unit."

Letting her head shake, Whisper peeked up at him. "I know that you believe that. But I don't belong here anymore than I ever belonged under my father's roof. I'm female. I'm disposable. I've got to look out for me because no one else will."

"I will."

It seemed like he was actually offended by the idea he wouldn't, which made her smile and slide her hand a little higher.

"After I walk out that door, I'm never gonna see you again," Whisper said. "So I'm going to do something that I've never done before. I'll deny it ever happened if you tell another breathing soul." She raised a pointed finger toward his face. "I swear I'll come back and haunt you if you ever repeat what's about to happen. I'll find a way to turn your balls green or keep your dick soft for eternity. I swear it. This goes no further."

Shaking her straight finger at him once, she made her point and then her hand fell to her side. It took a couple of tries for her hands to find his torso and slide around to his back. Edging closer, she began to regret her decision the moment her body sank against his.

Whisper had never held a man or been held by one. There weren't hugs in her house growing up, she hadn't even had a creepy uncle who'd think about trying his luck using one for cover. Given that she was short, men often picked her up on the way to bed. Situations like that were the only time she'd had her arms around a man. But this, it was something different.

Her eyes closed. Breathing slow, Whisper strengthened her arms, pulling herself closer, deeper into him, inhaling his scent and absorbing his heat. There was comfort there in that embrace; something she hadn't considered just touching another person could give. Her husband was broad and solid and felt indestructible, at least against her meager form.

But the moment his arms began to close around her shoulders, Whisper leaped back. She was mortified to feel a tingling behind her nose like maybe her emotions were thinking about manifesting themselves.

That was it. Over. Time to go. She eased past him, but only got a couple of steps before he grabbed her wrist to haul her back.

Whisper was about to argue when he curved an arm around her and yanked her off her feet to dump her down on the vanity. Her mouth opened, but there was no time to focus. He lunged in close and then his mouth was on hers.

His mouth.

Zaid was kissing her.

They'd been married for almost two months. Whisper had lost count of the number of times she'd given him head and they'd even had sex once. But kissing? She'd never kissed him. As she lost herself to the deep suction of their consuming kiss, she wished she never had.

Every emotion she'd damped down came rushing to the fore. Every feeling she hadn't let herself have about this man bubbled up. Her hands drifted from their places hanging in midair up and around his neck, pulling him closer, begging for more.

They'd never kissed. Why did he have to do this now? His lips were making her dizzy. The cradle of his hand around the back of her head gave her an intense sensation of security that she hadn't had before.

His other arm locked around her and he lifted her again. Her legs curled around him, clinging tight just like her arms that were coiling up and around his head, keeping his mouth engaged in the kiss she didn't want to lose for a moment.

SEVENTEEN

WHISPER LOST HIS KISS when he laid her down on his bed. That was when he pulled back to slide the cotton straps of her dress from her shoulders, easing it down over her hips, taking her panties with it.

She arched to unhook her bra while he shed his tee-shirt and shorts. They finished stripping at the same second, just as he dropped down over her to pick up their kiss where it had left off.

His long, hard form dwarfed hers. Nestled beneath him, lost in their kiss, she couldn't imagine ever feeling safer or more content.

Whisper was so consumed by his kiss, so enthralled by it that she didn't realize the route of his hand until his finger slid into her.

Her whole body slackened, even her mouth forgot to keep kissing as her head rolled back. "Oh God," she exhaled when he pulled it out to push it back in.

He'd never stimulated her like that, never used his hands to pleasure her. Whisper hadn't thought anything could be better than his kiss, but he was proving her wrong. Maybe it was the adrenaline and anxiety of the day, but the moment he touched her quivering clit, she went off. Bucking up and calling out in an orgasm she hadn't expected to achieve so soon.

He pushed her legs up and apart. Whisper was too boneless to think about objecting to anything. Not that she would anyway. The sensation of the engorged head of his cock pushing into her was medicine for everything that was wrong in her life and in the world.

It frustrated her that he left it there, just inside her opening, going no further. When she opened her eyes to seek the delay, she found he was there above her, just watching her. His gaze was heavy and as enraptured as she felt.

Opening her hands on his body, her fingertips traced up and down the defined lines of his torso and up over the globes of his shoulders to then slip down his impressive arms. It was a torment that she was too short to kiss his mouth, but she crunched up to let her lips taste whatever they could reach.

Her husband.

It was insane to be doing this when she'd still have to walk out the door, but it felt too good to fight. When she flopped onto the bed again, he pushed up, moving his hips slow so she'd feel every inch of him sliding into her.

It felt like she wasn't breathing though she definitely was; those short breathy inhales were hers. He was so long and thick that even she had to brace herself for the impact he had on her body. But Whisper adored every tingle and pulse that vibrated through her.

Once he was all the way inside and his groin was pressed to her, he stalled again. This time she wriggled, stimulating herself against the weight of his body, using him to take herself closer to the climax she craved.

One wasn't enough. She wanted two or three or four. Whisper would never have him again. Her husband was supposed to be the only man to ever occupy her body. Something about that clarity felt so right. But she couldn't make any promises to him or to herself. Life on the streets was hard and that was all she had to look forward to.

Turning tricks was likely her future. Her body was the only asset she had; realizing that broke her heart. She was going to share herself with other men, dozens of them, maybe hundreds. Not because she wanted to, but because she'd have to. It was the only way she'd survive.

Before Whisper could lose herself to the grief of that prospect, Zaid snapped her out of it by withdrawing and advancing.

He didn't stop, but didn't really pick up the pace. For the longest time, he pulled out and slid in, keeping their gazes as locked as their bodies. Whisper had never watched a man make love to her before.

She frowned. Make love. She'd never made love with a man at all. Whisper fucked, or screwed, or banged, she didn't make love.

As if sensing her confusion about what was happening or how she'd found herself in that position, Zaid withdrew and slammed into her hard. Her mouth opened in a sharp yelp.

It didn't matter what they were doing or why, what mattered was feeling it.

He sped up. She worked against him to work with him. Their contrary and harmonious movements matched each other in pace and rhythm until both were panting, fighting to get over the crest of climax.

Whisper crashed over it in the same moment he did. She didn't even try to silence her scream of need that went far beyond the release of her body venting the pleasure of her orgasm. She screamed for her life and the torture of having to leave it. She screamed for every hit her father had delivered that she'd had to take without fighting back. She screamed out her hatred for the Byrnes and her guilt over the way she'd treated her mother. And she screamed in disgust for Burl McDade and the frustration that his choices were forcing her into a corner.

Her lips closed as she opened her eyes to find Zaid still above her. He probably wondered at the insanity of the woman beneath him, who'd just hollered like a virgin being gang-raped. But he didn't question her.

He moved away. No, not away, he climbed off her, and took her with him as he lay in the middle of the bed. Easing her head to his chest and her arm across his body, Zaid slid his arm beneath her to hold her there. Seemed he figured the sex had erased her intention to leave.

Sitting up, Whisper wasn't going to let herself relax or bask in any afterglow. It was time to go. Now.

Knowing he wouldn't let her climb over him to slip out, she got off her side of the bed, closest to the window. Skirting the bed to grab her bra from the floor at the end, Whisper was quick to slip her arms into it.

"What the hell, Peanut?" he asked, rising to his elbows to watch her fasten her bra clasp.

"You're amazing, Zaid. I swear, I've never had a better lover," she said and meant it.

Despite it being true, the statement seemed to come off as insincere. Maybe it was because she was hurrying. Once her bra was on, she retrieved her dress and panties to put them on too.

"You're not walking out of here," he said, sitting up on the edge of the bed to snag his shorts and tug them on. He sat back down and bent to sweep his tee-shirt up. Whisper hoped his dressing would distract him, but as she was about to retreat, he lunged forward to lock his grip around her wrist. "Whoever wants to take you down, I'll take them down first, I guarantee it. Trust me—"

"No! Goddamnit! Stop asking me to trust you!"

Losing it wasn't the plan, but he'd switched on all these things inside her. Whisper felt overloaded, like she couldn't see or hear or breathe. Life was careening out of control; she didn't like feeling as if she was just along for the ride. Whisper had to take control, to be in control, or she'd never survive a minute.

He leaped to his feet, his tee-shirt in his fist. "Why? Why is it so fucking hard to give me your trust? The world didn't fall from its axis when I gave you mine!"

"I never asked for it," she said, trying to twist her arm from his grip and peel away his fingers, but it wasn't working, he just kept on holding her. "I never wanted it. And you're a fucking idiot for giving it to me."

"Why? Why, huh? Why shouldn't a husband trust his wife?"

Giving up her fight against his grasp, Whisper wanted to scream again. Instead, her frustration and upset cascaded out of her in a startling truth.

"Because I'm lying to you, asshole! I've been lying to you for weeks!"

It wasn't his fault, so the insult was unnecessary. Still, it worked, at least, her confession did. As his frown became a searching scowl, his fingers loosened. Good. That gave her the chance to slip from his hold. While he was standing there processing, Whisper took advantage of the opportunity to dash back into the closet to retrieve her bag.

She regretted the delay when coming out of the closet because Zaid was marching toward her. "Tell me," he demanded, pulling on his tee-shirt.

"No," she said and straightened the strap of her bag, intending to put it over her head. Zaid snatched it and threw it away again. "Goddamnit! Stop doing that!"

Whisper went after the bag, which gave him the opportunity to put himself between her and the door.

"I withhold from you all the time. There are truths neither of our families have shared, but that's business. This isn't business. You're not talking business. Business wouldn't do this to you." She didn't know what he thought 'this' was, but he wasn't wrong. "You're not lying to the family as a Doherty, you're lying to me as my wife."

"Yeah, pretty much," she said, succeeding this time in tossing the bag strap across her body. Whisper started back toward him. "Now we've established that I'm a lowlife, want to get out of my way?"

Zaid didn't move. "Why would your lie make you leave?" he asked, talking to himself. "You married me because your father threatened your life if you didn't. If you walk out of here, if you leave me, you're signing your death warrant with the Dohertys."

"So move aside and give me a fighting chance… a head start at least," she said. "You're under no obligation to, but I'd appreciate it if you waited as long as you could before telling them I'm gone."

That request made his brows rise. "You want me to

cover for you? Are you shitting me?"

Had Whisper known he was going to catch her, or refuse to cooperate, she'd have slipped out at night after Burl and Parker were on a plane and gone. If Zaid sounded the alarm before they got on that plane, they'd abandon their trip and come back. She'd be just as well putting a bullet in her head.

"Fine," Whisper said, taking off the bag to dump it on the floor.

Crouching to unzip it, she yanked her knife from its sheath and stood up. After holding the weapon up to give him a quick look, she grabbed his wrist to pull him into their bathroom.

"What are you doing?" he asked when she climbed into the tub and put the knife in his hand.

Whisper began to strip again. "Can you hit the aorta? You've got to be able to do that? Right?"

"What the hell—"

"A gun causes blood spatter," she said. "And I know it's nuts, but I've always had a weird thing about slitting my wrists. I wouldn't have the balls, it just weirds me out." He was still just standing there, flabbergasted, so she picked up his hand and pointed the blade at her chest. "You were a good husband, Zaid. Consider this mercy your last marital act."

Instead of plunging the knife into her, he swept his hand aside, tossing the knife to the floor.

"I'm not gonna kill my wife. I'm not my father."

Wearing a half smile, she climbed from the tub and went to retrieve the weapon. "Ain't I glad about that." Whisper got back in the tub and sat down. She was trying to align the blade when a sudden thought made her pause. "Wait, do you want me to write you a note?"

"A note?"

"To say the sex was consensual and I did this myself."

Protecting his future would lead to her writing the oddest suicide note ever.

He sank to a crouch outside the tub and took the knife from her. "I won't let you kill yourself."

Relaxing her hand, she leaned closer. "Zay, this is my

mercy. If my father finds me, it will take days, maybe weeks, I don't want that. I know you don't owe me anything, but—"

"No one is going to hurt you."

"You don't know what I know."

"Then tell me," he said, his deep voice almost beseeching. "Trust me with whatever this lie is."

She slid a hand to his jaw. "I've heard about some of the things you've done to people." She smiled. "When my father told me I was marrying you, I called you a psychopath." Now she knew that wasn't true of her husband but may be true of her father. Zaid laid a hand over hers. "I don't know what that is in your eye when you look at me, but I do know I don't want to watch it dwindle and die. Kill me, Zaid. Please…" Any softness in his gaze vanished. "I need you to do this before my father or yours gets the chance to strap me down and torture me."

"If you know something they need to know—"

"No, it's not like that," she said, shaking her head, then smiling. "The worst part is, there is no way for me to save myself. There's no magic bullet, nothing I can reveal that will make them spare me. They just want me dead… That's all they want from me."

"I don't understand why you think my father would… I saw him today, he said nothing. Whatever you think he knows, he doesn't, and if you think he'll find out—"

"This isn't what he found out. I discovered something and he knows I did and…"

Whisper was getting too close to the truth, so she shut up and took a breath. Figuring Zaid was going to keep on thwarting her efforts, she got out of the tub to get dressed. "Maybe I'll deliver myself to Madison," she murmured and smiled again. "As an early wedding present."

Snatching her arm, he whirled her around. "What fucking wedding?"

"You'll see," she said, stepping in to nuzzle his arm because it was all she could do. "Take care of yourself, McDade. And twist the knife in my father once for me, huh?"

Leaving the bathroom without looking at him again, Whisper didn't like going without her knife but would pick up another weapon along the way.

Retrieving her bag from the floor, she only got one step before he came out of the bathroom.

"You discovered something," he said, stalling her. "About my father… you think if you tell me, I won't believe you."

"It doesn't matter whether you believe me," she said. "I have a feeling that it would eventually eat at you enough that you'd get the truth from other sources. Even if you didn't believe me, after I was dead and buried, you'd always wonder. I'm not the only one who knows the truth."

That made him bound toward her. "Who else knows? My father? You think I'd confront him?"

"Your father and mine are too alike; two bullheaded, stubborn assholes. You'd never get the truth from your father. He'd never say the words."

"Then you think I'd get them from someone weaker. Someone who wouldn't hold up under torture."

That made her smile. "You're not going to torture someone in your own family. You certainly don't have it in you to torture a woman, not one who adores you."

But while Whisper enjoyed the joke, he processed what she shouldn't have said.

Clarity struck fast. "Nicole," he murmured. Panic shot through her. "Nicole knows."

Starting for the bedroom door, he was a man on a mission. Whisper tossed her bag to the floor and dashed after him, trying her best to block his route as he'd done to her so often that evening.

But she didn't have his strength or size. He pushed her from his path like she weighed nothing.

"No," she said, running after him when he opened their bedroom door and started down the stairs. "No! Zay! Don't!"

It didn't take him long to get to Nicole and Parker's bedroom. Without knocking, he threw open the door and marched inside, startling Nicole who was sitting on the bed surrounded by glossy magazines.

Getting right to the edge of the bed, he bent over and

grabbed Nicole's jaw to haul her onto her knees. "Say it," he growled.

The instant panic and consuming fear radiating from Nicole was palpable. "Oh my God," she whimpered, her frantic eyes darting sideways to seek Whisper by the door. "You told him."

Whisper opened her mouth intending to say that she hadn't, but Zaid spoke before she could. "I want to hear you say it."

Nicole's voice broke. "I wanted to have a baby," she wailed.

Zaid let Nicole go to whip around and look at Whisper like he didn't get it. And why should he? A woman wanting a child was hardly newsworthy.

But Nicole wasn't done. "Parker wouldn't… couldn't and… it had to be a McDade baby! He said it would be easy, and the baby would… even if it couldn't be Parker's, it would be a McDade…"

Slowly, Zaid's gaze cooled and crept around to the woman on the bed, who was turning and twisting the hem of her dress in her fists.

"What in the fuck…" Zaid said. "You've been fucking Doran?"

Blinking, the confused Nicole raised her attention from the bed. "What? I… no, I…"

She looked to Whisper; Zaid did too.

"It sure as shit wasn't me. Score's not even in the state. Who the hell else…" Horror hit him. His mouth opened as disgust contorted his expression. "You discovered something about my father…" he murmured to the floor, obviously replaying what had been said upstairs. In a flash, he whipped around to Nicole. "You're fucking Burl?"

Nicole pounced onto her knees. "I thought Whisper told you!"

"No," he drawled, sinister in every aspect. "My wife toed the line and kept the fucker's secret… Like we all keep his secrets." His attention snapped around to her. "He threatened your life?"

The truth was out, so there was no reason to lie. "He

wants Doran to marry Madison Byrne," Whisper said. "I'm out."

"Because of this?" She nodded. "Does Doran know?"

Folding her hands on the doorframe behind her, she leaned back against it. "About his upcoming wedding? No. About the affair? I don't know. I have no idea who else knows."

Spinning around, he turned his rage back to Nicole. "Does Doran know?" The tears were streaming down Nicole's face. The sight reminded Whisper of the blonde in Kitty's. Nicole didn't answer fast enough, so Zaid raised his volume. "Does Doran know?"

"No!" Nicole wailed. "No! No one knows!"

"Do you think Parker does?" Whisper asked.

Zaid was quick to answer. "A man doesn't find out his father is fucking his wife and just let that shit go," he said. A moment later his attention jumped up to land on her. "Tell me he didn't…" Whisper swallowed while doing her best not to look at him. A slow rumbling laugh vibrated in his throat. "Oh, I'll make him sorry he ever lived."

"Would you be careful what you're saying," she snapped and eyed Nicole. "She has access to phones and email. You can't talk like that when your father is away and has at least three days to come up with a plan before he gets back… or he could send people over here. Who knows what he's capable of? Besides, nothing happened. He made an implication that the offer was on the table. That was all. It was after I found out. He only wanted to keep me quiet. He probably figured if he was doing me too that I wouldn't have a leg to stand on if the truth came out. If I'd done it, he'd have been right."

His eyes narrowed. "But you said no."

"Of course I said no," she said, scowling in disgust. "I'm not sick enough to fuck my own husband's father… If your spunk doesn't work well then, we'll go childless. I'm not carrying another man's baby, McDade or not." It wasn't until the side of his mouth lifted in a semi smile that she rethought her words. "Wait, what did I just say?"

"You said you're sticking around," he said, but had his focus stolen when Nicole began to move. "You sit the fuck down, you're not going anywhere."

Whisper pushed away from the door. "Do you have a plan, husband?"

He seemed to be trying to figure that out. "We have to tell Doran."

Nicole leaped to her knees again. "No! Please! Please don't! Parker can't find out!"

Zaid gave Nicole a push, just enough to send her back to her ass. "Are you insane? No fucking way I'm keeping this from him. A man deserves to know what kind of slut he's married to."

"Husband," Whisper said, side nodding and edging out of the door. Zaid took her hint and followed her to the hall, though he kept one eye on Nicole in the bedroom. "You have a window. A couple of days breathing space to process this and figure out what, if anything, you want to do with the news... Take the window. Tell Doran, talk it out. You can't do anything while your father and Parker are away. To let them know you know while they're out of the city will hand them your only advantage..." She cast her eyes back to the bedroom. "But you'll have to make sure she can't communicate with either of them."

"What do you suggest?"

"Bring her upstairs for now," she said. "Until you can track down Doran and figure out what you want to do... Whatever it is, you'll need his support. You can't do it alone, and if he likes the idea of marrying Madison Byrne..."

Then he'd be on his father's side and the McDade civil war would be in immediate full swing. Subduing Nicole would be easy. It wouldn't be so easy to keep Doran from warning his father.

"I'm not alone," he said, touching the corner of her mouth with his thumb. "If turning around and walking out of here is how this thing has to end, we'll do it. But we'll do it together."

Whisper was at a loss. In every potential scenario she'd played out in her mind, this had never been even a remote possibility.

"I really didn't see this going this way, I…" Narrowing her eyes, she leaned closer. "You're really not mad?"

"I'm fucking livid, Peanut," he said and bowed to join their mouths in a brief kiss. "But I need you, Whis. I need my wife. I need an ally on my side who I can trust no matter what… The woman upstairs a while ago who asked me to kill her, she needs the same thing."

"You want us to be allies?" she asked. Zaid nodded. "That's a shame." He frowned. "I thought maybe we could try… being together."

She'd never said that to a man but meant it. It was right. It felt right. As confusing and intense as all this was, Whisper couldn't ignore that he'd supported her instead of blaming her. Her husband believed her. That meant what he'd said upstairs was true: he trusted her. And without the lie, Whisper could let herself trust him.

Curling a finger beneath her chin, he kissed her again. "You're ready now?" With a grin, she nodded. "Peanut, you pick your moments." He kissed the top of her head then grabbed her hand. "Come on, let's get her upstairs."

EIGHTEEN

NICOLE MOVED AT ZAID'S COMMAND. That was no surprise given the woman's feeble competence when it came to defending herself. Whisper followed her husband's orders too. He directed her downstairs to the unit by the front door to retrieve what they'd need to restrain Nicole.

On her return to the empty bedroom, voices in the bathroom drew Whisper in. Approaching, she listened to their conversation.

"Anything, Zay," Nicole said. "You can keep her quiet. I know you can. And anything you want—"

"You've been offering yourself to me since the first time Parker brought you home," Zaid said.

Nicole giggled. "Because you're so strong… You're so powerful. So much more powerful than all of them. I always wanted to be with you. It was always you."

"You think I'd get with my brother's girl?" he asked. Nicole's next gasp was filled with frightened pain. "You touch me again and I'll take pleasure in watching my wife destroy you. Do you know what she does to women who make moves on me?"

Whisper's smile curled. Proud of both herself and him in the same heartbeat, she loved his certainty of her dedication. Whether it had been a game before or not, whether it continued to be a game or not, she would enjoy taking apart any woman who made a move on her man.

Her man. Her husband. That's what he was. Now this truth was out in the open, it felt real… and she liked it. They could actually have trust. Real trust. She'd confessed a horrible truth to him. One he wouldn't have wanted to hear, but he didn't blame her or cast her out. He'd supported her. Her husband had supported her. Someone had stood with her rather than taking the easy way out.

"You know I… I love this family, Zay… My family… If you tell Whisper that you want me," Nicole pleaded. "Maybe you… you can have both of us."

There was real optimism in Nicole's voice. Could be that the suggestion excited her, or maybe she was just terrified of the alternative.

"What?" Zaid asked.

"Yeah," Nicole said, garnering speed in her hope. "Yeah, she's bi, right? Remember your reception, her friend, they were together. I could… I could do that if it made you happy. If it was what you wanted… Is it… what you want?"

"To watch you go down on my wife?"

"She has more experience, she could… I could let her…"

"My wife is a fucking goddess," Zaid said. "Why would I let her demean herself by going down on a slut like you? You don't deserve the pleasure of her mouth… Hell, I don't deserve it, but I take it because I can't fucking help myself around her. That what you want? To piss off a woman who can flatten you or order me to take you apart? I'd do anything she asked, Nicki. And until you feel like that about another person, you don't have the right to use the word love."

Flattered and stunned, Whisper couldn't move. No one had ever felt that way about her or even said the words. Zaid claimed he'd been watching her for three years and that a fuck wouldn't be enough. But what did that mean? What did he want?

"You… do you love her?"

"You're goddamn right I love her. I sure love her more than I love you or my fucking father." Though it was a compliment, it felt sort of underhanded. Of course he'd love her more than the people who were fixing to ruin the family. "I fucking love her more than I love the McDades, that's for goddamn sure."

Nicole gasped; Whisper almost did the same. For an heir to say that about his family was treason. Even while despising whatever was going on, he shouldn't take the family name in vain.

"You don't mean that."

"Why wouldn't I, Nicki?" he asked. Whisper smiled, appreciating that he'd started using the name their sister-in-law didn't like. "All this family has done is take."

"But you're a McDade," Nicole said like she couldn't understand him wishing for anything else.

Whisper sort of felt the same. She was so used to everyone being so proud of their faction, that it was difficult to imagine anyone questioning it.

"Yeah, for all the good it's done me," he muttered.

Whisper couldn't stay in the bedroom eavesdropping all day. Taking advantage of their lull in conversation, she went into the bathroom, holding up the supplies. She dumped them on the vanity, then went back to lock the bathroom door, trapping the three of them inside.

Whisper snagged the hand towel from its loop. "I'm going to be kind to you, Pretty Nicki," she said, walking between Zaid and Nicole to head for the shower. "Have you been held captive before?"

"I… I… no," Nicole said. "Captive?"

"Baby, will you come over here and make sure I don't crack my skull… Bring her."

Zaid shoved Nicki along, delivering her to the shower stall as Whisper slid open the large glass door.

"What are you doing?" Nicki asked with trepidation.

"Well, when I hold a captive," Whisper said, tossing the towel over her shoulder. "I always like to put myself in their position, you know, just to make sure there's no way out." Jumping up, she caught the top rail that held the runners for the shower door. "Your boobs are bigger than mine, so you weigh more…" Dropping to her feet again, she paused to point at Nicole's chest. "Those are fake, right?"

"My…" Nicole looked at the frowning Zaid and then back to Whisper. "My breasts?"

"Yes, they are," Zaid said. "McDade bought and paid for."

"I figured," Whisper said, brushing her hands together. "No matter. I'm stronger, so… But if this buckles we're all in trouble." Jumping up again, she caught the rail and swung her legs up too. Bouncing, the point was to pull it down. When it didn't budge, she lowered her feet, controlling her descent with her abs. "We're good."

Whisper didn't expect to feel someone touching her waist. Seeking out the source, it was a surprise to find Zaid steadying her. That kind of concern rattled her. Maybe if the whole thing had come down on her head, she'd have expected him to make contact. Otherwise, she didn't expect him to care.

"What… what are you going to do to me?" Nicole asked.

"We are going to keep you in one place for an extended period of time," she said with a mock gasp and bent to pick the towel off the floor to toss it up over the rail. "Can you tie that, baby?"

His reach surpassed hers. Having a tall guy around could prove useful. Zaid stepped in to lean over her and put a simple knot in the towel. He spread it just a little, then yanked Nicole forward, which forced Whisper out of the way.

"You… you can't do this," Nicole said.

Whisper pushed her into the shower while Zaid went to get the rest of the things from the vanity. He also grabbed her knife from the floor and brought everything over. After taking her hand to loop the duct tape around her wrist like a bracelet, Zaid pulled out a length of rope. He made a circle and cut through it with her knife.

"We could do a lot worse," Whisper said. "Keep your feet in the shower and you'll be fine."

The inside was slightly higher than the outside. Nicole was taller than her, so she should be able to stay on her tiptoes without straining too much.

Whisper noted how Nicole's attention dropped to Zaid's groin for absolutely no reason. Her husband didn't notice, he was busy tying the rope around one of Nicole's wrists. Once he finished with one, he raised it up to toss the rope over the shower rail and tied the other wrist on the opposite side.

She kind of couldn't blame Nicole for having sexual fantasies about Zaid. Whisper was guilty of having a few too, especially when pleasuring herself under his scrutiny. Even in the current situation of captivity and bondage, there was no way to dub Nicole's imaginings as rape fantasies. In spite of being their prisoner, Nicole wouldn't fight Zaid's advances if he made them. She might pretend to, but would probably be too afraid he'd change his mind about violating her.

Once he'd finished with the rope, he handed her what was left and retrieved the duct tape from her arm. He started to wrap it around Nicole's wrists, strapping them to the rail with the rope and towel inside.

He held up the roll when he was done. "Are you gonna make a noise? If you're thinking about screaming or crying, I'll gag you now."

Whisper hissed in a breath while concentrating on coiling the rope around her own wrists. "And that's good duct tape too, the professional stuff. It will really screw with your facial." When no one responded, she looked up to see they were both watching her tying her own wrists. "What?" she asked. "No reason it should go to waste. We have time to kill before Doran gets back… and there is a big bed right through the wall."

Nicole squealed. "You can't have sex! You can't! You just can't!"

She probably meant that listening to them going at it would be torture all on its own.

Zaid didn't seem to take it that way and grabbed the rope connecting Whisper's wrists to haul her closer. He jabbed a thumb into his chest. "Husband," he said, then pointed at her. "Wife… That's how it's supposed to fucking go, Nicki."

Without letting her go, he turned and stalked across the room, throwing open the bathroom door only to slam it as soon as they were through. Towing her across the room, Zaid whipped her around to toss her on the bed.

But he didn't join her, he marched around the couch at the foot of the bed and went to the window. Rising from her face, Whisper folded her legs underneath herself as she loosened her wrists from the twined rope.

"You're a liar, husband," she said.

He spun to face her. "Me? How long you been keeping this from me?"

"Not about that," she said. He didn't realize she was teasing yet. "You told Nicki you couldn't help yourself around me." Lying on her side on the bed, Whisper snagged one of his pillows to hug it to her body. "You've been doing nothing but help yourself around me since we got married."

"You've gotta stop eavesdropping," he said, sauntering towards her.

"Soon as you stop creeping," she said, rolling toward him when he sat on the edge of the bed.

Tossing the pillow out of the way, he laid a hand on her stomach to push her onto her back. "Your life is about to change, wife... Our lives are about to change."

Sliding a palm up the back of his forearm as his hand massaged her abdomen, Whisper hoped to offer some comfort. "Any idea what you're going to do?"

"Talk to Doran," he said. "Want to tell me what you meant downstairs?"

"Which part?" she asked, unable to remember what had been said on which floor.

His reply wasn't particularly helpful. "When did you find out about this?"

"When you were away," she said.

The seal was off. It was liberating to finally be able to talk to someone about the situation.

He watched his hand on her belly, his jaw moving like he was grinding his teeth. "Tell me everything... Tell me what happened. How did you find out?"

"Came home early one Wednesday," she said. "Had

a client cancel… I came in the front and heard a noise…" She smiled, running her fingertips over the hairs on his arm. "Funny thing is, I took my phone out my purse, I was ready to call you. I thought someone was breaking in or something… Instead, I found Nicki naked, bent over your father's desk with him coming at her from behind." Peeking up at him, she caught his sneer of revulsion. "Yeah, it wasn't a pretty sight."

"And you didn't think to finish the call?" he asked, letting himself look at her face. "Why didn't you tell me?"

Sitting up, her hand slid higher on his arm. "You know why I didn't tell you. Nicki came after me, I… I was ready to beat the shit out of her, but I didn't. I told her I was going to tell you… I think that I was, but… then your father kept you away the extra night. The next morning, he confronted me."

The sound of his teeth grinding got so intense it carried to her. "When he made his move on you?"

"He got too close… made some comment about my father." She licked her lips. "I told him I wasn't my father's to give anymore… that if he wanted use of my body, he had to negotiate with my husband."

Vicious determination seized his expression. "I would never—"

"I know," she murmured, raising her hand to his jaw. "I don't know how, but even then I knew I was… something to you. I don't think I admitted it to myself… He told me it would start a McDade civil war, that everyone would blame me… And that the Doherty alliance would be dust… He wasn't wrong about that." Whisper inhaled. "My father will kill me when he finds out I screwed this up… and that's not a euphemism."

Touching the corner of her mouth with his curled fingers on her chin, he made her look at him. "Your job was to play the dutiful wife, that's what he said at the door, right?" She nodded and he dropped his chin a fraction. "Bring that mouth here."

Kissing was still such a novelty that when she pushed up to press her mouth to his, Whisper couldn't hide her smile.

"Why does this feel so different?" she asked, trying to take another kiss.

Zaid caught a loose tendril of her hair and rested his fingers on her cheek to ease their mouths apart. "Tell me about the alley."

NINETEEN

ZAID HAD ALREADY stated that what she'd done in the alley wasn't about sex, but Whisper hadn't elaborated on her reasons for going out there with that guy. At the time, it hadn't made a whole lot of sense, even to her.

Having her husband's trust allowed her to be more honest with herself, which brought other things into focus.

"I went out to get trashed," Whisper said. "To forget life, I guess… The guy wanted me and I wanted to get it. I wanted to understand what was so damn good about screwing around."

"Did you figure it out?"

Mesmerized by the sight of her small fingers on his face, she lost herself to her thoughts. "It didn't feel good… It makes no sense… We didn't marry for love. Being faithful to you shouldn't have mattered. We hadn't even had sex."

"Maybe you just didn't want to be like them."

"My mom never cheated," she said, turning her hand to stroke him with the back of her fingers. "Not that I know anyway… I used to hear her crying, on the phone to her friends talking about whichever latest bimbo my dad had taken to Tahiti or whatever…" Frowning at herself, recalling the memories renewed her sense of guilt. "I used to get so mad at her… I used to think my dad wasn't doing anything wrong because my mom never showed that she was willing to fight for him. She never went out and dragged her man back, you know? I used to think she was so weak… I wanted her to go out there and grab hold of him. I wanted her to demand fidelity."

"Might have worked," he said. "Or she could've ended up like my mother."

"I know," Whisper said, hooking her wrist over his shoulder and resting her head on the back of her hand. "I was a kid. I didn't get it. I get it now. It wasn't like he didn't know what he was doing to her… I'd hear them fighting about it. She'd be sniveling and crying, begging him not to go to the bed of whoever… He liked it… He liked that she was dependent on him…He liked the power he had over her."

"My father was the same. Though he coupled his cheating with a helluva lot of psychological abuse."

"My father was definitely more of the physical variety… Though I guess you could say ignoring her for weeks on end was a form of psychological abuse. Even when he was home and talking to my brothers, he could go a whole month without saying one word to me or my mother."

"We're not going to be like them, Peanut," he said, finger-combing her hair away from her face.

Whisper raised her head from her hand. "How do you know that?"

Stroking her lip with his thumb, he brought their mouths closer. "I don't want anyone else."

"You say that now. But how will you feel after six months… or six years… or three kids. Won't you need some peppy twenty-two year old to make you feel like a real man?"

"My definition of a real man isn't the same as my father's," he said. "I want to be with you. Only you. I'm only yours."

Sitting back, Whisper met his eye. "That hasn't been my experience," she said. "Since we got married, you've been keeping me at arm's length… If you wanted me so bad, why not have sex with me straight away? It's not like I was going anywhere."

"I needed you to be ready," he said. "I know you. I knew how you'd be if I was like every other guy."

Sinking down onto her back again, her lips curled. "If you want to be like every other guy I've had in my life, you should probably punch me in the face." Arching her back, she stretched, settling deeper into his bed. "But please don't, your bed is too comfortable to bleed on."

Bowing over her, he brushed his lips on hers. "Never."

Before he could deepen the kiss, Whisper laid her hands on his shoulders to separate their mouths. "You wanted me to fall for you... to feel something."

Shifting around, he lay down on the bed at her side, looming over her. "Do you?"

"Do I..." Whatever was going on between them wasn't something she'd ever experienced. In fact, it was so unique, Whisper hadn't yet decided if she liked it or not. Drawing a finger over the shoulder seam of his tee-shirt, she breathed out. "Damn, I wish you hadn't kissed me."

"Maybe you weren't ready."

When he started to withdraw, she threw her arms around his neck to keep him near. "I can't feel anything for you, Zay," she said, fixated on his lips.

"Why not?"

"Because your brother will be home soon and maybe he'll like the idea of getting married to Madison Byrne. Maybe he won't want to confront your father or tell Parker about Nicole... If any of those things happen, I'm out. Right back where I started."

"You can't admit to feeling something for me," he said. "'Cause you still don't trust me."

While one arm remained around his neck, the other loosened so she could lay a hand on his chest. "I need you to do what's best for you, Zay," she said. "Your family is your life, and I'll be honest, I don't have a damn clue how this is going to play out. I can't see a way that everyone can make it to the other side. Something will have to give."

"You think it will be you."

"Makes the most sense... But that's not on you. If

Doran wants to get married, the Doherty alliance is over… The way your dad was talking, it's over anyway… My family will be coming for me. Even if you wanted to be with me… soon there won't be a *me* to be with."

"I can take on your father."

"And Caelan and Miles?" she asked, shaking her head despite his obvious determination. "I wouldn't want you to. You'd be committing suicide." He inhaled as though to object, so she put her fingers to his lips. "Even if you're ten times stronger than every Doherty that comes at you, how will your family react to you standing up for me? You're a valuable McDade resource and—"

He flew up off the bed, surprising her into silence. "Maybe I don't want to be a resource," he said and whirled around, opening his arms. "What the fuck are we doing, Whis? All of us! What the fuck are we doing?"

Pushing onto her elbows, the strength of his frustration was intriguing. "I don't know. What do you want to do?"

As the third son, Zaid would never be in charge of his family's businesses, not unless something happened to Parker. But her husband wasn't a backseat kind of guy. Whisper could only imagine how he'd gotten this far in life without asserting his dominance over all of them.

In contrast to the Dohertys, who had no rightful heir, the McDade side was brimming with them.

"I idolized my father too," he murmured.

"Not nice when they fall from their pedestal, is it?" she asked. "Figuring out they're human and you've been chasing an illusion your whole life… it's depressing."

"My father fell from his when I found out what he'd done to my mother… And then Score… What my father let Parker do…" He exhaled. "Guess we know why…" Whisper didn't know the full story there, but figured it wasn't the time to ask. "But what was I gonna do, Whis? Where was I gonna go?"

She understood that feeling all too well. "We've been conditioned since we were born," she said, sitting up in the middle of the bed. "This is what we are, Zay. You're a

McDade… I'm a Doherty."

Rushing back to the bed, he sat down facing her. "What if it didn't have to be that way?" he asked, scooping a hand around her cheek beneath her hair.

Though his words were more aspirational than optimistic, they did make her smile. "I had no idea I'd married an idealist," she said. "You have to spell it out for me, baby. What do you want? Hmm? Tell me and you'll get it…" That statement took on so much more meaning now that she suspected her husband had been invested in their relationship since long before they were married. He breathed in as if to speak, Whisper got there first. "Please bear in mind, we don't know who might be eavesdropping on us."

Nodding toward the bathroom door, she wanted to make sure he didn't say anything that Nicole may be able to take back to the other McDades. The plan was to keep her quiet until they came up with a plan of their own and got a lay of the land. Whisper doubted their plan would involve silencing the naïve adulteress for good.

He inhaled and released some of his negative energy. "Let's give her something to listen to, wife."

Easing the straps of her dress from her shoulders, he unhooked her bra and laid her down while dipping forward to kiss each of her breasts.

"Zay," Whisper murmured, running her hands through his hair.

When he lifted his lips from her breasts, she strengthened her hand on the back of his head to guide his mouth up to hers. She'd wished out loud that he hadn't kissed her, not because it wasn't incredible, but because it complicated everything.

He hadn't kissed her for so long. All her assumptions about his resistance were wrong too. He had wanted her, but wanted to wait until she'd come around to his way of thinking. Zaid hadn't just watched her, he'd studied her, he knew her. If he'd taken from her on their wedding night, Whisper would never have seen him as anything other than every other horny guy she'd ever met.

Waiting caused her to think. Her attraction to him

had time to simmer. Zaid had chosen not to fulfill her, which had built her anticipation, warmed her fantasies, and opened her to looking at him in different ways. Ways that led to guilt over the lie and a belief that they could never have anything real while that barrier was in place.

But the barrier had come down. Whisper couldn't love a man she couldn't trust and couldn't ask a man to trust her while lying to him. Except neither of those obstacles remained. Did that mean she could trust him and ask for his trust? It couldn't. If it did, then she could come to depend on him, could feel for him… could love him.

"We shouldn't," Whisper said, her voice weak within the pant that left her lips when his rose.

Her husband wasn't of the same mind; she could read that in his narrow heated eyes. "But we're gonna."

Kneeling up, he yanked his tee-shirt off over his head and leaned backward to grab the rope she'd left on the end of the bed. The corner of her lips rose when he stole one of her wrists and raised it to the head of the bed to tie her to it.

"What are you doing?"

"Proving that you trust me," he said, intent on his work tying one wrist to the headboard and then the other.

Whisper didn't equate sexual trust with other kinds of trust. Being tied up by her husband was exciting. Even if it turned sinister, she could turn herself off to whatever was being done to her. Numbing out was a particular skill that children in families like hers had to learn fast.

"Peanut," he said.

She looked at him, having not realized that her mind was wandering until his voice broke through. Pulling on her wrists to test his work, Whisper was satisfied that he'd done it well.

Curiosity tilted her head. "Why do you call me that?"

"Because you're tiny," he said. "At your best when you're salty… And lethal to anyone who doesn't have an immunity to you."

So much had changed so quickly. Whisper couldn't fight against him taking control; it was probably exactly what she needed while being so at sea. Somehow, he'd known that.

Zaid knew her. How had she missed that? He knew things about her that even she hadn't been aware of. He knew how to get into her thoughts, and into her heart, something no other man had ever accomplished.

The whole thing could be a ruse, but she couldn't figure out what benefit he'd get from conning her. The current situation was the first real and raw trial they'd had to face and they were doing it together. He wanted to do it together, like it was the most natural thing in the world for them to lean on each other.

"Can I ask you something else?" He nodded once. Given that she was tied up at his mercy, it made sense that he'd grant her request. It wasn't like running away was an option. Whatever his answer, she'd have to accept it. "Whose idea was our marriage?"

"You ready to hear the answer to that?" he asked. Her response was to bend her leg and bring her foot around to stroke his torso. "Your father came to us, proposed the alliance." Sliding his hand up and down her ankle and shin, he let her continue her caress until he stalled her foot in the middle of his chest. "Burl wanted the in, to expand our network. He recognized the power we had after…"

"The bloodbath," she said on a half shrug. "That's what I call it."

He nodded in understanding. "We couldn't ask for money or territory. The point was to join forces, so we'd be obligated to share those resources. Parker said the only way to judge whether Cyrus was serious or not was to ask him to give us what he valued most."

That was sort of dumbfounding because Whisper was low in her father's list of priorities. "And somehow all of you thought that was me? Boy were you wrong."

"Bosco was the first to suggest it. Can't say I didn't have the thought," he said. One side of his sinister mouth curled. "But he voiced it."

She waited a few seconds before asking, "Did he know?" Zaid just nodded and raised her foot to his mouth to kiss each of her toes. Bosco knew how Zaid felt about her. He'd been there three years ago when Whisper first got her future husband's attention, and the two were trusted friends. "I like Bosco." Zaid stopped kissing to frown at her, but she laughed. "Not like that."

"You scare him," Zaid said, kissing her big toe once more before sliding her foot down his body to the outside of his hip.

"Because I'm volatile."

He pushed up her skirt. "Because he knows there's nothing I'd deny you."

This time when their eyes met, she read an intense sincerity in his that humbled her. "If I was going to pick a man to love," she said, trying her best. "It would be you."

"Baby steps, Peanut," he said, shifting down the bed between her legs, working her panties off as he went. After tossing them over his shoulder, he slid his hands up the front of her thighs to expose her pussy to him. "I have waited too long to taste what's mine."

TWENTY

ZAID BEGAN TO LOWER, but Whisper tensed her legs, bringing them together a fraction to block his way. "You can have me anyway you want," she said. "But you will have to be willing to share."

His brow snapped down in a glare. "What the fuck? No, we're past that, Whis. You want to play and flirt and rile me up, that's—"

"No," she said, shaking her head. "I'm not talking about games or even desire; I'm being practical. You said that if we had to walk away, we would, but we'd do it together. The easiest way for us to support ourselves, at least at first, will be—"

"No," he said, tightening his grip on her thighs until she was sure his fingers were leaving their prints on her. "You will not whore yourself to feed us. I can think of ten better ways right off the top of my head." Lunging down, he got in her face. "You're my whore. No one else's. I have the paperwork to prove it."

Whether it was a naïve fantasy or not, it was nice that he wanted to keep her for himself, even if it couldn't be a reality. On their wedding night, she'd reprimanded him for calling her a slut because words like that only worked in dirty talk if there was an element of respect beneath them. Whisper felt that respect now, she felt him, and his possession of her. It heated her up so much that she wanted to claim him too.

"Understand that I'll do what I have to," she said. "To protect you."

All her life, she'd been vehement in her loyalty to her family. Learning that her family—which translated to her father these days—didn't have the same fidelity to her changed things. That was probably why she'd felt isolated and alone for so long. Whisper had no anchor. Zaid was offering one. He was giving her something to cling to, a lifeline, something to protect and be loyal to.

For the first time in her life, the person she'd die for was willing to do the same in return. It was intoxicating to be embroiled in something as pure as it was corrupt.

"Sounds like love to me, Peanut," he said, brushing his mouth over hers and pushing her legs farther apart.

Her eyes closed as she tried to steal another kiss. "I don't want you to love me."

For so many reasons. If he said it and she believed it then lost it, or he cheated on her, Whisper would be so broken there would be no return. But that was a pipedream compared to the reality of what was about to play out. In this bed, they could enjoy each other with ease. Maybe she had a few hours, maybe a few days, but as soon as her father caught up with her, she'd lose her life.

Whisper didn't want Zaid to love her because she couldn't promise to stick around and love him back. Losing her while their connection was still so new could ruin him. She didn't want to be the reason that such a magnificent, powerful man broke.

"Too late, Doherty," he said.

Whisper gasped when he thrust himself down her body. The next time she felt his mouth, it was feasting on her. She forgot about objecting and reality and good sense. Everything faded to nothing while he stimulated her clit with his tongue and fingertips. He pleasured her to paradise with a mouth more skilled than she could have imagined.

Still panting and vibrating with the thrill of orgasm,

Whisper couldn't breathe or see right when he began to kiss his way up her body.

"Ready for the entrée?" he asked and kissed her chin, then her lips.

"I can't believe you've been withholding that from me," she said, using all of her energy to force each of the words out.

"No more withholding," he said and kissed her again.

His hand moved between their bodies. Anticipation fizzed to excitement as she waited for him to take his dick from his shorts.

Before her husband could move onto the main course, someone came into the bedroom. "Zay, have we—oh, shit," Bosco said and immediately turned his back.

Whisper barely had time to register his identity because her vision was still blurry. Zaid pounced up to grab his tee-shirt, which he flung over her. He probably meant to cover her naked chest, but, in his haste, managed to cover her face too.

"Think about knocking?" Zaid demanded.

She guessed from the way the bed moved that he'd shifted to sit on the edge of the mattress facing his friend.

"That your wife?" Bosco asked.

"Yes," Zaid snapped. "What the fuck, B—"

"I'm sorry," Bosco said, a snicker in his voice. "I didn't know you were fucking her."

"I'm not," Zaid said. "Would be if you hadn't blasted that to shit."

"Can I turn around?" Bosco asked.

"You can fuck off," Zaid said.

"No," Whisper said from beneath his shirt. "We have to tell him."

"Uh, he knows," Bosco said. "I guess if she's talking you didn't drug her. The rope for effect or did she put up a fight?"

"Shit," Zaid murmured under his voice.

The tee-shirt moved from her face to her chest. Whisper smiled and blew her hair from her eyes while Zaid leaned over to untie her wrists. Her husband wasn't so amused if his frown was any indication. Bosco, on the other hand, was smirking, which widened her smile.

"Why do you look so pleased with yourself?" she asked.

Zaid finished freeing her and sat up to drop the rope onto the floor. Whisper took the opportunity to sit up, and didn't think anything of the tee-shirt falling away until Bosco's smile became horror and he spun around again. His sudden act brought Zaid's attention back to her. The sight of her naked breasts switched his scowl to a growl.

Grabbing for her and the straps of her dress, he clenched his jaw. "Flirt with other guys, fine, but they don't get to touch… or to see."

He glared into her eyes after thrusting her arms into her dress.

Wriggling to right the fabric, Whisper nodded, and offered him his tee-shirt back. "I'm trying, husband. I will try. I promise… But why does Bosco count? He loves you too much to take advantage of me."

"Every guy counts," he said, putting on his tee-shirt.

For a few seconds, Whisper considered asking about other women.

In a show of progress, instead of riling him further, she smiled and moved onto her knees behind him. "Okay, and just so we're clear: I'm not interested in a threesome with you and your sister-in-law."

Bosco didn't wait for permission to turn, shock brought him around. Whisper rose higher and slid her hands onto Zaid's shoulders for support.

"Stop eavesdropping," Zaid murmured.

"You already told me off for listening into that conversation," she said, ducking down to kiss the side of his neck. "You only get one lick of that lollipop."

Bosco's surprise became suspicion, he waved a finger side to side at them. "Something's different. Something changed. What happened?"

"I don't know what you could possibly mean," Whisper said, enjoying feeling light, yet energized. Safe, yet exhilarated.

An odd contradiction of thoughts and emotions zipped through her… probably because of the orgasm Zaid had just given her. That was the most acceptable explanation she could come up with.

"Don't play with him," Zaid said, his voice that usual deep, almost flat tone.

"Fine," she sighed, feigning petulance. Pushing away from his back, she started to climb off the bed. "I'm going to the bathroom. That should give you men a chance to talk."

Zaid grabbed her wrist and yanked her back onto the bed at his side. Aroused by his forcefulness, Whisper caught her lip in her teeth, experiencing an odd sort of rush. Giving herself over to the attraction she'd resisted for so long supercharged every moment between them.

Once she'd caught her balance on the edge of the bed, Whisper looped her arm around his and opened her mouth to dig her teeth into his upper arm.

"Don't play with me either, wife," he said, looking down at her as she sunk her teeth in deeper. "You're not going to the bathroom. You're going to tell him."

"Me?" she said, pulling her mouth away, keeping her arm coiled around his. "I'm not going to tell your friend about the thing that you found out completely on your own without my help."

"Still don't trust me, Peanut?" he said. "You can trust Bosco."

"I probably trust him more than I trust you," she said. Whisper didn't have to worry about her and Bosco breaking each other. "And he hasn't been inside me."

"You do?" Zaid said, interest lighting his smoldering gaze. "Why?"

"Because Bosco won't break me," she said. "And he'll let me go to the bathroom, which I'm going to do whether you want me to or not. There's nothing you can do to stop me."

"Nothing?" he muttered.

As she was about to head for the bathroom, Zaid put a hand on her face, pulled it around and landed his mouth on hers.

"Okay, okay," Bosco said, marching over. "Someone fill me in on what the hell is going on. You're flirting with each other? In bed together? Having sex? Kissing?"

Whisper took a minute to recover after Zaid stole his mouth away. With her eyes closed, she stayed in midair, struck by how deep his kiss touched her. It didn't feel like anything she recognized, which was disconcerting.

Zaid inhaled. "Bos—"

"I'm not done," Whisper said and grabbed her husband's shoulder to climb into his lap. Straddling him, she held his face in both hands and kissed him again. Angling her face one way and then the other, she kissed him both ways and then pulled his forehead to hers. "Why did you have to kiss me, jerk?"

Coiling her arms around his neck, she slipped her tongue between his lips and began to rock against his groin.

Zaid took her waist and twisted to toss her back onto the bed. "Peanut, cool your jets," he said and looked to Bosco. "Nicole's locked in the bathroom. We're keeping her there."

"Wh… why?" Bosco said, coming closer.

Whisper stayed on her back and stretched her leg, pointing her toes to the edge of the bed where she'd been sitting a moment before. Zaid's hand curled around her foot. So although he was looking to his friend, he was staying connected to her as well. Crooking her other knee, she rested her foot on Zaid's back, stroking him while he relayed the afternoon's events to Bosco.

Even when Whisper extended her leg and laid her calf on his shoulder, he kept on talking, explaining everything, including what she'd told him about her finding out.

Her eyes got heavy. It was crazy that she was so relaxed that sleep was an attractive option. But her stomach grumbled reminding her that a lifetime ago, she'd been heading downstairs for food. Forcing herself to sit up next to Zaid, Whisper stretched and yawned before boosting up to rub her face in his hair above his ear.

"I'm going to forage for food," she murmured, breathing him in.

Forcing herself onto her feet, Whisper bobbed her

brows at Bosco after Zaid smacked her ass hard.

TWENTY-ONE

ON HER TIPTOES, Whisper scampered down through the darkened house to the kitchen on the lowest floor. She made up some sandwiches and grabbed a six pack from the fridge while wondering if it would be wrong to mix margaritas. Though she herself was riding a high, it wasn't like they were celebrating. The potential for everything to go to shit still hung heavy in the air. Making the cocktail could tempt fate into screwing with them.

She heard someone coming down the stairs and chastised herself for not bringing her blade. There were a bunch of knives in the kitchen, but none matched hers. The sight of Bosco's outline in the hall relaxed her, so she went to begin chopping fruit.

Bosco didn't say anything, which wasn't like him. Whisper assumed he was absorbing Zaid's tale, so she kept cutting fruit and tossing it into a large bowl, giving him some time to process. A cabinet opened and she heard him retrieve what sounded like a liquor bottle. She smiled. Shock had been her reaction on first learning of the affair and the McDades were new to her. Bosco had known them a long time.

Glass hit glass, there was pouring, and then a bottle hit the granite-top hard. "I have never held information back from Zay."

Whisper stopped chopping and took a moment to absorb his words. Paranoid or not, his tone sort of implied accusation. So much for Bosco being open-minded about her.

"Wait a sec, are you…" She put the knife down and turned around. "You're pissed at me?"

"Whis—"

"I didn't tell him because you know this will blow the family apart. Burl wants me out and I was willing to go. I was sure that Zay would blame me for—"

"Nicki's on birth control," he blurted out.

Turned out she wasn't the one most clued up. Except the new piece of the puzzle didn't fit with what she'd been told. "What?"

Bosco moved away from the counter to get closer. Whisper leaned back to check no one was around the stairs.

"Zay is staying with Nicole," Bosco said, inching nearer. "Parker needed someone to get the drug, I got it for him. His father told him to do it. Nicole was going nuts about kids. Parker and Burl, they decided the business was more important. Parker tried to talk to Nicole about it, but… she was adamant… Burl suggested doing it without her knowing… Nicole likes her wine, it's not difficult for her husband to spike her… when she's out, he gives her the shot."

"Burl's suggestion," she murmured. "So while Burl is telling Nicole how important it is that she get pregnant with a McDade baby as quickly as possible, he's telling Parker to give his wife a contraceptive shot that she knows nothing about?"

Shed new light on why Parker wouldn't go to the clinic too; he wasn't just being a stubborn jackass.

Bosco bobbed his head. "Yeah, and… I didn't think it was a big deal. I take care of things for Parker and Doran once in a while. Zay's never been interested in his brothers' drama, so I just never mentioned it… I never mentioned it, Whisper."

Something made her reach out to rest a comforting hand on his upper arm. "Zay and I had sex," she said. The look of subdued panic on his face became a half frown when he squinted at her. "You know we weren't having sex… I mean we did, but then we weren't and…" She sighed. "Okay, so I don't know what you know about our relationship, but we weren't and now we are… Well, we did. I had sex with my husband. Great sex with my husband."

"Okay," he said, drawing out the word. "I figured that out for myself upstairs. Why are you telling me?"

"We've had sex and he didn't ask about birth control. He didn't ask before, during, or after. My husband has never asked me about birth control." Whisper leaned in to murmur, "And we didn't use condoms."

His head tilted in a shallow shake. "I don't…"

"He doesn't know about his wife's method of contraception, why would he know about his sister-in-law's?" She rubbed his arm. "You didn't do anything wrong… What did he say when you told him?" His lips thinned; she stopped rubbing. "Upstairs, just now, you… you did tell him… didn't you?"

He cringed. "I…"

"Bosco," she whined, sagging back until her hip hit the counter. "Zay and I are really working hard on this trust thing. It means something to him." Whisper feigned indifference with an eye roll. "God knows why, the man's a sap." One side of Bosco's mouth rose until he breathed out a laugh. "I know, right? Anyway, I thought the only way we could give each other a chance and maybe let this be real was if we could trust each other. As soon as this happened, when I saw Nicki and Burl, I wanted to tell him. Once I figured out I couldn't, I thought that was it. I couldn't trust him because I couldn't ask him to trust me. How could I when I was lying to him? I lied to my husband. The moment I lied by omission, that was it, our marriage was over."

"Doomed," he said. "That's what you meant in Kitty's… you said your marriage was doomed because of this."

She shrugged. "Not exactly, well… yeah, I knew the moment I decided not to tell him that our marriage was a sham."

"But you were honest, and he didn't turn his back on you."

Her attention wandered. "Yeah."

Thinking about that, Whisper turned around, returning to her fruit.

Bosco moved in at her side and took out another chopping block to begin working on the watermelon. "What does that mean?" he asked. "You thought it was doomed because you weren't being honest. You couldn't ask for his trust because you didn't deserve it. But you've been honest now. Everything is out in the open. You can ask for his trust because you're not holding anything back."

Bosco was giving voice to the exact thoughts running around in her mind. Since having a breakthrough with Zay, their future became less clear. Was it a breakthrough? So much had happened; so much was different.

Until that day, her future with Zay had been a non-starter. He'd stood by her. Whisper had said she wanted to be with him, that she wanted them to be together. Had she meant that? It had been an impulse. Saying the words just felt right. They felt right. Except, thinking about it, overthinking it maybe, Whisper couldn't figure it out. What did being together mean? What did she want from the future?

No matter how she tried to come up with an answer, she kept hitting the same wall.

She and Bosco finished with the salad and put it in the fridge. Whisper washed her hands first. As she was drying, he used the sink.

"Zay and I can't have a future," she said.

He glanced her way. "Because…"

Whisper gave him the towel when she was done with it. "Because Burl wants Doran to marry a Byrne. Because when my father hears that, he'll come for me. This marriage is over because my life is over. No amount of desire or attraction or honesty is going to change that."

Leaving him, she grabbed the six pack and the tray of sandwiches and returned upstairs.

***

"ONE OF YOU TWO better start fucking talking," Zay said,

moving his eyes from her to Bosco, back and forth.

In the bedroom again, her husband was seated on the couch at the end of the bed. Bosco sat in the window. Whisper was on the floor, leaning against the wall by the nanny's bedroom door, her legs stretched out straight in front of her.

They'd eaten the sandwiches and were drinking the beer. Having decided Nicole wouldn't want beer or bread, they figured they'd wait and feed her fruit salad later whenever Whisper went down to retrieve it. That was really just the mens' way of saying they didn't care about eating fruit salad.

For most of the last hour, Whisper had been thinking about what she'd said downstairs. She knew it was on Bosco's mind too. Though, if she had to guess, she'd say he was more preoccupied with what he hadn't told Zay.

Resting her head on the wall, she rolled it to look toward the window. "Do you think if I got pregnant my father would let me come to term before he killed me?" she asked the hypothetical question, but received no response, even after she looked to each of the blank men. "Seriously. I know Burl wants the alliance over. But a Doherty/McDade baby would be a difficult card for my father to ignore… He'd have to try to play it, wouldn't he? I might be out, but my child—"

"Our child," Zay said.

She pointed her beer at him, sitting up straight and crossing her legs. "Right! Exactly! Our child." Whisper smiled. "The child would be innocent. No man in his right mind would cast out a potential heir… That child would have McDade and Doherty blood." A thought struck her, she frowned. "Unless it was a girl… Hmm…" She slumped back against the wall. "Damnit."

"In what part of your hypothetical do you see me letting either man have any control over our child… or my wife?" Zay asked.

"Okay," she muttered, splaying her fingers around her beer. "Okay. It was just a question." Whisper drank some beer. "Doesn't matter anyway, I got my implant renewed right before we got hitched… No babies over here." She narrowed her eyes on Bosco. "Isn't that interesting, Bosco?"

"Why should he care about your method of birth

control?" Zay asked.

"He shouldn't," she said, raising her beer to her lips again. "But you should."

"Why?" Zay asked. "Why should I care? All your blood tests came back clear after we got married… You're clean and I know I'm clean."

"Because McDades are too pure to get STIs?"

"Because I got tested the same time and haven't been with another woman since we got married. Have you screwed another guy? You think you caught something?"

She scowled at him. "What does that have to do with birth control? Even if we're not passing diseases between each other, we might have got pregnant if I hadn't taken care of it."

"I don't give a fuck about getting you pregnant," he said and shifted to the edge of the couch. "I do give a fuck if you fucked another guy."

"No other guy. Tonight isn't about us, lover," she said, not too amused by his accusation, but she deserved it. "I just wanted to point out, for the record, that you didn't ask your wife about birth control."

"Because I knew you were clean and figured you'd want to get pregnant eventually…" He slid back on the couch. "But it turns out McDade sons shoot blanks anyway, so…"

Pushing out her chin, Whisper turned to Bosco again, urging him to tell the truth. "I wouldn't be so sure about that… husband," she said, widening her eyes.

Zay must have noticed her insistence. In her peripheral vision, she noted he turned to look at Bosco too.

"What's going on?" Zay asked. "What's she talking about, Bos?"

Bosco sighed and slouched deeper into his seat. "Parker shoots Nicole up with contraceptive," he said. Zay grew rigid. "More than a year ago, Parker came and asked me to get it. He said Nicole was harping on about kids, but he and Burl didn't think it was the right time. She refused to take any kind of contraceptive, so they decided Parker should inject her while she was having one of her episodes."

"Episodes?" Whisper asked.

Downstairs Bosco had talked about spiking Nicole

when she was drinking, but an "episode" suggested it was more than that.

Sitting up, Bosco caught his fist in his opposite open hand. "Few times a year, Nicole goes on a binge, gets emotional about the time she doesn't get to spend with Parker," he explained. "Sometimes she gets physical, lashes out or smashes up stuff. She gets drunk, goes on about the business and what it takes from her."

"Huh," Whisper said, wishing she'd seen that with her own eyes. "Can't help that Parker's putting drugs in her glass too… I sort of wondered if Burl sent Parker away on purpose, so he'd have a clear shot at Nicole when she was lonely and suggestible… She's probably always suggestible."

"I can't believe this," Zay said, running a bewildered hand through his hair.

His whole world was upside down. It was a lot for him to take on.

Whisper crawled across the floor toward him. "Baby," she murmured, and kneeled up to slide a hand onto his thigh.

He covered her hand with his own, keeping his focus on Bosco. "You're saying he knew. Burl knew she was on birth control and she didn't. Nicole couldn't get pregnant no matter how much he fucked her."

Bosco shrugged. "I don't think anything is a hundred percent, but… yeah."

Zay took some time to reflect. They all did. Whisper didn't like the churn of anxiety in her gut. She wasn't the type to get anxious; she was the type to take action. Realizing that the negative emotion wasn't for herself was disconcerting.

Whisper was worried about the man above her. "What do you want to do, baby?" she asked, curling her fingers around his hand. "Tell me and you'll get it."

He didn't acknowledge her at first. After a moment, his attention crept around her way. Even when he was looking her in the eye, he didn't speak. It didn't matter that there was something fierce and angry in his gaze, Whisper just sat and waited.

She didn't expect him to bend down and clamp an

arm around her waist so that when he stood up, he picked her straight off her feet.

Whisper wrapped her legs around his hips.

"Watch Nicki," Zay said over his shoulder to Bosco and then carried her through to the nanny's room, kicking the door shut behind them.

TWENTY-TWO

LYING NAKED in the nanny's room that had been her haven since moving into the McDade home, Whisper was content and relaxed. The moment she recognized herself drifting toward slumber, her eyes snapped open. Her rules had never been lax. They meant creating distance, she didn't know any other way.

Blinking once, she pushed away from the male chest under her body to sit up.

"What's up?" her drowsy husband asked.

After rubbing her face, Whisper slapped each of her cheeks and then sank her fingers into her hair. "I almost fell asleep," she said and scooted further away, tossing her legs off the edge of the bed.

"So?"

"So…" she said, slithering down to the floor to gather up the clothes her husband had helped her remove an hour or two ago. "We haven't fed Nicole and Doran could be home any minute…" Untwisting her dress, she tried to figure out if putting it back on was a good idea. Getting something more durable and warmer, suitable for being outside at night, might be a better plan. Whisper had no idea if and when she'd have to move, but it could happen fast. "I've never slept with a man in my life… I'm not about to start now."

The mattress shifted. She paid little attention and stood up to put on her underwear, figuring she'd ditch the dress and change clothes. Though that meant going through Zay's room to get to the closet. Bosco was out there and Zay seemed to have something against her skin being on show when other guys were around.

"I'm your husband," he said from the bed behind her.

Whisper wasn't sure what difference that made to her clothes, but was probably too caught up in her own thoughts to interpret what he was saying. The fog of hormones still pulsed through her, so making sense of any point was difficult.

Turning around, she set her hands on her hips to scrutinize his position lying on his side in her sheets, his head propped on a hand, his defined torso on show.

"How come you always wore a tee-shirt to bed when I was blowing you?"

"I knew if you saw the goods, you wouldn't be able to help yourself."

He didn't smile but was playing with her.

"I had the goods in my mouth, husband," she said. "And I've seen your body before, I knew you were hot."

Breathing out, he sank onto his back. "Having your mouth on me was enough… I didn't need your whole damn body rubbing on mine to remind me of what I couldn't have."

So it was his way of preventing himself from wanting more… from taking more.

"You could've had it," she said, crawling back onto the bed, blinking her sultry eyes. "I wouldn't have said no."

Whisper climbed on top of him and kissed him again.

"Exactly the problem," he said, scooping her hair away from their faces to hold it at the back of her head. "You've got so much respect for your family and so little for yourself."

"Blind respect," she said, pushing her body against him, her lips dancing within a breath of his. "I didn't think about it, but you're right. If we'd been screwing from the beginning, I wouldn't have had a chance to…"

Raising her hovering lips, her focus switched to his

mouth.

"A chance to what?"

"I have to get changed," Whisper said and tried to get out of bed, but he caught both of her wrists and pulled them together against his chest, forcing her to stay.

"A chance to what, Peanut?"

This man was intense and serious and determined. It didn't seem fair that she was such a mess.

"Why did you have to kiss me?"

"Because you were ready," he said. "I thought you were ready."

"You didn't want me to walk out," she said, twisting and tugging at her wrists. "Let me go, Zay. Jesus, you're hurting me."

His grip was so tight that it bruised her wrists, but he didn't care. Flipping over, he pinned her on her back, slamming her arms to the mattress by her head.

"I didn't think it was possible for any man to hurt you, Peanut."

"It wasn't," she said, struggling under him. "Until you fucking kissed me, you asshole."

"I was never gonna let you walk out on me. I never will."

"You don't have a choice," she said, trying to squeeze her knees under him.

The asshole was too strong. Whisper knew how to fight back when she got the chance. Her damn husband wasn't giving her one.

"I'm only yours. I fucking said it. You are only mine. Say it, Whisper. Say it now."

Words didn't mean anything. They weren't truth just because they were uttered. "Zay—"

"Fucking say it," he said, raising her wrists just to slam them down again.

Spitting her hair from her mouth, she stopped struggling to glare up at him. "I have to die for this. You don't. I will *not* take you down with me."

He bowed lower, bearing his teeth. "I am only yours."

What was that supposed to mean? Whisper didn't

want it to mean anything. She didn't want to trap him in any situation where he'd be forced to give up his own life.

"You still have a chance," she said, licking her lips. "You and Bosco can talk to Nicole, convince her to end it with Burl. If you keep his secret—"

"Why? Why would we want to keep his secret or let her off the hook for this?"

"Because it's what we do!"

The heat of his panting breath clashed with hers. Pinned there under him, matching her anger with his own, Whisper didn't know what was worse. Was it that she was asking him to save the McDades or that she cared about how their destruction would impact him?

"The McDades go down," he said with only a slight edge of frustration. "The Byrnes take it… Is that it? You asked me to burn their house down? You don't want them to have it? The Dohertys hate them that much?"

"You think there's any part of me that believes it's gonna make the slightest bit of difference to the Dohertys? We're done. Finished."

"Your father won't accept that."

She exhaled a whisper of a sinister laugh. "No. It makes me kinda sorry that I'll miss the meltdown."

"You won't miss a damn thing. Tell me and you'll get it."

The line was his, even though she'd adopted it on occasion. Her husband was asking what she wanted and only one thing came to mind.

"Let me go," she said. "Give me a fighting chance."

His head was shaking before she'd finished saying the words. "You said together. Downstairs, you said—"

"I know what I said," she snapped. "I was an idiot. For a minute, I thought…"

"What? That we could stop with the bullshit and be fucking honest."

"Honest," she said, tugging at her wrists. "Will you let me fucking go?"

Though Whisper asked, alight with the heat of infuriation, she hadn't expected him to release her and vault up onto his feet. Rising to her elbows, she watched him retrieve his underwear and tug it back on.

"You're pushing at me," he said, his back to the bed.

"Yes," she said. "Because I'm toxic. Persona non grata here, at my father's, everywhere."

"Okay," he said, turning to face her. "Then we get outta here."

Sitting up, Whisper shook her head. "You have a place here."

"I haven't wanted my place here for years."

That he could say it with such eerie calm knocked her off kilter. "You don't mean that."

But doubt wasn't fathomable in his expression or his voice. "I figured out none of this was about family the day Score was arrested."

No one mentioned Phoenix McDade, also known as Score, not in anything more than a passing reference.

"Your brother," she said. "He wasn't at the reception."

Zay cleared his throat. "Haven't seen him for years. Not since he was in prison."

"He did time for murder, right?"

"Yeah… Murder he didn't commit."

Whisper wasn't sure she'd ever heard the details. Caelan had mentioned it at their reception. Even when it was being talked about, she hadn't paid much attention.

"Parker set him up," she said. "Is that true?"

"Yeah," he said. "No way Score was coming back after that. Would you if your own brother set you up?"

"Did you know?"

"At the time, no," he said. "Later."

"Why did Parker do it?"

"'Cause Score's smarter than him, quicker than him, better than him. Burl still tries to bring him back to the fold… Score's afraid of no one. Not even Burl."

"You call him by his street name."

Zay backed up enough to lean against the wall by the door. "The only one of us who actually preferred it." His brow lowered in a semi-frown. "Not sure I've ever heard anyone use his first name."

Half a minute of silence passed. "What are you afraid of?" she asked, interrupting his reflection. "You said Score was afraid of no one. He made the break from the family. You never did."

"Score sees it that the family broke from him. Parker sent him to prison. Don't think Burl knew he'd set it up at the time."

"And when he found out?"

"Burl went nuts. Nothing came of it… But he was fucking the man's wife."

"It can't have been going on that long… can it?"

Whisper hadn't really thought much about when the affair started. Maybe because the idea of the two together was so sickening.

"Nicole wanted kids out the gate," Zay said. "They got married when Score was inside, but they've been together forever. First couple of years was okay, but it's always been a fight to keep her on birth control."

"Why doesn't he want kids?"

"He does what Burl tells him… the power goes to his head. Guess he played the loyal son all those years 'cause he knew the truth about Score's conviction could come out."

"And when it did, Burl let it go because he was sleeping with Nicole? That could mean it's been going on for years."

"Who knows?" he said, shrugging away from the wall. "I don't give a damn about them. It's all fucking sick."

"And incestuous," she said, taking a minute to process before looking up at him. "You can't deny that this is the safest place for you. Confront Burl if you want, tell Parker the truth, but you have to know that won't lead to anything good for Nicki."

"She made her bed."

"Same could be said for me," Whisper said. "Parker never taught her to fight, never wanted her to rebel. He does what Burl tells him. Nicole's witnessed that, witnessed how you all follow your father's orders without question. What was she supposed to do when he made a move on her?"

Though there was a chance Nicole had made the first move, Whisper doubted it. Flirting, letting her father-in-law know it was an option was one thing, actually laying hands, or lips, on the man first would be too risky a game for Nicole to play. That would be showing the patriarch that she was open to cheating on her husband.

"You did it," Zay said. "You told him to go to hell."

She snorted a slight laugh. "I put a knife to his throat."

Whisper wasn't really paying attention to his eyes narrowing until he came a step closer. "It was you… You cut him."

"What do you want from this?" she asked, neither confirming nor denying his suspicion. It sort of went without saying. "What's your end game? If Doran wants to marry Madison, it's over, right?"

"He won't. Doran's not much happier with what's going on than I am. He idolized Score."

"You know him and Nicki are close," she said, leaning back a little. "I know she said her and Doran weren't fucking, but that doesn't mean he'll be ready to watch her go down."

"He feels sorry for her. Always has… They're closest in age."

"Like I said, they're close. He won't want her to be hurt."

"And I don't want you to be hurt."

Sweet, but irrelevant. "Doran's nice to me. That doesn't mean he's invested in my safety."

"You've got a damn contradiction for everything," he said. "You did nothing wrong. Nicole has done something wrong. If anyone deserves to be hurt, it's her."

"Burl won't be hurt. Do you think he's innocent too? Because I gotta tell you, I'm no saint."

Before he could respond, there was a knock at the door. Zay backed up to open it an inch.

"Doran's downstairs," Bosco's voice carried from the other room.

Zay pulled open the door as he strode over to collect

his clothes to put them back on. "I'm gonna talk to him," he said, lifting his head to look at her. "Do I need to lock the door?"

She smiled and nodded past him. "Bosco's here. Where am I gonna go?"

He came over to brush a quick kiss on her lips and stayed low to look her in the eye. "You could take Bosco. Do I need to lock it?"

"I'll stay put."

Though she wouldn't guarantee for how long.

Zay kissed her again then stood up to head for the door.

"She couldn't take me," Bosco said, moving out of Zay's path.

"She could take you," he said, patting his friend on the shoulder once as he passed.

A moment later, the outer bedroom door closed. Whisper held her breath, waiting to see if he'd believe her word or not. There was no click. He hadn't locked it.

She grinned. "Zay has to say that. If I'm in a bad mood next time my husband wants to get laid, he'll hit resistance."

TWENTY-THREE

CLIMBING OFF THE BED, Whisper did a feeble job of making it, then strutted the unconvinced Bosco's way. She squeezed past him on her journey to the closet.

She was still trying to figure out what to wear when Bosco came to join her. Unlike her husband, she heard Bosco coming.

"You suit each other," Bosco said.

"He says after seeing us together for like an hour."

"You know about the first time he noticed you."

She glanced over her shoulder to find Bosco was literally just inside the door, sort of half peeking at her around the end vanity.

"Are you going to tell me that he cares? That he'll endanger himself for me? I've been saying the same thing. If you want to take a shot at telling him to cut me loose, go for it. You have my blessing."

"Actually, I was going to say the opposite."

That was interesting enough to take her focus away from the clothes. "What?"

"You've gotta stick with him, Whis. Both of us have to stick with him."

Until that moment, it hadn't occurred to her how she

and Bosco were connected. Zay and Bosco were best friends. Her being married to the former put her and the latter at a crossroads.

If Zay stuck by his family and she was cast out, Bosco would be his rock. As long as she'd known them, there had never been any doubt of their loyalty to each other.

"Where did you meet?" she asked, folding her arms. "You and Zay, what's the story with the two of you?"

"Known each other a long time."

Unconsciously, her observations of the friends brought her to a bunch of conclusions. "You're not loyal to the McDades. It's not the family. You're loyal to him."

Somehow that had translated to her. Bosco was a part of the family. Zay was his way in, his facilitator. Yet, his devotion to the McDades didn't eclipse his fidelity to his master. Something must have happened to connect the men on such a deep level.

"If he goes, I go, yeah," Bosco said.

His loyalty wasn't in question. Although he'd been worried about withholding, what turned out to be an important fact, from Zay, his friend hadn't punished him for it.

"It's more than that," she said, stepping forward to slide a knee onto the central bench, lowering herself onto it. "How long have you been at his side?"

"You don't want to hear about my history with Zay," he said. "All you need to know is we're solid."

"Staying with the family would be the smartest thing for him to do."

"Why?" Bosco asked, peering at her. "The way I see it, the family aren't exactly looking out for each other's best interests." That much sort of went without saying considering the patriarch was sleeping with his daughter-in-law. "I've been trying to get Zay to walk away for years."

She shook her head. "He wouldn't do that."

"Score's set up base, far from here, he's doing okay."

"And you really think he wants what he left behind to follow him?"

"He thought the marriage was a bad idea, your

marriage. He told Burl he wasn't going to weigh in, but once he got the news…"

Whisper hated it when people didn't finish their sentences. Sure, she was guilty of doing it too, but getting fragments and hints wasn't the best way to learn about the family.

"What? When Score heard the news, what?"

"He hasn't been taking Zay's calls. Never used to dodge him like that… Doran thought he would come straight home."

"Doran thought me and Zay getting married would bring Score home? Do you think that's what Zay hoped?"

Bosco flashed her a smile. "You and I both know why Zay married you and it was nothing to do with Score."

"He wanted in my pants," she said because it was easier to be glib than dwell on what her husband really hoped to get from her. "Why didn't Score come back? If Doran thought it was a sure thing?"

Opening his mouth to take a deep breath, Bosco rested his weight on the end wall. "I figured it was 'cause he knew coming back would mean never leaving. It's not an easy place to walk away from, especially if Burl gets his hooks in. Far as I know, Burl's stopped short of actually ordering Score back, but he seeks his advice on everything. Just like he always has."

Which was probably one of the reasons Parker had felt threatened by his younger brother.

"So maybe Score knows about the affair?"

Bosco shrugged. "Maybe, but I doubt it. Burl wants Score's input because he's smart and measured. He's just better at this… at everything. But if Score actually came back, I don't think any of us doubt there would be a showdown."

"Between Parker and Score," she said, thinking how interesting it would be to see that play out. "Burl would be stuck in the middle."

"He wants Score to be involved, but bringing him back would be risky. If Score takes Parker out and leaves…"

"All he's left with is Zay and Doran."

"Yeah, and Zay's been less and less involved, at least

he tries to be. Parker's starting to think he's too big to do the dirty work. Zay doesn't mind getting his hands dirty, but what he does for the family is a risk. And when you think the family doesn't have your back…"

"It's not a risk worth taking," she said, resting both hands on her thighs. "I can understand that. Score went to prison and I don't remember there being any kind of big effort to get him out."

"So Zay goes to prison for his father and brother… a brother who has a track record of throwing others to the wolves."

"Why should he take the risk," she muttered, reaching the same conclusion.

The McDades didn't have each other's backs. Throwing himself on his sword wouldn't earn him any gratitude or recognition. Every day Zay went out there to do Burl's bidding could be a day closer to him losing his liberty. If that happened, he'd be abandoned like Score had been. Any sane person would question their loyalty to the disloyal in the same scenario.

She sighed. Since they were having a heart to heart, figuring things out, Whisper decided to ask a question of her own. "The first day I was here, you were talking about Zay staying out all night. Doran said he thought it was over, where was he?"

"Zay was closing accounts. Burl wasn't a fan of him cutting ties with people he thought might be useful, but Zay got the bit in his teeth about their younger recruits."

She frowned. "What does that mean?"

"He took some of the younger recruits with him while he cut ties. People who borrowed money, people who had a running tab, he was putting pressure on them to settle up and then telling them it was over. Once the account was settled, he told them it wouldn't be opened again."

"And he took the younger recruits because…"

"He wanted them to see what it was about, what they were getting into. He didn't settle those accounts overnight, some of them took weeks or months."

And knowing how the Dohertys exerted pressure

gave her a good idea of what the McDades would do to get their money. Except Whisper looked beyond the bloodshed and the threats to understand the true outcome of Zay's actions. Cutting those people off freed them from their obligation. Sure, they could go to the Dohertys or the Byrnes if they wanted money or to keep using, but Zay at least gave them a chance to stop and think.

Most of the time, the rule was to keep people on the hook as long as possible. To increase interest, increase addiction, and keep them squirming. That ensured a steady supply of patsies they'd happily sacrifice. Often the debts got so big that there was no chance of ever paying them off, short of a lotto win. That meant pressure could be exerted in different ways. Victims took the blame for crimes they didn't commit when the McDades, Byrnes, Dohertys, needed a fall guy. Or the families—whose names were interchangeable in the setup—promised to clear or reduce a debt if a crime was done for them. Sometimes it was stealing or fraud, but it could go all the way up to murder.

Zay cut people off for their own good, even if they couldn't see that.

"And Burl let him do that? He let him cut those people loose?"

"Burl saw the returns; he was pleased with that. Zay let the clients know it was time to pay up. Most of them did… eventually. Since the, you know, Dohertys and Byrnes lost so many of their guys…" at the bloodbath, "Burl figured there were going to be a whole bunch of new desperate people out there."

Those who got their fixes or their loans from the Dohertys and Byrnes. They'd find themselves wanting with the families scrambling to protect their own interests.

She wondered about her husband and his reasons. Could it be as basic as compassion? Maybe he wanted to ruin his family from the inside, or it could just be spite that drove him to liberate others from the web.

Something he'd said earlier replayed in her thoughts. "He hasn't been happy here for years."

"No," Bosco said. "And if he loses you to this life,

he'll go nuclear."

Meaning he'd create the maximum amount of damage to his family. Whisper knew what it was to feel that way. Her own resentment toward her father had been growing for years. After losing so many members of the family, her perspective had shifted. The bonds that once held her to the Doherty name were gone. Loosened and free, Whisper wasn't a Doherty anymore.

Knowing what her father would do to her when he found out the alliance was over, she accepted being disposable. Some part of her had always accepted that. Yet, there, at Zay's side, she wasn't disposable anymore.

Leaping from the central bench, she got dressed and began to think about what they would need. "Can you get me suitcases?"

"What?"

"I need suitcases, luggage, bags."

"For?"

They needed to be able to move fast. "Whichever way this plays out, whatever Doran believes or Zay plans…" Whisper pulled her own clothes from the rails, then went to open Zay's side. "We won't be staying here for long. We need to get all the official stuff together. Do you know where Zay's birth certificate is? His passport? Our marriage certificate?"

All of her important documentation was in the lower drawer of the vanity.

"Yeah," Bosco said. "It's in the office downstairs."

"Get it," she said, opening a drawer. "Bring me something to put our stuff in and then go pack your own."

"Me?"

Whisper stopped pulling things out to look at him. "If you and me support each other, Zay won't think twice. We can't pull against each other, we can't do that to him."

Bosco's eyes lit. "You're sticking with him."

"*We* are sticking with him," she said. "Don't disturb him with Doran, let them talk as long as they have to. But you and me are going to make sure we're ready to move the second that we have to."

Bosco nodded once and disappeared out of the

closet. She'd fold and pack as much as she could and go give Nicole something to drink. The woman could wait for food.

Doran could decide to call his father and Parker. If that happened, her time in the McDade house would be limited. She'd flee alone if it came to it, but Whisper was beginning to accept that marriage meant more than she'd first thought.

Zay wasn't going to let her go anywhere alone and Bosco came as part of the deal. They'd have to watch each other's asses and be careful of who they trusted. All of their lives were going to change and there was no guarantee where the pieces would lay once the dust settled.

TWENTY-FOUR

BY THE TIME Whisper was done with the packing, it was dark outside. She hadn't seen hide nor hair of her husband since he'd left her in the nanny's room. Bosco had been in and out, helping her with things as he packed his own possessions. About twenty minutes ago, they'd been talking about what to do with Nicole when he got a message on his phone.

He hadn't said it. He hadn't said anything. He just read the message and made eye contact with her. Zay needed him. So Whisper nodded once and Bosco turned to leave her alone.

Doran would be more likely to trust Bosco to get involved. If she walked into the conversation, her own mouth would get her into trouble. Whisper wasn't naïve to the fact that Doran would blame her, just as Nicki and Burl would too. Maybe even Parker would focus his anger her way. Sure, she hadn't exactly told Zay about the affair, but her actions were what led him to confront Nicki.

Thinking about their options and how the situation could play out, Whisper couldn't reach any optimistic conclusions. That her husband stuck with her was a positive, though it might not mean much if they were all executed.

The length of time he'd been talking to Doran gave

her some hope. If the youngest McDade was going to dismiss his brother out of hand, he'd have done it sooner. Every once in a while, the voices of the brothers had been raised. Curious as she was, Whisper resisted the urge to get close enough to eavesdrop. Keeping busy had helped, and knowing Bosco was around prevented her from worrying.

No one had been in to see Nicole for some time. Whisper didn't care much about the woman being by herself, but she was on the hunt for things to do. Part of her unacknowledged self was aware that if she eavesdropped on the brothers' conversation, restraining herself would be impossible.

Getting Doran on side would take skill. Maybe her husband had it, he knew his own brother. Whisper didn't have it. Tact and diplomacy were not virtues she'd ever honed. Recognizing her own hotheaded nature was a sign of growth. At least that's what she told herself as she ascended the stairs, bowl of fruit salad in hand.

With the men occupied, Whisper decided it was her responsibility to take care of their captive. That was how she ended up entering the bathroom where Nicki was still attached to the rail above the shower.

Wearing a smile, Whisper stabbed a piece of fruit and took it between her teeth to pull it from the fork.

Nicki sneered. "I'm not hungry."

"No one asked," Whisper said, eating another piece of fruit as she moseyed closer. "Enjoying yourself?"

"You're disgusting. You're enjoying this."

"The fruit?" Whisper asked, raising the bowl in her hand. "Yeah, it's great."

Nicki wasn't amused. "Parker's going to rip you apart."

"Me? I think he'll be too busy filing divorce papers… If you're lucky."

"If I'm lucky? I'm not the one set on destroying the family."

"Uh…" Whisper ate some more fruit and propped a hip against the end of the shower stall. "I'm not the one screwing my father-in-law. McDade men don't like their women to cheat. I'm sure someone said that to me once."

That someone was Nicki, which made saying it all the more satisfying.

"Zay will blame you for this," Nicki said, full of venom. "Maybe you've got him under some spell now, but when you destroy everything his family has, he'll know there's only one person to blame."

Whisper responded as though she was on a game show. "Who is Burl McDade?" she said, eating the fruit, unaffected by the woman's poison. "Let's be honest, Nicki, you're just an idiot." The captive blinked in surprise. "If you'd thought this through, you'd have realized there's only one link the McDades will be willing to sacrifice. If someone is going to be blamed for tempting the old man, it will be you. He won't admit to seducing you. He'll play it down and you'll be tarred as the temptress." She ate another piece of fruit while giving her sister-in-law a few seconds to process. "You thought you were doing the right thing. Thought you were doing what was best for the whole family." Maybe that was true, maybe not, but it wouldn't hurt to give the poor fool some clarity. "You're not from this world. Sure, you've been a part of it for a while. But if this life was in your blood, you'd have figured out women are expendable long ago. You need to be smart, Nicki."

"Parker will understand. He will." Though her vehemence wasn't as potent as before. "Doran will talk to Zay, he'll make him understand… Parker doesn't need to know."

Pushing away from the shower, Whisper stepped closer. "Which is it? Parker will understand or he doesn't need to know?"

It was sad really. Feeling sorry for the confused woman, Whisper stabbed another piece of fruit. She offered it to Nicki and after a few seconds, the woman drifted from her thoughts enough to take it into her mouth.

"Burl said it would be okay," Nicki said into the silence that followed. "He said he'd take care of everything."

People in the family, and even those in the street, would think Burl McDade was a larger than life almost invincible character. But when it came down to the basics, he was a man, just like any other. Feeding the naïve Nicki false promises and assurances he'd never have to follow through on was just like any guy at a bar giving a woman a line.

Burl wanted sex. Obviously he'd been attracted to Nicki. Whether it was from early on in her relationship with Parker or the patriarch just took advantage of an opportunity, he'd thought more about his own needs than his son's.

The door opened. Whisper turned to see who was there and was surprised to discover Doran in front of Zay. The younger McDade didn't look at her though, his solemn attention was on their prisoner.

"Let's give them a minute," Zay said, tipping his head to the side.

Figuring her husband knew what he was doing, she headed for the door. Doran stepped out of her way, still focused on Nicki. Whisper slid the fruit salad onto the vanity, then went into the bedroom. Bosco was by the bed, his expression as somber as Doran's had been.

Zay closed the door at the same time she stopped, halfway toward the bed. Turning to the side, Whisper looked at one man and then the other, waiting for some kind of explanation.

"Well?" she asked when no one said anything. "What happened? What does he want to do?"

"Talk to Nicki," Zay said, focusing in the direction of the closet doors. "What's going on in there?"

Whisper had to turn all the way around to notice their suitcases were visible through the open door. "I packed."

His frown flashed to her. "What the hell did I say about—"

"Us," she said, approaching him. "I packed *our* things. Bosco packed too, he didn't tell you?"

Bosco was somewhere behind her. Whisper figured out it was harder for Zay to ignore her when she put herself right in front of him.

"Where are we going?"

"Don't know yet," she said. "But I figured if things didn't go well with Doran and he decided to call your father, it would be easier to run than to restrain him."

They couldn't indefinitely keep on imprisoning anyone who happened upon them in the midst of the uncertain time.

"Call Score," Bosco said, choosing that moment to contribute.

"You've said that already," Zay said, his focus sticking over her head. Somehow, Whisper could tell he was staring out the window rather than at his friend. "It's a bad idea."

"Doran didn't think so."

"Because Doran thinks the sun shines out Score's ass," Zay said, his brow strengthening. "You know what happens when we tell Score Nicki's stepping out on Parker?"

The man had put Score in prison, so it was unlikely he'd have much sympathy. Whisper would bet on crowing and ridicule. Though she didn't know Score. Maybe he could be the bigger man. From what she'd been told already that was doubtful.

"You keep on this path, you need allies," Bosco said. "You need someone to rally for you."

"You think I wanna call that asshole?" Zay asked, fixating on Bosco with such opposition that Whisper stepped in to lay her hands on his waist. "The guy who shunned my marriage?"

"Plenty of people don't like me," Whisper said, providing a buffer and an ally to Bosco. "You think I can't handle that?"

"Doran will stand with Score," Bosco said. "You know he will."

"What did Doran say?" Whisper asked, in need of more information. "Does he want to marry Madison?"

"Doesn't believe Burl really thinks that's a legit plan."

So Doran didn't believe her or doubted what she'd heard. That was fine. Burl would confirm it if his youngest son decided to call. Whisper could handle not being the most trusted member of the McDade clan. That wasn't the most apparent thing to her in Bosco's answer.

"He didn't say no," she murmured, her attention snagging on Zay's chest. For all the time the brothers had spent discussing the day's developments, one crucial decision hadn't been made. "Madison is beautiful. Maybe he thinks—"

"Nothing," Zay said, grabbing her chin to shove her head back so he could meet her eye. "Doran won't marry her."

"Did he say that?" she asked, but her husband didn't answer. "It's a lot for him to take in. The affair, the marriage… It'll take him time to figure it out." Clearing her throat, she began to retreat. "I should get out of here."

"Whisper," Zay warned. "You're not going anywhere alone."

"I don't have to go far," she said. "I can stay local. Give you guys a chance to figure this out. Doran will have to talk to Parker, he'll want to. It's the only way he can get perspective. Doran has every right to tell his brother the truth and to hear his father's proposal."

"If he wants to, he can do both. That doesn't mean you going anywhere."

Fear wasn't exactly the right word for what she felt while thinking about facing Burl and Parker. Between those men and Nicki, Whisper had the most sympathy for her sister-in-law. Parker would be mad and humiliated by the affair. If anyone would take the wrath of the revelation, it would be Nicki. Whisper would be the next casualty to face the McDade gauntlet.

From the first time he'd spoken to her about it, Burl had made it obvious he blamed Whisper for interrupting his cushy arrangement. Young Nicki was in his house and was at his disposal. Parker would do as his father said, which meant being away from home often. Burl had all of the convenience and none of the guilt. Men like him didn't experience guilt.

"I can take her to Cyrus," Bosco said.

Whisper whirled around. "If you want to watch him kill me slow," she said, scowling at him. "I thought we were gonna be on the same side you and me."

Blinking at her, Bosco was stunned for a few seconds before finding his voice. "The Dohertys need an heir, right?"

"You think I can talk him out of killing me by suggesting I'm pregnant? Newsflash, that's not even possible."

Technically, Bosco could argue that point. She and Zay had screwed outside Scooby's the night he'd taken down her almost-lover. But with her implant in place, Whisper was pretty sure her uterus was safe.

"And I already said I wouldn't hand my wife or kid over to anyone," Zay said, approaching to stand at her back. "Cyrus Doherty will not—"

"Your kid isn't the heir," Bosco said. "Whisper isn't either. You're the damn heir."

From the silence that followed, Whisper guessed Zay shared her confusion. The Dohertys were short of manpower and if the McDades were on the verge of civil war, they weren't a sure bet. Cyrus might consider letting her live if Doran married Madison, on the proviso that Zay became his lieutenant and heir-apparent.

"Oh, I get it," Whisper said, folding her arms and resting her shoulder blades on her husband. "*I'm* the one supposed to hand over her spouse." She laughed, though it wasn't out of genuine amusement. "Great plan, Bos. Brilliant. Superb…" Her smile was fast replaced by rancor. "Over my goddamn dead body."

No way would she push Zay into a position beneath her father, doing the bidding of a man who had no problem putting his hands on others in anger. Whisper couldn't imagine many worse scenarios. Not only would it piss her off to see her husband kowtowed by such a snake, but it would mean living in his invisible cell again. Her and any offspring she and Zay ever had.

Something about that thought shifted her perspective; everything came into focus. She didn't want to stay with the McDades. They were as foul and devious as the Dohertys. Her family wasn't a better choice. So all that left them with, if they wanted their freedom, was fleeing.

Spinning around, she set her sights on Zay. "Call Score."

TWENTY-FIVE

"WHAT?" Zay asked, amazed at her order. "You can't be serious."

"We have to get out of here. We can't stay."

"Parker has to know what Burl and Nicki have been doing."

"Send him an email," Whisper said, though she didn't really mean it.

Parker did deserve to know the truth, but it was unlikely he'd thank the messenger. Telling Parker would put him in an impossible position. He loved the life and wanted to take over from his father in time. That meant he'd have to make a choice between his wife and his future. Nicki would be an easy sacrifice for him to make. Except would he ever be able to trust his father again? Something like that would eat at a guy's insecurities. A normal guy's anyway.

"Whisper will be the first target," Bosco said, approaching at her side. "Even before they decide what to do with Nicki, they'll want Whisper subdued."

She scoffed and folded her arms. "What a polite way to say fucked up."

"Burl will be back Monday," Bosco continued. "If Doran calls him, or Nicki does, they might come back early.

But you know it doesn't make a difference. If they want her taken down, they don't have to be anywhere near here to do it."

Because the McDades had plenty of people they could call up to come do it for them.

"I won't go quietly," she said more to herself than anyone else, which was why she didn't expect Zay to yank her chin up again. The heat behind his discerning gaze wasn't passion, not sexual passion anyway. "What?"

Her husband did like to glare, but he seemed to be trying to figure something out. "We need to put you somewhere."

Like she was an out of place casserole dish. "Yeah? Like where? I won't go to Cyrus."

Talk about out of the frying pan and into the fire.

"Can you trust the McDades?" Bosco asked in a way that suggested he wouldn't.

If they couldn't trust the Dohertys and couldn't trust the McDades, they definitely couldn't trust the Byrnes. That left... no one. Everyone in the city who might be capable of secreting her were loyal to one of the families.

"One," Zay said. "But the fucker won't answer his phone."

She blinked once. "Uh... Score? Didn't I just fucking say—"

Zay put his hand over her mouth and looked to Bosco. "You have to go with her."

"Yeah, because if Score sees a Doherty, he's likely to kill it."

"Thing about my wife is people don't need to hear her name to feel that way about her."

Without so much as cracking a smile, Zay made a joke and cut her down at the same time. As he walked toward the closet, his hand fell away, so Whisper turned a glare on Bosco.

"What are you looking at me like that for?" he asked, surprised to be the object of her wrath. "He said it, not me."

"You were thinking it," she said, narrowing her eyes. "I can tell."

Holding up both hands in surrender, he gave

innocence a shot, but she saw right through it. "I've never wanted to kill you."

Whisper tilted her head to the side. "Never?"

"Bosco doesn't believe in murder," Zay said, reappearing from the closet, proving he'd been listening all along.

"Then you have an odd friendship set, Bos," she said, not objecting when Zay took her hand.

When something cool and hard touched her palm, Whisper looked down to see he was sliding a sapphire ring onto her finger above her wedding ring. During her packing, she'd put the band back on. Just like on the day of their wedding. Thinking about it, the sapphire was probably the first ring he'd ever put on her finger himself.

"You sure about this?" Bosco asked.

Raising her attention away from admiring the ring, she could tell Bosco was surprised. Yet, there was something solemn about the question and the way he looked at his friend.

Zay slipped his hands into his pockets. "She'll need something." Whisper held up her hand, asking about the ring without saying a word. "It was our mother's."

Her lips circled in a silent "oh." "So this is my passport to getting in to see Phoenix."

One of Zay's eyes narrowed in a semi cringe. "Don't call him that. You call him that and no amount of jewelry will save your ass."

Broadening her smile, Whisper smacked Bosco's arm. "I'll have Bos-Boy with me, what could go wrong? We'll be great."

Bosco rubbed his arm where she'd hit it. Zay just shook his head. It seemed acceptable to joke until she thought about what her husband was actually telling her to do and what it meant for him.

"That means you're planning to stay here," she said, thinking about the distance that would be between them.

Wherever Score was, it was out of state, too far for her to get back to her husband if he needed backup.

Except who would tell her if he did. No one would be left behind who'd look out for Zay's interests or for hers.

If the brothers confronted Parker and Burl with information of the affair while at the same time refusing to accept the marriage between Doran and Madison, any number of things could go wrong.

"All of us should go," she said, the joke long forgotten. "You can't stay here by yourself."

"I won't be by myself," Zay said. "Doran will be here."

"And how will Parker react when he finds out you figured out the affair because of me? If I'm not here to blame, he'll focus that anger on you."

"I can take Parker."

Maybe, but it didn't seem to her that Parker was the type to fight fair. He'd stabbed one brother in the back, nothing would stop him putting a bullet in another. Probably when he was least expecting it.

Whisper shook her head and grabbed his hand. "No. I don't want you to stay."

"If I have to gag you and stuff you in a steamer trunk, you're going, wife." He looked over her head at Bosco. "Call the airline."

Maintaining her attention on her husband, Whisper heard Bosco start for the door. "Zaiden McDade, I will not abandon you here."

The bedroom door closed as his gaze dropped to hers. "I'll always be stronger than you."

She gritted her teeth. A noise in the bathroom tried to take Zay's attention, but she yanked on his hand to tell him she wouldn't be so easily cast aside.

"I don't trust them, Parker or Burl. You need someone in your corner."

"This is how it's gonna be," he said without hesitation. "Dutiful wife."

Yeah, right. If he thought laying down the law would work with her then he hadn't been paying attention.

Whisper quoted his words, giving him one last chance to change his mind. "If turning around and walking out of here is how this thing has to end, we'll do it. But we'll do it together."

"We will be together," he said. "I'll be right behind you."

"Not good enough."

Just that morning, Whisper had woken up troubled and alone. Yet, there they were, facing off, matching frown for frown, set in their determination to protect each other.

His hand twisted so he could lock his fingers between hers. The contact startled her so much that Whisper had to look at their link to really register it. His broad, capable fingers spread her digits; his palm pressed against hers.

Whisper couldn't remember the last time a man had held her hand in that way. The twine of their fingers was too intimate. She tried to pull away, but he wouldn't let go.

Zay came even closer. "You can't argue you're worried for my life then pull away from me."

There was a truth that hurt to admit. Still, the words came from her throat anyway. "Makes me feel weak."

"To feel something for me," he asked, picking up her other hand from her side to press it flat on his chest. "That's because you are weak."

Despite her instant tension, he strengthened his hold, forcing her to stay against her will. "Let me fucking go, asshole."

"It's what love does to you, Peanut," he said. "See how worried you are 'bout me being here on my own, that's what I feel about you staying."

She relaxed, almost amazed by his calm. Somehow his acceptance aided hers. "You're saying we make each other weak?" As far as Whisper could figure out, that was an argument against ever feeling anything for anyone. "If you stand up for me, Burl will turn his back when Parker wants to…"

"Burl already turned his back on Score, I know exactly what he'll do."

"He expects you to fall in line," she said, recalling what had been said by the men before they left. "Parker tried to tell him that you wouldn't want to give me up; Burl said he made the decisions for the family. Your father expects you to…"

If Zay stood in front of Burl and refused to give up on their marriage, his father or brother could turn violent. But if he stood in front of them and couldn't do it, she'd be with Score, apparently under his protection. One phone call and she'd be a sitting duck if Burl ordered Score to eliminate her.

Trust. Looking into her husband's eyes, registering his determination, she couldn't deny his certainty. But he wouldn't be the first man to sell out another to save himself.

"If my father hasn't noticed how I feel about you, then he deserves whatever he gets," Zay said. "I won't betray you."

Either he could read her thoughts or he was thinking the same thing about how the scenario could play out.

"You and Doran need a plan," she said, tightening her hold on his hand and curling her fingers into the fabric of his tee-shirt. "I won't leave you until I know he'll have your back."

Not something the McDades were particularly good at.

"Doran is the softest of us all," he said, like that was a bad thing. "He'll keep the coolest head."

A mediator might be a good thing. From her observations of Zay and Bosco, usually the latter kept the peace, which included stepping in front of his friend when necessary.

"I don't need Bosco," Whisper said, thinking it might be better for Zay to have as many allies as possible. "You should keep him here with—"

"Score doesn't know you're mine," he said with a shake of his head. "Bosco was right. If he sees a Doherty—"

"How will he know I'm a Doherty?"

"I'm gonna bet he did his research the minute he heard about the marriage. You heard me say Score was smart, right?"

"Why should he care?" she said, assuming her husband was overestimating his brother. Seemed Doran wasn't the only one to idolize the second McDade brother. "I can handle myself."

"Not around Score you can't. Don't ever

underestimate him."

The weight of his certainty brought her up short. If Score was so smart and capable, and so untrustworthy, it didn't make much sense for her husband to send her there.

"If I can take Bosco, Score sure can," she said, regretting leaving her blade in the suitcase rather than strapping it to her thigh. "And if he's ducking calls, he won't be pleased to see us."

"Long as he sees Bosco, he won't hurt you," he said, though the twitch in his brow wasn't as positive. "Or he shouldn't."

Translated, that meant she'd get a window, probably a small one, to explain herself. If she didn't come up with something Score liked, her stay there would be short.

Anywhere else would be a smarter option. Except there was nowhere else. The Dohertys were done. The stragglers still alive were loyal to Cyrus.

Talking more about it was a waste of time. What would be, would be.

"I have to call Mariana and Paula," she said.

Zay disagreed. "Call them later. After we know how this goes."

Her girlfriends would worry if they didn't hear from her. Though it wasn't exactly as if she was the most reliable friend. Since being married, there were plenty of nights out that she'd missed. Even when she did turn up, Whisper had a tendency to disappear at some point. That wasn't exactly a new trait, she'd done the same before being Zay's wife. If some guy caught her interest, she'd wander off with him without reaching out to her friends to tell them what happened right away.

Unreliable though she was, her friends had confidence in her safety. Once upon a time, Whisper had been able to do what she liked, when she liked, sure that no one would mess with a Doherty. Those days were a distant memory.

"I should take Nicole with me," Whisper said. From his startled expression, he hadn't expected her to say that. "Yes, she's an idiot and I don't like the way she looks at you, but you know she'll be the first casualty of this."

"She could be a casualty at Score's. You're delivering Parker's weakness straight to his enemy."

Odd that she couldn't quite equate Parker and love. Thinking of him as weak was easy, he was definitely spineless. But Zay was just through telling her that love made people weak. Nothing she'd seen of Parker and Nicole's relationship betrayed much more than an affection. They'd been together a long time according to Zay. Could be that was what marriage was years down the line. Wasn't like she had a role model to look to on what a real marriage should be.

"If she stays here, there's no way she'll say anything that will help her case," Whisper said. "Think about it, Nicki apologizes to Parker and blames it on Burl. What happens then?"

"Burl takes her out."

"Or Burl gets there first and blames her…"

"Parker takes her out."

"There's no way this ends good for her. Score won't kill her, not right away, not if he's as smart as you say."

"He'll want to use her against Parker," Zay said, considering the scenario.

"So Parker gets a chance to fight for her… or forget her. Either way, Nicole has a chance at freedom."

"And Parker gets a chance to stop and think about what's important to him before acting. If he decides she's meaningless maybe Score lets her go," he said, then inhaled. "Take her with you."

Whisper smiled at her husband. "Good idea."

TWENTY-SIX

NICOLE WASN'T A FUN travel companion. As much as Whisper was tired of hearing her sister-in-law's voice, she imagined it was worse for Bosco who'd put himself between the women more than once. Whisper had never noticed just how short her fuse was before. Maybe it was the situation, maybe not. But as soon as they picked up their rental car, Whisper dug her blade out of her suitcase and strapped it to her thigh.

She felt better after that. Relaxed.

In contrast, Nicole seemed to tense.

Whisper did the driving while Bosco navigated. She wasn't much of a driver and didn't enjoy it. Only when Nicole started nitpicking again did Whisper tip her hat to Bosco's strategy. If he'd been driving, separating the two of them would've been impossible.

They drove up to a tall, sleek building made mostly of glass from what she could tell.

"Wow," Whisper said, trying to peer up at the place from their position parked in the pickup point outside. "Nice work if you can get it, huh? You sure he's on the up-an'-up?"

According to the quick history Bosco provided on the flight, Score was walking the straight and narrow… ish. He hadn't wandered too far from his roots and did still do the occasional task for Burl while cleaning McDade money through the nightclub he apparently ran these days. But for a guy from their background, that was positively saintly.

"He got a settlement," Bosco said. "Something from Texas, don't know the details, know it was enough to set him up."

"Apparently," she said, snatching Bosco's phone out of his hand. "Which apartment is his?"

He'd put the address into the navigation on his phone. After committing it to memory, Whisper went to his browser to check out what she could about the building.

During their journey, it had been the job of both of them to keep Nicole under supervision the whole time. That meant sharing a ladies' room stall at the airport and refusing to let her use the restroom on the plane.

Before leaving the house, Whisper packed some stuff for Nicole, ensuring to leave the woman's phone off and in a drawer. They'd been careful to ensure she didn't get hold of any phone, either from them, strangers, or payphones. Yeah, it had surprised Whisper too that there even were still payphones at the airport.

"What are you looking at?"

"There's a bar in the building," she said, reading real estate listings that included floor plans. "That's fucking amazing." Raising her attention to Bosco, who was trying to peer at the phone, she smiled. "When this is done, we should move somewhere with a bar in the building."

"Yeah, I don't think Zay would be wild about that idea."

Turning Bosco's phone off, Whisper freed herself from her seatbelt and reached over to grab her purse from the foot well under Bosco's legs. The child locks were on the back doors, so Nicole was stuck inside until one of them let her out.

"What are you doing?" Bosco asked when she pulled the door release. "We can't park here. All our shit's in the trunk, we'll be towed if—"

"Yeah, there's a valet around the corner." The one behind them that they'd driven past. Getting there would require a detour. "You should probably take it there."

"Uh, me?" he asked as she pushed her door open. "Where the hell are you going?"

Whisper slung her purse strap over her shoulder. "I'm gonna get us inside. Take the stairs furthest from reception," she said, winking at him then leaping out of the car to strut through the grand glass entrance.

Elevators and stairwells were security protected. Residents fingerprints granted them access to their own apartments. Guests had to check in at reception, which was exactly what she planned to do. Going through another set of doors, Whisper pulled her top down to accentuate her cleavage when she registered a security guy was manning her destination on the right. According to the plans, if she went around behind that reception desk, she'd reach the access to both stairwells.

To actually get in there though, she'd need what was dangling from the security guy's belt, his master key. It came in the form of a plastic card, and would be easy enough to swipe. Instead of going to the front of the reception desk, Whisper went to the open end. The security guy spotted her, or rather her tits, but she pretended not to notice.

Whisper pasted on a smile and propped an elbow on the opening to the reception desk. "Sugar, you couldn't help a lady out, could you?" The guy's eyes widened. "See… I had a little bit of fun with one of your residents last night…" Sashaying a little closer, she watched him tense, but he didn't back off even when she got into his personal space. "You probably know him, on the third floor?"

"David Lennox?"

"Yes," she said, boosting onto her tiptoes while allowing an excited giggle to escape her lips. "See, he said these things to me…" Whisper ran his tie through her fingers, one hand and then the other, easing herself closer. "He said all these wonderful things and I… You know how it is, I'm all alone and scared to trust, to believe he could really feel that way about me."

He frowned. "He's married."

Dropping down, she snagged the keycard without

breaking eye contact. "I knew it! It's always the same with these guys!"

The elevator opened at the other side of the reception desk, and he turned, presumably to see who was coming out of it. Taking advantage of the opportunity, Whisper reversed and swerved around the back of the desk to hurry down the narrow corridor and through the doors that would grant her access to the stairwells.

The keycard got her through one door and then the other. Fitness was her life, in work and in her spare time. Her favorite form of exercise ended with an orgasm, which, unfortunately, wasn't on the cards that day. Still, her condition meant making short work of the stairs.

The security guy probably wouldn't notice his keycard was gone until the next time he tried to use it. Just in case he was more astute than she gave him credit for and he didn't just shrug off her disappearance, she wanted to be quick.

Getting to Score's floor took no time at all. The stairs were a better option than the elevator for a couple of reasons. First, it was easier to disappear from the security guy's view. The front of the reception desk stood perpendicular to the elevators, giving him prime position to see everyone going in and out.

The second reason was personal. Whisper didn't want to announce herself and give Score a chance to draw first. If she could get a lay of the land, maybe listen in or figure her could-be host out, then she'd take every advantage open to her.

Using the keycard, she opened the door from the stairwell into Score's apartment, and was thankful that it didn't beep or make any sound. Anything that could herald her arrival took away the element of surprise.

Opening the door slowly, Whisper dropped her purse from her shoulder, using it to prop open the door. She wiped her fingerprints from the keycard with the hem of her dress then tossed it into the central void of the stairwell. It would fall and land somewhere, hopefully far from her, and maybe the guy would just think himself careless.

Stepping over her purse to creep inside, Whisper listened, waiting for a clue as to where the residents were. A voice came from the room to her right. A female voice, singing something under her breath.

She'd just pulled her blade from its sheath and felt her dress flutter back to its place when the door opened. The brunette who appeared was about Whisper's height. Short, but pretty, and no good at hiding the fright that tinged her surprise. A stack of towels in the brunette's arms provided her only shield. Hardly worthy.

They stood staring for a few seconds until eventually the stunned woman's attention dropped to the knife.

"You are exactly what I need," Whisper murmured.

Lunging, she grabbed the woman and yanked her forward. The neatly folded towels scattered to the floor; the woman yelped as Whisper slammed her back against the wall.

"I don't know what—"

"Where is he?" Whisper asked, pointing the tip of her blade to the groove at the base of the woman's throat. "McDade. Where is he?" Credit to the brunette, she curved her lips into her mouth, showing a defiance Whisper wouldn't expect between employee and employer. "You're fucking him." Whisper's amused smile was quick. "You're a lucky, lucky gal… I know that from experience."

Before the brunette could reply, Whisper reached around to grab a handful of her hair at the back of her head. Keeping her prey just in front of her, she held the knife to the beauty's throat.

"Let's go find him, shall we?" Whisper said, dragging the woman into a hallway.

The plans told her there were bedrooms to the right, the living space was to the left. Eenie meanie… it wasn't long after two in the afternoon, so she picked left.

The brunette squealed as Whisper hauled her along. Light came from the massive windows circling the apartment. As the external view emerged, she stayed alert, expecting someone to be there. The first person she saw was some kind of stiff in a suit. He didn't spot her, not until she went further and discovered two men sitting at the island in the kitchen.

One shorter and younger than the other, she fixated on the other guy, the one nearest the window.

Her target was the first to notice her, though it was just a fraction of a second before the younger one turned. Score rose from his stool, not showing any glimmer of reaction in his expression, yet Whisper could see him prickle. It was in his stance, across his broad shoulders. Zay was leaner than his older sibling, yet there was no mistaking they were brothers.

Whisper couldn't confuse his lineage. "Nice setup, McDade," she said, yanking the woman closer to her, angling her hand to show she wasn't afraid to use the blade.

"Oh my God," the younger guy said, obvious in his alarm. "Oh my God, Shyla! Let her go!"

Without shifting his focus, Score put a hand to the younger guy's shoulder, telling him to quiet. "What do you want, Doherty?" he asked, unequivocal bass in his tone.

Whisper laughed, but gave the woman a shake when the stiff stood up too. "Zay said you were smart," she said, drawing her eyes back to him. "He was right, you really do your homework."

"Where is he?" Score asked, probably expecting his brother to be on her heels or dead already.

"Home last time I saw him," she said.

"What do you want?"

"That any way to greet your new sister?" Whisper asked. "Heard a rumor if you met a Doherty you'd kill it."

"Exactly what I plan to do soon as you let go of my woman."

"Phoenix," the Shyla woman said.

He raised a hand. He didn't even look at her, yet the woman silenced and stilled.

"Shit you're good," Whisper said and shook the woman again. "Said you were fucking him, didn't I?"

"What do you want, Doherty?" Score asked with more force. "You just come here to fuck around?"

"No. I came here because my husband told me to," she said, tucking herself slightly more behind the woman and raising her blade higher, forcing Shyla's chin up. "And to bring you a peace offering."

Stepping around the other man, he opened his hands at his sides. "What? I see nothing but a parasite."

"You don't have to do this," Shyla said, presumably talking to her. "We can work this out. Whatever you need, this isn't the way to get it."

"Shy," Score warned.

"You're scaring her," Shyla said, surprising both her and Score.

"Me?" he asked. "She's the one holding a weapon."

"You are a weapon," Shyla said. "And she's alone."

Whisper tugged her back to murmur in her ear, "What makes you think that?"

A few tense breaths past while she let that notion percolate through to all of them. The room remained on pause, the air thick with resentment and fear.

TWENTY-SEVEN

NO ONE WOULD MOVE. No one would break. They could've stood there for the rest of the night just staring each other out.

The tension was only shattered when another voice joined them.

"Fuck, seriously, Whis?"

She stepped back enough to look sideways at the man stalking up the hall cajoling their captive along in front of him.

Whisper smiled at the guy who'd sort of become her friend. "Come on, Bos, don't pretend to be surprised."

He just glared and passed the end of the hall to come into the others' view. With Nicole in front of him, Bosco kept hold of her shoulders and was tall enough to see over the beauty.

Watching Score register Bosco's identity and then catch sight of the woman was strangely satisfying.

"Told you," Whisper said. "Peace offering. You wanna say thank you or just lay waste to her?"

"Who is that?" Shyla asked. "Who is she?"

"Nicole," Score exhaled her name.

Nicole objected to Bosco's grip. "You said he wouldn't kill me!"

Bosco held her firm. "You gotta hear me out, Score."

"I don't gotta do nothing," Score said, his chin descending an inch. "Not while the Doherty's hands are on what's mine."

Everyone turned to her. Well, everyone who could. Shyla was still shielding her.

Whisper focused on Bosco. "What?"

"If you were gonna kill her, you'd have done it already," Bosco said. "Zay told you to play nice."

Those had been his last words to her after kissing her goodbye that morning. "He also promised to love, honor, and obey. Haven't seen any evidence of the last one, have you?" she asked. Bosco tilted his head and raised his brows. "Fine."

Letting go of Shyla, Whisper held up her hands, though the knife stayed in one. The moment she was free, Score strode forward to get hold of Shyla. He cupped her face and crouched to make eye contact. He must have got some kind of answer because he quickly released her and swept her around behind him.

With his sights set on her, Whisper didn't back off or back down. She expected to be struck, expected pain, expected to be punished. She didn't expect Bosco to step in front of her, using his whole body to block Score's way.

"Listen to me," Bosco said.

Score was forced to stop. As his jaw tightened, his nostrils flared, proving his anger was rich and hot.

"What the fuck is he doing?" Score snapped at him. "Why the fuck would my brother—"

"To protect her," Bosco said. "Zay sent her here to keep her safe. Don't make a liar out of him."

His attention shot up over Bosco's head to land on her. Widening her smile, Whisper raised her hand in a finger wave.

"Why is she wearing that?"

Whisper hadn't thought much about the ring Zay had put on her hand the previous day. Score must have noticed it during the threatening thing.

"I'm already married to my McDade," Whisper said, taking the ring from her finger. "Maybe you can use this to see if yours wants to marry hers."

"You're a Doherty," he snarled, but at least he hadn't flattened Bosco to get to her.

He could. If Score wanted to take Bosco down, he could. Whisper didn't like agreeing with her husband. Yet with his obvious muscle, it was clear to her that Score could snap her in a second if he chose to.

"Please don't engage her," Bosco said. "She has a problem with her mouth."

"My mouth is just fine," Whisper said, strutting up to him to put an arm around his waist. "My McDade has no issues with my mouth. He loves it. Especially when it's loving him."

"You're disgusting," Nicole muttered. "We should've strung you up the first day he brought you home."

After a slow blink, one side of Whisper's mouth rose in a smirk that she landed on Nicole. "Sorry you picked the wrong McDade? Must upset you that you can't complete the set. Two of five isn't so bad. Mine is off the table, but you can take a run at the other two if you think you've got something they want."

"Shut up!" Nicole said, stomping her way. "Don't you say a word!"

"You want to fight?" Whisper asked, tucking the ring in Bosco's pocket before backing away from him. "Oh, please, sweetheart, bring it."

"No one is going to fight," Bosco said, hurrying away from Score to get between her and Nicole. "You already know she can't defend herself against you."

Whisper's head snapped to the side to track Shyla's movement in the kitchen, now on the other side of the island. "What is it with McDade men picking frail little delicate flowers…" She sighed. "Here's hoping Madison puts up more of a fight."

"Play won't do it," Score said, side-stepping to interrupt her line of sight. "He won't marry Madison Byrne."

His inner knowledge turned her smile sly. "Oh, you are good," Whisper said. "Maybe I picked the wrong McDade." Folding her arms, she glanced at Nicole. "I get it now. Good idea to shop around."

Nicole just glared.

Bosco came to her side to grumble in her ear. "You want to turn it down?"

Whisper patted his chest. "Don't worry, honey. Score won't beat me in front of his Shy."

She took pleasure in showing her brother-in-law her satisfaction.

"Don't bet on that," he growled her way.

"Maybe we should talk," a lighter female voice came from the kitchen. Had to be Shyla. "They've come a long way." Score turned. He and Shyla made eye contact. "If you still want to kill her after we've talked, you can do that. But your brother sent his wife to you for protection."

"Yeah," Whisper said. While Bosco was distracted, she went over to hook an arm around Nicole's neck. "And let's be honest, of all your sisters-in-law, I bet you'd want to take this one down before me… Why do you think I brought her? I've wanted to kill her since the moment we met and her husband didn't put me in prison… just saying."

"Shyla is right," the stiff said. "We should talk… Find out what's going on."

"I guess the Doherty figured out that Burl's plan to hook up Play and Madison means she's out."

"How come she's Madison and I'm *the Doherty*?" Whisper asked, folding her arms. "You're playing favorites."

Score's gaze zeroed in on her. "Madison has never threatened someone I love."

"Because she left her threatening to her brothers… when she had them." Whisper opened her arms. "I'm more hands on."

"You wanna stay here, you keep your hands off."

Shyla appeared just behind him. Running her fingertips down his forearm seemed to calm him, at least until they touched his wrist. In a snap, Score grabbed Shyla's fingers to yank her arm around his torso while using his elbow to tuck her in at his back.

"You know, Bos, remind me to punish my McDade for not being so protective of me."

"He stopped you committing homicide in front of a hundred or so witnesses," he said. "I'd say that's love."

"I say if I'm still alive when this is over, I'm gonna track Blondie down and finish the job."

"Still smarting about it?" Bosco asked, keeping an eye on Nicole. "I'd say that's love too."

"I'd say no one asked your opinion, Bos-Boy."

"Why would Raze send both women here?" Shyla asked from behind Score. "Did Parker send his wife to you too?"

Whisper scoffed out a laugh. "Parker is on business with Daddy McDade. He's in for a surprise when he gets home. Right, Nicki?"

"Parker wouldn't be that stupid," Bosco said in response to the woman they couldn't see.

Score still held her arm around his waist, his flat hand lay over hers on his abdomen. The two were close, more than just fucking from the looks of it.

Whisper wandered back their way, putting some distance between herself and Nicki. "Zay know about your little chippy?" she asked, earning herself another glare. "What? I'd love to have a sister-in-law not hell bent on killing me."

"Think you nixed any chance of that when you put a knife to her throat," Bosco said.

"Put the women in the guest room," Score said.

His focus hadn't moved, but Whisper doubted he was talking to her. The younger guy from the kitchen jumped to attention. As he raised his arms like he wanted to herd Nicki without touching her, Score opened his hand to her.

Whisper looked from his palm to his face. Kicking the women out was so standard for men like him that she almost wanted to spit. His desire to unarm her was more understandable.

"Uh… I probably wouldn't leave Whisper alone with Nicki," Bosco said. "They need a buffer."

Score closed his eyes in a blink that saw them open again on Bosco. "Anyone alive who doesn't want this woman dead?"

Hesitating, Bosco curved a hand around the back of

his neck. "Uh… Your brother probably… I don't mind her most of the time."

"Wow, am I blushing?" Whisper asked, bounding closer to sock his arm. "Remember what Zay said…" She pointed a finger at his face. "I will embarrass you in front of all these people. Right here, I will."

She was only playing and even Bosco responded with a smile.

In spite of the teasing, Shyla's curious voice floated from behind her lover. "Why is she so angry?"

"She's a Doherty, baby. It's how they're born."

"Better that than backstabbing, two-faced psychopaths," Whisper argued, expecting a quick return. Except almost as soon as the words were out of her mouth, she turned to Bosco. "I just insulted Zay. Damnit!"

Bosco laughed. "Never bothered you before."

"Insulting him to his face is more satisfying."

Because some part of her got aroused by irritating him. Score didn't have the same effect on her hormones.

Bosco put an arm around her. "She's still coming to terms with her new reality."

He slipped a hand into his pocket and pulled something out. Only when he released it into Score's palm did Whisper realize what it was: their mother's ring.

"New reality that what?" Score asked, letting go of Shyla's hand to turn on the spot and seek her other one. "The marriage was bullshit." He took Shyla's left hand and slid the ring onto her finger while still talking to them. "A sham. Setup by Burl."

"Yeah," Bosco said. "That's what most people thought." He tugged on a section of her hair. "Give the man your knife so we can get to talking."

"Zay says anyone who can be taken down by a little girl deserves to go down."

"He's also going through enough right now without having to worry about you going to jail."

Whisper nodded past him at Nicki. The younger guy was still standing next to her with his arms wide.

"We can blame her, there's plenty of witnesses,"

Whisper said. "Parker sent Score to jail, next best thing is sending Parker's wife to jail."

"Yeah, 'cept the one Score's worried about is Shyla," Bosco said. "You think if you kill her, he'll be in the mood to watch you walk?" That was a good point. "Half the reason we brought her here was because we're not all that sure Parker won't want her dead when he finds out what she's been doing." Another good point. "And, as much as you'll hate me for reminding you, it was you who pled her case to Zay and got him to agree to bringing her here for her own safety."

"She'd be safe in prison… ish," Whisper said. "She's pretty."

"And wouldn't survive a day," Bosco said, then switched his interest to Score while she admired Nicki. "If you'd picked up the phone, Zay would've told you everything."

"He can tell me soon as these two are tucked in."

Whisper put a hand on her hip. "Zay and I are sort of in a shirking the norm phase. I know more than you do at this point… and more about what he's thinking."

Though he didn't smile, Score coughed in amused disbelief. "Yeah, right, you forget you were just a sacrificial lamb? Cyrus handed you over because he couldn't care less what my brother did to you."

"Mm," she said, half-nodding in agreement. "That's what I thought too. Turned out my husband had a different motivation."

Score's frown jumped to Bosco who just sighed. "He's in love with her. Has been for years… God knows why."

"Because I'm purtay," Whisper said, pleased to register Score's surprise.

"He's in love," he said, looking her up and down in disgust. "With that?"

Nicki started laughing as Shyla got close to lay her hands on his torso. "Phoenix…" His lover's words influenced him, Whisper could see it. Her intrigue about the couple grew. "I can take them both down to the bar to give you some privacy."

Whisper raised her hand. "I'm in."

"No, you're not," Bosco said. "When you piss someone off—let's face it, we both know you will—Nicki won't lift a finger for you. Down here you're anonymous, this isn't your regular beat. You can't hide behind your name."

She gave his arm a reassuring pat. "I can look after myself, Bos."

"Yeah?" he said. "You gonna watch Nicki and keep Shyla safe? She's not anonymous down here. Anyone who wants to get to Score will go through her, like you proved the minute you got here."

"Okay, so we stay in," Whisper said, leaning back in a twist to scan the room without moving her feet. "There is booze somewhere in here, right?"

"I can pour you a drink," Shyla said, but Score snatched her back before she could move.

"You're not going anywhere until she gives up the blade," Score said, presenting his hand to her again. "You want me to take it from you?"

"I don't think your brother would like that," Whisper said, putting her hand over his to sacrifice the weapon. "He likes to watch me fight."

Until the words came out of her mouth, she hadn't really considered it. But he did. From the light of interest in Zay's eyes the first time she'd taken him on, to the delay in him stepping in between her and Blondie, it was obvious. Her husband liked to see her defending herself... or what was hers.

TWENTY-EIGHT

BOSCO'S PHONE began to ring, so he quickly retrieved it from his back pocket. No sooner had he answered than he was holding it toward her.

Whisper took the phone to her ear. "Mi amor," she said without even bothering to look at the screen.

No one else would call her. Period. Not through Bosco's phone.

"Quit the attitude."

Her mouth fell open. "How do you know I—"

"You think I can't tell by the tone of your voice that you're screwing around. You give Score the script yet?"

"How do you know I've even seen him?" she asked, but hit on the answer and said it in time with his response. "You can track my phone." She narrowed her eyes. "You're creepy, you know that? You didn't tell me that Score had a live-in lover."

Whisper didn't even care that the others could hear her. Though she did turn to saunter toward the elevators.

"Shyla," he said. "She started out as his housekeeper."

"Well, she's doing more than keep his house now," Whisper said, running a finger along a side table beneath the mirror attached to a wall perpendicular to the elevator. "Keeps his bed warm too."

"Burl knows," Zay responded.

"Should I tell your brother that?"

"Can't have been there long if you haven't realized he's switched on. He'll know Burl knows."

"Hmm," she said, spinning around to stroll back the way she'd come at the same lazy speed. "Miss me yet?"

"I didn't call to shoot the shit, I called to check Score hadn't killed you yet."

"He's only threatened it two or three times; that's a glowing welcome where I'm concerned."

"Peanut…"

Just the way he said the word stopped her. The timbre expressed that he needed something.

"What happened?" He didn't answer. "Baby?"

"Doran and me are gonna do something."

"What?" she asked, not sure she liked what his tone implied. "You did not send me down here just to keep all the fun for yourself."

The statement should've been said as a tease, yet she spouted it as an accusation. It infuriated her that he'd think to magic her away just to put himself in danger. If Zay got hurt or killed, she didn't want to be far away. She wanted to be there with him, to have his back or do whatever needed to be done.

Doran might be his brother, but Whisper wouldn't trust anyone to keep Zay safe. Not the way that she would.

"Relax," he said. "It's not dangerous."

"Walking down the street is dangerous for you," she said. "Especially now. Parker doesn't think you'll fall in line. He's had nothing but time to convince Burl of that. Goddamnit, Zay, why did you send me down here?"

"You know why," he said. "You're where you need to be."

"You said you'd be right behind me. I'm here. Where the hell are you?"

"Let me talk to Bos."

"No," she said. "No, whatever you can say to him,

you can say to me."

"I can't tell you to protect you. To look out for you before everyone else," he said. "I do that and you'll probably jump on a plane just to spite me."

Whisper frowned at the floor under her focus. "I'm considering it."

"I know you are because it's what I would do if I was you. Trust me, Peanut."

"I hate it when you say that."

"You keep Nicki alive and away from phones. She's our ticket. If we have to trade her to Score for him to give you up—"

"He doesn't care about me."

"No, but the longer you're there without me, the more likely you are to piss him off."

So maybe he'd want to finish her before Zay was around to step in.

Her husband wasn't the only one who could see through his spouse's ruse. "You're trying to make me feel involved, pretending like I have some role to play."

"Your role is to keep Nicki under wraps."

"That's Bosco's role," she said and coughed. "No way you'd ask me to restrain myself."

"Bosco's role is to keep you alive so you're around when I need something to ride."

She exhaled. "You're a lousy husband, you know that?"

"And you suck at the dutiful thing."

Her lips curled until a whisper of a laugh escaped her. "I want you here."

"Soon, baby," he said. "Put Bosco on."

Though she didn't want to, Whisper stomped over to thrust the phone Bosco's way. As he took it and turned away to talk to Zay, Whisper looked at Shyla.

"If I promise not to touch you, will you show me where to find the hard liquor?"

Shyla didn't reply until she'd got the nod from Score. Leaving his side, she headed up the room, away from the hallway.

Shyla paused to look at her. "Follow me."

Unfortunately, she couldn't forget what Zay had asked of her. So after backing up a few steps and grabbing Nicole's arm, Whisper stalked after their hostess.

***

WHISPER HAD ELECTED to take the decanter of good Scotch over anything else in the bar. She liked that her brother-in-law had a bar in his apartment. Sure, the guy might be a homicidal psychopath who hated her and everything she came from, but his priorities aligned with hers.

Out on the terrace with Shyla and Nicole, Whisper sat on a patio chair, lounging in the sun. Just for kicks, and because she needed a break, she'd put Nicole on another chair around the corner in the shade. Probably pissed her off, but Whisper thought it smart to take advantage of the glazed walls. Meant she could monitor her prisoner without actually being anywhere near her.

Shyla stood with her back to the view, her arms wide, so her hands rested on the aluminum rail above the glass of the terrace.

"How long you been screwing my big brother?" Whisper asked, raising her glass. "I know he'll hate me calling him that. I really can't help it."

Aggravating her family, and more specifically, her father, was the only way she'd ever got their attention. More than that, it was the only outlet for her resentment toward them. Only since her marriage had she realized just how deep her anger towards them ran.

Maybe it was because Whisper had an opportunity to let go, something she'd never had before. It changed her perspective. The Doherty chains that had allowed her the freedom to be as offensive as she wanted were loosening. Once they were gone, she could give up her need to be callous and bitter… in theory.

"About three months," Shyla said. "Well, I started working for him three months ago. We haven't been sleeping together that long."

"Yeah? Your McDade know something about seduction?" The half-smile that Shyla tried to conceal by looking away wasn't missed. "Lucky you, mine's idea of seducing me is throwing me to the floor and stuffing his cock in my throat… and he's got plenty of it." This time Shyla tried to hide her widening smile by curling her lips into her mouth. "As does yours, I figure from that face."

Shyla took her hands from the rail and threaded her own fingers together, pushing them deep against each other. "We thought the marriage was part of a plan."

"It was," Whisper said. "Something cooked up by Burl and Cyrus… my father."

The petite beauty frowned. "But Bosco said Razer loves you."

"He does," Whisper said, swigging from her glass. "How could he not?"

Leaving the rail, though still fidgeting with her fingers, Shyla crossed to sit on the patio chair next to hers. "Score worries about him. I know he does."

"McDades don't worry. Dohertys don't either."

Worrying suggested caring. Caring for another person was a weakness. Whisper frowned at herself. How could she get the Doherty mantras out of her head? Hadn't she told herself to trust her husband, to work with him? His belief in her had seduced her. For a while, she'd wanted to trust it. Wanted to have something uncomplicated and pure. Zay cared for her. Even Whisper could admit to herself that she cared for him. But the chances of freeing themselves from Burl were so remote that she was afraid to let herself believe they would ever be free to be together without the patriarch's interference.

"Bosco said Razer loves you," Shyla said. "He didn't say how you felt about your husband."

Whisper couldn't answer that question. Not to herself. Not to anyone.

"Because I'm a woman of mystery," Whisper said and offered her glass to Shyla. "Want some?"

The hostess's gaze moved beyond her, to something inside the apartment. Whisper twisted around to see the men in various positions around a glass coffee table. Score was looking their way. Not her way. Toward the woman opposite her. She wasn't even sure Score saw her, his focus on Shyla was absolute.

Bringing her attention back around, Whisper took another drink from her glass. "You gotta ask his permission?" Shyla didn't seem to hear her at first. "Hey!"

"What?" Shyla asked, snapping out of her trance. "I'm sorry."

"What you looking at him for? Scared he'll fuck off somewhere without you?"

"No," Shyla said, curling her fingers around the hem of her dress on her knee. "He always comes back to me."

"Ain't that a loaded statement," Whisper said. "So how'd you two hook up? Bored one night? Drunk? He's got appeal, I get that. Seems sort of caveman next to you, but sometimes that works."

"What's Razer like?"

Dodging the question with one of her own was an interesting tactic. "Not like your McDade," Whisper said. "He doesn't go by his street name. Doran either… Not to family anyway… So what's Score's plan?"

"His plan?"

"Sure," Whisper said, swirling the liquor in her glass. "He doesn't let things go. McDades aren't good at doing that full stop." Not that Dohertys were. "But Score's known for leveling the field, righting wrongs."

"That's who he used to be."

"He still uses the name."

"Habit," Shyla said.

In Whisper's opinion, although the woman wasn't exactly being defensive, something lingered beneath the surface of what she didn't say. The answer came just a little too quickly. Intrigued as she was, Whisper was impressed too. The fidgeting was a giveaway about the brunette's anxiety. Whisper could forgive Shyla that, she wasn't always the most personable individual.

"And what about you? It's Shyla, right?" Whisper asked, attracting a nod. "Where are you from? What's your story? Your folks got a name down here?"

Though she asked, Whisper already knew the answer. Nothing about Shyla said capable or dangerous or at ease.

"My folks are dead."

"Hey," Whisper said, raising her glass in time with her smile. "Lucky you!" That was an honest first reaction. About as honest as she got. Shyla's blinking surprise reminded her that not everyone had a bad relationship with their family. "Oops, guess that was a bad thing for you."

"Not all bad. I wondered what my life might have been if they'd lived. But we were raised by my grandfather, I loved him very much."

"Dead too?" Whisper asked, noting the use of past tense. "Who's we? You got siblings?"

"A brother."

Zay would never have gotten along with the Doherty brothers. Though if they hadn't died, the marriage would never have taken place. At the time of the bloodbath, at the funerals of her family members, Whisper never thought for a second that anything positive could come out of such loss. Thinking of so much death as positive was wrong, yet she didn't feel negatively toward her marriage either. Not at that exact moment.

"He get along with your honey?"

"Phoenix?" Shyla asked and shrugged. "They haven't met."

"Makes sense," Whisper said, taking a shot at supportive. "Even the most protective of brothers would think twice about warning a McDade off."

"Oh no, it's not like that. Wyatt is…"

Another curious response. Shyla was hesitating. The words had been on the tip of her tongue before she snatched them back.

Spinning on her butt, Whisper put her feet on the floor, almost parallel to Shyla's. "Don't be shy, Shy," she said. "We're practically sisters." Except Shyla's conditioning came from Score, who wasn't her biggest fan. "You can tell me anything."

"Score doesn't trust you," Shyla said. Hardly breaking

news. "I trust him."

Following the steps to their conclusion, Whisper got the message: Shyla didn't trust her. "Zay and me were married about a month before we had sex." Shyla blinked in surprise. "He didn't tell me he even knew who I was until after we fucked… like a day after. I married Razer McDade believing he was a psychopath."

Shyla swallowed. "That's all I knew about him at first."

"Score told you that?"

She'd figured one brother would know about the other. Zay was a lot of things, incapable of emotion wasn't on that list. For Score not to pick up on that suggested he wasn't as astute as Zay believed.

"Fish," Shyla said, picking up Whisper's question by the way her eyes narrowed. "The younger guy from inside."

"Who is he?"

"Works with Score. He's a friend."

The information lodged in Whisper's memory bank in case it became useful later. Even coming to Score's for protection, asking for their trust, she still couldn't get out of the Doherty mindset. People outside the family couldn't be trusted. Any opportunity to double-cross them for the benefit of the family should be taken. That was what her mind went to whenever she learned something new.

"Who's the other guy? The suit?"

"Amos Beeks," Shyla said. "He's a lawyer."

"Score's lawyer?"

Shyla nodded. "And Fish's."

A smile curved her lips. "Fish did time?"

Shyla's fingers curled tighter then loosened over and over; her anxiety was raising its head again. Maybe she hadn't meant to reveal anything. Or it could be she was worried what Score would do to her when he learned she'd been giving the Doherty details.

"I don't know that I—"

"Hey, don't worry about it. I know plenty of guys who did time in prison, believe me… Though, I guess, a bunch of them are dead now, but… Doran did time in prison too. Play." Shyla nodded, probably not trusting herself to open her mouth. "What else did Score tell you about Zay?"

Finding out how the older brother felt about her husband could be useful. If there was any chance Score couldn't be trusted, Whisper needed the inside track so she could warn Zay.

"They were close," Shyla said. "It's complicated, I guess."

"Isn't it always," Whisper said on a sigh. "I should count my blessings my family were massacred, right?"

Shooting for genuine was one thing, hitting the target was another.

"I'm sorry," Shyla said, squirming. "Phoenix told me what happened. It's awful, I… I can't imagine."

"I didn't have to, I heard every second of it."

"Just you and your dad left?"

Whisper bobbed her head. "Basically. Don't think the uncle my father hates or my idiot cousins count." She sucked in a breath. "And now that I've fucked up the Doherty-McDade alliance, my father will be looking to reduce the Dohertys by another number with one more fatality."

Once again, she raised her glass. After tossing the rest of the liquor into her throat, she uncorked the decanter to pour more into it. As she was putting the stopper back into the crystal, a shout came from inside.

"Sounds like they're having fun," Whisper said, rising to her feet, glass in hand. "Let's go get in the way."

TWENTY-NINE

STRUTTING THROUGH the terrace doors into Score's apartment, Whisper didn't declare herself. She didn't have to.

Score spotted her within seconds. "Get outta here."

"You boys don't seem to be playing nice," Whisper said, only slightly aware of Shyla coming in a dozen feet behind her. "What are you fighting about?"

"Babe…"

That warning tone was unmistakable. Zay still occupied Bosco's phone line. The device itself, she noticed, lying in the middle of a chess board on the glass table the men were congregated around.

The suit Shyla had identified as Beeks was on the couch next to Fish. Bosco was in an armchair with his back to the window. Score was on his feet opposite Bosco's position.

Whisper tossed some Scotch into her mouth. "I'm playing nice," she said, continuing toward the group.

"How much has she had to drink?" Zay asked.

The question stunned her to a stop. Glancing around, she wondered where the camera was because the phone wasn't lit up, it wasn't a video call.

"I don't know, she's been on the terrace," Bosco answered.

"I heard a rumor," Whisper said, swinging her hips as she got walking again. "That someone owns a nightclub."

"No," Zay said before she could even look at Score. "Stay inside."

"You haven't seen the weather down here, babe… Did you know there was a bar in the building?" She squeezed past Score to approach the phone. "In the fucking building."

"Do what Score tells you to do," came his voice from the handset.

Whisper scoffed. "Yeah, right." The glass was on its way to her mouth, but it stopped when a thought struck her. "You don't actually mean that… do you?"

"Why do you think I sent you down there?"

"She doesn't give a fuck," Score grumbled from behind her.

"How the fuck would you feel behind enemy lines knowing the whole damn world wants you dead?" Zay snapped. "She's screwing around because she's terrified."

"Uh…" Whisper didn't like being so central while he declared her weak. "Tell me you're not talking about me."

"I don't have time to tiptoe around it," Zay said. "Interpreting your insanity took me years. Score doesn't have time to learn Whisper Doherty-McDade."

"Hmm," she said, tilting her head. "I hadn't thought about the hyphenate."

"I already changed it once," Bosco said as Whisper dropped to her knees. "I'm not doing it again."

"What's the plan?" she asked, leaning in closer to the phone.

"We're trying to figure that out."

"And you don't think I should be in the room while you do that?" she asked, ignoring everyone else. "We got this far together, remember?"

"Yeah, and I know you're less likely to get drunk if you're occupied. You have my trust."

That last short sentence told her exactly who didn't want her in the room.

Twisting around, Whisper crossed her legs to end sitting on the floor, looking up at Score. "Just because Shyla defers to you doesn't mean we all will. You get some sort of kick out of smothering your woman?"

Score's elbow began to bend, but before he could bring his arm up, Shyla stepped in to thread her fingers between his.

"We don't know you," Shyla said, keeping Score's hand. "You came to our home to ask for our help. I defer to Score because I trust him and he knows me. It's important to both of us to do what's best for the other… I don't know how your relationship works, but I don't have to second guess Phoenix. I know he'd never do anything that would hurt me… And I know if I asked him to do something, even if it maybe wasn't in the best interest of his family, he'd do it."

"Like kick us out on our asses," Bosco said. "That's what she's saying."

"Yeah," Whisper said, wondering where the hostess got her fire. "You might be happy for your guy to make all the decisions. While you're busy doing that, I have to worry about mine walking himself into danger. See he doesn't live in a fancy condo a million miles from the action. Right now, he's square in the middle of it. Unfortunately, I've learned recently that mine also tends to put me before himself. It would be easier for him to forget everything that's happened in the last couple of days and toss me out on my ass. Doesn't seem to matter how much I tell him that, he's determined to do right by me. He's an asshole."

Shyla's brows rose. "An asshole? For caring about you."

"His insistence on doing what's best for me makes me feel guilty. I'm not good with guilt, it screws me up, so I start saying and doing things that can only lead to my own destruction."

"Hey, I never thought about it that way," Bosco said.

"You been paying attention?" Zay asked down the line. "Why do you think she's such a bitch all the time? Trusting means a chance she'll get comfortable. Then she could be caught off guard… Someone could fuck her over… No one has ever had her back."

Her girlfriends might argue that. Except Whisper

would never let them. In her mind there was a division between her life connected to her family and name, and the her who could be frivolous with Mariana and Paula. Whisper would never ever go to them with real issues or endanger them in any way.

"She's a Doherty," Score said.

Whisper hooked her elbows onto the edge of the glass table at her back. "McDades aren't all that different from where I'm standing. Your brother sent you to prison. Your father is fucking his son's wife."

Shyla reacted with an intake of breath; Score tightened his grip on her hand. "Oh my God," the hostess murmured.

Drawing her eyes away from Shyla's surprise, Whisper took her focus back to Score. "And your brother is asking for help, but you're too focused on the Doherty in your midst to hear him. I didn't go to the Dohertys for help. Sure, there aren't that many of them left. But I was given to the McDades as payment for an alliance that your father now wants to dissolve because I caught him pepping his pecker. Only person who's done nothing wrong in this is me, yet I'm the one everyone wants to kill."

The familiarity of the words brought a frown to her face. Whisper had argued with Zay when he'd said the same thing. That was just the previous day. So much had happened since then, it felt like a lifetime ago.

"No one's gonna touch you," Zay said, his voice solemn.

She tipped her chin his way. "Yeah, including you? Not sure I signed up for that."

"We'll help," Shyla said without consulting her other half. "But we have to respect that Score and Razer know their own family better than we do."

That was questionable. No one present had known about Burl and Nicole's affair before she did.

"Maybe," Whisper said in a nod toward diplomacy. "But my husband is the one out there about to take this battle on because of me."

Whisper hadn't told Zay about the affair, not

outright. He'd have had to make a choice when Burl told him about his plans to marry Doran to Madison. So whichever way it went, they would've ended up in basically the same place.

Like she'd said to him in their bathroom. He'd have been curious enough to pursue the issue. Burl's switch from supporting the Dohertys to exiling them would've piqued his intrigue. So even if he'd cast her out at his father's will, Zay would've found out about the affair eventually.

Still, Whisper couldn't erase her guilt. Zay planned to confront his father about the affair and his scheme to kick her out of the family. Doran was at his side. Whether he'd stay there when it came to it, Whisper couldn't be sure. Part of her maybe didn't want him to remain loyal to Zay. She didn't want her husband to be betrayed, but either or both of the men could pay the ultimate price for defending her.

Score was just a name before arriving. Whisper hadn't known a thing about Shyla. But there they were pledging their support. Even thinking about trusting Zay, who'd been in love with her for years, was a big step. Yet, there she was faced with the prospect of trusting even more people.

"Go to them," Score said.

Whisper had been sitting there on the floor, staring into nothingness. For a second, she'd forgotten about her audience. Seemed they weren't that worried about her. Score anyway. Shyla was looking at her with such sympathy that Whisper got nauseous.

"We call and they'll come back," Zay said. "We don't have to tell them anything—"

"That's the home field advantage," Score said. "Just like you said at the start of this. In the city, they have too many allies."

"Could work for us too."

That voice was new. It didn't take her long to figure out it came from the phone or who it must belong to. Doran.

Whisper turned to face the phone again. She finished her drink and reached over to put the glass down on the other side of the chess board. "You know how close I was to stealing the phone into the restroom? You should tell me when your brother's on the line, husband. I could've switched to video and taken off all of my clothes."

"Nothing we haven't seen before."

That muttering came from Bosco, so Whisper narrowed the evil eye on him. "Just because you get your kicks hanging around Zay's bedroom waiting for me to strip and walking in on us when we're having sex, doesn't mean I'm happy to get naked for just anyone."

Though her past behavior didn't offer much definitive evidence of that.

"You walk around naked up there," Bosco argued.

"Because my husband told me to."

"Enough," Zay said. "Bos, you've gotta learn not to engage her."

Whisper just showed their grimacing friend a broad, proud smile. "I know I'm growing on you. I'm like the tattoo you get when you're drunk. Next day you're embarrassed and upset with yourself. Over time, it just becomes a part of you. You'll be proud of me eventually."

"You go to them, they don't have time to plan," Score said, doing an excellent job of steering the wayward conversation back to its relevance. "You wanna see Parker's face when you tell him too. Don't want to give the old man a chance to break it to him gently."

"How do you do that?" Whisper asked, folding her arms on the edge of the table, staying focused on the phone. "Hey, son, you know the woman who sleeps next to you every night you're home? Yeah, most nights she comes up there filled with my spunk… You're dipping your cock in a pussy swimming with my jizz."

"Okay, this is disturbing," Bosco said. "And he's not even my father."

Whisper caught a side glance at the duo on the couch who hadn't said anything. "Why are you here? Does Zay know that he's talking to a room full of people? Maybe that's why you wanted me to stay out because I'll tell him the truth. You've got a lawyer and an ex-con listening in… Three ex-cons if you include the McDades who have done time."

"We trust them," Shyla said. "And we might need their help."

"We don't need their help to make a decision about what's best for the family," Whisper said, planting her hand on the table to hop onto her feet. "We should be careful who we include in the plan."

"If they were spies for Burl, we would know it," Zay said. "He'd have told us already."

"And he wouldn't need to call Score to get his input," Doran agreed. "If Score trusts those guys, that's good enough for me."

Not good enough for her, but it didn't matter. Not really. In her new family, this new circle, she'd always be outnumbered. Zay's plan would work or it wouldn't. The truth was that until the moment in Nicki's bedroom when Zay had chosen her and offered his trust, she'd believed her life was on borrowed time. Anything she got after Burl and Parker were confronted was bonus time.

Whisper snagged her glass from the table. "Okay," she said, giving up being the only one on guard. "We want to trust everyone, let's let the world in. Who cares?"

Striding back the way she'd come, Whisper went out on to the terrace and retrieved the Scotch. If the McDades wanted to play happy families, they could. She was used to being on the outside looking in. Her time of honesty with Zay was too short to make any permanent difference.

Whisper couldn't be seduced by it. She wasn't a McDade and never would be. She didn't think like them, didn't trust like they did. They didn't plan her way either. The Dohertys didn't want her; it would only be a matter of time before the McDades felt the same way.

THIRTY

WHISPER WASN'T MUCH in the mood for following instructions. That was probably why, despite being tied to the bed and under supervision, she was sitting on her pillow, twisting and working the knots from her wrists.

Nicole was lying in the bed beside her. Much in the same position, the woman had her wrists tied to the headboard. So much for trust in the McDade family.

The young guy Shyla had called Fish was sitting in a chair that had been brought in and angled to face the bottom corner of the bed. His job was to watch the women as they slept. Not an exciting mission or a riveting one. The poor guy would probably have his ass handed to him, but he'd fallen asleep before Whisper was sure Nicole was slumbering.

Still, he'd done her a favor, which was appreciated. With him and Nicole asleep and night shining from outside the massive windows, Whisper planned to split as soon as she could get out of the bindings. Giving Score credit, she acknowledged that he had skill. Men like him had no doubt been tying up prisoners for a long time. Whisper came from the other side of those knots. Since her toddler years her father and brothers had been tying her up to keep her in place... or out of the way.

When it suited her, Whisper knew exactly how to manipulate her hands and the ropes to free herself. It was especially easy when attached to a padded headboard. The padding offered more leeway and meant she got out of the ropes in under three minutes.

Slipping off the bed was easy enough, moving without making a noise was another talent she'd picked up young. As a teen, she snuck out almost every night. Every night her father had grounded her anyway… which, yeah, was basically every night. Thinking back, Whisper couldn't deny she must have been a nightmare adolescent. Like she'd said to Zay, her father put up with her shit for twenty-nine years. It was no wonder he'd turned to violence.

Creeping to the door, she hunkered down to look at the lock. Her brother-in-law had credited her with the setup. The ropes, the guard, the locked door, the combination proved he suspected she could have skill.

That skill took her to the closet area. The evidence left behind suggested a woman must have once slept in the room. Hazarding a guess, Whisper assumed the room had belonged to Shyla before she tripped into Score's bed. Not bad for such an uncertain woman. Shyla revealed herself with the fidgeting and the way she looked to Score for confirmation on everything. It was incredible to imagine how she must have been before the relationship if she was still so nervous while in a safe place with a man capable of killing for her. Surely being with a man like Score would increase a woman's confidence. Poor thing must have been afraid of her own shadow before finding her McDade.

Poking around at the leftover knickknacks and toiletries, the bobby pins tucked against the join in a shelf brought a smile to her face. Grabbing what she needed, Whisper dragged the plastic ends off with her teeth and spat them to the floor. Being quiet and careful was inherent, but not that important. The other two people in the room were heavy sleepers. They had zero awareness of what was going on around them.

Hunkering down at the lock, she used her bobby pins to pick it. After just a few seconds, a yelp sounded from somewhere in the apartment. Whisper froze, wondering who was out there and if they'd wake everyone else. When it was followed by a moan and a squeal, her lips began to curve. That was no one breaking in to cause trouble. That— if she wasn't mistaken— was their hostess.

Returning to her picking, she couldn't stop smiling. The noises got louder and more urgent and were quickly followed by a rhythm of movement. Damn. Whisper hadn't really been thinking about her McDade until she heard another woman enjoying theirs. Pleased to have some cover, the lock popped and she opened it an inch.

Fantastic.

Standing up to slip out, she suppressed her snicker at the continued yelping and panting coming from the room opposite the one she'd just snuck out of. Not even remotely modest, she paused to listen for a few seconds. Shyla began to call out her lover's name with such desperation, Whisper wasn't sure what she was asking for, mercy or satisfaction.

Much as she'd like to loiter and hear how the story ended, it was a tale she'd heard before.

Their things were in the laundry room; that was where they'd been piled after being brought up by some lackey from the lobby. Living the high life wasn't so bad. People did things for her family because they were afraid or because they were paid.

Score's settlement had set him up. Whisper thought about that while changing her clothes and retrieving her backup weapon from a pocket inside her suitcase. It was a smaller piece, a switchblade. One that she didn't like half as much as her primary weapon. She hadn't seen where Score had put it. Wasting time looking for it would increase the possibility of being discovered and she wanted to get out of there fast. Once changed, Whisper retrieved some folded bills from another pocket and slipped them into her bra.

Traipsing down the stairs, she didn't have any fear of being discovered or worry about being on the streets by herself. From a young age, Whisper had known there was always a possibility she'd be targeted. In a new city, far from home, that knowledge was still relevant. Being aware and indifferent at the same time was an engrained trait.

One place called to her more than any other. True, she didn't know the city, but Whisper trusted herself to get along anywhere. Not with *anyone*, people were more complicated than bars. Or nightclubs, which was the real goal for her that evening.

It didn't matter that she didn't know where McDade's club was, she hailed a cab and asked the driver to take her to Score McDade's club. The guy started driving without asking anymore questions. Why the destination was so straightforward became clear when she departed the cab.

"Score" was the name emblazoned above the wide entrance. Maybe she should've realized that, but the obvious wasn't always her first thought. The McDades had a name and had similar protection to the Dohertys. Still, putting your name on the place was sort of asking for trouble. She couldn't imagine things were so different just because he was in another state.

Only one way to find out, Whisper figured. Paying her way inside, she took the place in. Not bad. Not Scooby's, but tolerable. The bar stretched along the right hand wall, tables were spread out in front of it. At the back was a stage where women strutted and danced, tempting the revelers. They weren't stripping, but they weren't covered up either. Above was some kind of second floor that overlooked what went on beneath.

Getting there was most of the battle won. She'd have time to explore and figure things out after downing a few drinks. The locals were friendly enough. Even over the loud music and the humidity, more than one guy tried to pick her up. Whisper knew exactly how much to flirt to get herself a drink and exactly how to shut a guy down before he started to think she owed him something.

On her third drink, Whisper was moving to music, settling into the rhythm of the place when someone snatched her arm. Her glass dropped as she swung around, ready to thrust the heel of her hand upward. At the last second, she stopped herself making contact when she registered the guy's identity.

Whisper exhaled. "You made me spill my drink!" she called over the music.

The guy Shyla had identified as a lawyer, named… Beeks or something, didn't know her well. He couldn't know that he'd taken his life in his hands grabbing her like that.

He probably didn't hear her. He shook his head before tipping it sideways and giving her arm a tug, implying he wanted her to follow. Curiosity took Whisper in the direction he'd nodded. Seemed this Beeks was a quick learner because he didn't let go of her arm. Bolting would be easy with the crowd around for cover.

How someone like him got mixed up with a McDade was a mystery. Delving into that mystery would have to wait for another time. She still didn't understand what kept her husband and his best friend together or how their paths had crossed. Beeks would have to take a number.

With his hand firm on her arm, he guided her through the throngs of dancing partiers and past the stage. In the corner was a dark door that she hadn't registered before. Whisper hadn't got to exploring or even thinking much about the layout. There was usually an office for the boss somewhere and it seemed that was where Beeks was leading her.

Once they were inside, he closed the door behind them. The low ceiling and dim lighting gave the room more of an ominous feel than an intimate one. It was a decent sized space with a solid desk at one side of the room and a long couch at the other. Black blinds hung above the couch. Closed black blinds.

"How did you know I was out there?" she asked, following him when he passed her to go to the desk.

"We have cameras all around."

"Huh," she said. "Wouldn't think you'd notice me mixed in with all those people… How can you see in the dark?"

There were flashing lights around the club. The bar area was dark. It caught only glimpses of the light that swung around the busier dance areas.

"We can switch to night vision if we have to."

"And you recognized me on night vision?" she asked,

sitting on the desk when he descended into the chair.

Wearing a look of incredulity, Beeks studied her, probably perturbed that she was so entitled in a new place. What he didn't understand yet was that fitting in meant faking it. Not that she was uncomfortable. Nightclubs were sort of her home from home.

Even being ensconced in the office didn't ruffle her. As she'd almost proven at the bar, she could take Beeks down if necessary. Unless he gave her reason, she'd leave him be. Another sign of growth, Whisper thought. Not so long ago, she'd have flattened him just for sport.

Pulling himself closer to the desk, Beeks moved the mouse to bring up a box requesting a password on the black screen. He typed in his password: Lobby2926. Watching his hands was habit. Still always looking for the upper hand. Whisper didn't need to log in to Score's system, but the lawyer had given her a way in if the need ever arose.

When he glanced over his shoulder at her, she tipped up her chin to look the other way. He didn't need to know that she'd been paying attention.

"See."

Beeks' word brought her focus back to him. On the screen were a bunch of little boxes. He clicked on one to show her the bar area, after a second, he minimized it to show her another from a different angle.

"Cool," she said, thinking it could probably be a lot of fun to watch people when they had no idea they were being scrutinized.

Gave her an insight into Score's mind too. Most bars and clubs around the country would have some form of closed circuit system. Whisper could tell from the images and from the number of boxes that clubbers that came to Score were always being eyeballed.

Power. Men just couldn't resist.

"What are you doing here?"

When Beeks posed the question, Whisper had just noticed text in the corner indicating that the screen filled with camera-feeds was just the first of twelve.

Her first instinct was to ask where else she should be,

but the answer to that one was obvious.

"Wasn't tired," she said, pushing her shoulders up in a shrug when she clutched the edge of the desk beneath her thighs to push herself up and off the desk. "This is a decent place."

Whisper wandered around the desk, taking in the features of the room. Nice rug here, some kind of art there. Somehow, even though everything was where it should be, she didn't feel like any of it was accidental. Score could just be a fastidious guy, yet it didn't feel like that. Whisper couldn't put her finger on what she was feeling; something about the space just screamed contrived.

"I'm surprised that Score let you leave the apartment… alone. Are you alone?"

"Wasn't alone at the bar," she said, stopping in front of a black and red canvas on the wall, trying to figure out what the image was supposed to be. "Guys around here are real friendly."

"Have you called Razer?"

Whisper winced. "You all call him that. Does Score call him that? Is that why?"

"I… never thought about it."

"I used to call him meathead," she said and spun around, giving up on the canvas. "To myself anyway."

"I haven't met him."

"You will," she said, sauntering toward the desk again. "Providing he doesn't get himself killed."

Beeks pushed himself back in the chair to regard her progress toward the door. "I don't think you have to worry about that. When Parker wanted Score out of the way, he went to great lengths to do it. I suspect it would've been easier just to kill him, but he chose not to."

Whisper stopped between the end of the couch and the door to open two slats of the blinds and peek out at the stage. "Score seems like an easy going guy," she said, without believing the words. "Not hot headed or quick to temper."

"Most of the time."

Withdrawing her fingers from the blinds, she twisted on the spot to glance his way. "My husband is less restrained."

"You call him your husband a lot."

"Helps to remind me I'm not single," she said, strolling past the couch toward the painting again.

Like an animal in a cage, Whisper's subconscious seemed aware of her limitations in the restricted space. It wasn't a small room, yet it was contained in an inconvenient position. Figuring there had to be a way out, a back door, some kind of exit that she couldn't see, Whisper became more particular about eyeing the walls and the lines of the art pieces.

A man like Score, one who'd spent time in prison, and spent his life involved in criminal activities, wouldn't leave himself cornered. If he did, that would be another strike against his brother's perception of his smarts.

"Do you have an issue with that regularly?"

Regular was a relative word. She and Zay had been married for less than two months and already they'd both confronted each other in the midst of potential infidelities.

"Bet Score gets plenty of pussy down here," she said, ignoring the direct question. "I'd think a guy like him wouldn't need to open a club to get it. But, hey, guess we all have our weaknesses, right?"

Beeks frowned just as she redirected to check out the walls behind the desk.

"He would never touch a woman here," Beeks said. "He's devoted to Shyla."

Whisper smiled, unsure if he was naïve or the couple were really that entwined. "You shouldn't tell someone like me something like that."

"Why not?" he asked, turning the chair to follow her movements as she ran her fingertips along the wall.

"Because I'm the type of person who won't hesitate to do whatever I need to. Hell, sometimes I hurt people just because I can."

Though she hadn't done that for a long time. It was more a feature of her youth. The only time Whisper saw her father's pride was when she displayed sadistic tendencies. It had never been one of her favorite things to do and often devastated her mother. But back then, Whisper had wanted to be in with the cool kids. That meant her father and brothers.

All she'd wanted to do was prove herself a worthy Doherty. Funny how things turned out. Now she couldn't imagine anything worse than being compared to her father.

Beeks spun his chair back to face the desk. She paused at the sight of him reaching for the phone. Before he could get past the first number, Whisper leaped over and pressed the button to disconnect the line.

The lawyer hadn't expected to be interrupted. When he blinked up at her, there was enough surprise in his eyes to give her an impression that he wasn't entirely at ease anymore.

"I have to call Score," Beeks said. "Let him know you're okay."

"He was getting his when he left," she said. "Don't think he gives a shit where anyone is. Anyone except the woman under him."

Thinking of that took her train of thought to Zay. If she could, Whisper might have called him, just to keep the cavalry from charging at her. But she'd learned her lesson about carrying her phone when she wanted to go off McDade radar.

Something flashed across Beeks' expression. "Fish was watching you, wasn't he?"

"And you're only now wondering if I did something to hurt him. Damn, I can tell you're not a McDade by birth. No, the idiot was asleep before Nicole. I couldn't have hurt him to get out, Nicole would've screamed her head off. There's no discreet bone in her body."

From her revelation about Score getting his, Beeks was probably reassured that Shyla wasn't hurt either. Score could've taken her down, but Whisper wasn't lying about his level of awareness as she snuck out. Zay would never be that distracted, even if they were in the midst of sex.

"I can't lie to him," Beeks said. "I'll have to let him know you were here."

"Were," she said and shrugged, retrieving the phone from his hand without meeting any resistance. "Past tense is fine by me. Nobody cares about getting in trouble after the party is over."

"Your husband must be very different to his

brother."

"Why? Because I don't bend to his will like Shyla does to Score or because I might be somewhere without his permission? Just what is the deal with that? Score can't be the insecure type. And if he's jealous, well, he's a McDade, he knows what to do with the competition."

Zay sure had when he'd found her pinned to the wall by the Scooby's guy.

No sooner had Whisper put the phone down than it began to ring, saving Beeks from answering the question. The lawyer reached for the handset, but her hand got in the way, blocking him from picking it up.

Beeks looked up at her. "It's an internal line. Look at it."

Doing as he suggested, she read the digital display, which said "internal." That didn't really mean anything. A phone could be programmed to display anything. The joy of the night was gone. Whisper couldn't go out to enjoy the music and alcohol knowing Beeks could call his McDade master any time.

Relaxing her arm to take her hand out of his way, she watched him pick up the receiver and slowly raise it to his ear. Only once it was there did he lower his attention.

"Beeks," he said into the phone. "Yeah… Okay. Give me a minute." He hung up and stood. "There's a problem at the door." He took his suit jacket off the back of the chair to put it on. After that, he reached down to press a button on the keyboard, switching the screen to black again. "Can I trust you alone in here for a few minutes?"

"Sure," she said, bouncing aside when he began to walk away.

"I'll just be a few minutes," he said, fixing his collar. At the door, he stopped to look back at her. "Please, Whisper."

She smiled and dropped into the seat. "Take your time."

With little other choice, Beeks opened the door and went out into the noise and humidity of the thumping club. Once the door was closed, she smiled and planted her hands on the desk. She might not have bothered with the computer if he hadn't been so quick to lock it in front of her. If there was something he didn't want her to find, she planned to make the most of her few minutes alone.

THIRTY-ONE

THE CAMERA FEEDS were tempting. Rather than amuse herself watching whatever trouble Score's horny drunks were getting themselves caught up in, Whisper minimized the program and began to look through the rest of the system.

Accounts weren't that interesting. Employee files weren't either. Checking out the browser history was enlightening. Someone had been doing a lot of research on the Doherty family. Not only that night, but on previous nights, like around when she and Zay got married.

Not shocking or incriminating. Whisper already knew that Score was the type of guy who liked to be prepared. Just like she'd said to Shyla, his street name came from his reputation. Score should want justice. His own brand of it. But unless his status was just complete bullshit, she couldn't imagine he'd just walk away from what Parker had done to him.

The guy still had buttons, still had a temper, she'd provoked him enough to see that. Yet…

The word processor yielded more in the way of results. A file near the top of the recent documents simply called "Chrono" drew her attention. Opening it up, she began to read. Drawn closer to the screen, she frowned. Everything in the list related to the McDade family. To what had gone on recently. Whisper hadn't been around for everything. Some of the details came from before she and Zay were married. Reading the dates and the notes in the table, she recognized the weekend the McDade-Doherty alliance intercepted the Byrne shipment. The weekend she'd cleaned up men from both sides.

Score hadn't been a part of that. As far as she knew. Whisper hadn't heard his name often in the McDade house, yet there was information about deals and conversations that took place there. Not only did it include events Score hadn't been a part of, it also included notes of contact he had with Burl. Phone calls. Emails. What was discussed. What was advised. On top of that was detailed information about tasks carried out for Burl including figure amounts of cash cleaned through Score.

Whisper didn't like it. She didn't like scrolling through pages and pages of information laid out for anyone to see. Anyone to find. Score should know better than to commit any of it to paper. Especially on a computer. Paper could be burned and destroyed, files on a computer were never really gone. They could also be accessed by anyone on the outside. Anyone who wanted to amuse themselves by hacking into his system would have years' worth of blackmail material. Sure, going against the McDades meant taking one's life in their own hands, but delving into a McDade system in the first place suggested desperation.

More than a few minutes passed; Beeks still didn't return. In the back of her mind, Whisper was aware that could mean he was doing more than just defusing an altercation. At the same time, she wanted to maximize her opportunity to read the details of her spouse's family presented in the document.

Printing and stashing it would be the best route. Trouble was, she couldn't see a printer around and the document was almost a hundred pages long. That would take some time to print... maybe more time than she had.

The phone would be a great help. Except she'd left her own cellphone at Score's apartment and didn't know either Zay or Bosco's numbers off the top of her head. They could be saved on the phone itself, though she doubted it. Before finding the document on the computer, Whisper would've thought Score would be too smart to leave evidence of his connections lying around. Apparently, she'd have been wrong.

Skimming the text, it became obvious that she'd never be able to read it all. Quickly opening the internet, Whisper logged into her own email and sent the document to herself. Zay probably had email, but she didn't have his address. Sending the information without explanation would confuse the hell out of him and he could get the wrong idea.

Thinking of her husband made her search the file for his name. It didn't appear, not in any of its forms, full or shortened, not his street name either. Parker's name was there, in all of its configurations. Like Zay, Doran's name was absent.

She didn't get it.

Zay had been involved with the operations. For sure at least one of them because she'd been with him that weekend. That was the same weekend Doran had been hurt, so he'd been involved too. Why would Score be cataloguing the events yet omitting his brothers' names. Two of them anyway. Why would he include his father and Parker, but skip over Zay and Doran's contribution?

It wasn't a boastful document. The facts were presented in a detached manner. Business, not personal. Few observations were noted. The details were fascinating, but laid out in a fashion that suggested they were being relayed to a stranger. There wasn't any familiarity or anything that gave any hint as to the author's opinion.

With the way it was written, she could only guess that Score was the author. Maybe Beeks, definitely not Fish. Shyla? Could be, but how often was she at the club? Whisper didn't imagine it was often. The place didn't have any female flare. If it was another employee, it had to be created at Score's instruction. Notes like the ones she read were so incriminating, it would—

The office door opened. Torn from her reading,

Whisper turned to see Beeks in the doorway. Standing still, his brow drawn down, he was absorbing her position and what was on the screen. The noise and scent of the club behind him carried to her. She didn't flinch. Apologies weren't on her mind, not from her side. If he wanted to, Beeks could sure apologize to her.

After recovering from his surprise, Beeks came inside and closed the door. "What are you doing?"

"What does it look like?" she asked, slouching against the back of the chair to give him an even clearer view of what was on the screen. "I'd really love to hear your explanation for this."

Beeks rushed to the desk and went around her to lean over and close the file. Didn't matter, she wouldn't get to read any more of it now that she'd been discovered. The whole thing was winging its way to her email anyway.

"How did you get into the system?"

"I don't think that's really the issue," she said, rising from the seat to put space between them. "The issue is what it's for. Obviously you knew it existed. You didn't even read it, but you knew from the other side of the room what it was."

"None of your business," he said, taking her place in the seat. "You shouldn't be spying on us. When Score—"

"What?" she asked, stopping on the opposite side of the desk. "When you tell on me, he'll be mad? He's mad anyway. I didn't have to do a damn thing, he hated me on sight." Because he hated her name. "And what the hell do you think my husband will do when I tell him his brother is keeping tabs on every little thing the family does. What the hell is Score's plan? Blackmail? I'm guessing it's something to do with his scheme to ruin Parker 'cause he was never just gonna let the death row thing go…"

Something about ranting aloud realigned her thoughts. One terrifying prospect chilled her through to her bones. Her words were gone. Whisper wasn't sure she'd be able to pick them up again even though her mouth was slowly opening.

"You shouldn't be here," Beeks said. "You shouldn't be here and you shouldn't be looking at other people's computers.”

“Oh my God,” she whispered, finally able to speak again. “He’s gonna testify.”

The sentence had come out all on its own. Her mind hadn’t even caught up with her voice. Beeks’ attention snapped from the screen to land on her. For a lawyer, he had a lousy poker face. She’d caught him off guard, both with her actions and with her deduction.

A sudden urge to flee struck her. Getting out of the club would be the first obstacle. She had to get to Bosco then get out of the apartment, out of the state. Zay, she had to tell him and…

“Whisper…” Beeks said.

She’d begun to retreat toward the door, walking backward, maintaining her focus on him. “Stay where you are,” Whisper warned.

“Please you have to stay here, you have to listen.”

“No, I don’t,” she said. “Zay sent us here because he trusted his brother to look after what he cares most about. How the hell does…” She couldn’t wrap her head around it. “How could he do this?”

“To his family?” Beeks asked. “Look what his family did to him.”

“Parker,” she said, pausing a few feet in front of the door. “What Parker did to him and what Burl let his son do. Zay wasn’t involved. Doran wasn’t involved. He plans to take down every McDade for what they did.”

Anger heated every single atom vibrating through her. Whisper couldn’t believe it. All her life, all their lives, they followed a set of rules. The first one was to never turn against the family. Doing anything which could undermine or weaken the family was a cardinal sin.

The instinctiveness of her reaction came from her father. From her brothers. From her family. She shouldn’t care that the McDades would be ruined. Burl and Parker deserved everything they got, but Zay, her husband, the man who’d loved her from afar for so many years…

“You should hear him out,” Beeks said, ascending onto his feet one slow inch at a time. “Don’t jump to conclusions, you have to—"

"Talk to my husband," she said. "If I can. What's the plan? When are the feds swooping in for their arrest?"

"It's not as simple as that."

"What an idiot," she snapped, still fuming so much that thinking straight or even listening was difficult. "What kind of an idiot leaves a file like that lying around for anyone to see?"

"No one left anything lying around," Beeks said. "You were snooping where you shouldn't have been."

"Please," she said, holding up a hand as she exhaled her disgust. "Do not make this about me. All the damn McDades and their buddies are determined to blame everyone else. If that wasn't there to find, I wouldn't be this mad and you wouldn't even know that I'd touched your precious computer. This is about Score, about what he's doing wrong—"

"And what would that be?"

The bass of Score's voice so close to her back brought her whirling around. Somehow he'd snuck up behind her. Zay was good at the sneaking thing too, but he didn't usually have to contend with concealing the sound of a nightclub. She hadn't been listening, she wasn't paying attention. The shock of the truth sent her senses careening off in a dozen directions of their own.

"I'm out of here," she said, snatching for her confidence.

Before she got so much as one step around Score, he had hold of her arm. McDades weren't gentle, but he had some nerve dragging her across the room to throw her down on the couch. The asshole was turning on his own kin, yet he had the audacity to treat her as the aggressor.

"I should've put a bullet in you the minute I set eyes on you."

Shoving up from the couch, she swept her hair aside and didn't blink as she sought his gaze. "Maybe you'd have done both of us a favor. Shame your fed buddies wouldn't like that."

Without giving up his position of blocking her in, he

looked to his friend at the desk.

"I don't know how she did it," Beeks said. "She found the chronology."

"Yeah, and from there it was a quick hop to figuring out what it was for. Parker was the one who screwed you over. Biz acted on his own. Zay told me he didn't know anything about it at the time and I believe him."

"So do I," Score said, his voice no less threatening despite its calmer hue.

Whisper hadn't expected him to agree with her. "Then why the hell would you take him down? Him and Doran trust you. If Zay didn't trust you, he wouldn't have sent me here… Maybe you don't believe he cares about me, but would he have sent Bosco? They've been close for years."

"Since Bos pulled Zay out of one of his own fires."

She didn't know about that. Score still wasn't looking at her, he considered his lawyer friend who remained tense and wide-eyed. Maybe he didn't want to witness the murder Score was considering.

"You can't keep me here forever," she said, deciding that escape was more important than answers. "Kill me or let me go."

If he chose the first, he'd have a lot of explaining to do. Bosco would wake in the apartment and ask for her. Zay would eventually call and want to speak to his wife… even if it was from a jail cell.

"I pick door number three," Score said, bringing his focus back around to her. "I'm gonna make you listen."

Usually people abducted or imprisoned others to make them talk, not to make them listen. If her brother-in-law thought he'd convert her or force her to turn on her husband, they'd be there for a while. Bosco would wake in a few hours. Score couldn't keep her there against her will indefinitely. Either he had to present her to Bosco or explain her disappearance.

Score could try to convince him that she'd run off on her own. Zay wouldn't accept that so easily. Even if he believed it, that didn't mean he'd let her off the hook. Her husband would find her, one way or another, dead or alive. If it was the former and he found her before Score executed his plan, he'd need divine intervention to save him from her husband's wrath.

THIRTY-TWO

"YOU CAN TALK at me from this millennium to the next," Whisper said. "Nothing will change."

"You think," Score said, walking away from her and across to the desk.

Despite Beeks being older, he leaped out of the executive chair to make way for Score to sit down.

"What do you think you can say to change my feelings on this?" she asked. "We don't squeal. No Doherty would even consider testifying against their own blood."

Whisper didn't blame him for being angry with his brother. She didn't know how many exactly, but Score had lost years of his life to prison. Years he wouldn't ever get back.

A bunch of people on the street, and probably more than a few ignorant civilians, still connected the name Score McDade to death row… with murdering a woman who'd shared his bed. That would be a tough pill to swallow for anyone, especially when it was fed by his sibling.

Zay was quick to reject any notion he was like his father. Hence why he'd refused to kill her on request. It was possible Score felt the same way. Whatever his reason, Score had a right to take revenge against Parker, maybe Burl too. Still, nothing would change her mind about his betraying her husband.

"Few months ago, you'd have said Dohertys and McDades kill each other on sight."

"A sentiment you subscribed to until today."

"Sometimes things change," he said, infuriating her further with his composure. "My brother trusted me. All I ask is that he do the same."

Whisper didn't know what was truth and what was baloney. Score was a blank page, fathomless in his intensity. Zay might be able to read him, she hadn't been close to him for long enough to trust her gut. She'd never have guessed his intention, never believed it, unless she'd seen the evidence herself.

"Zay might do it," she said, unable to imagine a situation where he'd hang around long enough to hear anything after the phrase *"cahoots with the authorities."* "He might trust you. But I don't."

"You don't need to trust me. You have to sit down and think about what's best for you."

She almost couldn't believe her ears. "For me?" Glancing Beeks' way, Whisper didn't miss the opportunity to be snide. "So much for devotion. This guy can't know anything about loyalty to a partner if he's asking me to turn on mine." Her attention snapped back to Score. "Maybe Parker was right to get you out of the way. What will your precious Shyla think when she finds out your loyalty doesn't run deep?"

"Shyla knows about all of this," he said, resting his elbows on the arms of the chair. "I don't lie to Shyla."

Didn't mean he included her in all of his decisions either. Being told or commanded wasn't the same as being involved or respected.

"I don't believe it. Shyla loved her grandfather, she told me. She would never have turned on him. But that's exactly what you're doing. You're betraying your family."

His expression grew harder, his brow strengthened over his dark eyes. "Listen to yourself. Listen to what you're defending. You're sitting there, talking about my betrayal, when you've done the same thing to your own family." Her mouth opened, though she said nothing. "Your father didn't want you, he threw you to his enemy. All he wanted was what he could get. I'd bet this club that he didn't have a damn clue that Zay felt anything for you."

The tone of his words implied he wasn't all that sure his brother really did feel for her. The world was so upside down that she was in no hurry to argue that truth.

"My father chose to hand me over to Zay," she said. "Just like he'll choose to kill me if I go back and tell him the alliance is over. My father betrayed me."

"My father betrayed me," he said. "My brother did too."

"So that gives you the right to destroy people who had nothing to do with Parker setting you up?"

His head shook slightly. "I have no intention of hurting Zay or Doran," Score said, opening a hand toward the computer. "Did you see anything that incriminated either of them?"

Whisper wasn't stupid and had made that observation without his prompting. Still, she wasn't naïve and was surprised to learn Score was. "They live in that house with Burl and Parker. They can't claim ignorance."

"Sure they can. I didn't always tell Shyla the complete truth. She lived with me and knew nothing about this club or what I was doing with Burl."

Burl adored his son. He knew of the animosity between Score and Parker, which was why he didn't force the former to return to his place in the family. But Burl still wanted his input, wanted his opinion and guidance. Whisper had been told that Burl was in regular contact with Score, always conscious of including his perspective in decision making. The Chronology document provided further evidence of that.

When the feds did swoop in to take Burl down, it would be a sight to see. Whisper wouldn't be there to witness the moment he learned of Score's betrayal. Imagining it wouldn't do the spectacle justice. Seeing that would almost make the treachery worth it.

"Shyla doesn't share our background," Whisper said.

"No, but she's not stupid either," Score said. "If Zay

and Doran plead ignorance, the feds won't be able to prove anything in court."

"Burl and Parker will incriminate them."

"I'd be surprised if either say a word," he said. "That's the advantage of arrogance. They will always believe they'll get off, that they'll be set free on appeal even if there's an initial conviction. Both will assume that they'll be running the business again one day."

True. If Burl could screw his son's wife in the house they all shared and still believe he'd get away with it, the man was capable of convincing himself of anything.

"They'd sacrifice anyone for their own freedom."

"Not like they have the best credibility," Score said. "Though there is an alternative."

An alternative to working with the feds? When Score looked to Beeks, Whisper followed his line of sight.

The lawyer licked his lips before speaking. "We have contacts. People we've been working with for some time… Agents who know what's going on… who trust us."

That point was debatable. How anyone in law enforcement could trust Score McDade was beyond her. Maybe he hadn't committed the murder he'd done time for, but he had committed others. Whisper didn't need details to be sure of the veracity of that.

"What do I care about your buddies?"

"You probably don't," Beeks said.

"Because she's not thinking past her anger," Score said. "What he's saying is, the case gets stronger the more of us there are."

She frowned. "Us?"

"Brothers."

The McDade brothers. The more of them… Incredulous didn't begin to describe her shock. "You want Zay to join you? You think there's even the slightest chance—"

"Would you use your head?" Score snapped. "You're so fucking determined to be angry that you can't see how this works for you."

"For me?"

Planting his hands on the desk, he pushed up out of the chair. "You're a target. For the Dohertys and for the McDades. Whatever the hell you think Zay is going to say to Burl doesn't matter a goddamn. Do you think there's any chance Burl will just let you walk away? With Zay? You think he'll let you take Zay from him? Burl needs people to control. He needs people to do his dirty work. You might think Zay choosing you is some big romantic whatever when the truth is, if he even tries to walk away, Burl will do everything in his power to pull him back. That means the end of you, Doherty. Burl erases you, Zay has no reason to leave."

"If Burl lays a finger on me, Zay would never forgive him."

Shoving his hands from the desk, he straightened up and folded his arms. "My brother always did go for beauty over brains." He spat out a sound of disgust. "Burl won't do it himself. Fuck, look how Parker set me up; no one knew for fucking years it was orchestrated by him. Putting you in prison would be too much effort. They don't care about you that much. So they take you out. Make it look like an accident, maybe even get it done by your own side. That would make Zay real mad. Mad enough to go back to his family and dedicate himself to ending every Doherty. Burl would be thrilled to help him out."

Gritting her teeth, Whisper listened to her breathing. She couldn't object. Couldn't argue that Zay would keep her safe or that Burl wouldn't be that conniving. Of course he would. Even if the McDades did let her go, there was no way Cyrus would. Zay intended to confront his father. To tell him that he planned to be with her, even against the patriarch's wishes.

The other part of the plan involved revealing the affair to Parker. Either Parker would accept it or he'd join Zay and Doran in spurning the family. Doubtful. Whisper wouldn't be able to trust him. Parker would probably have notions of ousting his father in that scenario. He wasn't going to retire to the beach and live happily ever after with the cheating Nicole.

If Parker took over, either by killing or incriminating

Burl, he might expect Zay and Doran to help him maintain the McDade empire. He may still want Doran to marry Madison. If the youngest McDade was dead against that, maybe they'd find another way. However it panned out, Whisper had no place in the McDade house. Zay could choose to stay loyal to Parker. But after what he'd done to Score, how could any of them trust the eldest McDade brother not to sacrifice them if it pleased him?

"Cooperating with authorities takes them out at the knees. In the worst possible way," Score said. "They'll never see it coming." She wouldn't have. "And it ties them up for years… To strengthen the case, we'd be best to have as many allies from the inside as possible. Allies with firsthand knowledge of the most recent goings on."

Her eyes narrowed. "You can't have been intending to recruit Zay and Doran this whole time."

"No," he said, descending into the chair again. "I hadn't made the decision to consider it until you interfered." But her interference had apparently strengthened Score's hand. "You're not going back there. There's nothing for you. Your loyalty to the McDades is limited to your husband." Whisper wasn't all that sure her brother-in-law believed her fidelity. "You'd be better staying far away from the Dohertys."

His pitch wasn't practiced; it couldn't be if he'd meant what he said about her interference. His intelligence worked fast. He didn't hurry her or race through a speech meant to sway her. The facts were there and she couldn't argue he was wrong. The only way she and Zay would ever have the freedom to be together and not in danger was to get rid of Burl and Parker, who may blame her for revealing the truth of the affair to her husband.

Killing them wasn't an option. It would be easier and much quicker. But it would lead to too many questions, especially if Score's fed buddies were watching. Prison would keep her in-laws out of the way. It wouldn't eliminate the chance of them trying to retaliate, but their options would be limited; especially if Score, Zay, and Doran fostered their own connections on the streets.

Lost in her thoughts and trying to figure out every

possible eventuality, Whisper sank down onto the couch. "He's been closing accounts," she murmured. "Bosco will have the details, but Zay has been… He's been letting people go." Something Score understood the significance of if she read him right. "Whoever those people are, they might think they owe him a favor."

Not all of them, but some would be grateful for their freedom from the McDade yoke.

"Maybe they'd want to tell their story."

She shrugged, though it had been more of a statement than a question. "Zay won't go for it," Whisper said, second guessing herself. "I don't even know how you would… How you would raise it with him."

"I wouldn't," he said, which seemed like a contradiction. "But you could."

Her smile was slow though her mind connected the dots in a second. "So if he doesn't go for it, he thinks *I'm* disloyal?" Whisper shook her head. "No. No way."

Half a minute went by before Score took a breath. "Do you remember what Shyla said today?"

"If she asked you to do something, you'd do it."

"I haven't seen you and Zay together. I didn't know he had feelings for you, I still don't know it. But if he does, if you believe he does, he'll do the same for you."

In just the short time she'd been a McDade, Whisper had gotten embroiled in the deepest mire of the family's politics. Her first thought wasn't for Zay's counsel, it was for Bosco's. Her husband would have an emotional reaction to the topic, either fury or agreement. Hashing out the details, figuring out if it was best for her husband, Whisper needed Bosco for that.

"I have to talk to Bosco," she said.

Score and Beeks made brief eye contact. "You open your mouth to him, you can't put it back in the bottle," Score said. "It will be out there."

Whisper stood up, inhaling through her nose. "I guess you'll just have to trust me."

THIRTY-THREE

IT WASN'T UNTIL Bosco started to yell that Whisper realized she'd never heard him raise his voice. Her belief that he was mild-mannered and any kind of pacifist were brought into question when he went on a rant about her sneaking out and snooping on Score's computer.

She guessed that he fixated on that because her suggestion of recruiting Zay and Doran to Score's cause didn't go over too well.

Bosco wasn't the only one revealing hidden qualities. Whisper's ability to remain calm and be diplomatic surprised even her.

Score didn't trust her, but since she'd discovered his intention, he had no other option. Killing her or casting her out would lead to too many other problems.

Score, Beeks, and Whisper all stayed at the club until closing. She'd have returned to the apartment earlier, except Score kept her in the office. He wasn't forceful about it, not physically, but any time she mentioned going home, he rejected the idea. That was how she knew he still didn't trust her.

Shyla had been waiting up for them to return. Well, her and Score anyway… probably more likely Score. Beeks went back to his own place, wherever that was, after assuring them he'd return to Score's apartment later that day.

While Shyla and Score stood toe-to-toe in the foyer of the apartment murmuring to each other, Shyla removed his jacket. Despite their serious expressions, probably related to Score's revelations of the night's events, there was something charged about the moment that made Whisper feel like she was intruding.

So instead of hanging around perving on them, she'd gone to the third bedroom, where Bosco had been sent to sleep. She'd considered waking him and having the conversation there and then, but after lying down next to Bosco's slumbering form, Whisper had drifted off to sleep. He was more like a brother than a boyfriend, so her lifelong streak of never sleeping with a guy was safe.

Bosco's exclamation of surprise had woken her. He'd been going on about how she was supposed to stay where Score put her and how unhappy Zay would be to learn she was sleeping with other men. That made her tale of the night seem all the more dramatic. As her friend had slept, Whisper's discoveries had changed all of their paths.

After she recounted the story of the previous night, he read her the riot act. It took some time to calm him down and fill him in. Her ability to handle his objections and convey Score's perspective also gave her a chance to think the situation through.

Neither of them could guarantee how the situation would play out. Even Bosco wasn't sure how Zay would react to the suggestion. Her gut reaction had been angry and accusatory. Bosco dealt with the news by focusing on aspects that did make sense to him—like her not doing as told.

After a good couple of hours of arguments and discussion, she and Bosco were still at an impasse.

"Think they've got coffee in this place?" Whisper asked.

Bosco shrugged and pushed his shoulders from the window he'd been leaning on. "Let's go find out."

As she stood from her seat on the bed, he put a heavy arm around her shoulders and they left the bedroom. Shyla was in the kitchen, Score and Fish were seated at the kitchen island, much like the pair had been when they'd arrived.

Shyla and Fish stopped to watch her and Bosco's progress down the living area. Score wasn't as interested.

"Coffee?" Shyla asked.

"Thanks," Bosco said and relayed how they both took it.

Whisper went to the window beyond the dining table. Staring out into the sunshine, she wished life could be so simple. Simple as the sun and the sea. Everything looked so happy from that perspective. Inside, she was anything but.

"Reach any conclusions?"

Shyla's voice came from right next to her. Whisper glanced her way and took the proffered coffee. Bosco was seated at the dining table. As she took a sip from the steaming mug, he answered Shyla's question.

"Too many," he said. "Sounds like a great plan in theory."

"It's more than that," Score said, though he still didn't bother to turn around.

He had coffee in front of him and his phone in hand. Didn't seem like he was dealing with the same turmoil they were, which angered her.

"We didn't ask to be pulled into this crap," Whisper said. "This is your crap, McDade. Not our crap."

"If you love your husband, it is your crap," he said like he wasn't so wild about that.

In her conversation with Bosco, something had become clear. It wasn't something she'd voiced to anyone, but Whisper was certain. She didn't want to influence her husband's decision.

Something like this could thrust him back into line with Burl and Parker. If he despised Score for his collusion with authorities, Zay could realign with the patriarch to rebel against it, to hold the empire up while Score tried to tear it down.

The alternative was that he cooperated. That he went along with his brother's plan, gave the feds what they needed, maybe even stood up in court against his own blood. Any ideas from the previous night about that scenario offering them relief had become dark. Wanting freedom from the McDades was selfish. Whisper didn't like Burl. Simple as that. Maybe because the man was too like her own father. He personified everything she despised about the life they all led. Driven by his own selfish needs and desires, the man deserved to be brought down.

Score's beef with Parker was his own. Whisper wouldn't lose any sleep over whatever happened to him. But she did care about what happened to her husband. What life could they hope to lead if, in a few years, he came to regret what he'd done? Being free was one thing, but what would come after? Where would they live? What would they do for money? She didn't know the details of Zay's financial solvency. If it was anything like hers, it relied on her father's whims. The feds would probably tie up the McDades cash, freezing it pending investigation at least. Then what? Were they to live with Score forever? The man might tolerate his brother. He wouldn't tolerate her.

Then there was Doran. He'd be in the same position as them. All of them. Bosco lived in the McDade house. He relied on them for an income, he had to.

"This will never work," she murmured, interrupting the discussion that had been going on between Score and Bosco. Turning around, her eyes met each of theirs in turn. "It won't work." She exhaled and put her cup on the table. "We should get out of here, Bos."

Nicole wasn't around, Whisper had no idea where the other McDade wife was. Score wouldn't have let her go far.

"Where are we going?" Bosco asked when she started around the dining table.

That was a valid question. Didn't mean she had an answer. "We'll go to the airport and get a flight." To anywhere. She paused at the mouth of the hallway. "I'll need my blade back."

Because she wouldn't go anywhere without it. Their cases were still stacked in the laundry room. Whisper pulled hers out and crouched to root around for clothes. If Score would allow them to shower, she'd use what could be their last opportunity for a while to clean up.

"I can't imagine what you must be going through."

Twisting to look up at the female who'd spoken, Whisper didn't so much as smile at Shyla. "Yeah, right," she said, returning to her rooting. "This the part where we have a heart to heart and become best of friends?"

"I don't know. Maybe," Shyla said. "Shouldn't really matter whether you like me or not. We've both made our positions clear."

Whisper exhaled a laugh and zipped her case after scooping her clothes onto her lap. "You were in a pretty damn fine position when I left last night," she said, standing up, her clothes bunched in her arms. "Couldn't tell if Score was fucking you or murdering you."

Shyla's shoulders moved a fraction. "You must miss Zay."

Breathing in, she shrugged. "We'll catch up with each other eventually."

"You're amazing," Shyla said, her eyes narrowing. "No matter what you just… everything just rolls off you."

Best she could do was show exaggerated sympathy for the naïve woman. "You're sorta sweet. Like a cartoon. You've never lived in the real world at all, have you?"

"Just because our worlds were different growing up doesn't mean we can't identify with each other."

It was beginning to bug Whisper that the woman was in the doorway, blocking the exit. Wasn't that she couldn't shift her if she wanted to, but her brother-in-law wouldn't like her threatening the brunette beauty again. Twice in two days was maybe a little much.

"Look, Shyla," Whisper said on an impatient sigh. "I need to take a shower. You want to say things at me so you can tell Score you gave it a shot, go for it. But can I shower while you do it? It would really help me out if we could multitask."

"If you have nowhere to go, what's the hurry? There will be flights available no matter what time you get to the airport."

"The more distance I can put between myself and my

past, the better," Whisper said, moving up close to Shyla, expecting her to move out of the way.

"You know what you're running from," Shyla said. "You've probably been running from it your whole life." One thing Whisper despised to hear was pity, especially when it was aimed her way. "But what are you running to? It's not your husband, you can't be going back to the McDade house. Why take Bosco? If you want to be rid of the McDades—"

"This is not about being rid of them," Whisper said. "I have to leave. It's the only way to protect my marriage."

The revealing answer caused Shyla to become more discerning. "So that's what you think."

"What I think is none of your business," Whisper said. "I'm guessing Nicole is still locked up tight in the same bedroom she was in last night, so I'll use Bosco's shower."

"You think bringing it up with him will turn him against you?" Shyla asked, neither moving nor responding to what Whisper had said. "Your marriage isn't that secure if you can't communicate with him."

"You know nothing about my marriage or my husband."

"Maybe not," Shyla said. "But I know about my relationship with my McDade, as you call him."

Any hint that the little woman was laughing at her would be a mistake. "Think it's clear one McDade isn't like another," she said, then raised her chin. "Though I guess maybe they're not that different. I was going to comment on Parker sending his brother to jail, but Score plans to do the same thing. They're not that different after all. Are you going to move or do I have to move you?"

"If they're the same, what makes you think Zaiden is so different? Could be he's happy to send his brother to prison."

Leaning closer, Whisper put her face near to Shyla's. "You're so sure about that, tell your honey to call him up and share the special plan… If Score's so ready to let me do the asking, why won't he do it himself?"

"Score used to be close to Zay. Just like he and Doran were close. He lost a lot during his time in prison, but he didn't lose his loyalty to them. Why do you think he didn't mention them in any of the notes?"

"How the hell do I know?" Whisper asked. "I don't care. I don't care about his plan. I don't care about his buddies. I don't care about his loyalty."

She tried to muscle past, but Shyla pushed herself against the door frame to stay in the way. "If you didn't care, you wouldn't be this emotional."

"I'm mad," Whisper said. "You said it yourself, I'm always angry. Well done, whatever, now get the hell out of my way."

Without being polite about it, she shoved her clothes into one arm and used the other to thrust Shyla aside. The woman was an idiot if she thought Whisper would respond to some kind of sisterly appeal. She'd never had a sister. Never wanted one. The last few days had taught her how important it was not to be influenced by others… or to do the influencing.

Stalking up the hall, she intended to go to Bosco's shower, just like she'd told Shyla. Except as she passed the foyer, the elevator doors opened, taking her by surprise. On instinct, she stopped to see who was arriving, figuring at the last second it was likely to be Beeks. He was the only one of Score's posse she hadn't seen since coming from Bosco's room.

Her mouth swung open when she absorbed the identity of the guy in the elevator. There was someone behind him, but Whisper couldn't tear her gaze from the man in front.

He marched across the lobby, reached around her head and grabbed a handful of her hair to yank her head back. "I can't leave you alone for a fucking second," he said then bowed to plant his mouth on hers.

Whisper didn't know why her husband had come or how he'd known that she was about to leave. At a loss, she didn't even realize she was responding to his kiss until his tongue curled around hers to beckon it into his mouth.

Confused, tense, angry, whatever she'd been before didn't matter. The clothes in her arms must have fallen to the floor because her hands were free to grab hold of his neck.

Yanking him down, she felt his resistance and used it to bounce off the floor and coil her legs around him.

It shouldn't be right to need him, to want him with such a ferocious heat, but all of her screamed for him. She hadn't realized it, but she'd been screaming for him since the moment they'd parted.

"You want to take a left and keep on walking," Bosco said, somewhere in the background. "You'll find the bed from there."

Loving her friend and eager for her lover to follow the instructions, she dug her nails deep into him. Instead of turning or traveling the path Bosco suggested, Zay ripped his mouth from hers.

Whisper fought it, her lips still craved his, but he used his grip on her hair to jerk her away. "I came because they said you needed me," Zay said, fierce in his intensity. "Tell me what you need, wife."

"I want you to take a left and keep on walking."

His attention fell from her eyes to her mouth. He wanted her. She was coming to understand that he always wanted her, yet an internal conflict raged behind his eyes. Her husband wanted to satisfy their desires, but he'd been summoned, apparently, and wanted to get to the bottom of what was going on.

THIRTY-FOUR

"WHAT'S GOING ON?" Zay asked. "Tell me and you'll get it." When Whisper didn't respond, he looked beyond her toward the kitchen island. "You told me to come."

"And you did," Score's voice came from behind her.

Exhaling, Whisper loosened the lock of her legs and slithered down her husband to put her feet back on the floor. He didn't let her walk away. Instead, he clamped an arm around her, holding her to his side.

Shyla was standing just inside the kitchen. She must have followed Whisper out of the laundry room. After leaving there, everything else was hazy. Fish wasn't sitting at the island anymore. Either he was watching Nicki or running an errand. Possible he'd just run for his life when he saw an opening. With the madness of this place, Whisper wouldn't blame him.

"You're not angry anymore," Shyla said, smiling at her.

Whisper wasn't sure she liked the knowing look in the woman's eyes or the not-so-secret satisfaction they held. She might have lashed out at the comment if she didn't suddenly realize that Shyla was right. The tension. The ball of venom that had been embedded in her gut from a young age, didn't weigh so heavy.

She looked up at Zay who was scowling in the direction of his brother. "You came," she murmured, getting to grips with what was actually happening.

Whisper wasn't naïve to Score's conniving. Zay said his brother had told him to come and that someone had said she needed him. That wasn't exactly true, not by any external measure. Even she hadn't known how his presence would alter her attitude, so no one else could've known it. They'd used her relationship with Zay to lure him there.

Her husband blinked and when his eyes opened on her, the set of his harsh brow was more relaxed. "Why wouldn't I come?"

One side of her mouth rose. "You came because they said I needed you."

"Still don't believe it, do you?" he asked.

Her muscles loosened. "I'm getting there."

"I'm guessing you're Bellamy."

The new male voice brought Whisper's attention around. Doran crossed past Shyla to open a hand to his brother. Score slapped a palm onto his and stood to give the youngest McDade a one-arm hug.

"Please call me Shyla," she said as the brothers parted. "Would you like coffee? Something to eat?"

Shyla rounded the island to produce more coffee as Score returned to his stool.

"She's something, brother," Doran said, his gaze sliding down Shyla and back up. The woman missed the appreciative once over because she was busy with coffee. "Ring looks good on her."

Zay slipped his palm under hers to pick it up and look at her finger. "Looks better on Shyla," Whisper said by way of explanation. "I'm only likely to hock it anyway."

"When you getting hitched?" Doran asked, taking the cup of coffee Shyla offered to him.

Her cheeks flushed and she tipped her chin down, catching a glance Score's way. "Soon," came the deep, certain reply.

"Phoenix," Shyla murmured, probably trying to scold him. It didn't come across as that. The woman was too soft and gentle toward her lover to ever be mad at him. Whisper would bet anyway. "Thank you for coming, Doran."

"No problem," he said, turning in a slow circle to scan the place. "Wanted to check out the boy's digs anyway."

"You know I am actually married into the family," Whisper said. "You weren't this nice to me when we met."

"I offered to take you to bed the first time we met," Doran said without looking her way.

Though Zay tensed, she soothed him by stroking his torso. "Offering a dose of McDade protein was just your way of being crude… Didn't mean you liked me."

"Nicole sure didn't," Doran said, fixating on her. "Where is she?"

Whisper shrugged. "Tied up somewhere, I think."

"She's safe in one of the bedrooms," Bosco said, laying his displeasure on her. "Everyone's too fried to handle your usual feisty self. You didn't get a full night's sleep, so you're probably not at your best anyway."

"That's what sleeping next to you gets me."

"I should never have left you alone," Zay grumbled.

Whisper turned a grin up to him. "I've had a whale of a time," she said, squeezing herself close. "Not sure my hosts would say the same."

"She's very welcome here," Shyla said. "All of you are."

How someone could be so sunny and optimistic all the time was beyond Whisper's comprehension. Being with a man like Score had to take its toll on a woman. The sex sounded fun, but he wasn't exactly a conversationalist. Last night he'd been more accusatory and threatening than calm and interested in debate.

"At least for now," Score said, which sort of proved Whisper's point.

"How did you get down here so fast?" she asked her husband, finally catching up to the surprise. "If Score called this morning—"

"I called last night," Score said. "After we came home from the club."

She couldn't help but glare at him. Of all the devious,

scheming—

"Thought I said no club," Zay said.

He could be as unimpressed as he liked; he'd still come running when he thought she needed him.

"What can I say?" Whisper asked. "I'm curious… I didn't go to the bar in the building, that has to count for something, right?"

No, not by the scowl on Zay's face. He obviously figured there wasn't time to fixate on that and he was right.

"We have to talk," Score said, finishing his coffee and rising to go around Shyla to take the mug to the sink.

He just put it down on the counter, proving he had no intention of washing the thing. His woman went after him, putting herself in the perfect spot to accept his kiss after he slid a finger under her chin to tip her head up.

Whisper's default was to cringe at their easy, almost choreographed affection. Except for some reason—most likely related to the man still holding her—she wasn't disgusted by the sight anymore. Score was an overbearing, arrogant jerk and Shyla was the complete opposite, yet it worked. She didn't know how, but it did.

Sliding her hand from Zay's waist down to his ass, Whisper gave her husband a squeeze. "Want me to show you where Bosco's bed is now? It's empty."

She was occupied, waiting for her husband's response when Score came around from the kitchen to stop a few feet away.

"You've got talking to do too, Doherty," Score said.

"I have packing to do," she said. "If you thought bringing him here would change anything, you're going to be disappointed. I have time for sex if your brother's willing to give it up. If he's not, I'm showering and hitting the road."

"Hitting the…" Zay's arm fell away as he stepped back to look at her. The fact that he was parallel with his brother rankled. It looked like the two men were standing against her. "What's going on, Peanut?"

"Nothing," she said, retreating to swipe her clothes up from where they'd dropped. "I'm done with your brother… figured I'd try somewhere else on for size."

"Whisper," Bosco said.

He was the next to rise to his feet. That brought the count to five against one. She exhaled and opened her arms, clothes clutched in both hands.

"Talk if you want to talk," she said, sort of bowing at them. "I'm going for a shower. I don't want any part of it."

Score was the first to respond. "Doherty, he'll do the same for you."

At the club the previous night, Score had reminded her of what Shyla said about him doing anything for her. Although Whisper thought Zay could maybe be influenced by her, she didn't want to push or cajole him.

She shook her head. "I'll support whatever he decides. I'll always support him. But I won't be the one to ask. I can't do it."

Shyla moved up to Score's side and laid a hand on his arm. "She doesn't want to be responsible for his decision. Don't ask her to use her relationship capital on this… She's worried it'll backfire… If he comes to resent her…"

Zay had said on the phone that it had taken him years to learn Whisper Doherty-McDade, Whisper wasn't sure how she felt about Shyla's interpretation or the speed at which she'd picked up the clues.

"Okay," Score said without even pausing for a second to think or argue with his girlfriend. "I'll do the talking." He pinned a glare on her. "But you stay put until we've thrashed it out."

A compromise. Hmm. Not something Whisper had ever imagined herself coming to with Score. Still, she could be fair. It wouldn't be nice to pose Zay a dilemma before Score even got to telling him about the real cause he wanted his brother to subscribe to.

"Not like I have a hot date," Whisper said and widened her eyes before glancing back and forth between everyone. "Can I get in the shower now? Maybe? Please?" Score nodded once and Shyla relaxed. "Thank you." Her gaze found Bosco's. "Stay with him."

Zay was about to get the shock of his life. The guy looked confused as all hell and she didn't blame him. He'd showed up at his brother's request to help his wife. At least, that's what he'd thought. But it wasn't true.

She offered him a tight smile and then turned to stride up the room. The decision was Zay's; Whisper didn't want any part of it. If he chose to stand with his brother, she'd accept that. As for actually coming to that conclusion? Whisper didn't envy him the quandary.

***

SHYLA WAS STILL in the kitchen when Whisper came out of Bosco's room. She'd taken the longest shower of her life, killing time and hoping to stay out of the vicinity of the brothers' discussions. Only seconds after walking into the living space, the vibration of raised voices carried through the apartment.

Shyla paused to wince. "It's been coming and going."

Whisper continued toward her and eventually put her butt in the central island stool. "You're really okay with this," she said, watching Shyla mix something in a bowl. "Score said you know what's going on."

"I do," she said. "It's like you said, we support them in whatever they decide."

Though it went against her nature, Whisper sucked up her discomfort and forced herself to say the difficult words. "Thank you," she said. Shyla paused. "For backing me up with Score."

"He's a good man, you know," Shyla said, stirring again. "I know that hasn't really been your experience, but none of this is easy for him."

"Could've fooled me," Whisper said, selecting an apple from the fruit bowl that hadn't been on the island earlier. "Seems like a pretty sure guy to me."

Shyla smiled. "He's always sure. It's one of the things I love about him. I can be indecisive, uncertain… He gives me confidence, knows how to hold me up, how to… be everything I need him to be."

Whisper nodded once. "Does seem like opposites attract with you two. Never told me how you two hooked up."

Shyla stopped stirring and thought for a moment before putting the bowl down and wiping her hands. "He made it happen. I would never have made a move on him, never in a million years. I didn't even know he was attracted to me… not for sure." Coming closer, she propped a hip on the island and hid her not-so-secret smile like she'd tried to before. "I was so nervous… Sometimes I still am. The way he makes me feel is so overwhelming…" Sliding her hip down the island, Shyla edged closer. "Do you ever get that way where you look at them and are just so overwhelmed?"

"I don't look at Score and think that." Whisper took a bite from the apple and shrugged. "He's hot, but my husband wouldn't like that, you know?"

Shyla's slight smile came with a head tilt. "With Zay. He's yours. All yours. If he didn't feel the same overwhelmed way, he wouldn't have abandoned his plan to get to you. He came down here for you and dragged Doran along, doesn't that mean anything to you?"

That being a McDade, or more accurately Mrs. Zaiden McDade, wasn't a straight forward transaction. It was going to be a lifetime deal. Staring down into her apple, Whisper frowned at herself. A lifetime. Once that hadn't meant much. The future wasn't something she spent a lot of time considering… not until Zay.

But she was thinking and she was wanting. Him. A future with him.

A door opened and a loud bang followed like it had hit the wall. Fast, heavy footsteps came up the hall. The moment Zay came into view, she leaped from her stool, casting the apple aside.

He paused and looked to her. "We have to talk."

THIRTY-FIVE

WHISPER COULD TELL he was angry. His tension had been apparent from the second he'd grabbed her hand and dragged her away from the kitchen stool. As far as she knew, he hadn't been in Bosco's bedroom, yet he found it without wavering and marched on inside.

He'd tossed her onto the bed and gone back to slam the door. Unfortunately, he didn't join her and went to pace in front of the terrace access instead. Whisper sat up and pushed herself to the middle of the bed to lean back against the headboard. Discovering Score's purpose would hit Zay harder than it had her, so she waited for him to pace it out and process. Whatever he needed, she'd do her best to provide.

"I don't even know what to say," he said, though Whisper wasn't sure he was actually talking to her. "Where the fuck did he get this idea? What the hell would make him…" He exhaled. "This is fucking Parker. The fucking asshole set himself up. What the fuck was he thinking taking Score on?"

That was going back to a time long before her. Funny how far the ripples of one decision could reach and how long they could keep on going.

"Did you talk to them? Before you got here? Parker and your father?"

He shook his head, but kept on pacing. "Doran and me planned to go to them. We were gonna leave today, then Score called…" Zay stopped pacing to set his sight on her. "You figured this out at the club." She nodded once. He ran a heavy hand through his hair. "Geez, baby, you're like a magnet for McDade secrets."

Which could be a positive or negative.

Draping her arms wide on the pillows, Whisper arched her back in a pose that matched her sultry eyes. "A McDade magnet… I think I might like that."

"Why didn't you call me?"

"I wanted to," she said. "I didn't take my phone to the club, for obvious reasons." She didn't want to be tracked. "When I tried to walk out, Score got in my way." His wandering attention snapped back to her. "He didn't hurt me."

"You stayed," he said. "You listened to him."

She shrugged. "Had nothing better to do." Her smile widened again. "Your cock wasn't waiting for me at home."

Zay tilted his head, taking her flirting in his stride. "What did you think? When he told you."

Losing her playfulness, Whisper waited a second before sitting up straight and crossing her legs. "This is about you. About what you feel and what you want. They are your family."

"I know you, Whis," he said, approaching the end of the bed. "You have an opinion."

Downplaying the situation wouldn't be genuine. "Course I do."

"And…"

She shook her head. "You heard Shyla. I don't want to be responsible for this."

"Why not?" he asked, sitting on the end of the bed, twisted around to look at her. "This has to be a decision we make together."

He wasn't wound as tight as he had been. Being with him calmed her too. Still, that didn't mean she could drop her guard.

"No," she said. "If I have any input on this, you can

use it against me later. There's no way I want that to happen."

"You ever think the opposite could be true too? Whichever way this goes, I need you with me. Whatever it takes, I don't want to lose you. I can't lose you."

Score's play would lead to Zay losing someone. Either his father and Parker or Score and possibly Doran. Whisper hadn't considered the opposite, but he was right. If she stayed silent and didn't offer support to hash out his decision, he could come to regret his choice and decide to put the blame onto her.

Taking a deep breath, she crawled down the bed and hooked her linked fingers over his shoulder. "I can't tell you what to do because I don't know how it will turn out either way. If you go against your father and Parker, they could incriminate you. They could put a hit out and cause all kinds of trouble."

"But?"

"Not supporting Score could lead to you being drawn into the web with your father. Even if you aren't or if your father isn't put in prison, he's never going to let you choose me. We'll be looking over our shoulders for the rest of our lives… Score has connections, he's already in contact with the feds. You know they're going to descend on your father eventually. So…" Sitting straighter, she took his hand from the bed to clasp it in both of hers. "We have to pick a side. We have to. We can't know and not warn your father if you choose his side. We could try to stay quiet, but it would be too easy for Score or the feds or whoever to turn them against us just by telling them we knew and did nothing. Then we'd have both sides against us."

"Standing with Score means talking to feds. It means everyone loyal to the McDades turning against us."

She smiled and cast her attention down to their linked hands as she ran her fingers through his. "The people you cut loose, they won't turn against you."

"Bosco told you?"

Whisper met his eye. "Baby, you've wanted an out for a long time. You told me that yourself. You freed those people because you could, because you couldn't free yourself. You did for them what you couldn't do for yourself."

Zay brought a knee onto the bed to twist further toward her. "You've thought a lot about this," he said, combing his fingers through her hair.

"Not really. Score's scheme didn't make sense to me at first either. I was mad. I yelled. I told him he could talk all he liked, he'd never change my mind."

"But he did."

"He called me on my anger, made me see that my initial response was habit. Cyrus might be a long way away, but he's still in my head."

Zay bowed forward to kiss her hairline. "We've gotta work on that."

"We'll get there."

"You know," he said, leaning back to find her gaze. "You talk about *us* now. You talk in terms of *we*."

"Thought that was what you wanted."

Tipping up her chin, he touched his lips to hers. "You're what I want, Peanut."

As though asking him to prove that, she gathered up her skirt to pull her dress up over her head. Once she'd tossed it aside, Whisper slid back on the bed to lie down, presenting herself to him. Her husband didn't need her to say a word. He stood up to pull off his tee-shirt and shirk his jeans. More naked than she was, Zay came down on the bed above her as she wriggled out of her panties.

"We'll need to meet with Score's contact," he said, his mouth hovering above hers.

"Mm hmm," she said, skimming her fingertips up his arms and down his torso. "I don't want you to open your mouth until you have immunity… or at least a deal that won't take you from me."

"Doran too."

Raising her hips to push against his, Whisper writhed. "We have Nicole, what will we do with her?"

"We'll tell Burl we all took a vacation… our honeymoon. He doesn't have to know it's at Score's." His voice was just a deep hum of desire. Kissing her one way and then the other, he pushed his pelvis down to lock hers in place.

"Might only buy us a couple of days, a week at most…"

"Burl will blame me anyway," Whisper said, draping her arms around his neck. "I'm okay with that."

Misdirection could be their best friend. While Burl was busy cursing her for delaying his plans to hook up Madison and Doran, he wouldn't notice the greater scheme at work.

"Means hanging around here a while."

In the glorious sunshine just a stone's throw from the beach in a city with some of the best nightlife in the country, in the world?

Whisper struggled to contain an excited laugh. "There's a three bed place for sale the floor below this one… A four bed place on the floor above."

Something close to a smile moved his lips, which were still sampling hers. "Not that you've looked."

"It was reconnaissance."

That wasn't a lie, she'd looked up the listings the day they got there to figure out the best way in. Just so happened that she remembered the gorgeous apartments that were vacant.

"Not sure I'll have the kinda money to make that dream come true for you, Peanut."

"Score might. Let's face it, he's going to owe you one."

"We'd be his tenants, maybe he wouldn't want us up close."

"We give him the choice," she said, linking her fingers together around his neck. "We can live downstairs as tenants or upstairs as roommates."

Squeezing his hands between her and the bed, he rocked her body against his. "You know how to get what you want, baby."

"I'm trying," she said, taking a shot at reaching for his dick, but their bodies were too close. "Think you want to make me beg."

"That'll come later."

Sliding down her body, Zay got to the point fast. Tasting her, arousing her, he did what any good spouse should, prioritized her over himself. Whisper was learning to put him first too. Having someone to rely on felt nice, still not totally familiar, but she'd get there.

What would come next was a rollercoaster none of them had ridden before. The McDades could rely on each other, the ones present in the condo anyway. Whether all of them would accept her would be another matter.

THIRTY-SIX

THEY GOT TEN DAYS of leeway. It helped that Burl and Parker went off to do some other thing before returning to the city, so they didn't realize no one was home.

Whisper got a better understanding of the loneliness of Nicole's life too. Mrs. Parker McDade knew something was going on, she had to. Still, they couldn't take the risk of cluing her in. Score took Zay and Doran out every day. In front of Nicole, they said it was club business. Whisper and Shyla knew better.

Bosco split his time, probably at Zay's request. He spent a lot of time with the trio of McDade brothers. Whisper liked seeing them together. None of them were exactly warm and fuzzy, and she wasn't sure Score was a fan of hers yet, but there was an enviable ease between them. Despite the fact that Score hadn't been part of the fraternal circle in such a direct way for years, they slid back in to sync with each other without missing a beat.

The responsibility of monitoring Nicole fell on her shoulders. Most of the time that was easy. She'd just lock Nicole out on the terrace with a bottle of sunscreen and a pitcher of sangria. The woman complained the first few times, but quickly figured out that her objections were pointless.

Fish and Beeks lived elsewhere. Whisper wasn't sure where. They always arrived for breakfast, which happened at like two in the afternoon, and were dedicated to Score and Shyla. Both proved useful in their own ways. Fish was young and gullible; she liked that about him. Sometimes it wasn't so bad to have a naïve perspective in the conversation.

On arrival, Whisper would've given that crown to Shyla. But she'd have been wrong. The brunette beauty didn't have Whisper's confidence or her stylish attitude. Her life was dedicated to doing chores and accepting Score's cock any time he wanted to use it. As Whisper was getting in the latter habit with her own McDade, the two women had found common ground.

"It wouldn't be so bad for all of us to live together," Shyla said.

The decision about which condo Score would buy was still up in the air. Whisper wouldn't mind her and Zay finding their own place. Wherever they settled, Bosco would come with them, which was fine too. But even she missed the buzz and activity of the Doherty house. The McDade men would no doubt be the same.

"Whether we live here or not, we're still coming for dinner every day."

Seated together on the terrace, the table between them held a chess set. A new one. Not the one from inside. For some reason, Shyla was protective and particular about that one. But when Whisper had shown a casual interest, Shyla had offered to teach her to play.

"You'd be more than welcome."

Shyla was still smiling at her when Whisper noticed movement in the apartment. Expecting it to be Bosco or maybe Fish, she didn't anticipate seeing both Score and Zay arriving back.

A chill stole the smile from her face. "Something's happened."

Shooting to her feet, she hurried around the patio lounger and went inside. Zay was already halfway across the room, heading her way.

"Peanut—"

"What?" she asked. "What happened?"

Rather than answer, he put his arms around her and pulled her to him. Hugging wasn't their usual way of saying hello and his severe expression was more intense than usual. At least that's what she'd got from the glimpse she'd had before being lost in his embrace.

"Babe," Zay said, curling a hand around the back of her head.

Whisper planted both hands on his chest and pushed hard to get a look up at him. "You're scaring me. What is it?"

Zay glanced at Score who appeared more solemn than she'd ever seen him. Her husband cupped her face to join their gazes. "Your father's dead."

Whisper heard the words. They made sense. Except… they didn't. "What happened?"

"Murdered. Shot."

"By?" she asked because it seemed like an obvious question. Before Zay could answer, Whisper stepped back, out of his embrace. "Forget it, I don't want to know. Excuse me."

Turning around, she strode away, trying not to rush, or at least trying to make it seem like she wasn't rushing. She needed space and air and peace and… Something.

Going into the room she'd been sharing with Zay, also known as Bosco's old room, Whisper went straight out the terrace doors opposite the end of the bed.

It was late. The sky should be dark but was polluted by too much of the light glowing from the bustling city below. People were out there having the time of their lives, without a care in the world.

"Peanut."

If she'd thought about it for more than a second, Whisper would've realized her husband would follow her.

"I'm fine."

"I know that," he said. "You're always fine."

Yeah, she was, and it was good that he'd noticed. His hands rested on her shoulders and slid down to stroke her arms.

"I'm not upset," she said, somehow prompted to talk just by his touch. "He was a horrible man. Cruel. Violent. Sadistic. There's nothing to mourn."

"He was still your father."

"Is that how you would feel if Burl was killed?"

"There's a part of you thinking about retribution, that it's your responsibility to avenge him."

If that was true, Whisper had a helluva long list to work through. "That's not it... I... I think I'm relieved."

Zay stopped caressing her arms. Did that make her a horrible person? Maybe. Probably. Wasn't like she'd ever aimed for any Daughter of the Year award. Her father had grieved her brothers in his own way. His rage over their loss saw his anger fixate on the Byrnes, who were also responsible for the death of her mother.

Yet, Whisper didn't care. Not that she didn't care her family were dead, but that it all seemed so futile. A Byrne killed a Doherty, so the Dohertys picked off one of theirs. It had to end. At some point, someone had to say the killing was too much.

"You should be," Zay said, his hands skimming up to give her shoulders a squeeze. "Can't say I was unhappy. The way he treated you..."

He trailed off as she turned around to face him. "You know there's a chance this could be—"

"Burl?" Zay asked and nodded. "Score left a message for him to call as soon as we got the news."

"How did we get the news?"

"Doran got a call from one of his guys," Zay said. "We left him at the club to come tell you."

"Score didn't have to come with you," she said, tilting her head. "Unless you're worried the McDades might be on the hit list too."

"All I care about is you," Zay said, holding her face again. "I think maybe Score's warming up to you. He was worried about how you'd take the news."

She wasn't so sure and smiled. "Probably worried I'd wreck his apartment or hurt his girlfriend."

He bowed to kiss her. "Don't be too sure about that,

Peanut."

They were still enjoying each other's mouths when someone spoke. "It was Parker."

Breaking the kiss, Zay turned to look into the bedroom. Score was standing at the end of the bed. If she wasn't still processing what he'd just said, she might have made a mental note to go striding into his bedroom without knocking sometime soon.

"Parker," Zay said. "How do you know?"

"Burl," Score said. "He called back. He's at the airport."

Whisper stepped in front of her husband. "Who's at the airport?"

"Burl."

"Why?" Zay asked. "Why now? Why would he—"

"Burl told him."

The men didn't say anything. Seemed they both understood what that meant; Whisper wasn't fluent in the looks the McDade brothers exchanged. Blinking first at Score, then tipping her head back and around to look at Zay, she waited for one of them to translate.

Neither opened their mouths.

Whisper ran a hand through her hair. "You know, the intense eyes thing really does it for me, Shyla too, but I'm gonna need a little bit more information." Score's brows shifted closer when his attention fell to her. "Not like there's not a whole bunch of stuff going on right now. What exactly did Burl tell Parker?"

"That he fucked his wife." That was low on the list of possible things Whisper would think Burl wanted to confess. "'Parently Parker was having a fit about Nicole. Saying he didn't believe his wife would take off with Whisper."

Tipping her cheek nearer her shoulder, Whisper's eyes left his as they widened. That wasn't a major leap. She had to give Parker some credit for recognizing his wife's animosity toward the newest McDade.

"She didn't take off with Whisper," Zay said. "Me and Doran are with her."

"Yeah," Whisper said, still not looking at either man.

"But unless she thought you were going to fuck her, she'd rather stay at home…" Her head moved the other way. "Maybe that's what Parker was worried about: keeping it in the family."

Zay put his hands on her shoulders again. "You said he was at the airport. Where is he going?"

"He's coming here because he thinks Parker is coming here."

That made even Whisper frown. "Why would he come here?"

"'Cause he's tying up loose ends. Burl said he took a shot at him, they got in some fight," Score said, focusing on her. "Burl told Parker you found him and Nicole together."

"Trying to blame me," Whisper said because it was what they'd expected. "You think he went to my father looking for me?"

"Or because he set up the deal that brought you to Zay," Score said. "Don't know, don't care."

Nice. But she had just told Zay that relief was the emotion overwhelming her. Wasn't like Score owed Cyrus more than she did.

"If Parker's coming here, you better get Shyla—"

"She's packing," Score said. "Beeks is on his way to pick her up."

"I'd send Fish and whatever other muscle you have with her," Whisper said. "If Parker wants to hurt you, she's ripe for the picking."

"I won't let that happen," Score said.

Whisper had never believed a person more in her life. His absolute certainty that he'd protect the woman he loved hit her like a two ton truck. That was love. Real, raw, instinctual love that drove him harder even than his own need for revenge.

"You should go with her."

That from her husband.

Whisper's brows rose as she twisted his way. "What? Are you kidding me? And miss all the fun? No way. If you're staying, I'm staying."

"I already called McNeill," Score said.

"Who's McNeill?" Whisper asked, bumping her butt back against her husband.

"Score's guy at the agency."

"Oh…" It didn't take her long to figure out why he'd been called in. "I suppose it does make sense to take them down now. Parker's delivering himself."

"It'll take him time to get a team in place and all the warrants he needs."

Which left the McDade brothers sitting ducks.

"How long until Parker gets here?" Whisper asked.

"We don't know," Score said. "Maybe he's not coming here at all."

Which would be kind of embarrassing for McNeill, if he swooped in with a whole team ready to take the eldest McDade brother down.

"But Burl's coming," Zay said. "What does he think? You're the next best bet with Parker off the reservation?"

"Maybe. He knows you're out of the running."

"Because of me," Whisper said and narrowed one eye. "I don't think Shyla will be wild about the idea of you going back there, even if it is just to draw Parker out."

"Let me worry about Shyla."

Because everyone had to be good at something. Whisper hadn't realized that she was worried until Score put it that way. She didn't usually care about others wants and desires, not more than her family's. Except, she was it. The whole Doherty family. Dallin would try to step in, but he'd send the whole thing to shit before Cyrus was cold in the ground.

THIRTY-SEVEN

"I HAVE TO GO BACK," Whisper said. "After the Parker stuff is through, I have to go back home."

"Why would you go back? There's nothing there for you," Score said, but only paused for a few seconds before voicing his conclusion. "You wanna take over."

"Yeah, that's what it is," she said with full-on sarcasm. "Please, brother-in-law, I couldn't give less of a shit about the Doherty empire or the McDade one."

"You'll be a suspect," Score said, proving again he had a way of being one step in front of her. "You had most to gain."

"What did I have to gain?" she asked. "My Uncle Dallin and his idiotic sons will try to take over."

"When was the last time Cyrus updated his will?"

Far as she knew… Whisper's thoughts crashed to a halt. Last she'd heard everything of Cyrus Doherty's was bequeathed to his children. Dallin had asked him about his will once, not long after the bloodbath, Cyrus shot him down declaring he wouldn't be following his sons any time soon.

"I don't know," she said, figuring he must have done it despite what he'd said to his brother. "He inherited everything Adan and Keegan had."

"And if you're the only kid left in the will… Unless he stated otherwise, you're his closest living relative."

The Doherty money wasn't all held in the bank, but Cyrus did have a lot of property. Several businesses, all of it was in his name. Everything. Her brothers had some in their names, but that would've reverted to Cyrus after their deaths. Her name was on some of the less lucrative businesses, but she hadn't ever had a controlling interest.

"I can have Beeks look into it," Score said. "If you want him to."

Zay squeezed her shoulders, pulling her from her thoughts. Whisper gave a loose nod.

"Could be you're rich, Peanut," Zay said and kissed the top of her head. "Maybe we can get our own place in the building after all."

Whisper swallowed, still trying to get to grips with what was and what could be.

"Phoenix!"

The feminine shout from elsewhere in the condo startled all of them to attention. Score was first to turn and stalk out. Neither she nor Zay could match the urgency of his gait, maybe because the only person to ever use his first name was Shyla.

As she turned into the apartment, Whisper slowed to a quick stop. Score was a dozen feet in front of her, fixated on the same sight that rooted her to the spot. Zay came up against her back hard. Whisper opened her arms to wind them back around him.

For a score of seconds, maybe minutes, everyone stood assessing each other.

Parker was by the dining table, holding a gun on the woman he had pressed to his chest. It wasn't Shyla, thank god. His hostage was in a pant suit and had a tag on her lapel, suggesting she was an employee. From the fear in her eyes and the tears on her cheeks, Whisper guessed Parker had used his hostage to get from the lobby up into the apartment.

"I shouldn't be fucking surprised that this is where you brought him, Doherty," Parker spat, fixating on her.

"Brought?" Whisper asked, spying Shyla near the

open terrace doors, just inside the apartment.

Score's body had blocked Whisper's view of her before. Either the woman had gone outside to breathe in the night air or had walked around the terrace from their bedroom to the living space. Whichever way it was, Shyla had been the first to see Parker and he must have seen her too.

"What the fuck does she have?" Parker spat, his attention on the man behind her. "You don't have a fucking clue what she's done."

"What do you want?" Score asked, interrupting Parker's wrath. "You didn't know they were here. You came for me."

"You fucking started this."

"You started this!"

Shyla's exclamation took all of them by surprise. An arm rose from Score's side in Shyla's direction, but there was almost the full width of the room between them.

"Go outside, Shy," Score said. "Go through our room."

Their room? Smart. Score was telling Shyla to get the hell out of the apartment without being explicit in front of Parker. If Shyla went onto the wraparound terrace, she could go through their bedroom and creep up the hall to get to the stairwell.

Shyla didn't move more than a few inches before Parker's arm sprang out to aim the weapon her way.

"She stays," Parker said. "All of you stay."

"Please," the woman he was holding against him begged. "Please let me go."

Parker's elbow bent, there was a quick shot and then he was aiming at Shyla again. The lifeless woman dropped to the floor. Though furniture impeded her view, Whisper didn't need to see blood to know Parker had just shown his level of mercy.

Shyla's hands leaped to her mouth. Despite both being layered over her lips, the horrified gasp of surprise still made it out into the ether.

"Who's next?" Parker asked.

The sly smile on his smug, satisfied face was more

than Whisper could tolerate. Without thinking too much about it and before her husband had any chance of getting hold of her, she took a long step away. Heading for Parker, she didn't flinch in response to his threats.

"What is it you want, McDade?" she asked, far enough away from Score that he couldn't touch her either. Not that she'd expect him to hold her back. "You came here to kill Score? His woman? What? You've figured out that Zay and me are here, what about your wife? Wanna know where she is?"

"That bitch is nothing but a pathetic whore," Parker said, his aim still trained on Shyla.

"Maybe," Whisper said, stopping just ten feet from him. Folding her arms, she shrugged. "But are you gonna let the whole world know that Parker McDade is a pussy who let his woman run around on him?" She relaxed her head. "Thought McDade men didn't like their women to cheat."

"Whisper," Zay warned from far behind her.

She didn't blink. "She fucked your father."

"And I killed yours," he snarled.

If he was waiting for a reaction of grief or fear, he would be waiting a long time.

Whisper just kept on going. "I saw it, you know. I watched your daddy fucking your wife… heard how she called out for him, how she begged for more, how good he satisfied her…"

"Shut up!" Parker hollered, swinging the gun around her way.

One of the McDades behind her might have signaled Shyla, or the woman was being smart and taking advantage of Parker's distraction. From the corner of her eye, Whisper noticed Shyla retreat one tiny increment at a time.

"You can kill me," Whisper said. "And Score and Zay and anyone else you want… Then Nicole gets away with it… You'll never find her."

Nicole was in the same bedroom she'd spent her first night in. It would be easy to find her if he took the time to look, but Whisper wasn't going to let him steal any advantage.

"I'll find her," he said. "After I put a bullet in you and

one in Score's whore too."

Shyla froze when Parker's focus leaped back to her. She was right on the threshold of the terrace. The damned glazed walls that she'd so admired were not going to work in their favor even if Shyla managed to get out.

"All women are whores now, huh?" Whisper asked, trying to get his attention back. "Hell, I think I've been missing out on all kindsa fun. I'm the dumb idiot who's been faithful to her husband. I know for a fact Shyla's been loyal to Score… Guess we got with the wrong McDades."

"Shut her up, Zay," Parker called. "You fucking shut her up or I'll fucking kill her."

"I'm not like you," Zay said, his voice coming steadily closer. "I don't demand my woman defers to me. She's fucking strong… Wild? Sure. But she's got balls bigger than yours… bigger than any McDade's."

"Not difficult with the likes of him," Whisper said. "He couldn't outsmart or out maneuver Score, so he took the pussy way out. Setting him up rather than facing him like a real man."

Parker's lips thinned. Whisper didn't mind pissing him off. Actually, she sort of enjoyed it.

"I'm here to do that right now," he growled.

"No, you're not. You're aiming at his woman. Not at him. You're still afraid of him. You should be. Just pointing a gun Shyla's way is reason enough for him to kill you slow. I've seen how much he loves her. You can't even begin to imagine it. Big mistake. So far all I see is you killed an innocent woman to come up here and wave a gun around… that's 'cause you know that short of death, you'll never win against Score."

"He's smarter than you," Zay said, coming up closer behind her than she liked.

Whisper didn't want her husband to be hurt… didn't want any chance that Parker's rage could be directed towards him.

"We can still talk about this," Shyla said. Whisper hadn't expected her to get involved. "No one else has to die."

"Tell me where Nicole is," Parker said to Shyla, no doubt assuming she was the weakest link. "Where is she?"

"Why would we tell you?" Score asked.

It was nice that everyone was coming together in a show of support against Parker. Sort of uplifting, like a corporate team-building exercise… except for the guy waving the gun in everyone's face and the dead body on the floor.

"Tell me or I'll kill your woman," Parker said, pulling back the hammer of his gun.

"And what do you think will happen next if you do that?" Zay asked.

Parker didn't know where to look, so many people were talking at him from slightly different angles and distances that he appeared disoriented. Whisper wondered if he was on something or having some kind of psychotic break. After finding out his father was fucking his wife, she wouldn't blame him for losing his mind.

He shook his head then brought the gun around to her again. "You get over here."

"Oh, I'm the chosen one," Whisper said and raised a foot intending to comply.

Zay grabbed her shoulders, holding her back. "No fucking way."

"Let her go!"

"It's okay," Whisper said, tipping her head to press her cheek to his knuckles. "I'm not afraid of him."

"Let her go or I put a bullet in her," Parker demanded, taking a step their way.

"You lay a finger on her and I'll rip you to shreds."

"She's gonna come over here and sit her ass down."

Parker leaped to the side and yanked a chair out from the dining table. "Long as you have my woman, I'm keeping both of yours."

"She's your woman?" Whisper asked, slipping away from Zay's loosening fingers. "I wouldn't be so quick to claim a gal who spent so much time under your father."

"Shut the fuck up, bitch!" Parker tried to come meet her, but she pivoted out of his path. Whisper wasn't surprised to be quicker, though she was surprised that he seemed unsteady. "I'm gonna end all of you!"

He started to turn again. Whisper went the other way,

confusing him. Crisscrossing meant they passed close to each other; it was then she got the whiff of alcohol. The idiot had come to face his nemesis completely hammered.

Just behind him to the side, Whisper waited to see what he would do next and considered rushing into the kitchen for a weapon. Before she could move, a shot went off. An exclamation of pissed off pain snapped her focus around to land on her husband. Clutching his arm, blood seeped between his fingers.

Somewhere a cellphone rang, Parker glanced around, trying to figure out what and where it was. Whisper was still staring at the blood darkening Zay's hand. Rage equal to nothing she'd ever experienced speared her like a red-hot poker deep in the gut. Pressure built in her head. Nothing except the sight of that blood registered in her consciousness.

Lashing out, Whisper snatched one of the decorative candlesticks from the dining table. Without even thinking about it, she swung it in both hands up and around, smacking Parker on the side of the head.

The fucker went down next to the woman he'd murdered. The candlestick dropped beside them a fraction of a second later. Whisper didn't care about any of the mess, all she wanted to do was get to her husband.

"Baby," she exhaled rushing across to peel his fingers away from the wound.

"It's a flesh wound," Zay said, trying to touch her.

Whisper swept his hand away. "Sit. You need to sit."

"Whis…" he said, a glimmer of a laugh in his voice.

She definitely wasn't amused. Her glare locked onto him. "Few inches the other way and you're in a body bag." With the heel of her hand, she socked his shoulder. "Asshole."

"Careful, Peanut… sounds like you care about me."

Narrowing her eyes, she intensified her glare just a second before snatching his face in both hands and pulling him down for a kiss. Her tongue drove his back into his mouth. Whisper was in charge of that kiss. The fool didn't understand what could've just happened. What it would mean to her to be without him.

Pushing his face away from hers, she kept hold of it.

"You're all I've got, McDade."

A flash of surprise in his eyes made her wonder if she'd revealed too much of herself. In the intense moment, the truth was all she was capable of.

"Yeah… You've gotta…" Score said. Whisper whirled around to see him on the phone, standing over Parker who was still out. "Sure."

Score hung up the phone and tossed it onto the dining table. "Doran's closing the club and calling in the troops. Come help me move this fucker."

Whisper planted a hand on Zay's chest to stop him moving. Her concern lightened his eyes, he really seemed to like seeing her upset.

"Love you, Peanut," he murmured, amusement dancing behind his eyes.

"If you did, you wouldn't be in such a hurry to abandon me."

He bowed to kiss her. "I'll be back for you to play naked nursemaid in a minute."

"Don't hold your breath," she said, stepping aside to let him go help Score.

THIRTY-EIGHT

SCORE USED METAL chains and padlocks to secure Parker in the bathroom attached to the room where Nicole was holed up. A man prepared for every eventuality always impressed her. Not that she was quick to let her grumpy brother-in-law know that.

Shyla gave Whisper medical supplies. So when Score and Zay returned from trussing up their elder brother, Whisper sat on top of her husband to patch up his arm. The bullet had sliced through his skin, tearing just a little of the muscle. Maybe he should've gone to hospital for stitches, but he was happy to let her do it.

The four of them had nothing to do but wait after that. Doran would return and Score had put in a call to McNeill to update him. The feds were on their way. Burl was on his way. Everyone was heading for them and they just waited.

"Feels like we should be doing something," Whisper said, lying on the couch with her head in Zay's lap.

Shyla was kneeling on the floor while Score sat on the opposite couch. The two of them were concentrating on the game of chess they'd started without so much as a word. Whisper hadn't been allowed to touch the glass chess board, now she knew why. A familiar charged energy zapped between the silent couple who kept catching brief glances at each other.

"What do you wanna do?" Zay asked. "You hungry?"

"I was thinking of something more physical," she said, rolling her head to look up at him. "Sex?"

On a shrug, he stroked her hair.

Whisper was about to get up when Shyla spoke. "He's injured."

"I'll cut him some slack if it's not his best work," Whisper said, rising into a seated position.

"McNeill's on his way," Score said.

As though on cue, the internal intercom buzzed. Score stood up to go over to it. The guy never showed much reaction to anything. Zay was good at that too. They just let everything roll off. Only after having the thought did Whisper realize Shyla had said the same thing about her. Looking at her husband, she was struck by their similarities.

Zay parted his lips to inhale as he took her hand. "Remember this guy is a fed… and he'll probably bring feds."

"So don't confess to any unsolved murders," she said, tossing a leg over his lap to straddle him. "Is that what you're saying?"

"Something like that," he said, looking down the front of her dress. "They don't really need us for this part. All they gotta do is setup their crap to arrest Burl."

Whisper pushed her pelvis closer to his, rocking against him. "Mm hmm," she said. "Feels weird not doing something about the body before the feds walk in."

Zay put his good arm around her, skimming a splayed hand up and down her back, pulling her to him. "Just like calling pick-up."

Leaning in, she married their mouths. She'd strapped his injured arm into a sling, so it got trapped between them. Still, somehow he found a way to fondle her breast while pushing her hips close to his.

"Oh, shit."

The new male voice, she guessed, belonged to McNeill. Breaking the kiss, Whisper peeked over her shoulder to see half a dozen guys in plain clothes. The dark haired one in front was next to Score, fixated on the floor, right about where the murder victim lay.

"Concierge from downstairs," Score said. "He used her to get in."

Which would be shown on security footage if they were lucky.

"You couldn't have told me there was a corpse in your apartment?" McNeill asked and stepped aside to gesture at the woman, sending the minions over to her. Score and McNeill wandered their way. "Where's Biz?"

"Wrapped up ready to go," Zay said, drawing attention to them.

McNeill looked from them to the kneeling Shyla, then back to her. "Whisper Doherty," he said, some kind of awe in his tone.

Tilting her head, she wondered about the agent. "Doherty-McDade," she said. "Crime's about to take a nosedive, should our McDades get some sort of award for what they're doing?"

"Maybe, but I hear I owe *you* a debt of gratitude."

Never one to miss an opportunity, Whisper climbed off her husband to turn their way. "Every man should be grateful to be in my presence… that what you're talking about?"

"I hear this operation only stayed together because of you." She wasn't sure who'd said that. It was news to her. "You could've blown the whole thing to hell, but you listened to Score and recruited your husband."

"I wouldn't say recruited exactly," Whisper said, folding her arms when he stopped a few feet away.

Score went to help Shyla up from the floor. The two were murmuring to each other again as Score led her away.

"I was sorry to hear about your father."

She laughed. "Well that makes one of us… I doubt you were a fan of his work."

"You've lost a lot in a very short space of time," McNeill said.

"Gained a lot too," she said, thinking having her

husband's trust, his faith, meant more to her than anything the Dohertys had ever given her. "Hear I could have some legal trouble of my own when I go back north."

McNeill frowned. "You're going back?"

"If you didn't already hear, my father's dead. Soon as I know my husband's situation is stable, I'll have business to take care of."

"Parker confessed to the murder of your father."

"You have that on tape?" she asked, noting his withdrawal. "Yeah, I figured. Wouldn't hold my breath expecting him to confess anything to you any time soon."

"He confessed to us and to Burl," Zay said, standing up behind her. "This wasn't Whisper's crime. She hasn't left the state since we got here."

"Should be easy enough to prove," McNeill said and slipped his hands into his pockets. "Don't suppose I can tempt you into turning over a few Doherty rocks for us."

Whisper smiled. "One step at a time, agent... Let's see how you do with the McDades first."

"We let Burl come to us," Score said, sauntering back their way, now alone. "Maybe we'll get him to verify Parker's confession."

He stopped next to an intrigued McNeill.

"Where's Shyla?" Whisper asked. "She shouldn't be alone, even if Parker is chained up."

"Unpacking," Score said. "Doran is on his way up with Beeks and Fish."

"I still think you should get her out of here," Whisper said, feeling protective of Shyla in a way she'd only ever felt with Mariana and Paula. "None of us can guarantee how this will go down."

"We'll do what we need to with the victim and take Biz out of here," McNeil said. "Then we'll just need an hour or so to rig the place... Burl's plane's still two hours out."

Plenty of time. After landing, he'd have to make his way out of the airport and it was still a half hour drive to the apartment building. McNeill retreated, presumably to give his guys updated orders.

"Time to get Shyla out of here then," Whisper said,

giving Score a pointed look. "You don't do it, I will. No way she should be anywhere near Burl for anything."

Zay slid his hand from her shoulder along her collarbone to draw her back against him. "She has a thing about protecting people who can't take care of themselves. Especially women."

"I do not," she said over her shoulder.

The problem was, when Whisper tried to come up with an example that would contradict him, she came up blank. Even learning that Nicki was unable to protect herself annoyed Whisper. Sure, she didn't show it in any traditional way, but she still showed it.

Pushing away from Zay without confessing her pique, Whisper passed the agents who were taking samples and photographs of Parker's murder victim. She was heading for Score and Shyla's room, but was stopped when McNeill came out of the bedroom opposite and met her in the hallway.

"Anyone want to tell me why Biz McDades wife is tied to a bed in there?"

Whisper shrugged and pushed out her lower lip. "Because she was never taught how to look after herself."

Walking right through the guy, she went into the second bedroom where Nicole was seated on the pillow, her wrists tied to the padded headboard. A bunch of agents hung around the bed.

"Whisper!" Nicole called when she saw her.

"Don't freak out," Whisper said, sighing to show her impatience. Climbing onto the bed, she began to work Nicole's hands free. "These guys will take you somewhere safe, far away from us. They'll ask you questions and if you play nice, they might let you loose."

"What's going on? I don't understand what's happening."

"Your husband and your lover are both going to prison," Whisper said, freeing the last knot and pulling the rope loose, liberating Nicole's hands.

Nicole didn't appear any more aware. "I don't…"

Whisper cupped her face. "Do not let yourself live under a man. Any man. For any reason. Not ever." She was about to go, but had another thought that took her back. "Oh, and please don't try to fuck your way out of this one." Crawling off the bed again, she found McNeill waiting between her and the door. "Parker's in the bathroom… Nicole's an idiot, but she's not a criminal."

Whether they chose to believe her or not, Whisper had no control over that. Departing the bedroom, she went straight across into Score and Shyla's room. She found the latter in the closet.

Shyla gasped when she saw her. "Geez, Whisper, you scared me… Phoenix freaks me out with that creeping thing too."

Maybe Zay was having more of an impact on her than she'd realized. "You need to get out of here."

Shyla put down the sweater she'd been folding and frowned. "Me? Why?"

"You don't want to meet Burl. Trust me, no one wants to meet Burl McDade. Doran is bringing Beeks and Fish. Grab whatever you need for an overnight and we'll send you to Beeks' place."

"And Score isn't suggesting this because…"

"Whisper got here before I did," Score said, bringing Whisper's attention around. "You don't need to pack, but I do want you out of here."

"Phoenix…" Shyla sighed.

Sensing it was better to give the couple their privacy, Whisper sidelined her urge to eavesdrop and crept out of the room. The apartment was full of people. Not that crowds worried her. Coasting on straight past them, she returned to Zay who was sitting on the couch again, his phone in hand.

"Score's sending Shyla away," Whisper said, sitting down next to him, then leaning over to check his wound. "Are you sore?"

"Told you I don't want pain meds," he said, putting his phone on the end table. "How come Score gets to send Shyla to safety, but you're staying right here?"

"Because there's nowhere else for me to be," she said, hooking an elbow over the back of the couch. "You really think you're going to get rid of me any time soon?"

"Hope not, Doherty," he said, finger-combing her hair away from the side of her head to pull her mouth to his. "You ready to admit it yet?"

"That we're stuck with each other," she asked, touching the neckline of his tee-shirt. "I never thought you'd ever stand by me."

"Yeah."

"I thought Burl would tell you to kick me to the curb and you wouldn't hesitate."

"Yeah."

She exhaled. "How did I end up falling for a man I was raised to hate?"

"Lucky for you," he said. "Lucky for me."

Difficult as it was, she found his eyes. "I do love you, Zay. I hate being so weak. Hate that I let you in."

"You weren't willing," he said, touching her lip. "I had to storm the damn castle."

Her lips curled until a laugh escaped. "Yeah, I guess you did." Narrowing her eyes, she leaned closer. "You're so devious, husband... Such a schemer. Forcing me to marry you then making me fall in love with you."

"I do what I gotta do," he said and kissed her slowly. Once their lips parted, he still kept his attention on hers. "And what does that make you? You never did say it."

Seemed like a lifetime ago he'd demanded she reciprocate. But he was right, Whisper never had. Weak or not, she couldn't deny it, not if it was what he needed to hear.

"I'm yours," she whispered. "Only yours."

"Damn straight," he said, taking his time about kissing her again. They might have kissed for a while, but it wasn't long enough for her liking. "What do you wanna do?"

Whisper was angry in her offense. "I'm staying here with you. You're not kicking me out when—"

"After. Once we're done with this crap. What do you want from our future?"

That was a big question that she wasn't sure she'd ever be able to answer. "This city isn't so bad."

"You like a party town?" he asked without nuance. "What a surprise."

She laughed and edged even nearer. "Think I could invite Mariana and Paula down, see if they like it too?"

"You could. I'd say things at home won't be right for a long time. They'd probably appreciate the break."

"And Shyla needs more girlfriends… Not fair for her to spend all her time with males… Maybe some of my spunk will rub off on her."

"Oh, and Score will love that."

"I think you were right," she said. "He might warm up to me… if given enough time."

"Doran won't want to go back, not if Score's staying here," Zay said. "So I guess the Doherty-McDades just got a new base."

Whisper leaped to her feet. "Great!" she exclaimed, offering him a hand. "What do you say we go christen it?"

In spite of all the men and activity in the apartment, Zay didn't hesitate to take her hand and rise from the couch. They had time to kill before Burl got there, she couldn't think of any reason they shouldn't make the most of it.

THIRTY-NINE

WAKING IN THE SHEETS she'd torn up with her husband, Whisper yawned and reached across the bed for him. Her arm went as far as it could, her hand widened, but she didn't touch anyone. Opening her eyes, she slammed her hands into the mattress and pushed up. Looking around, Whisper found she really was all alone in bed and in the room.

Jumping out of bed, she sought the short silky robe Shyla had loaned to her earlier in the week and pulled it on to hurry out of the room.

She expected her husband would be with his brothers and maybe surrounded by feds. Instead, she stopped at the sight of the McDades all seated around the dining table, various drinks in front of them.

Burl was at the head of the table, which presented him the perfect angle to view her surprise.

"Good evening, is there a problem, Miss Doherty?" Burl asked, his smugness outmatched even his son's.

Zay's shoulders shifted. He wasn't looking her way, but she didn't have to see his expression to know he didn't like his father diminishing their marriage.

"No," she said, folding her arms. "I'm just sorry I missed your arrival. Looks like you're settling in."

The bar was behind her, so she went that way to fix herself a drink. Obviously they were going for nothing being out of the ordinary. She'd noticed Zay wearing a hooded sweatshirt. If he'd taken his arm from the sling, his wound wouldn't be visible in the long-sleeved garment.

"Heard about your father, what a shame," Burl said without a shred of sincerity.

"Shame you didn't get to do it yourself?" she asked, picking up her Scotch and spinning to face the men again. "Don't deny you wouldn't have loved to pull the trigger yourself."

Swaying her hips, she sashayed down the room at a languorous pace.

"As you would've," Burl said. "You weren't close."

"You're in no position to know that," she said. "Let's be honest, just because a man lifts his hands to a woman doesn't mean he doesn't love her…" Whisper paused to ponder the point. "Or does it? No one I know is more qualified to answer that… What did you do when you discovered your wife's infidelity? No less than Parker will do when he finds his wife, right?"

Burl wasn't so smug anymore, which only widened her smile. "My wife got what she deserved. I don't regret killing her. Parker won't regret killing his whore either."

"That why you're here? Looking for your lost little sheep? Bet it was a surprise to find your other boys here with the one Biz framed. Why was it you let Parker set up Score for murder? Because you were fucking Nicole… Fucking her, telling her you'd get her pregnant, even though you knew Parker was drugging her and pumping her full of contraceptives…" Whisper sneered. "You're sick. You and your oldest son. You disgust me."

"Won't be your problem for much longer," Burl said, pushing back in his seat. "Once we calm Parker down, the McDades will be stronger than ever."

"Stronger?" she asked, her brows rising. "And what makes you think the Dohertys will let your murderous offspring get away with murder? Cyrus Doherty was an asshole… as sadistic asshole, but he didn't deserve Parker's bullet." Burl's flash of surprise encouraged her on. "Yeah, I know who's responsible for the murder of my father… Your favorite boy… or is Score your favorite? Tough to remember. I suppose you'll be telling Doran he's your favorite if you're set on him marrying Madison Byrne."

Burl's shoulders went back and his chin rose. More than surprised, he had to wonder how the hell she was so clued up.

"Parker killed your father because he deserved to die and because you weren't there to take his place."

"Oh, so Parker wanted to kill me?" Whisper asked. "Why? Because I was the one who saw you fucking his precious wife and had the audacity to tell my husband."

Burl surged to his feet and slammed a hand on the desk, an act reminiscent of Cyrus. "You ruined everything! I will not let some Doherty slut destroy everything I have built! You will not get away with it!"

"No?" Whisper asked, continuing to the table to lay a hand on Zay's shoulder. "He believed me… He didn't wait for you to talk him out of it. My husband believed me."

Zay picked up her hand and took it to his mouth to kiss her palm. "I always will."

Burl frowned. "You cannot listen to this slut. You can't choose her over your own family!"

"Whisper is my family," Zay said. "My wife and future mother of my children. Doran's family, Score… even his woman. We're the McDades now. We're what's left. What matters."

"What are you saying?"

Burl was still glancing between his boys, searching for answers when men appeared from the hallway.

"FBI!" one of them exclaimed. "Hands in the air! Burl McDade… do it now!"

The frown on his face was surreal to see. Keeping their weapons trained on the McDade patriarch, the agents surrounded him. One moved in to slam their target down on the table to frisk him, all the while Burl didn't say a word.

Zay pushed back his chair and hooked an arm around her to pull her into his lap.

Burl was yanked onto his feet again. "You!" he screamed as he was being dragged away. "You! Doherty! This was you!"

Wearing a smile, she kissed her fingertips and blew him a kiss. "Bye, daddy!" she called, offering a finger wave as he was hauled into a waiting elevator.

The doors closed and just like that, he was gone.

A couple of other guys came from the hallway. McNeill and someone she didn't know.

"Wow, that was…" McNeill looked her way. "You are the cherry on my shake."

She frowned. "How dare you, Agent McNeill. I'm married."

Zay tightened his half embrace. Just as she'd thought, he wasn't wearing his sling. His hand was free in the sleeve of the hoodie. Assuming it had to be tired, she slid her palm under his and held his hand to her chest for support.

"I mean we got everything," McNeill said.

Score and Doran were on their feet, approaching the fed who switched his focus to them.

"You didn't wake me," Whisper said to Zay.

"I wanted to keep you out of it. We told Burl Shyla was asleep too."

"But she's not, right? Score did get her out of here?" Zay nodded. "How long was he here?"

"Around an hour," Zay said. "We covered a lot, updating Score on current operations. Burl didn't hesitate to tell him everything. We were sorta struggling with how to segue into your father's murder—"

"That's what you get for benching me," she said, mesmerized by the proximity of his mouth.

"You did good, Peanut. Perfect."

"That's right," she said. "Now you know things have to change if we're gonna start over."

"Change?" he asked. "We're starting over?"

"Yeah," she said. "I think maybe we should date… You know, go out together, get to know each other."

One side of his mouth rose. "We're married, Peanut. Too late for takebacks now."

Looping an arm around his neck, she pulled herself close to whisper on his mouth. "No takebacks. Just because I'm dating you doesn't mean I'm on the market… and neither are you, husband."

"I'm only yours?"

Whisper's eyes closed as contentment washed through her. "Damn straight, McDade."

They were never supposed to make it. At the time of their marriage, Whisper hadn't realized they were being set up to fail. Whatever the motivations of their fathers, they'd found their own in each other. Whisper needed Zay's certainty and he needed her heart. After all they'd endured together, she was definitely ready to hand it over… providing he gave up his in return.

Zay had confessed to loving her for years, so she had some catching up to do. Whisper didn't mind being a little behind him. It was a great way to keep an eye on his fine ass, and keep him wondering about what she might do next.

Thank you for reading this tale!
If you can, please take the time to review.

~

Ask your local library for more Scarlett Finn
novels!

~

For all things Scarlett Finn
check out:

www.scarlettfinn.com

MORE FROM
THE MCDADES

OUT NOW!